Roadman

Colin McGinnis

Fomite
Burlington, VT

ISBN-13: 978-1-942515-04-3
Library of Congress Control Number: 2016939434

Fomite
58 Peru Street
Burlington, VT 05401
www.fomitepress.com

For my Mother,
Elizabeth Jane Mitchell
The foundation of this book who gave me life

&

my wife,
Sandra Patricia Ricardo,
Who returned my life to me when I had none

"'Forget what is behind you,'" the preacher said. "'Have more hope than memories.'"
— a quote from a letter by Vincent Van Gogh

"If you take [a copy of] the Christian Bible and put it out in the wind and the rain, soon the paper on which the words are printed will disintegrate and the words will be gone. Our bible IS the wind."
— Carol R. McGrath

"Old friend, what are you looking for? After those many years abroad you come with images you tended under foreign skies far away from your own land."
— George Seferis

Part One

Sima de los Huesos

Prolog

My father?

Yes.

Died a long time ago?

He did.

Was he a good man?

Gathering her daughter closer Velvet answers,

Good. Rare and exceptional also!

What was he like?

Velvet smooths her hair before answering.

An untamed man. Not willing to take the bit.

What's a bit?

A cruel piece of iron we force on horses. It bites into their mouth and makes them turn left or right. Stop or continue at the rider's whim.

A maverick?

Her mother doesn't reply for a moment. Enjoying instead the hot oklahoma sun overhead and a delicious. All too rare northerly breeze. An uncommon peace unbroken except for the drone of a distant plane.

Later. Eyes closed. Velvet turns from her willowy daughter as if consulting a book for a decision and out of legion gathers just one.

Listen. During tonight's ceremony. I will give you a little peyote.

Will it bite?

Velvet crinkles her eyes. Then stills her teenage daughter's fears.

No but it might singe you a little!

Guess I am old enough.

Her mother nods and waits for nightfall's come what may to instruct, guide and perhaps enlighten Autumn Bright about her father's life and death.

Since she herself only knows what was told to her when they were once or twice together in the cab of his Hercules she now possesses or during one long night and stretched morning of intimacy and close council, it will not be easy to convey from limited firsthand experience, as the rest's gathered from his aging friends, rumor and disjointed account, just what to say knowing that none of which will be enough to still her daughter's hunger to learn about the man whose last passing month sparked her eventual entry and gave her a rough equivalency of his form and spirit.

ET somnus

Chapter One

His station wagon follows rutted road like a train on track along arid valley and memory haunted hills with no bird overhead nor animal glimpsed except a solitary dust devil. A pocket full of secrets even his three–by–nine smile can't check sprinting toward distant horizons clotting like old blood cross sky blue as a widow's shadow.

Handsome. Distracting pageantry conceded and noted yet apprehensive of worn tires and suspension. He slows. Carefully unscrews his battered canteen. Then takes a long pull of warm water over a stretch of teeth rattling rock and hard clay. An abandoned secondary eroded by man, weather, and time. Till darkness and windblown *paoyn* stop him.

Without remedy for lonesomeness all deliberations dissolve and turn instead to distant parishioners near fort sill. Remaining unbroken by a dart of manumissioned, long nosed mexican bats.

After a glance into his rear view mirror. Its tally's accepted without reservation along with a certain liberty or libel. Accrediting his face's topography to spiteful occurrences mapped by victory and sorrow, it's neither handsome nor ill featured but strong and dark like good coffee with a prominent forehead, granite jaw and a sharp nose dividing two far seeing and watchful twenty-twenty amber flecked eyes.

Man's middle aged or a shade more. A presumption derived from grizzled hair cut short over his right ear. Nary the rest gathered in a long braid under his black cattleman's hat matching the rest of his somber rig tucked into paper–thin leather boots.

Definitely not a cigar store Indian or reservation shirttail. Instead. He's a wheeled lanky shanked so and so heading east not looking for trouble but not backing away from it either.

Downwind windy prank he stands vigil while lengthening shadows slake the waning day.

Later. Inhales–exhales. Stretches to draw cold dusk like a draft of freedom. Then takes a long deserved piss.

Rain starved branch and scrub's strop behind him. Echoed by poaching memory's trespass. It's an eerie sound reminiscent of frozen clothing's chafe on a forgotten or unattended clothesline.

Later let's fly at a rusty can. Kicks it into old ash. Burying it under cold gray–black grit before widdershining round his Hercules. Later leans against it to watch diurnal flocks break westward against early star prior night's capture and first light's release; a timeless humbug trotted out back east etched into stone by time and pressure.

He too hungers sin regret for pasts faltered on compunction. Guessing each day's renewal is a relentless clocked, brooding, and restless necessity but wastes no time with useless remorse. What's done cannot be amended and best not recalled far from friend and kin as evening crimsons. Ultramarines to violet. Brimming fathomless as a mechanic's pocket before stirring gold. Sterling. Later field gray skyward.

Nearby. Bloody motes rake stubbled patches too runty for the sporting abandons bullying lankier scrub and thorn into carless, sculptured pattern marking passage of stronger winds whilst nosy parkers and flannel mouthed blusters vie for attention.

Evenhandedly he grants each their due forewarned against owl or picketing specter's cry and listens for warning notes but there are none. Only a subtle unheralded change of guard showcased by a lone cooper hawk astride unpitched taint of distant farm, ranch, pond and arid crop, all carted by evening heavy with seasonal change and the cooling promise of moisture, tempting as an answered prayer.

Smells late. Little airish too this autumnal dying day around him and well it should with crowding nigrescence. Pungent grasses and felled birds. Particularly a desiccated crossed eyed rusting crow. Singular from other countless carcasses reaped by winter's culling and while acknowledging these fell signs, he glances away with a shiver. Then walks quickly back to his truck.

Time and season are not beyond him or outside his own miserly conception. It's just that he chooses to ignore or only casually reflect on mortality like a leaf. Or seasonal bloom. Accepting *Pa' hy's* pale glimmer as banked surety for day's return and if no moon brightens his way. Holds with what will like a cupped flame against this eat, shit, strive, hemming world's darkness until illness or age gathers him homeward.

Grounded from more fancies by nagging discomfort. Man stops. Digs a pebble out of his boot. Finds it. Then fishes it out while sorting lessons and winnowing trivials from the profound as would his mother hunched over a basket of pumpkin seed. Chirking gruff assessments with a penny's forfeiture,

Harvests seeded anew by cagey cycle's writ

"Particulars that matter we disregard. False omens. Lies festooned with church bazaar rustica. Chased. A feral dog scenting rabbit. It's the same with all other half–baked nonsense. For example. This malarkey. Twilight is peaceful. Honestly," he counters, "It's only day's labor ceasing and a signal for night's hunters and prey to slip sleep. Slumber, dream play their circuited, appointed role." After tossing the offending pebble away. Regretting that he hadn't questioned Donna Torbellino earlier, grumbles, "Should have asked Saynday if he courted *Maw-Toye-Gyah* before fever's bite. Eating horse and star fall. Whilom. Before nuisance and trouble settled lean and hungry. Like vultures over us."

Bit by banded copperhead melancholy, starts back to his truck with memory a sadness behind perched like bent crow's shadow. In its place guarantees are gathered from sunrise or dusk's unsure. Tentative promise and garnered from first light's coffee or bitter tea. Grub sizzling in a cast iron skillet. Fuel in the tank with a new road ahead cleansed anew. Bleached by sun. Or scavenger's picnic.

Wind dies. Show over. Claps his hands. Grabs a canteen. Then uses the last water to clean his windshield.

Later pressing on steering with both hands under darkening sky with his cargo of drying peyote nestling safely covered with horse blankets resting as might children, while stronger, autumnal winds congregate and startle dust into dark spray above his disfigured, uncertain road.

Chapter Two

Far away. Undreamed of, a longhaired fellow crosses a span of scorching new mexican sand. Barefoot. Toughening feet. Snaking prints behind him. Leading to two bodies' ugly sprawl. One male. Other female.

Feverish heat swelling already.

Woman a Paipai from northern mexico. Raped repeatedly while alive. Hell he even took her a few times after he slit her throat. Damned if he could tell the difference. Sour milk clogging his throat. The only moisture around for miles or more hers.

Reunioned back in alamogordo. They had shared a meal of Indian fry bread and at first all was amity until matters of faith were disputed. Then the two men. Other Lipan. Fought a singing duel. Lipan lost and Comanche did him and now slung over his back. Everything of value they once possessed.

When a ragged crow settles on his shoulder. Allows familiarity. Smiling a crooked welcome. Believing that the bird embodies the soul of a blind witch left behind in tucson. Since she's too much trouble to cart along. He hires out a careworn mestizo couple to cook her a meal once a day, clean up her stews around the wicker rocker she sits in night and day and to see that hungry crows don't peck at her too much.

The Lipan had sported a pair of handsome Arizona jaguar boots. Probably what caught his eye with a sly yearn even more than his scut. Thin thing. Pock marked by small pox.

Thirsty. Tired. Hungry. The Comanche needs to get out of the sun.

Find a place to shack up and ready himself east where a band of fellow coreligionist. *Numunahkahni*, are meeting up with him near fort sill oklahoma.

Till then there's lots to do.

A few peyotists to meet with.

Later calculates how many miles needed to walk before his feet singe. Blister. Toughen like the feet of *Napwat Tu*, warriors generations back. Before the white man corroded their hardness. Sentencing Comanches to rot.

Untroubled by what passed last night. Man's a visionary after all. Don't those dirty lying anglo–saxons say that means justify the end and that you have to break a few eggs to make an omelet?

Twice Born. So christened because he died at birth and was resuscitated by his mother's handmaidens. Uses or is used by the emerging peyote cult to cauterize the suppurating wound of white culture dominance. Rebuilding tribal affinity. Rearming. Getting to it before it's too late!

"War in europe getting bigger every day. Distracting our overlords. Now it's time to saddle up!"

Picking up the pace. He heads along the shoulder of a two lane east.

Man up ahead. Needs recruiting. Kind of a milksop from what he's heard but perhaps salvageable.

Tonight. If *Seni* pleases. Send a message. A spiritual telegram if you will. Letting him know a brother is knocking.

"Krist start this way?" He demands. Looking back at the two corpses now only two small and dark indentations against glaring sand. Doubts it. Yet he didn't shit on their faces. Hell! Even pulled the woman's legs into a more decorous posture so that passing whites won't have a scowl. Maybe he's calming down. Stretching toward beatitude

Chapter Three

Needing gas. He pulls up beside a converted farmhouse selling fuel and groceries. Possessing a single hooded pump, it reminding the roadman of a Navajo *Yei* figurine or a Hopi *Kachina*.

Waiting for the attendant he gets out, dusting off and stretching. Taking time to watch clouds colored by red top soil. Many a poor farmer's dream. Blowing westward toward california.

Finally an old white woman comes out and greets him wiping her hands on her long apron.

"How do?"

"Fine Mam and you?"

"Just pepper and vinegar thank you! Except for all of the storms. We have been having. Gas?"

"Please. Fill it up."

"Ok." After locating his gas cap. She fills his tank.

"A handsome truck. What is it?"

"A Hack Hercules."

"Hmmm. Don't see many round here. Heck! Never seen. Pardon me. One of your people driving anything but a wagon or riding a horse."

Responding guardedly to her question, her customer mutters "Money."

After finishing pumping the gas she asks, "Anything more. Tobacco. Coffee? Got last week's El Paso newspaper. Talks all about the big war breaking out in Europe!"

"Well, as to the first. I used to roll and smoke tobacco because cigarettes let me judge mileage."

"Do tell?"

"Well Mam. You see each cigarette, hand rolled, burns for twenty to thirty miles depending on one's speed. I learned to roll them uniformly. Enough that these punts were a dependable gauge of mileage. But I had to give them up. Heart pains. Now," he says rapping on his pickup, "It tells you how many miles you have made. As for the news of this war. Is it not more of the same?"

Her piercing blue eyes peer into his as she first frowns and later comments, "Well. I lost my husband in Cuba. That was war enough. Sides. What do folk like us know? I never thought I would see cars. Edison lights and all these new electric gadgets everywhere. Why sir twenty years ago. If you would have roared up here when I was alone. I would have shot you," she adds with an arid chuckle.

"Perhaps I would have returned your fire."

Afterward, pump jockey gruffs, "You betcha! That will be one dollar with or without fresh coffee. Anything else?"

"Well. Got any licorice?"

"Red or black?" old dame solicits.

"Either one. But if you got black I'll take half a jar."

While paying her, the roadman glances at the newspaper she had proudly thrust into his hands and studies a drawing of men marching toward war and looks away before remarking, "They haven't even finished this one!"

Chapter Four

Untouched by the cramped empty bellied nation east and west. As sky. Wind. Cloud. Sun. The roadman bides. Posing silently on a knoll's edge–a living, breathing remington print or a drawing off the front cover of a penny dreadful.

Satisfied all's well. Lowers binoculars. Wipes their lenses clean and puts them away in a case fastened to his belt. Later resting his weight on his outstretched right leg. Watching a bank of clouds pass.

Assigning them pattern. Form. Unbecoming nicknames. Distraction from more pressing thoughts is obtained. "There's old Mr. Rabbit. Skedaddling east like this waddy in about an hour or so and over there," he declares. Pointing to a rather fat and sassy laggard for his Hercules's attention and benefit. "That one? Let's see. A fat banker's wife dressed up for church. Go on. Pop your corn! Opine all you want. It's a free county ain't it?"

Crotchical except for a pop or creak. His Hercules is otherwise silent.

Weary of this game. Hitches his pants up. Wipes off his boots. Then turns with a look sufficiently bitter to sour milk, "Whenever time's foretold hand strikes boy. They'll drown. Bury us and sweep away our language. Culture and history–done that a bit back along the trail don't you think amigo? Just about along with everything else gulped down like a corndodge or slurped up like hominy right out of the can.

"Not if I can help it!

What then old hen? Sit here with a thumb up my–yes sir! Ok. Just sit around. Waiting for your number to come up. Lucky seven?

And what's this "Ok" you're always throwing around?

Shaking head. Answers his own question, "I asked once. But no one really knew. Anyhow—lot of folk—hungry. Craving hope and a little assistance before first snowfall.

Better get a move on then!

I'm bushed.

Simmer down. Rest a while. Take them boots off.

He ignores this suggestion not wanting to get too comfortable with a long ride ahead of him.

Fuel?

Quarter of a tank. Maybe less.

Money?

Not much. Gave too much away. Always was a soft touch for hungry children.

Pretty widows you mean!

Now wait a second there—

Just joshing. Moving on soon?

Figure to!

Notice sky's color.

Yes. Blue. Clear as old mexican turquoise. Clouds far as an eye can see. —handsome.

Yes it is. Camped here once. Put coffee on the boil. Heated up some canned cow and beans—" pauses before adding in a confidential laugh, between pork n beans and licorice. I admit that I've succumbed. Bent a little but considering all that I could be aholding too. Whiskey. Wine. Woman and song. Figure in these last years. Instead of resting in one of them marble orchids of theirs. I've scraped by with little owed on that score. Considering—

But now there's places to see. People needing ministering. Got a whole winter's worth of ceremonies and blessings back in the truck and chances are and with this I can offset at least a handful of misery.

If I had. More—I would do more. Buy up a lot of food. Medicine.

With whose money. Yours?

Now just wait a cotton picking minute! You know that all I got is in this truck. The peyote. Fuel. Food.

Ain't much pal!

A bowl of chili now and then" This said lightly to keep the peace, "not too many signs of folk about. Amarillo's behind us. Old house hereabouts. As I said. Camped here before but did not investigate.

Why! Scared?" He shrugs. Weighing his response before answering, "Lots of spirits around. Not human. Or at least no more they ain't. Souls make camp here just like us. Liking the view. Safety. This here's an old place.

The circles nearby you mean? He nods. "When the moon is out. I've seen a couple.

Don't talk about them! Get their attention. They might take an interest—

Already have! Poked around mucho plenty.

Naw. It's just more likely some are mossing around like horse flies because I killed them or maybe they're lonely and want me to rejoin them. This thought saddens him for there are many he would give everything but his last reserves of honor and courage to embrace again. "Them that come in familiar".

Chuckling nonchalantly adds, Beloved forms—K'ou—m—tou—are the most dangerous and let's say the most persuasive.

Unconcerned. Hunted. Run to ground. There's not much a soul can do in the long run but defray or plank the bill in the best manner possible.

Looking down at the empty plains below. He remembers an related incident with a near smile, "One should have seen our faces when we were pushed and shuttled through museum corridors stacked high with dead tribes people remains at the nation's capital (Well—theirs)!

—Her?

Now you dredge her up. My wife!

He stops. Clears his throat and spits over the side. Then sits back on his haunches like one not trained to sit in a chair.

Saved a few people.

That's the truth. That little girl in arizona.

Sure enough. She netted me my truck.

Along these lines he sits for a spell with a stick of licorice whistling a tune learned from his father. Who in turn mastered it at his sire's side. Music. Old and timeworn as the land. Independent of any known tonal scale. He imagines it's a singular wind's composition exchanged long ago with a straggler in token of friendship when both needed assurance. Mutual companionship.

Pair of traveling german musicologists asked him to let them listen and write it down using Italian notation. He refused. Rather never air it again. Than allow it to be dissected and studied by men to whom music is no more than a scrubbed and dismembered corpse.

Marooning. A cold sourmilk biscuit in his hand. He stops and gathers a handful of stones. Flinging them at a pile of rusting junk at the edge of this whelky knob well along day's end while crisp leaves tumble. Somersault and fall at his booted feet.

Can any soul blame him lazing in the late sunlight before hitting the road for another thirty or forty miles? Stopping for a lonely supper sopped up with only star and moon for company?

Later solemn and silent. 'Cept for sporadic winds. Blue Jay's spat and sidewinder's rattle. His vantage. An empty acreage high above the flats below. Unflustered by trespass. Too introspective to acknowledge occasional callers. Aloof. Uncaring. Idyll gusts. Warming as saltbeef and misleading as a fair weather sailor's grief. Attracting eye. Heart. Not a few local prejudices discriminate against this locale. Generally following in this vein. Traditionally. After a few nights alone on its heights. Most folks. Move along. Feeling that they have been rebuffed in a matter not easily explained or understood.

Former settlers were driven away by a relentless disdain. Poor harvests and a lingering propensity for pets and children.

Ancient stone circles hint of earlier occupation and usage but this fact is generally ignored. On the other hand there is a certain coolness roundabouts. Creating an island of calm and a refuge for wild life well as for men and women cut from the same cloth as himself who camp here on occasion. Providing a sanctuary and shelter for exiles and outlaws. Long as they follow house rules and keep abreast of check out time. A fact garnered by the number of fire pits left around and complaints to the local sheriff concerning the notoriety of this locale for attracting no–accounts of many breeds and inclinations.

It's only a matter of time before this affront to the good citizen of this county is addressed by a committee and remedied by stomping and burning till this eyesore's reclaimed.

There's considerable indication of human habitation hereabouts if a body cared to look. Dirty old amarillo. Not too many leagues behind girt by a sand blasted scrubland of yellow sand, thorn and *mucho llano estacados* far as the crow flies. Peckish prairillion. Frequented by Arctic winds from canada. November through may. Fit only for hardy cattle, goats, men and woman with little other option.

Amarillo's not a town he cares for. Why? Despite folks being largely of mixed ancestry. They're apt to put on the dog. Simply because they purchase kit from sears and roebuck. Enjoy the occasional nicked half dime shave, rough cafe blue plate special (Yesterday's if lucky) and bob their hair at a dime a throw just out of reach of that god almighty stock yard stench.

Later solicits more diversion but none's forthcoming. Only a blanketing stillness and mystery posed by the abandoned homestead and its outbuildings under clean lonesome sky and rushing cloud. Like him. Oklahoma bound.

Warming hands on his truck's hood, dawdles, brushing flaky crumbs from his lap. Mindful of winter's proximity and neighboring Jaynuts' empty bellies. Liberally scatters his lunch at his feet. Mixed flock of birds overcome their mistrust and desperately feed.

One big bold cuss eats more than his share till the roadman fixes him with a hard stare. Shooing the bird away. Allowing others a taste.

In the high north. Wild things overcome all fear of humans and eat directly from one's hand before the first bite of winter as if tame.

Lunch over. Gets up. Hitches first one shoulder then the other. Looking around and takes a heads up toward darkening and quickening sky ignoring the birds' plea for seconds.

He simply turns. Displays his empty hand and swears, "No more amigos. Sorry!" They're incredulous at first. But as one nervously faces the other, disbelief turns to disappointment and one by one they fly away seeking other victuals toward promenading cumulus clouds or as he has it, 'a court in attendance. Preening showy as a gaggle of oklahoma city slicks accompanied by their painted dames visiting the opera or a tin horn tribute to far and fabled broadway.'

"And why not gussy up this world a little? There's too much misery and ugliness about. Like honey. Folk need imagination's sweetening once in a while."

Finishing. Lays his thoughts to rest like a good father and bids them good night while hue and color exit overhead with considerable fanfare as a sickle moon rises.

Cold nemesis. Forgotten huntress. Post-menopausal deity shorn of worship and sacrifice left to fend for herself

Wary of her he never the less asks *Pa'hy* to grace his way tonight while later thanking her in turn for aiding many a close scrapes lit only by her light in the past before picking up a long blade of grass and glancing again at the waning moon with a pensive prick acknowledging that the hour's late and it's time to get going.

***

Some of what's seen on the peyote road ain't there. At least not summarily agreed upon by a majority opinion, a fact that doesn't bother him a hill of beans. In fact the roadman snorts and laughs even while conceding that his own people. More than half of 'em view peyotists as empty headed, misguided fools or worse. In turn, he divides their varied detractors roughly into four opposing camps. The traditionalist. Waiting for some great spiritual miracle to save them. The conformists next. These busybodies dancing the white man's jig. Every full and quarter note. Dress like them. Talk like them. But they're never going to be them! So why bother? Lest he forget, the "Don't give a damns." Folk. Usually older or the bitter young. No longer giving a flying—yes sir! This last group is self–explanatory. And then there are the rebels. Either daring continued resistance. Or men and women cut from the same cloth as he is. Trying out divergent synthesis. Likes the word. Smiles at how it plays. Between the old world. Which in their view is forever gone and the new. Which is open to interpretation. Limited trial and error. And experimentation as long at such attempts don't fly in the face of the law, (Capital "L," please) or cultural norms with their sunday gone to church day to day mandated certainties. Falling somewhere between the cracks their emerging peyote cult.

Stops fancying. Relishing instead this pleasing savagery. An evening warm and lingering for a panhandle fall. "Yes it is. "And this closing solitude's wild sage and buffalo grass. An agreeable balm. "Indeed." An elixir or livener against isolation and loneliness begging this question, "If I was not here to witness this. Sky's last colors washed away by smooth thickening darkness. Would these wonders waste? Or do gods and devils watch this closing solitude and pause their rivalries–" Resting this thought. He inserts a silent aside reaching under his seat for his canteen filled at the old woman's gas station and takes a drink before stating flatly, "Of course there's no knowing."

October winds sweep by without so much as, "A beg your pardon," a real crow footed humdinger. It dosey–does. Then rings around the prairie striking distant windswept headlands before heading toward vanishing points beyond even his considerable range where play and eddy the long brush strokes of they who move the wind, stage clouds and laugh with *P'ay* and *Pa' hy* beyond human senses yet the wild know them gathered close at night, huddled or hunting alone, or while shivering as their strange ribald humor, inside jokes, and cruel jests wash over them uneasily. Even wolves protest their passing. "Why do you think they howl so much?"

They spin a disdainful. Unfocused levity without mal-intent beyond our limited sense of humor as are certain ranges of sound and light

With this and other thoughts and in mind and frowning with concentration, he squats down and draws two intersecting circles. In one writes an English word. God. Using Harrington's unwieldy script next writes *Dawkee*. Its near equivalent in his own language.

Never cared for this lexiconist's handiwork. It's awkward to write. And most of all though it's sanctioned with a purposeful meaning created obviously as a helpful. Long winded undertaking with the best of intention. Protesting, "It's from outside." A stranger's gift. As if a visitor dressed your children in outlandish finery after discarding their own well wove cloth.

"No," he cautions, "this isn't the right example. It's more as if one our dearest poems or sacred prayers were stolen. And rendered forever "without parole."

Unsatisfied with his handiwork. He erases it. Then draws two new circles. Not transecting but separate. Though of competing size. "There's our problem. Conflicting cosmologies."

Afterward, licks his lips. Relishing the word. "Ours and theirs. And the devil himself and if this gent truly exists. He must sit around and laugh himself sick after trying to make sense out of this buzzard poop labeled science."

Mountains. Endless sky. Ponderosas. Great oaks. Eldest pines. Whales deep in the sea. Bears. Cold glaciers. Untold seasons' kiss and chafe

Cottons that it's a very complex world. Round from the smallest motes to what's mirrored by the intricate, grand, lordly humbling structures, and living critters of all shapes and sizes .

Frustrated by any lack of success he quickly stands up and stamps out his drawings. Sulking away like a crossed schoolboy, "Christ almighty! You need to dust out your bin friend!" he nods in agreement but continues on unabated, "If the crap they write up isn't the most cantankerous nonsense proclaimed outside a drunken saturday night's romp. I mean excuse me but I looked into their books of science," foldout dioramas of a courted chief. The sun circled by planets. Moons and stars. Held up to light a half dollar sized sun shone while cardboard planets and moons orbited as stiffly as shy children decked out in holiday finery all at the pull of a satin ribbon. Later laughed and was reprimanded and left to brood outside for days.

Below all this intellectual going ons—two horses wrestle a wagon westward while its passenger's apparently half–asleep bob up and down like corks with their mouths open.

Watching, gathers their sawing away and letting their team pull their own way home. Witnessing this steadily decreasing occurrence he addresses his truck with a slight reproach, "We won't be seeing much more of this," he points out and just to show there aren't any hard feelings, gives his Halk Hercules an even handed appraisal. While informing it offhandedly, "Guess your kind will rule the roost in a couple more years."

This off his chest. He clears his throat and spits out a gob of phlegm. Feeling better he apologies, "Don't mind me truck. I'm just ornery sometimes. You can't help what you are. Where you come from any more than me."

Later after inspecting his ride from rear bumper to front grill, finds nothing amiss. "No sir! You're sprung tight as a mule's—yes sir!"

If there's a wrinkle or rub lurking in this entire one wonders. Hell yes! Oh he knows. He's aware. Well acquainted with the facts of the matter. Yet there's many a mile between here and the mexican border. How else to transport these uneasy. Unconsecrated hosts north out of some goldtooth, backroom rootseller's tar paper shack and back to his people waiting for the year to fold as it has for many an age on broken promises and stillborn hopes?

Badgered by sudden curiosity his carefree parole ends and redirects nearby. Protests are hopeless but he takes a stab at it, "Listen no account! Go on. Play elsewhere. I don't have the time of day to spare. Want me to take a look over there don't you? And feel sorry for them. Hold a wake. Tell you what son! If all of them poor souls would head back east. Get off the crapper. Roll up the carpet. Turn off the light. Sail back over the brine. We'd all be a sight better before the week's out!"

This settled, the roadman walks down a faint path toward a majestic oak shorn by lighting ringed by a miniature forest alive with birdcall. An Echoing, melancholy confederacy of sound eerily ample to set him on edge scouting toward pale chimney and partially glimpsed house bravely whistling another off key tune birds find particular and taunting.

Whereas Sapsuckers ignore his affront flirting tree–to–tree gathering their netted prey as the less prideful flee. Hesitating over a crimped fern he muses dryly, "Clever devils! After drilling holes into trees. Plug up with sap. Later. When bugs stir, taste or smell these inducements. They fall in. Lick away unconcerned till the birds scoop them up without even, "a beg pardon," using tongues frilly as painter's brush."

"I am any different?" he asks then quietly stands for a moment with his ears pitched for any warning sound but there are no owls about so discovery pulls easy and nice as a huckleberry pie's boarding house reach. Hauling him a stone's throw away where weed choked trails branch and circle headfirst. To a derelict chimney. Towering above feral grasses. In its shadow. Funny headed dandelions. Dusty sunflowers' rough heliotrope at the knee of a thin screen of scot pine. Planted long ago to break winds blowing off the plains below.

Later with each respectful step, he categorizes. Weighs and judges forward into slanting light the color of old honey. Striding over with his hands in pockets. Finishing a longish tune. Tries for another but his mouth's dry. Spooked. Never liked stepping around these old abandoned places. Not knowing who or what waits.

Pa' hy's up. Playing second fiddle to the fourth of july shenanigans overhead. A sliver of measured worn silver defaced by thousands of hands' over eager, clumsy clinch till smooth and yet accountably older than the roman specie he long ago traded for on a whim just to see cesar's face. Kept in his vest pocket to take out on those occasions when there is no one else about to confide in or tell a story to.

Discovers downwind old swing folded against great oak. One rope tied to a strong branch in a hangman's knot. Other's aground.

Oak? Once king of the hill. Now a tattered giant drawing wind and lightening's constant furry.

Tricky tree. More in its beard than on its plate

Listening awhile to its complaints, touches its hardened bark and with a long sigh, offers a limited rationed comfort, "Would like come back here on a warmer day friend and sit under your branches and rest a spell. Maybe eat an apple and take a long drink of water against summer's fire but not today. It's too cold!"

True for there are many ever–changing shadows about and after a prolonged reconnaissance the roadman decides this property went bad long ago.

Ground's ashy. Tainted with salt, "Some land's just trouble. The whys and what for's of it are beyond my grasp. Probably anyone else's for the matter." Spoken while he stepped warily, keeping ears and eyes cocked up until finding the small house. A no account structure abused and beaten by time and weather.

Shielding his eyes from momentary glare he stops and gathers his thoughts glancing upward checking the lot's remaining assets. Its strength weighed against coming winter's. Found wanting. He turns away sadly disappointed. Wishing it wasn't so. Because families hereabouts lack shelter. Yet realizing that somewhere a deed. Or title waits and just as winter's first fire would catch, its smoke run up the chimney, there would be that knock at the door. So he shrugs these thoughts off as just one more empty pocket gesture. One of so many made when desiring to help yet having little in the way of meeting any one's needs more than wishes costing but little. Though promising much. Tired. Closes his eyes and gives them a brief massage while running a bitter notion or two.

Nearby farmyard is no inducement for a prolonged stay. Littered yard returning to glade. Bent forest's writ. High grass's warrant. Miscellaneous animals' whim and strange woven circles that he guesses but wouldn't place a bet on it. Molded by relentless winds' cast.

Hearty insolence or heart breaking submission all about as well. Broken glassware. Scattered chips from a blue patterned enamelware set. Perhaps a spring day wedding present or good will notion. Additional clues to a hardscrabble life crackle under footfall: cracked porcelain washbasin. Rusted tin coffee pot. A broken cradle–scythe. A badly carved hobbyhorse darkened by rain and ice's touch. And one large green glass marble shot with bright red bold as mexican chili pepper. This he picks up and places it in pocket. A ready thing for another child another day. Standing up. Glances around sighting a puzzle or two. "What's this? Don't shy. No hoodoo. Just plain old forgetfulness. Or easygoing recognition that someone wouldn't be chewing breakfast. Lunch or their cold supper warmed up on that old stove in the corner."

Placing his hands behind his back in a parolee's parade rest he bends closer to a broken window and takes a look at what surely is evening's or at least today's oddest exhibit. A mason jar set in the empty window holding a set of false teeth. Shrunk and brittled yellow into a forlorn. Embarrassing token of fragility surely as a pair of Anasazi mummies.

His father once related finding two children sitting atop a new mexico mountain. "Pop thought they were just two lost children. A boy and a girl. Asleep. Waiting for a passing friend to lend them a hand to he peered lower and discovered that this hansel and gretel were long past saving. Figured they were sacrificed to gods long since bleached away by time and occurrence. Said their clothing was as fresh as or fresher than his." So he left their lonely vigil after his brief and momentary interruption. Hopefully unnoticed after multiple seasons beneath sun. Moon. And sky's ceaseless meter above their little heads slanted forever toward reservations of the dead.

Someone. Perhaps with a sense of whimsy or in a fit of artistic license left three small heads carved from apple cores next to the denture dusty jar. One's an old man. Lips cruel. Eyes hard. Another a child's head. But slack mouthed. Colicky. The last. A fat woman with plump cheeks. He pokes at her dimples before picking them up and pocketing them but stops since there's something too personal. Or ill charmed about this trio's placement. Again there's their oddity of expression so he leaves them be watching and waiting for the next stranger. If any. Moved to visit here.

On his final circuit he discovers a child's reading primer and tips it upright with his left boot. Nothing to cry over. Just a sodden chapbook stained with rain and mold. Now a lattice for eager fungus. Behind it there's a wooden table set for six. Centered cobbler pitcher sprouts a riot of white mold.

All a tumble its doorway invites him in but he only shakes his head. Simply replying, "No. Not this time thanks." Next ponders questions posed by its forlorn rustle. Tar paper scupper. Tall oak's rice paper shadowy reach. Lacy and dark against stilling light but doesn't venture in. Too wary of spirits clinging like soap on a mug's rim. Walks swiftly away stiff legged through thighhigh dying autumnal grasses recalling another homestead burned by his own hand long ago.

A telephone line stretches over his head. Sleeping blackbirds ranked in close quarters. Sit on its thin swaying cable.

Nailed below a faded sign promises nickel phone calls. Despite predisposition, he strolls over and lifts a boxed phone's receiver off its hook. Cranks it. There's not a peep. Wait though. Something or someone's there. Stubborn. He tries again, "Hello!" The faintest of whisper cracks dryly, "*Tovt–Sar're*." Next a woman's scream. Followed by a burst of static. After a marked change in pitch and accent. One word or name, "*Kayshaunt*," growled later by a deeper and unmistakably masculine voice.

Fed up. Demands sternly, "Who this," straining to hear each weakening voice before they disappear. He'd swear they spoke in Comanche before another word, "*Haits!*" captures his attention again.

Frowning with concentration. Tries to remember other languages from his more ambling days before the line susurrates again with three words or phrases, "*Tuyaaitu – Eit–ma–han'it– Tovt–ti'vo,*" again suggestive. But untranslatable since Kiowa as he's often informed by busybodies. You know those barber's cat. Spectacled types with a thousand question on their lips but never a nickel to pay for them. Is an isolate. Possessing a rather unique idiom.

Stubbornly though, he clears his voice and tries again, "Who's there?" but the voice or voices fade with a high hat sibilant hiss.

Frustrated and a little put out, starts to place the phone back on its cradle just before a snippet of tinny music bursts form the receiver and then fades. It and each stolen voices were sent a tumble across the very continent and this disturbed him.

Sulking, he angrily chides himself. Having read accounts of other natives. Or what a good doctor. Met long ago called indigenous folk. We? Well. Both dislike having our pictures taken by camera.

"Still," he argues, "there must be something in such seemingly childish beliefs. Old values are not always foolish nonesuch," he stubbornly insists, "not always."

Resonating like a Ladder Back woodpecker. Phone rings. But the roadman pays it no mind. Only quickening his pace concerned about the toll of such a call.

Weary. He doffs his hat and steps toward another outbuilding nearly tripping over a stack of records under an old rust stained washtub.

Bending down he picks them up. Blows off the dust and clears away their webs. Almost puts them back down but checks his motion. Instead, dusts them off and puts them in his shoulder bag since he has a friend back in fort sill who loves spicy creole music from new orleans.

Economic triage. There's only room for so much in the wagon when the bank forecloses. Rent's due. Mortgage's overdue

Guesses that the folk who once lived here took what they could and what they needed.

Scratching with the itch of conjecture without any possible answer. He steps around the property and gives it a rough and ready appraisal before speculating, "A white cast of hope, Twelve Nation gamble or a Cherokee replanting after that bastard Sharp Knife forced them west!"

Against a flimsy leather hinged door he finds the expected outsized crudely carved letters "G.T.T."

Satisfied that at least part of this puzzle's solved, Kuy walks away.

Holding's small barn is better roofed than the main house in long sheeted tin and sound despite continued beating from summer's flash storms, hail and patch lightening not to mention winter's miscreant attention.

Gingerly looking about for nails or late lingering rattlers or banded copperheads not yet burrowed deep and lulled back by a last chance of delicious warmth soaked up on a flat rock or old plate steps forward until a rustle stops him in his tracks.

"What now?"

Mangy curs. A pack actually! Nosing around silently without even a whine. Don't look like they cotton to strangers. And it's the silent ones you have to watch for since they have relearned what brother and sister wolf never forgot, "Make noise only after you are sure of your prey and not before!" So he back tracks and turns away from the barn led by the creaky–crack of a slowly turning windmill and like saul on the road to damascus.

Hesitates before returning to his truck troubled by a prickly mood darkening as if scratched by a malevolence. "Whites leave behind their brickwork. Goods and whatnots. Doodads. Gewgaws which stain the land for many a year while we leave only shallow imprints passing in a season or two's grace and whim gathered by the wind and rain."

Chill williwaw bites. Shuts him up. Sends him back hurriedly to his truck and glancing back while buttoning up his coat he realizes that there's no placating winter's momentary approach. Nature has her ways irrespective of our needs and desires. "We're just fleas on the back of a dog. The dog scratches. We jump and dance the three step jake. Dog gives itself a good shake. We're flung around from hair to hair. Are we any different?" he asks even as the dimming light sets directly over oak, and windmill alongside the old house. Till his view is colorless as a silent film. Eagerly once paid a half dollar to crowd into a back roll where colored and tribes people were allowed to goggle and gaggle with their betters as a hesitant. Coughing projector astounded wits by the giant image of a crashing ocean wave. Can't help but chuckle remembering, "Sakes alive but me and a cart load of other fools ran out of that school gymnasium when we saw that wave coming!"

Dusk's stark scenery brings other memories. Crude missionary school indoctrination. Halloween namely. With its spooks. Witches and ghouls. "Funny. They don't believe in ghosts or spirits. But dissemble a watered down–greeting card supernatural to the children under their care."

He often argued with the well–meaning but culturally naïve young men and woman spreading their traditions and customs. He felt that they were actually poisoning minds and perceptions of their charges with egregious nonsense and cluttering their students' minds with glue and paper foolscap.

Ready to hit the road he checks his tires and draws wick. Oil's fine. He first scrutinizes evening's promise. Weather. Narrowing bands of banded color–apple green. "Fussed dark this evening ain't it?

A good deal of hard nighthawk driving ahead on a worn road laid over an even older trail. Taking a last look. Fairwells before climbing back inside his truck. Before he can shut the trucks door, burst of light blinds him. Justly alarmed. Hastily covers both eyes. Afterwards checks his head and neck for injury frantic to discover what the hell happened. By and by, after looking wildly about. Except for setting sun. There's nothing. Chastened that there's no lingering physical pain or mark upon him. Just expectation there's something amiss. Heightened by cock's crow. He shrugs. Warily reexamines his mirror's reflection.

Movement. Where? Across the twilight freckled fields beside him barefoot and toting spotted long heeled boots slung over hunched shoulder as if lord of all it surveyed and arrogance it's pennant.

Not a little surprised and alarmed at this unexpected apparition the roadman reaches under his seat for his rifle but belays this. Instead. Opens his door and gets out but it's only his shadow that's cast and his breath heard.

No one about. Was there ever? "Had a black hat similar to mine," he insists. Before he can add more or exclaim. It appears again. Then winks out with the audacity of a spent military flare–its afterglow burned into his retinas.

Pondering this experience he orders his thoughts for any resulting contingency, "Deuce take him or her! What type of trampous whim–wham borderland bravado is this," he demands, "If this is some long nosed witch. Haint or living and breathing cantankerous soul drawing me a line in the sand. If so. Why don't they stop playing around and get to it!"

Dreams occasionally leak carelessly crisscrossing day from night and though peyotists don't believe in dividing wakefulness from sleep. They do like to keep their hierarchical concepts neat and tidy as any other school of thought and so slowing his windowing heart and lungs with a quick dismissive laugh, he later upon reflection, tries to codify this experience or rationalize it away. Later failing. Bids it unclassifiable. Phenomenon beyond ken or at least something not to brood over alone and far from home. So gets back in and later tries to recall any reverent facts or stories concerning the experience just underwent.

Taradiddles speak of a group of roadmen and roadwomen perverting peyote's potential into nothing more than petty quests for power and domination. Several deaths have been reported as a sad outcome. Used not as a beneficial sacrament. They denigrate it opening doors better left closed or so he's heard. "This one?" he demands while shaking his head in despair. Saddened that even this remaining purity. Bastion of hope and sorely needed beacon is under siege by selfish. Twisted individuals. He acknowledges that peyotists and roadman are a finicky lot. Hell. They have to be! When meeting fellow pilgrims at some god forsaken spot. It's unfortunate that they often have to dance around like dogs sniffing each other out until they're reasonable sure that the other isn't a sorcerer or black hearted witch bent on stealing their powers and reputations after duels sometimes lasting for days armed only with song and ritual.

Wouldn't you? Troubled. Throws a quick backward glance behind him and then airs a penny's worth of unease, "It's unfortunate though that we do believe! Dead things call the dead!"

Afterward. Takes the marble out of his pocket. Scoops the records rolls out of his bag. Circles around to the front of the house in his truck and quickly places these items inside out of rain's reach. Then gets back in just at the nick of time as members of the mangy pack lunge at his folding legs a second after his door's slammed shut.

They chase till the first bend of the road and later honor served, stop on a dime then pivot and retreat under moon's glow as their intended victim drives off.

***

Some distance away. Dark under bright star, twisting and turning over broken crowned highlands and ascending moon—except for occasional reflections mirrored in the eyes of passing animals, the roadman's alone on a road stretched like an endless dark tributary.

Frankly moments such as this, alone with only persnickety notions for company; displaced thoughts, fancies and daily experiences coalescing into internal monologues and in turn argufy while he debates and struggles with fundamental questions haunting everyone: where have I been? Where am I going and how do I get there? Yet now and then. The sheer spectacle of a day's end or a night's beginning captures his attention and for these usually brief instances, all doubt and speculation end.

Example: uncountable stars circling overhead. Pintsize lights similar to mission school Christmas twinkles rimmed by wise old hills.

Counting each crooks his neck. After two hundred stops.

la bola de fuego   Firedrake. Easy as a lost lucifer. Drops into the next valley. Its downward trajectory brings to mind an old lecture. His father's. A cold day's topic selected after they wandered along a long windswept mesa fruitlessly hunting for strayed horses. Before inadvertently discovering a blistered rock fallen long ago from the dark. His Father explained that the stone fell long ago from cold night before whites numbered so.

The meteor's glow lighting his way he volunteers a new thought, "I wonder if all creation is a collective–whole. Hold on. Listen now! That is neither in any way ordinary or bizarre. This comet buzzing over my graying head is perhaps no less remarkable than a lamp held aloft by some kind soul to light my way home."

" 'Eit–dei th' peitgyH."

***

Eastward. Pick–backed contraband runner. Rogue priest of a proscribed twilight religion sailing under a slice of moon thin as a rich man's gift, given short shrift. Stifled by careless committee. Judge or sheriff's warrant–prying wrung hand against heathen practices. Frequent delinquency. Misbehavior–remembers–that–if literate. They were encouraged to read religion and philosophy and with time on his hands. He studied foxed texts in the humidity and warm rain under palmetto shadow–reading musty tracts on the deists. For example, "'Jacobi then threw down the gauntlet to the deists.'"

"Well he did! For president jefferson and his circle believed god was only a fantastic clock maker."

Shakes his head now as then after he first studied this passage long ago knowing there is too much spirit and graceful providence to ever be misconstrued as parts of a soulless machine. Perhaps, he argues, "We are instead part of a massive being or the beating of a colossal heart inclusive of all creation."

Coasting sleepily to familiar spot he pulls over. Discovering that he is too all-in to prepare food. Instead, pulls out his fleece–lined bedroll and makes camp while stars above sketch old familiar tales.

He searches for *Sayn–Day's Arm* later and the Seven Sisters before sleep but decides it too early for the first so concentrates on locating the latter.

Comforted by these familiar ancestors close enough to almost touch loneliness slips away while he settles down securely with his great grand-parents overhead. Stretched far away other lights offer anecdotes, family gossip and legends but dog–tired he rolls instead into dream.

Chapter Five

Morning, slows at a crossroad hunting for a small community where lives a certain woman named Velvet Horn. A scarred and badly mutilated medicine woman. She had attracted his attention as she milled through a rough assortment of typical border town riffraff asking a lot of stiff questions. Strong willed. Crusty tongue cypher. She cut off their bullshit. With indifference and shielded interests but did not win any friends. Or gain acceptance into their trail worn fraternity. One edged on mysterious ritual. Rumor, furtive practices, unwilling as horntoads to be rousted and face scrutiny.

Outriders with feet planted on both sides of the border ready to skedaddle depending on circumstance and whim—a scruffy–princely hodgepodge of peyote dealers. Roadmen and road chiefs. Outlawed. Proscribed. Indifferent to Law and strictures drawn up by cigar smoking big shots.

"Hell. We smiled dismissively at her questions and then turned our collective backs on her!"

Armed with a lively. Intelligent interest. She possessed a mysterious. Furtive quality. Enforced by habitually wearing a dark slouch hat and a marked fondness for men's bandannas.

The roadman always a sucker for the mysterious and uncommon kept an eye on her from the first. Considering his stake hold in this odd woman. He rolls over the incident that brought them relative reciprocity while slowing to look at his map. Satisfied that he is on the right tract he drives on considering the first time they shared an intimacy not of either's choosing. "The patriarchal nature of our tribe's people as well as the chauvinism–" likes these two words captured from an old dictionary wrapped against weather and ruin back of him "–of the assembled, gave her the brush off. I should have stepped in. Introduced Velvet all around. But to what end? They would only ape acceptance and then play her hard if I did not squire her every minute she circled around with her dollar a question sincerity. Slit nose. And knife scars across her face freed her from men's attentions–at least at arm's length and if free from molestation. Sleeping like a wild denizen of field and plain. Wherever willed and where need demanded. Living against the dictates of at least three cultures was not without considerable risk."

Changing the topic, alludes later to a troubling attack on the poor unfortunate by two men, "Dark night that one and those two drunken mexicans–policemen from across the border attempted rape. Velvet's screams woke me. And let me tell you it was a dangerous fight! Stabbed one maybe! Not sorry for it either after what she told me about her trouble and how she got her face cut up!"

Fact of the matter he beat the other unconscious then used his raw and broken knuckles to calm her down and later smoothed her hair and face as would a father a frightened child. Dried her tears and slowed her sobs to ragged hiccups.

"But in the end boy (listen now) what really counted was that I pulled her to safety not–"

Morning he let her sleep in the cab of his truck. Afterward they struck up an abrupt friendship after he promised to visit to her small community and bring her as much peyote as possible and instruct her on its proper usage and ceremonies. An undertaking triggered after he was informed that her village was racked by poverty. Alcohol. Infighting and losing any semblance of communal spirit.

What's worse she added, drinking and hopelessness had started to infect younger members of the tribe as if despair was a contagious disease such as typhus or gripe. Ailments known nothing about before forced into army–overseen reservations and posts.

Watching his gas gauge creep to low wondered for the umpteenth if he is on the right road and asking all the while why this gal. This woman. This healer? When so many others have passed through his life since Dancing Woman his first and only wife died long ago.

"And Velvet?"

"She's all cut up."

"Me too amigo! Yeah. But beneath the skin. Listen hot shot! Someone as noble as she. Risking everything to learn about the peyote way is a rarity in these soulless n parched times."

"We's just stock on the way to our equivalent of chicago slaughter-houses unless we check our fall–running on empty.

"Yeah. And not just on gas."

"I can't hack this loneliness anymore!"

"And this healer going to fix you up?"

"Listen Sport!"

"She and I got a certain amity. Understanding. Simpatico. Understand!"

"Ok. I get you drift. We got enough fuel to make it?"

Doesn't answer. Just shifts into lower gear.

Winds thicken while he turns left trying to remember if this is the way or is memory playing tricks. Reservation lands often lack any distinguishing features and are composed of erased plains. Treeless scrublands. Nothing to hold the earth from joining sky. Land bakes when summer. Bogs when spring. Fit only for black fly and mosquito. While winter`s a long season ripe with death and his brides cold, hunger and sickness.

Almost out of fuel he stops. Reckoning he can hunt up a little kero-sene and mix it with what gasoline's left in his tank hoping it doesn't foul his carburetor.

Off the main road into trackless badlands fuel is hard to find. Used to keep a galvanized water can for it but some so and so stole it in el paso while he was wheeling and dealing over the price and quality of the peyote now in the back of his truck.

Judging that there's just enough fuel in the tank to retrace his track back to a small hamlet avoided earlier because they are unfriendly to natives he gets out. "Hell. As if we'd want to cohabitate with people to whom we are no better than coyotes or other vermin and not even worth the price of a bounty!"

Grabbing a sack of peyote buds, slings it over his shoulder. Before forgetting, reaches under his seat, grabs in order of its perceived importance. His canteen. Then his long shot never knowing.

'Gone spooky.'

This is how Velvet described her tiny villa last time they had a word.

Moseys. Glad for sun and clean sky overhead.

Not much rodent or bird life around. "

"What is it about these reservation lands that our generous benefactors planted us on that are so bereft of life and hope?" Really no knowing since had given up on resettlement long ago after his own family had a visit with typhus and typhus rode off with them.

Hour gone by he encounters the first signs of human habitation. Broken farm implements. Rusting milk cans. Conked–out wheels well as a spindly windmill and a rusted galvanized stock pond ringed by scrawny woebegone cows.

But no houses or people.

Just more rusted machinery. Finally he spies a group of kid's ahead intent on some childish game and walks up to their bent and furtive circle unnoticed.

One of the ragged children. Girl or boy? Peeks up at him with one eye half closed with a cyst. Yet the rest of the little urchin's face is perfectly formed.

Black Wolf wonders what's got their attention before offering a polite greeting, "Howdy!"

The children look at him shyly or guiltily depending on one's perspective. Only one youngster returns his greeting–the child of uncertain gender,

"Hello mister. Got any candy for us?" Kuy snaps his fingers. Regretful that he did not bring any from his truck.

"No. Sorry not this time!"

Another child demands, "Money?" Despite this irregular propensity for asking gifts from total strangers. The roadman hefts the peyote higher onto his shoulders and grabs the end of the sack with his strong teeth and digs into his front jeans pocket. With his free hand, he takes out some change and fishes copper from silver. The *plata* he needs. The copper. Well he was once a child. "Here *SyH–n*! Here's six pennies for six!"

"Give me!" a rather impudent lanky boy child demands while grabbing at his free hand.

Reacting with a measured calm. Black Wolf frowns. Not a little angry at this rude behavior. Again, so different from the expected behavior of his culture's social dictates for children toward adults. Especially strangers and outsiders.

Later questioned. They answer distractedly.

Satisfied. He then carefully thrusts a penny into each grubby hand. Having to stop the taller boy form forcing the bright pennies from the other children.

This boy. Around twelve he reckons. Livid, picks up a stone, and threatens the roadman. Not willing to get into a fracas with an ill–mannered youth, Black Wolf turns on his heels. Moves on.

Indeed something amiss here he surmises walking past this noon's furtive sport. A battered cat's head drawing a cloud of black flies.

Arriving finally at a no account square. Dusty. Surrounded by the usual suspects, dram shop, pawn shop, government agency shack, apothecary, he stops suddenly. Digs his boot hills in to the hard earth and waits.

A bunch of men of various ages meet his questioning gaze. Putting aside other considerations Black Wolf greets the men, "Hello."

"Hello. Yourself stranger!" a few of the men either squatting or standing reply.

Possibly Kiowas though one or two could pass for white. Of the lay-about. N'er do well variety.

"Help you?" One reasonable friendly asks.

"Yes. I am looking for Velvet Horn."

"Got business with her?"

"Said I did!" Black Wolf answers determinedly.

"Name?"

"Black Wolf."

"You are a *Q–gop* aren't you fellow?"

The roadman considers his response carefully before answering.

"Father was *TsH–'H–ga*. Me! I am just a drifter. Listen. Is Velvet Horn around here? I have something for her."

"Like what?"

Scratching his head, the roadman starts to agree with Velvet Horn. This settlement is cantankerous and obviously fallen into bad habits. Impolite address and empty–headed hostility, "I did not know that gifts brought to others were so discussed."

Angered a big fellow gets up. Hitches his bowie knife to a rakish tilt and walks toward Black Wolf with considerable menace.

Unfazed. Kuy smiles. Then tilts his Sharp carbine without aim a few degrees off his shoulder.

Catching sight of his rifle, Bully licks his lips, ignoring the questioning looks of his fellows, circles around as if lost or on another errand all–together before looking back. Wandering down the dirt road toward another cluster of buildings and shacks just as unpromising.

After this little pissing contest another man offers a friendly suggestion, "Don't mind them any," from his perch atop the shaded porch.

With a forced smile the roadman turns to him and demands, "What gives round here?"

Gent shrugs. Waves his hand around as if to include their surroundings before answering, "Nothing much. Just a bunch of sour pusses. Waiting around with nothing for nothing."

The roadman nods. Seen this before. "About Velvet Horn?"

The outgoing fellow looks at his friends. Shrugs and then offers to lead the roadman to her house. "It's just up toward that little round hill. Not far!"

Agreeing, Kuy follows.

"You're from around fort sill right brother?"

"Yes. On my way back. But I promised Velvet that I would bring her a gift."

"I ain't going to ask. But she spoke of a peyotist coming through soon. You he?"

"That's right *amigo.*"

After this exchange the tall man steps over and greets the stranger, "Good. We need some good medicine round here! I'm Two Cloud. Glad to meetcha friend!"

The roadman puts his sack of peyote down and shakes his new contact's hand with a strong grip, "I'm George Black Wolf. Glad to meet you as well."

"Kuy"

"Same brother."

Continue walking toward a hill. They pass a few stragglers but no one pays them any mind. This in itself is odd for any community of Kiowa. For the roadman knows that his people are inquisitive to a fault and always interested in strangers for the news. Tales and possible means of profit or barter.

But not here.

Not now.

Finally bent knee up a slight rise. Two Cloud knocks on a wooden door. Off a large parking case because it's stamped US MAIL.

"Who's knocking," a strong but clearly feminine voice calls out.

"Hello yourself Velvet. A fellow here to see you. One you spoke about maybe!"

A furtive bustle. Hurried husbandry follows before the door creaks open and out steps a tall, lithe woman wearing a bandanna of blue and turquoise silk covering her face below her eyes. A long dark green blouse and an old mexican skirt just covering sharp toed cowboy boots completes and compliments her rakish air or nonconformity.

Particular eyes greet them. One's cobalt blue. Other black as a raisin. Wide mouthed as well. Alluring till one sights her nose he recalled. Just a torn stub where it once graced all the rest. Flurries of scars across her face mar as well. As if her face's flesh was sloshed water stilled. All in all it hard to meet her head on but the warmth and friendly spirit emanating from her wide smile and merry sparkling eyes dispels much of its shock.

"Kuy!"

Smiling, drops his sack for the second time, then chastely kisses the healer square on her mouth.

Watching, Two Cloud slightly embarrassed, readies his exit.

"Well. I am here. Said I would," the roadman exclaims happily.

"Yes. You are! Those them?"

"Yep. About twenty pounds from the heft of them!"

"Enough. How much do I owe you for the lot?"

"Nothing."

"Sold. Want to come in?"

"Reckon."

Feeling like an intruder. Two Cloud. Though a close friend of Velvet—with a little more stake in the pot if truth be told—not wishing to interfere. Since whatever notions these two strange folk are up to. It's probably not his business and perhaps not of his liking so he excuses himself. Yet before he can retrace his steps downhill. Velvet thanks him for showing her guest to her door and then ushers the tall peyotist inside.

Stooping low, he crosses pass her threshold after making a particular. Involuntary sign.

Inside the ceiling is just high enough for him to stand up. There's only one room. Well swept and hung with countless bundles. Strings of dried grasses. Herbs. Knots of roots. Even dried animals and other bundles and bunches that only nameless spirits could name.

"Like tea roadman?"

"Yes. Pleased to."

"You walk all the way from mexico?"

"No Velvet. Trucked."

"Where's your stead then?"

"Left it down a way."

"Why?"

"Gas"

"That short?"

"That short!"

"We could scrape up some money from some interested parties."

"No."

"Why not?"

"This is a gift. A seed."

"Well. You have seen what type of soil it will have to spring from–"

Nodding, inquires curtly, "Things that bad here?"

"Yes. One or two more bad winters. Another fallow summer without rain or too much rain. Then people well sell out and run from here as from the white's devil!"

"*Seni* will help Velvet!"

"Might! But things bout finished here," she informs him sadly. Though not all together resignedly.

Though her face is ruined. Body still like a young woman's and much to his chagrin. Her full breasts' tug at her blouse. Catch his eye despite. Another annoying distraction. Velvet's hair. Long. Clean. Glossy as a colt's. A dark screen of silk to hide her ruined features.

Returning his gaze. His uninvited, unfamiliar admiration burnishing her body, she shyly ducks her head and looks away with embarrassment and confusion.

In tandem Kuy swallows. Wondering where his thoughts have strayed before reining them in with an embarrassed cough, "True everywhere. We're not farmers. Never were! How do they expect us just to change horses in the middle of the stream as a matter of speaking."

Glancing at him. She shrugs before sitting down cross–legged on her hard dirt floor and beckoning him to join her. Later after lighting a small charcoal brazier she prepares tea as they enjoin kindred expression and field studied questions.

Concerned about his truck. He looks at his watch. Notes the time and decides that he will just have to risk his Hercules' safety to wind, night, and star.

Smoothing her hair back from her face. Velvet asks a simple question, "Truck worrying you?"

"A little."

"Don't! No one here knows how to drive. Hell. We have never seen a truck let alone–"

Shifting their conversation back to matters more pertinent, they lower their voices, speaking about many subjects.

Seni

Old legends

Mexican and indigenous ceremonies and as their discussion grows more nebulous, Black Wolf watches her from the corner of his eye. Velvet always averts her face when speaking, judges that this must be a habit of long standing because he cannot break her of this. Irked by her continued discomfort, Black Wolf brings his hand up. Cups her chin. Gently forcing her to face him.

Velvet tries to turn away from him but he does not allow her. "I am getting hard of hearing. So face me if you want me to hear you clearly."

"This true or do you want just to be kind?"

"True!"

She smiles. Relaxes a little. Later. Shifts her weight from one leg to another. Moving closer to the now silent, dark featured man sitting on her left as her lamp flickers, dies and shadows soon flank them from every corner.

Black Wolf senses her body`s warmth. Notices her scent as well. Similar to the grasses and herbs hanging above them.

Night's warm. Soft and gentle. Little wind. Although a breeze. Now and then rocks the eaves above them.

More relaxed than for many a month Kuy allows himself a degree of license by removing his boots and hat. Laying them by her side as she watches him silently with eyes hinting shyness and fear hidden within her, demure, sure exterior, well as emotions long denied from being forcefully segregated most of her young life from the joys, normal occupation and trials and tribulations of other young women smolder though like charcoal in a banked fire.

Yet behind this mask Velvet softens. Wishing not for the millionth time that either the occurrence that cruelly maimed her so did not happen or that she had died afterward and not had to face this life so different from the one envisioned or promised by general expectation. Despite herself. She feels her breasts shifting free from the cloth that binds them and with a chafe that is not unpleasant her sex moists with mirth and desire not of her choosing.

Uncomfortable with her gender's ordained role she reverts with courage back to another possible capacity. That of a healer expressing a matriarchal concern for her community. Though they too disdain her until illness or need spurs them uphill or seek her out on dark nights after the whiskey or gin is gone and temptations for any outlet even it's marked and cut up. Still she's better than nothing it's often alleged meanly and matter of factually down below in the village.

Kuy too longs. Harried priest that he is—aware of her bundled form warming the cool night air a foot away partially obscured by this night, spice rich with dried essences of flower, and strong curative plaits put aside for winter's cruelty and mishap's fancy.

Guiltily aware of each other and mutual longing, they move apart and resume their leaned discussions as if other occurrence stirred them not as nature commands as salmon toiling upstream. Bird entwined with bird or fox arched and mounted with the calibrated need.

Ignoring flesh's usual ruses. Velvet bends low. Husky voiced. Irritated.

She had thought these annoyances banished or long buried, asks, "This peyote. These new ceremonies. More of the same Kuy? Buffalo Dances. Ghost Dancing. Calling old spirits with songs best forgotten and buried with the bones of our ancestors?"

Man disagrees, "No! We are speaking of matters both old before knowing and as new as my truck Velvet. I call *Seni* seeds and they are! Peyote can stop drink. Fighting and violence. It helps to dispel disappointment and despair like a balm drawing poison."

Velvet Horn glances at him with a light in her eyes that makes him a tad uneasy. Hero light. Admiration. For him?

"Nothing earth shaking Velvet! But maybe on the other hand salvation for those otherwise without!"

"You peyotists are rebels. You know this?"

"Yes!"

"It's only a matter of time before whites try to put a stop to this."

"They already have. Had to spend twice as long as I wanted to find and purchase as much *Seni* as I was able." Kuy then changes the subject. Uncomfortable with so much or their conversation focusing upon him. "How's things with you?" he asks softly.

Apprehensive by his unsolicited insight into her loneliness. Disfigured exile from her sex's normalcy, little joys and life's normal course, Velvet screws her eyes up and spreads her hands helplessly, "I am going to move on soon if people here don't take to peyote."

"Why?"

She shrugs. Then answers frankly, "Look at me man!"

Does. Shooting her a candid stare.

"With my face. Not a man wants me except for a late night, drunken jape! And with people leaving week to week and never returning. Any means of earning a living is now beyond me! Who needs a healer, or if they do. People are more apt to hitch a team or walk to a nearby medico for treatment–"

He disagrees but she cuts him short. "No wait," she begs. Holding up her hand to halt his sincere. Though meaningless and polite negation of the truth, "No fellow or woman really would want someone like me."

He smiles sadly as she continues. "Though when liquored up a man or two might stop and bother me but I would rather dry up and blow away than let them touch me. Get with child. Then two would starve than one!"

"How old are you Velvet?"

She bids him quiet again while tallying up her years. "Reckon thirty–five or a little more."

Black Wolf courtly denies her self–depreciation with a flourish, "Still young!"

"No. Those Pawnee scouts that did my face busted up my insides and my cunt's just as scarred as my face!" During her outburst, Velvet's features coarsen and stretch into a frightful mask. Boiling over emotionally, she hisses with hatred, that only evaporates slowly like steam as the hour passes.

Looking away Kuy, saddened and embarrassed, doesn't know what to do or say. But he's spared any embarrassment when Velvet, regaining control of herself, briefly turns away from him before asking softly, "Want to stay stranger till morning walks again with us?"

Looking at his watch again. Sighs. It will take how long to teach her the rudiment of basic peyote ceremonies both specific and general.

"Yes."

When dark outside, a small kerosene lamp is lit. It casts only a small measure of light. A glow too low to enable them to read each other's features or expression until she turns up its flame.

Man and woman stop speaking as it brightens anew. Then resume. Mostly, she listens as he explains. Teaching patiently.

***

Hours past, tired of instruction, he offers her a first hand of sacrament. The taste of knowledge. Sweet and acid as experience itself.

"Try some?"

"Is it like lightening? Will it sear me?"

45

Ruefully, he smiles at her ignorance. Slightly offended answers, "No. I won't give you much the first time. Some take to it. Others no. A few. Take no affect what so ever."

After considering her opportunity, aware of what is at stake, inclines her head demurely. Accepting his proposal, "Yes Kuy please."

Nodding, he then carefully takes out his long bladed barrow knife and cuts first one portion and then another. After a number of buttons have been carefully segmented, they share the sacrament. Each ingesting at least eight buttons.

After an hour or more, Kuy feels spirits coil in his gut. Then spread from limb to head. Velvet. Silent. Still. As if waiting important visitor.

Private reverie.

Dark. Darker still. Her lamp just a sputtering nuisance to tired and travel strained eyes.

Velvet? Across from him she transforms into waves of color beyond measure or easy accounting.

Warm and lovely, glowing molten with spring flowers' hue or the last band of sunset after a dust storm's passing, cast adrift and gathered by *Seni* to fête this moment's actuality.

Kuy gasps, "But I knew this. I knew!"

"What?" she asks. The first word passed between them in over an hour.

Before answering her, again he marvels at her strength. What degree of pain she must carry. As if it's equal to the measure of water carried by her sister's day in and day out, however, her burden is not liquid for cooking or washing but sorrow and regret for a life cruelly dictated by pointless violence.

Without warning. Velvet crosses over to him and caresses his face and Black Wolf after a moment of surprised inactivity responds slowly. Changing tempo with a fury of unleashed emotions he thought long dead and buried as she confesses softly, "I love you Kuy!"

"Me! Why? I am just an old stumblebum!"

"Just do!"

Grins. Then warns, "Loving a tumble weed might get you a little winded."

"No listen," she says tenderly. Placing her perfect. Graceful fingers on his lips to stop him from talking, "Ever since that night you saved me from those mexicans."

"Hell! That was a tough tussle."

"–since then. I thought about you. Wondered if you would truly pass by."

"Said I would!"

"Most men say many things but don't live up to their word."

"Well. I try. Father taught me to follow my words with action or shut up."

"Your father was a wise man."

Black Wolf accepts her comment with a curt nod before adding, "Reckon so hon, but they don't make his kind anymore!"

Then without pause yet with considerable bravery, Velvet simply repeats what her pounding heart spoke before, "I love you Kuy."

Responding to her soft, terribly vulnerable words with a softening of eye, he places his right hand on her left shoulder while Velvet in turn slowly unbuttons the front of her old calico cowboy shirt and slips his callused and scarred right hand inside against her left breast.

Black Wolf, no milksop once the table's laid, kisses her again till she's all smiles and mouthing silently, "Yes," before kissing him and letting her tongue play deep till rooted fully into his throat. Sharing breath and measured pleasure.

Assured, eased by her acceptance, summoned by her banked heat, Black Wolf takes his hand again and firmly places it back on her flesh.

Her thick hardening nipples respond. Welcoming. Guiding as he slips her shirt off, kissing each breast before tracing her ridged stomach and the flanks of her long, fine boned thigh below the waist of her somehow displaced and discarded spanish skirt. Much to his delight her skin's smooth as pulled satin and colored like old honey or smoke gathered on the skim of water. In the dim light her scars are not as visible and her clipped nose no disfigurement. Now an embellishment as if carved by the hand of a stern artisan. Its sharp defile acts as a signpost for her mouth both warm and inviting. Its breath sweet. Her breasts full. Playfully sharp against his now half unbuttoned shirt.

Love. A feast after great hunger for this man and woman a quickening release after a paucity of longing.

Afterward he crowds her wrapped in an old mexican blanket on her hard floor, warning, "I came in you several times."

"I know."

"What if you have a child?"

"Doubt it but if I did?" she demands.

"Keep it!"

"Why?"

"Man should leave something behind of himself."

"No others?"

"Once!"

"What happened?"

Near shadow remains silent as the night around them.

Grasping his unspoken response Velvet's eyes narrow. Spark. She gently drops her question, "I understand." Tugging her hips and freeing herself from him. "Anyway what if I do?"

"Send word to either Old Smoke or William Buffalo. They will see to it that your message reaches me."

"Who are they?"

"Good friends"

"Fort sill folk?"

"Yes."

"And if not?"

"Velvet. I'll swing back around again in two or three months' time."

"Three months is a long time Kuy."

"Yes it is," he admits while listening to her heart thump buried beneath her old shirt she chose to sleep in. "Don't worry though," Velvet says with a catch in her throat, "you won't have many rivals!"

Kuy kisses her again deeply and leads her into sleep. Then whispers but she does not hear his words, "Nor you love."

Sleep long both and for once in a great while Kuy doesn't rise at dawn. Instead gets up when it's truly another day. Dresses. Slings his rifle over his shoulder and leaves. Though her eyes are shut she watches and hears his going waiting.

Chapter Six

Leaving Velvet, filled his tank before starting a hard day of driving. Now with night pouring deep like molasses overhead, whistling along, inadvertently offending a pack of rowdy canines. As his taillights recede hunger whips them forward, sleepy laggards trailing behind yawning and stretching, stirring reluctantly into an assembly of need.

Fighting to stay awake at the wheel Kuy summons his father's strong voice for a winter's tale to keep his eyes open and on the road,

'Fought kit carson once that son of a bitch! Listen *Tahlee*,' Iron Knife stormed, 'Many years ago we camped near Red River in the middle of a long winter like this one. Part of our camp was laid out along a frozen creek. Our main camp was further away. Game was scarce. The buffalo slaughtered. We were hungry. Not looking for a fight! Just to live.

One night I couldn't sleep. Felt uneasy. Hell. It was hard times all around. Hearing neighing from the stockade. I went to check on our horses. *Ahoow*, I spied soldiers coming to attack us so I turned around and raced back to our camp to give alarm. All of our men ran out with whatever they had on to fight. In them days we slept with guns more than woman. You and your mother—you were just a child—ran in the other direction away from the battle. We reached our horses and fought until pushed back.

We abandoned everything; carson burned our camp and everything in it! They made us poor. We nearly starved and froze the next couple of days before we could remedy our calamity. We were able to save half the lodges in the other camp. We rode down the Red River and started a new camp by the Wolf and Beaver rivers. We spent the rest of the winter hiding there. Licking our wounds. We helped and shared with each other. Trading wild horses for supplies wherever we could.

After the battle. We found two old people burned up inside their shelter. Guess they chose to die together rather than trying to start over with nothing. There were a lot of needless deaths on that day,' his father added deep in remembrance as night brought more cold and sleet.

Snapped back. Kuy swerves hard to avoid hitting a hawk. His Hercules lurches left up a widening rut. Challenging unsound front left tire as he cross steers.

Unmannered the dark raptor with no apology at all soars over a barb-wire fence. Following its upward flight, the roadman, a long–suffering man, moves on without further comment.

***

After camping for the night with a small brush fire for company and a quick breakfast of resinous coffee and leather britches beans, he extinguishes the remains of his fire and drives on.

Wind's heavy. Throwing sheets of dust.

When younger, say fifteen, wind was an ally and not an enemy–helping to screen them from marauding cavalry as desert gusts carried the scent of enemy mess fires and the smell of shit from their overfed tethered *tsainñ* as the echoes of lonely soldiers' curses and their ribald jokes foxed over silhouetted scrub and narrow defiles where his band crouched silently in a dry gully behind a wind scoured rise like captured shadows. Passing time. Waiting for the soldiers and fires to sleep and for darkness to blanket their enemy's camp so they could kill them.

Behind their informal lines of watch. Army pickets both black and white if not asleep loitered; soldiers heard only waking desert wayward winds. Coyotes. Which to city–bred ears were strange. Disturbing the night with unfamiliar measure.

Bored with long watches posted men turned their thoughts to home. Loved ones. Favorite saloons or green hills soft with spring rain or over-ripe ports rich with woman and whiskey.

Usually only the youngest or least popular soldiers served picket duty. On watch. Their gaze grew tired–ears lax. Heads nodding–folding into sleep. Too late they heard the whispered command, "*Ahoow*, kill them," as his people lurched forward to kill or die trying.

Kuy knew these small wars and grew to manhood and bled in them. Final stands against the imprisonment of their nation. A last gasp of resistance before forced acceptance of resettlement near fort sill oklahoma.

Angry. Gritting his teeth, Kuy banishes all to the white man's hell as he steers. "At what price is a nation's death redeemed?"

Later as morning becomes day and day afternoon he exclaims softly, "I must be careful. People need me," before cautiously scouting an orphaned valley ahead. It's an unlucky territory woven into a tapestry of conflicting forces which the roadman divides into several mercurial categories. Benevolent. Undecided. Neutral. Baneful and downright dangerous. Their roles are not static. Shifting allegiances. Acting on skittish whims not clearly understood.

Ancient land. Battlegrounds. Especially the surrounding windswept shallow valleys and worn knolls stretching below his descent.

To his people. These are dangerous grounds–not to be taken lightly. Wondrous and treacherous earth rife with nameless devils and saints. Here a night crossing is very dangerous and only a strong individual or a fool passes these haunted lands alone and unprotected rather than awaiting day behind walls or stretched hides guarded by small aromatic brush fires. Sentinels against the closing dark.

With so many miles ahead and with so little collected from his poor congregation at the last ceremony. The roadman can barely buy the meager supplies needed except for gas. "Yet if my congregation had offered more I would not have taken it." For he realizes that starvation stalks them. Their quick evasive smiles could not shunt his chary eyes away from the looks of fear and concern they cast toward their thin children crying and coughing in the shadows while listening to their elders' low and careful voices, "Winter is coming following these times of hunger and cold," they whispered.

Grimly he tightens his grip on the wheel as the highway degrades into a narrow defile skirting the lap of dwarfish hills.

With this road grown silent, mulish and of little counsel, he hums a tune picked up from cafes and dry goods stores frequented on his travels to keep him company. Pleasant and sometimes graceful. These songs. Like drink and cheap clothing issued from reservation stores, they are snares of forgetfulness, failure and self–loathing, and so he stops.

As he turns a curve later a long white feather flutters into his cab. He catches it and after a quick glance thrusts it into his hatband for luck as he debates which route to take back to green county and fort sill.

He could take one of the newer paved roads cropping up like the barbwire. Electric lights and white communities over spreading the vast plains but aware of what awaits him in this new emerging world he out of habit chooses to take alternative, less traveled routes.

Trying to place experience into perspective, Kuy scowls-"townsfolk mistreat the People." Rankling him and his considerable pride masked beneath meekness while their eyes follow him or shunt him outside with a tin plate of sour beans and cornbread on the back porch with other people of color or mock him as eases his backside on a stool drinking hot bitter coffee.

"There are good people among them but a stray dog never knows which hand will scratch him and which hand will strike him. A wolf knows better for all hands are raised against his kind."

In towns and lonely diners strung along his highway detractors don't see the knife and bullet scars earned by combat from dead men. Unaware as well of the foot long Bowie or *k'oo* hidden in his boot. Nor of the powerful Remington kept oiled and hidden under his front seat. Though of little or no use since he has turned away from violence. War and armed combat just as surely as from whiskey. Abrasive or corrosive pursuits serving no purpose since his nation is buried and its people scattered and their victorious enemy pays them no more mind than if they were cart horses. Humbled. Obedient servants pastured out awaiting their next block of hay resigned to fate's idylls.

"Violence and revenge are a waste of time," he admits, slowing down to turn off a main artery onto a gravel drive.

Tired from driving up from the border and feeling the long miles. Hard on both truck and constitution, the Kudwa twists in his seat, getting comfortable since there is only more of the same ahead. Yet his parishioners need peyote and even though new troubles follow roadmen and road chiefs since the american government has begun to harass and sometime impede peyote traffic. Someone has to gather their principle sacrament.

"Hilarious," he comments driving down a hard clay lane, "or just tragic," before adding caustically, "Whites drink from dusk to dawn. Whoop it up. Sell their poison or make it as they please but if we gather *Seni* from the ground we're in the wrong!"

Would have driven further south and bypassed texas altogether but trouble in mexico made driving down there dangerous so he bought cactus from a *mestizo* root doctor he knows on the texas side where *Seni* goes for about ten dollars a crate.

Seni doesn't grow too far north. Only in a few places above the border and they have long been picked over or are located on unfriendly–posted land.

Even now he marvels how land can be partitioned with invisible lines by selfish hands. Even borders are nonsensical. For example, the frontier between texas and mexico.

Bets a hundred dollars to any taker that they could not spot the difference between the two countries while standing on what a map or globe would represent as a two–color division where one nation began and one ended.

In the past he rode over their imaginary borders like an eagle or falcon without noticing but now with each year. Officials on each side of the border attempt to corral people like branded cattle.

With winter coming, even here, there's a subtle change in the weather despite the boiling heat; most of his parishes will suffer from poor harvests, failing stock, hungry kids and needy elders this coming year and they will need all the help he will bring.

Sanctioning that, "White churches only give handouts paid for by submissions that are too costly. Cultural and spiritual death. While peyote offers another path to salvation and pride to reweave our culture to fight poverty, alcohol, despair and hungers both physical and spiritual, thus allowing me if not the ability to heal, then at least to offer my people a respite. How it all started. How prisoners long ago in florida furtively sketched the peyote way?"

This he happily clarifies, "It's funny," speaking from remembrance, "When they had us locked up. All of us bad "injuns" from different tribes. Old pratt did not know what he was doing! Sure christianity, well as reading, writing, and arithmetic and all of their pap were forced down our throats but little did they know that teaching us english opened up the door to for us to talk to each other."

Afterward, he tips his hat and spits, "Kill the Indian and save the man!" and later down road continues, "At night we discussed many matters. The promises of prophets. Ghost dances. More importantly of *Seni* and old Lipan rituals brought up from mexico. Why! This became our university for rebellion and not for assimilation!" he adds with a bitter smile, "More than worth the price of admission!"

Parks then steps out. The owner of the hash and chili stand he had stopped for is white but he doesn't pay mind to whom he serves and he's married to a big fine mexican gal and has a pack of young ones who could pass for reservation children.

Kuy steps up to a screened partition and rough wooden counter where food is served. Prices have gone up a little since last month's circuit he grumbles.

Not a soul around so he calls through a rusty–screen service window, "Hello. Anyone here," to induce service.

Except kids playing somewhere though, it's quiet with no other customers around. Finally after catching the attention of the owner and his wife, the roadman orders and after being served strolls away from the stand to take a seat on a tilting wooden table ringed by dusty cottonwoods.

After stretching and yawning he takes out a couple of road maps and spreads them out on the table to study them. Trying to find a better route north. Examining the maps, he thinks about all of the people waiting for him, "Well. There will be a lot of ceremonies. Lots of healing and singing with this load," he promises.

Tilting back on the hard bench. Closes his eyes. Feeling worn all of a sudden asks, "Is it age?" For he has been feeling ill used and tired. "Hell. With all the mileage I put on me and the truck. It's a wonder either one of us are running full bore!"

While scraping his bowl clean, two small dogs beg for a bite. The chili would only make them sick so he shoos them away and afterward, sits back; loosens his belt and wonders about his life that was furtively cast long ago in florida with other desperate men locked away in an old spanish dungeon.

Tilting back his hat, watches children play tag in the shimmering heat behind the little stand. One reminds him of his own son long dead. Bitter, Kuy turns away and watches a flock of black birds fight over crumbs.

Worried about money. He'll have to find work. At least a day or two to scratch up food and gas money to reach his flock and return home.

He's confident though. Since taking up his calling one salutary fact manifests itself. The road always provides.

Digesting, Kuy wonders about past associates—other jailbirds. His peers or rephrased, his fellow apostles of the peyote way. "Sometimes. I wonder what happened to my wild fellows. White Goose. Good Teeth and Old Bad Eye. All of us locked up under president's grant's Order 88" Kuy grows grim while recalling the fate of one friend. "Setkopte. Old friend. When you coughed your lungs out on a cold new york winter did you ever believe we'd make it even this far? All that we promised and fought for hasn't come about—yet," he pauses to take his last drink of tea. "We're still fighting. Rest easy Setkopte. I for one will never turn aside!"

Chapter Seven

 Young man startled reluctantly covered with powdered, crystalline snow without remedy or deliverance and wept tears that froze unless wiped away with a clockwork regularity before being allowed to settle.

Raw earth and clay clung to both hands from his dead son's grave as well. Foxing his ribboned and slashed clothing. Cut in mourning. As was his head. Crudely shorn. Pale scalp showed through like a scar under black stubble.

Caught in a storm. He cursed himself for being desperate enough to have sought medical help so far from home.

Socked with sleet his full–length rubber mackintosh shielded his pale wife cradled in his lap. Her face once beautiful was ravaged by emotion and illness. One of her slender fingers bled. Sliced off in bereavement.

Formally part of a committee helping the sick and old with food de-liveries, burial parties and other crisis services, Black Wolf abandoned serving on the diminished, and scattered emergency council after his son's death and his wife's grave illness and focused instead on frantically searching for every possible remedy. Buffalo doctors and witches. Even bribing a white doctor to come to his house.

Doctor did little or nothing. With a dismissive tone. The bleary eyed. Unsympathetic for hire medico pronounced typhus. It was an easy as-sumption. When so many were either dead or dying from it. Though it would be hard to qualify his diagnosis in the face of their spotless white wood frame house lit by two–floor length catalog ordered glass windows and the fresh, vinegar sharp scent throughout. Nor withstanding the clean wash hanging outside frozen fast as forlorn sails on a dead ship.

After his son, *YiHgyH–dou* or "In Four Places," so named because of his almost magical ability to be in four places at once died. A group of family and friends built a great bonfire to thaw the ground. His father did not want him like so many to await spring like sacked grain.

Disdaining further help. Kuy no longer cared frankly about other unfortunates under the shadow of disease, cold and hunger. An effective trinity in place after fall's disastrous harvest. Poor rains and early frosts. Effectively stilling hope and stealing lives.

After In Four Places' funeral. Black Wolf dismissed attending family and friends to carry *Kuan–mH*, his wife back to their house.

Her parents rested in the back of his gig also awaiting burial but gusty, blizzard conditions drove mourners and attendants away to find shelter.

On return Black Wolf managed to get his feverish wife inside. Light a fire and tend to her slowly diminishing needs. Before nightfall. Another blizzard set in. With a desperate decision, Black Wolf heaved her parents' corpses onto his front porch and forced his reluctant horses into the settlement's tired, withered heart to its sole besieged clinic.

Flurries all but concealed the ramshackle council and bureau buildings' outlines while frantic fathers, mothers, sons, and daughters milled about. Heavily bundled. They beseeched attention from any white shuffling by in the cold.

Bureau headquarters. School. Dispensary. Mission. Informal saloon. Trading post. Were sketched by sleight of hand fires burning fitfully in old kerosene drums. This dispelled some of the cold. Though not enough to warm the sick and dying crowded inside every shelter. But it too was arked with dead and dying stacked on desks, tables well as covering the unpainted wooden floor–air thick with the suppurating, sickly sweet odor of disease and death.

No outside medical help had come to their assistance. Pellagra. Rubella. Not to cast an aspersion but often–called german measles. Whooping cough. Tuberculosis. Scurvy. Typhus. Once unknown as their name, these fevers fell with the first snow like avenging spirits and overwhelmed them.

As winter deepened . The dead and dying were propped up or lay draped or uncovered in front of their community's small dispensary and clinic.

Inside. Beleaguered doctors and nurses struggled to cope with both the ravages of contagion and their patients' traditional attitudes toward healing and infectious disease. Bureau agents sent several desperate telegraphs requesting aid but no assistance reached them.

It was deliberated and later judged that lack of any concerted effort to mitigate the outbreak of typhus was intentional. Cynically reasoning that there was a lot of land in question and the tread bare promises from washington and local authorities had fallen into apathy. Why give them seed grain. Instruction and government land grants if the only return were sallow furrows. Weeds. Rusting plows. Gaunt horses and sickly cows ringed by thin, expectant children. Loitering elders and unremitting flies.

Even the more indifferent among them faced with the cold, hunger and suffering around them. Cursed pointlessly. Calling down both temporal and spiritual wrath upon the perceived heartlessness of officials both military and civil charged with maintaining their virtual charges if not in the pink of health, then least free from scourges of communicable or nutritional based maladies such as pellagra which struck children and the elderly fed almost exclusively on government provided grain or seed corn roughly ground into meal darkened with mold and the patina of age and neglect.

Dutifully they had organized burial parties. Food distribution and general councils but to no avail. Anger spread yet escaped a specific focus or target. Each doctor was faced with an impossible task. The weather and the mixed, savage epidemics attacking them had created a deadly combination.

Against this grim setting Black Wolf staggered into the sleet and rain with his wife to fight their way to the dispensary. Vowing that he would not be turned away, Kuy forced his way pass two native constables inside. Knowing him. They ignored his trespass.

Inside, a hurried nurse stopped him. Hysterically, she pointed back outside and screamed at him to wait his turn.

"Where am I to wait," he demanded. "My wife's sick! She's dying–"

"Outside!"

"It's cold and raining outside–"

She shrugged while suggesting, "In the schoolroom!"

"Full of dead!"

"Not my responsibility," she irritably replied.

Hearing their argument. A tired. Slovenly medical orderly, marched over and attempted to force them back outside.

With one arm, Kuy grabbed him by the throat and brought him to his knees. The orderly. Recognizing him, apologized, then lurched away like a tired short–tailed stoat. Afterward a hemic stained doctor enraged at this breach of protocol stood in front of Black Wolf and read him the riot act until he noticed the look of pain and desperate concern stamped on the Kiowa's face and relented after Kuy pleaded with him to take a quick look at his wife.

"Go home!" The doctor ordered afterward. Placing the blanket back over her. "Can't you tell she's dead? I'm sorry," he commented with a rationed degree of sympathy. "She's gone sir! There are many more waiting. Please take her and go," he commanded, before turning his back on him to arrest a hemorrhaging cough of an old woman.

Grief numbed, Black Wolf carried her back to the wagon and carefully laid her in its bed. Returning with their horses, surprisingly no worse for the weather after being tied under a porch, hitched them to his wagon and with a hard, "Hah," lurched homeward as the snow. No longer ragged; individual flakes, fell like a winter army in unbroken, serried ranks.

Home. Black Wolf placed *Kuan–mH* on their kitchen table. On its two wooden benches her parents' corpses dressed the occasion.

Stirred later from fretful, disturbed sleep in the pitch–black to answer a loud, determined knock, Kuy after pulling a blanket closer around him, demanded, "Who's there?"

"Old Smoke!"

"What do you want?"

"Let me in. I heard about–"

"Come in–" Black Wolf said and opened the door and let his friend inside. There was just enough moonlight to hint of the tragedy inside.

"*Kuan–mH*. Dancing Woman. *YiHgyH–dou?*" Old Smoke demanded frantically.

Black Wolf remained silent.

So his friend asked again in disbelief, "All!"

"*Pééy–*"

Old Smoke embraced his friend while steadying him, "Sorry I came so late. I was not near but when I heard–" he cleared his voice choked with sympathy and then added, "What are we going to do?"

Black Wolf clinched his fists. Didn't answer. But the wind did. It howled.

"Your boy," Old Smoke demanded, "*YiHgyH–dou?*"

"Buried! Before the storm."

"And your wife?"

"In the kitchen with her mother and father–"

"I can get some men together. Help you. Tomorrow if the weather lets up–"

"No. The ground is too hard–"

"We can light a fire. Melt the ice and then–"

"No!" Black Wolf shouted.

Old Smoke noticing the wild, grieving look in his friend's red–rimmed eyes, didn't like the tormented glare and wild sorrowing, hesitant gestures so uncharacteristic of his young friend and so reasoned with him, "Listen. Storm's getting worse! Come with me to my place before we are forced to spend the rest of the night here and when the weather dies down, we'll come back with some brothers and lay everyone into winter's embrace!"

Black Wolf shook his head, "I have other plans!"

"What plans?" Old Smoke asked worriedly.

"Fire this house!"

"Are you crazy–Where'd you go?"

"Away–"

"In winter?"

Black Wolf pulled away from his friend's restraint and gently pushed him into the kitchen.

Old Smoke noticed the three dead on the table and shuddered with supernatural dread. Mastering himself, he tried to convince Black Wolf to take more immediate action, "Listen! You know that we have to do for them as tradition demands–Come with me and then we will return–"

"In this weather. I will not leave her alone." Kuy stated, first pointing to his wife. Then her mother and father shrouded beside her before adding, "Or them either. Good people! Can't leave them with only the night and wind for company–"

"Then tomorrow. Right now, we can sleep in the barn–"

"No–I built this house."

"I helped!"

"True–"

"Every other nail driven into these walls is mine," Old Smoke reminded his friend.

Black Wolf half smiled. Also recalling that late summer's hurried apprenticeship with carpentry.

Remembering as well Old Smoke wistfully replied, "We didn't know how to use hammer! I lost half my fingernails. But we became pretty good carpenters by summer end we did–"

All the while. Only half–paying attention to his friend's consoling words, Black Wolf silently crossed over to his kitchen and took down a box of kitchen matches.

Alarmed, Old Smoke watched, guessing his intent, protested, "It would be a waste–"

Black Wolf ignored him and looked out through a framed window at the gusting snow. The moon shined through for a moment like the wink of an eye.

"No. Not a waste," he argued while motioning toward the dead. "I built this home for her. My son. Now they're gone–"

"Many have died. I'm sorry but–"

Black Wolf didn't listen or reply. Instead, he rushed into the back and grabbed two saddlebags, his heavy coat, knife, and rifle and then rejoined Old Smoke in his cold dark kitchen. With a growl. More warning than threat. He ordered Old Smoke outside.

Resignedly. His friend joined him on the front porch where both stiffened in the cold and braced for what was to come bundled up as best as possible as they made torches from fireplace logs. Thus equipped. Black Wolf splashed coal oil around the inside while Old Smoke stood apart helplessly watching. Later warming his hands with his breath, he again attempted to assist his friend, "Listen, I built half of this. Let me help!"

"No!" Black Wolf replied exhaustedly. "Just stand and watch with me–"

First started a blaze in his son's bedroom. Ignoring its contents assembled with loving hands. His grandmother's quilt. His father's bow. A half–completed wooden carving of a bull elk–he looked away for the last time and then torched the lot. Later treated the main bedroom in a similar fashion. Disregarding the tableau of *Kuan–mH's* reading glasses perched between the pages of her rice paper bible. Then kitchen and front room. Using his torch like an erasing brand. Enraged with loss. Empty with sorrow. He expressed his conflicted emotions with savage swiftness.

And as a result, within minutes, arid pine. Dried by winter and warming hearth. First smoked. Then burst into flame. Erasing any physical representations of laughter, fellowship, and family spirit collected within.

Crackling flame followed by thick black smoke rolled out of the rooms, forcing the two friends back outside to watch from the porch.

The house's two windows, glowed like fevered eyes till the heat and smoke drove them further into the frozen yard where they silently watched the conflagration contest winter and push back the blizzard's strength.

But they knew that this was only a brief respite.

Black Wolf said nothing. Didn't move. Displayed no emotion and said not a word as his beloved house burned.

Old Smoke kept a respective distance and watched with a mournful consideration. At that moment more concerned with the living than the dead. Reasoning that you cannot aid them, those who were called away to wait.

As the last rafters smoked and sizzled. There was a long, plaintive cry from the flames. Like a soul's final expiration. Followed by more pops and whistles.

Red faced. Chapped. Dried and roasted by the fire's heat they edged further way. Wary of the now roaring fire and its escaping cinders and flaring sparks despite the flurries and cold around them. Occasionally they looked over their shoulders but soon relaxed again into a stolid, waiting vigil unmarred by an owl's cry or errant animal's call. Surrounded only by the falling snow and its handmaidens—cold and dark they watched silently as the flames died and the cold returned even more intense and threatening.

By and by, bundled figures silently joined their vigil. Neighbors. Drawn by the light and flame on the horizon. At first believing that the fire was accidental, they braved the weather to help put out the blaze, but after their arrival, one by one or in pairs, they soon realized whose house was afire and most importantly, why and after surmising the situation, they held back from putting it out. Letting their water buckets and axes fall at their side and silently stepped back and let flame eat.

No one spoke. Recognizing Black Wolf's mourning and loss they ringed him without word or touch. Some were friends of his wife or his wife's family. Others were relations. Whose presence conveyed concern and shared sorrow and if not abetting his misfortune, least shared it throughout the freezing night till one by one they returned to their farmsteads silently and wordlessly as ghosts returning to the grave.

Old Smoke left alone by his friend's side in the closing circle of diminished light and warmth asked worriedly, "What are you going to do now?"

Black Wolf watching snow and sleet's final assault on the remaining dying embers at first did not reply. Then placing his bags and rifle over his should. He pointed to his small barn, "I am going to sleep inside with my horses till tomorrow. Then ride off–"

"Where?"

Black Wolf didn't answer for there wasn't one.

The two men despite their thick winter clothes felt the wind's bite and retreated to the barn. Only Black Wolf glanced back over his shoulder with a shudder.

The dying fire. Waked by ash and thick, failing smoke was soon smothered. Heat failed. Light hightailed it. Extinguished. Cold returned. Ice and dark prevailed.

Not wishing to revisit pain banked like fire, Kuy struggles free of sleep, then hastily stands and curses, "Hyh!" before getting up to pour water over his head and roar away quicker than the ghosts who troubled him.

Chapter Eight

Velvet`s happy. This true?

Her smile declares it. Her long limbs as well. *Tambien–tambien.* Moving with unaccustomed freedom she heads downhill with an empty water bucket held in hand to a small wooden building neighboring woman took over for laundry and a place to take an impromptu shower if it's not too cold or inclement outside.

Toward her immediate goal Velvet meets a few residents. They exchange pleasantries with no real warmth or concern because she is outside their immediate frame of reference. Truth is; both parties prefer it this way.

Afterward she walks over to their communal tap. A sure source of water courtesy of the us government. Turns it. Fills her bucket and sloughs it back to the bathhouse. There's no one else inside at the moment therefore she fills an overhead tank with water. Strips. Stands under the tank and then opens a caulk to let the water splash over her. Later grabs a bar of lye soap. Dilutes it with water and gives herself a good scrubbing. Cleaning his dried semen off her taut belly she next carefully scrubs her sex with a rueful smile of remembered pleasure. Glad that he was gentle for she`s easy hurt inside.

Thought we`d dispel bitch! Because some tumbleweed fucked you night when he could not see you. Guess again!

Tracing the scars on her face. Slowly. Reluctantly. She reaches for an old metal pocket mirror and studies her features. One cruel scar crosses from her left check to her right. Originally it crossed the bridge of her nose as well but she later lost this segment to an untreatable infection despite the attentions of an old army doctor and his wife treating her for weeks without charge or stint. Below these cruel lines. Her mouth. Once beautiful and a catch for many a gaze, unsolicited desire and envy, fogs the metal as she moistens her lips. Turning her face this way and that, mirroring not the ruin above until later, with soap stinging her eyes, burning her skin. Sobbing uncontrollably, Velvet cowers against the bath house's hard stone floor with her knees drawn defensibly in front of her.

Later when an older woman enters. Recognizing the heart wrenching cries' source, she debates offering a minute's dab of solace but dinner is due. Old man's not sympathetic. Got troubles of her own and this has nothing to do with her really. So old *Donna* melts away with only a minute or two's pang of guilt–thus all cruelty excused and staged for more beforehand and after forever and ever.

Velvet? Hate and desire cut her up left for dead and bleeding. For sport. Because she was not tribe or kin. A lone woman captained by no hand but her own. Gathering wild herbs and grasses to heal sickness. Still ravish. Sooth pain. Run fever off.

A group of three Pawnee army outriders caught her off guard and carried her off to an old abandoned cabin. Drunk off several days' pay and not considerate of their actions–immediate outlawry or death within their own community. Or swift death among white justice. Lust and penned up hate tore her clothes. Entered her. Played knife across her face and even reached deep and cut her inside between her legs–an agony like fire–without remedy–until Velvet's screams silenced their laughter and limited their strained humor until they rode away on painted horses the color of spring awash and bit with shame and eventual perplexity at their handiwork as they sobered back to their unit after promising each other that they would never boast about this one.

Their merciless act later caused two their deaths and one to become a common drunk in salt chunk frisco though of princely line and feature.

Cringing on the bottom of the shower, she throws her mirror away as hard as she can but it doesn't break because it's metal. "Well," she stammers, "then neither will I!"

Velvet stands and turns thoughts away from stinging memory. Dries her tears and lets more water splash over her and washes away the grit form the floor.

Water used up. She replaces the caulk. Steps away. Dries herself off and then wraps the towel around her head.

Later studies her body. Not to take stock for herself but for another. Promising him if he wants everything, her breasts, and the rest of her body are without scare or blemish a maddening hint of what once was.

Velvet carefully shaves her underarms even her legs though trembling with morbid fear of blade. Then washes her hair.

Her one vanity since her body has until recently been locked way and at the pleasure for only her hand on those sad, lonely nights when she weeps until regaining the strength to accept her lot.

Finished, she ties her bandanna around her lower face. Hides her nose and scars. Then puts on her clothing. An old but clean shift. No brassier. Likes her tits to swing free. Then another of her long dresses but no boots. Just soft as paper moccasins slipped on with grace and practice.

Outside, menacing shadows are left behind in the bath house and recovering most of her former elation and with a renewed purpose, Velvet plans a counter attack against the apathy and despair around her.

Washed clean and knowing that one man. Handsome and stern and cut above the average. Cares for her. Perhaps loves her for it was in his eyes. And in his heart.

We
Hurt-her bad. Fucked her. What a scut. Heard her scream? Good though wasn`t she? Kuaka another crack at that! Why the knife brother? Don't know. Like someone else moved my hand. Shit'n die. Best thing! We fucked up! No witness no crime. Remember-that was the worst thing I ever did. Whisky boy! It was the whiskey! Sides, she's Kiowa. Forget what they did to us back awhile?

She smiles. If he would but listen and let it ascend against his own loss and pain. Though she knows. Heart quickening. That his road is long and hard.

He is not without hazard. For what are they be entwined? The sum of two parts but two desolate priests. Cut adrift. Peddling a new rough edged gospel to men and woman lost and at loose ends.

Shaking doubts away like dust from a broom, Velvet sets her bucket down. Looks east.

He's gone. Black Wolf. Squinting her eyes. She looks toward the horizon but gives up with a shrug. If she ever sees him again it will not be for months.

Why he would overlook her mutilations, gentle her with love and not lust, or pent–up need. Then kiss her mouth. Suck her stub nose. Capture her tongue. Turn her with strength and command as she in turn bids his thrust and play.

There's no answer. So picks up bucket again and saunters off with a school girl's sway looking for Two Cloud. The one man hereabouts she considers fit for friendship and confidence since he would never press her against a rude wooden wall and feel her up or try a hand up her skirt as so many. Now that their social fabric is torn and cast adrift and the men edgy from confinement, forced unemployment or just adrift without remedy waiting for another handout or stipend.

Two Cloud found at the other end of their community labored over an old wheel. Catching sight of her, he stops his refitting. Stands up and wipes his hands on his dusty jeans and then smiles while deliberating silently, yet aloud greets her–"Velvet–"

"Two Cloud."

"Fine day."

"Yes it is."

"He leave?" Two Cloud asks just this side of jealous.

Catching his glance and demeanor, she smiles and then answers softly, "Yes."

"Bet he rode out at dawn!

"Don't know. I was asleep when he left."

Two Cloud takes this in again while wondering why he gives a hoot and holler. Obviously though strange and unbridled, Velvet is a good lady and it's not only her unfortunate past that separates her from man and woman alike. Undeniably there's a coldness about her. Even her "home" is purposely remote. Emanating a disdainful, studied coolness.

Afterwards he offers a curt comment, "I bet! Them peyote fellows are a strange lot."

"How so?" she asks, interested despite herself, since her beloved is one.

"Well for one thing they move about free as hawks. From place to place. Bringing a lot of crazy notions."

"Are they–" she interrupts.

Her friend shrugs then answers, "Naw. Guess not! But to most–"

Listening to him her expressions sours. Later, after her friend had belittled the peyote cultist in no uncertain way, she defended them, "Of course they are considered wild and crazy. Since they want to shake up our pens. Close the dram shops and force us to look inward and walk through our bars and not stare through them!"

Two Cloud whistles appreciably at his friend's outburst–then adds his own take on matters, "Why. Velvet ain't you all fired and full of beans and bacon this day!"

In turn, she grins at her friend, prior to turning aside to check behind them and once assured that no can over hear them, pleads–

"Listen. I need your help!"

Straightening. Two Cloud stares at her. Slouched hatted. Bandanna worn like a *bandito* across her face. Before joshing, "What now Lady?"

"I want to call a peyote meeting."

"Really?"

"Yes!"

"He brought you some didn't he?"

"A lot really!"

"Then–"

"It isn't good sitting in a burlap sack. Have to use it or dry it. But he said that fresh was better than preserved."

Two Cloud ruminates before adding, "I went to a peyote circle once."

"And?"

Since wind carries secrets man tilts his face aside prior to whispering, "Not good! Me and a bunch of Mescaleros tried a bunch."

"Was there a priest among you?"

No a shake of his head says. Then, "Not really!" Scratching his head trying to remember, adds-"No priest but some wild Comanche fellow. Unprincipled. Full of bull shit about how peyote was the key to the white man's lock."

"And," she demands.

"Well!" he answers ruefully, "no one paid him much mind; we ate a sack full and waited."

"Waited for what?"

"For it," he says and then continues.

"Hell. It kicked in slow but when it did—"

"Crazy?"

"Crazy like fire! We danced around like a room full of cats and rockers. Hell! Men took off their clothes. Some rocked themselves like children and others screamed or cried."

All the while, saying nothing, Velvet just listens.

"It was a sight Velvet! But the next day—"

"What?"

"Next day we were plain kilt."

"How so?"

"Stuff got a kick like liqueur. The next day we could barely raise our heads. There were a lot of fights the night before—" He considers his next statement yet being on good terms with Velvet, spits it out, "Rapes. Even a child done dirty."

At this she stoically squares her shoulders and stands unfazed because she will not allow herself to be cowed. Instead, lets her hair whip behind

her strong shoulders and then faces him with a firm expression of decision blazing above her checked handkerchief. "Yes! Everything under sun
and moon is two edged Two Cloud. You had no guide. No– what`s that
word, "Presence" to lead you!"

Her friend looks at her with worry. Then asks unabashedly, "Things
bad here. Velvet. You know this. You really want to a call a peyote meeting with this wild lot we got here. Hell! Before everything fell apart most
of them would be outcasts and their woman scullery for higher castes.
Not a fit man or woman here!" This broached, Two Cloud then takes a
rag from his hind pocket and gives his nose a honk, or two before adding,
"Ever pay a mind to the kids here?"

Grimly, she answers, "A hard. Misbehaved and unruly lot."

"Then?"

"What better ground to start."

While digesting her suggestion, he stares at her in wonder. Wishing
that she was man so he could express himself more openly or that they
were man and woman. So he could lead her way to another community
or set up house with her and have children that they could mold firmly
between their writ and hand. But it's not to be. She's too ornery. Strange
even by his openhanded register.

"We start next full moon!"

"Three days!"

Agreeing. She concedes, "Yes! In three days."

"Ok where?"

"They built a meeting house didn't they?"

"Yes Mam! Thick with lay abouts like a dog with fleas."

"No matter! We'll–"

"We?"

"We will sweep it clean and smoke it out."

"And?"

"And hold our first ceremony."

"Who will?"

Standing straight. She fastens mismatched eyes on her only friend and smiles.

"We will! Who else?"

"Oh yeah! The town *bruja* and its handyman can't wait till our council gets wind of this."

Velvet laughs. Then demands, "What council?"

This outburst is answered in a lower tone, "Our council!"

Countering with dismissive cruelty. Velvet sneers, "Them! They're so deep in the pocket of whites that if one of our benefactors sneezes. As one they dig for handkerchiefs and present it with a servile whining posture!"

Two Cloud gets a tickle out of her rashness and wonders where her strength comes from. Most women. Cut up. Raped and left to die like her without family or a husband probably would have died. "But not her! So how? By what unknown resource or deep. Unsullied channel does she abide?" he asks silently watching the sun play behind them while she challenges him with a continued and frank stare,

"Ok!"

"Ok?"

"You hold this ceremony."

"Me?"

"Yes Two Cloud. You lead the ceremony!"

Incredulous he sputters, "Me!"

"Yes you!"

"I know nothing about it!"

"I will teach you."

"Why me?" he persists.

"Because you are good and strong!"

"I can't even read Velvet! Those missionary school swells look at me and want to put a broom in my hands whilst they sign away more of our land rights and traditions fast as ink can be sloshed or another parcel of onerous regulations and statues can be slammed down over us as if it's the law of moses himself."

"Woman! I am a woman man! Women cannot do this at the moment. Hell! Men round here either look at me like I'm *loco*. Or when the moon is away. Scratch on my door looking for my cunt as if my face's horror can be ignored if another whiskey's drank!"

Embarrassed. Two Cloud looks away. Aware that her words are true, considers for a minute, then agrees,

"Yes!"

"Yes. You will?"

"Yes!"

After their exchange, Velvet steps over, lifts her bandanna, then plants a kiss on his cheek.

Grimacing like a boy under a barber, her friend wraps his strong arms around her shoulders and makes a quick promise, "We hit them over their thick skulls with enough peyote to stir 'em up Velvet! Either this sorry excuse of a place wakes up and fights it out or we's dead in a season or two."

"I know it!"

"True," he says, "I am about ready to high tail it west myself–"

With a worried frown she demands, "Where?"

"Californias reckon!"

"You–" she hesitates. How much should a woman in her place condone? Yet. Human. Souled and hearted like any other *she* needs comfort and shared confidence as well as anyone else. "I will wait another season. Then if we can't shift things here–"

"Go on," he prompts.

"Then I will head to fort sill."

"Hell. Why there?"

She doesn't answer at first and though his seed is long dried in her. It's there and so are the bruises and bites along her thighs are breasts aching even still under mid–day sun.

"He`s there!"

"Who? That roadman I brought to you yesterday."

She silently nods. Two Cloud in turn. Gives her a hard. Demanding look. "For one man. One night?"

She looks away before addressing his question. Then turns and answers him, "No not only one night–"

Afterward, Velvet quickly relates how she met Black Wolf.

Two Cloud listens silently. Aware of a steady jealousy beating its drum in his head till he pushes it way as unworthy of her confidence and trust.

"Look at me Two Cloud!"

Does while she pulls down the kerchief covering her face. "Look at me!" Again he faces Velvet head on. Staunchly. Without affront or avoidance. "Seen your face often Velvet."

"And?"

"Hell woman! If you ever gave me the chance–"

She smiles at his confession. Yet stills more–

"I am a healer! Witch. Medicine woman. Whatever you want to call me Two Cloud. Never settled for long. Always adrift. Till caught for a stay. Then on again–"

"I know this."

"Then?"

"'*Ata*! Two Cloud. I would spare you."

Half pleased, grumbles–"Me?" Yet guessing that her reluctance is anchored elsewhere, states flatly, "You would. But what if I don't want sparing?"

She laughs and then steps back from her friend to suggest, "Maybe not but as to–"

"Three nights!"

"I will inform our people."

"Don't expect much! A few might come for novelty. A few out of spite or meanness. A couple. Perhaps a handful will come out of desperate need."

Two Cloud agrees, "We have to start somewhere."

"Listen. Come later and let no one see you if possible. Come and I will teach you what you need."

"Is it hard?"

"Well. It is involved. But not more than a few hours study to sketch the basics. Besides. I gather that *Seni–*"

"What?"

"Peyote or *Pioniyo*. Has a will of its own. Like a deacon. If we call. Set the alter. Will it. He or she will take care of the bigger details."

Chapter Nine

Oncoming highway's swept clean as a giant's broom and now just visible on the rise ahead a hunched over man battles both blustery weather and ornery, pernicious grit.

"What have we here?" hazards Kuy slowing down to offer a lift, "Need a ride?"

Trusting not to luck and who would especially after a rather cantankerous run of *suerte mal,* this dust anointed pilgrim accepts gladly, "Mind if I do Mister!" Once inside introduces himself, "I'm Walks into Walls but my friends call me Billy. I'm a rodeo clown. Just gotten out of a jam. Broke my leg sometime back and three ribs," and after glancing furtively discloses, "I'm only a few hours out of the jug for vagrancy."

"Well I'm glad to meet you Walks into Walls. You must sure have been a trial to your mom with a name like that. Mine's *Kone-gyah-daw-kue'.* Means Black Wolf. Or just plain Kuy as my amigos call me, even George," he says adding, "but prefer Kuy if this is all right with you!"

Letting fly a dry chuckle, Billy studying Kuy again between bands of light snatching dust, offers a compliment as well. "You could be a buckaroo yet!"

"Thanks son! Played around rop'n and ti'n once upon a time. Where are you from?"

"Don't rightly know. Ma Mandan. My pa Mex. They met in las cruces new mexico. Hell! Might say that I am a traveling man. You?"

"Oh. Round fort sill oklahoma."

"Kudwa?"

The roadman nods.

"Well. Mister. Guess you and I are of a similar breed."

That said. Exhausted, the clown turns toward the station wagon's window and massages his aching legs.

Billy's turned out much as a *hombre* of thirty or forty years ago, daily braving this uncaring globe draped in a fly blown duster, black derby worn as the passing hills outside, and large high heeled yellow boots coated with grit from out-there's sand blast, and truthfully folk, pinch me if I'm lying, his unshaven mug don't elicit trust either.

Furthermore Billy's tired and crusted eyes mimic dark commas and his left jaw's missing or broken teeth gives him a habitual sour expression ofttimes mistaken for his general outlook.

Why so? See Billy's a carefree and rather careless fella oft not knowing or caring where his head will next lie or plate of grub await.

***

Magical ain't it how the road passes effortlessly once settled in and Billy would be the first one to agree while looking out the window rocked and lullabied drowsier than a plate of snakes on a hot rock by the Hercules's motion.

Guessing he's reluctant to speak. Worn out as well. Kuy lets his new acquaintance slowly nod off without interruption. Soon the rodeo clown's eyes roll behind crinkled lids into nevermore where Billy is young again chasing ponies into a box canyon with his brother and sister screaming shrilly besides him and later when his dream tumbles into dullness and pain shadowing his waking reality, sore footed again with only the remains of campfires, tumbled down ruins, half empty bottles and another chill night for company–who wouldn't trade actuality for dream's varied comfort.

Me? You?

As the Mandan naps Kuy doesn't mind the lack of conversation. The clown's physical presence is company enough.

Anyhow all land hereabouts is posted and protected. Still necessitated by parched machinery the roadman stops at a windmill and saltlick for water and gets out to fill his radiator and canteen and when finished, cranks his Hercules, and climbs back in. Noticing that his passenger smells like an old polecat. A bum's stench. Soiled clothing. Cheap whiskey and a general air of defeat, Kuy shrugs. Mean what's a soul do about it? Just hopes Billy don't carry any of the biting variety of critters. Now this would surely ruin what had otherwise been up to now a fine as you please day.

Upcoming stretch is a lonely one so he tells stories to pass time and once in gear, see, he grabs several sticks of licorice and happily chews a mouthful watching bands on the horizon flatten and spread out into more emptiness marred only by the occasional house or abandoned building and yet on guard at all times for tricks of wind and weather waiting for the unwary.

Who knows though. Maybe they won out by orchestrating another attack of remembrance. When? A hot and dry fourth of july under the crack, boom, and pyrotechnical display of fireworks. Where? Small railhead. A bad night for one of the People. Usually on big celebrations like this. He stayed away all though it's also a time that is important for Kiowas everywhere.

Weaving drunks and fights broke out yet no one bothered him. This fact's recalled with a broad, smile expressing pride for his reputation predating turning "holy."

Down wide main dirt street, a tall drunk cowpoke pointed him out to an equally boozed up amigo, "Hell Tom. See that Indian? That's one bad son of a bitch," he said jabbing his friend's ribs to get his attention, " 'member what that sonabitch did to them Walker twins! Damn law said it was his right coss of self–defense!"

Never the less as the roadman walked past them; that buckaroo slid into the shadows pulling his friend with him slick as a snake in a stump.

Drunks mocked Kuy.

Neverminded and smiled his cold crooked grin. Luckily, tall frame and stern face gave even the most persistent Indian baiters pause. Ignorant rowdies who had challenged him and cornered him in the past had been cut up by his blue steel Bowie. He'd sliced their mouths wide open with his sharp *k'oo*. Cut off an ear or two. Maybe sliced the tip of a nose off like a cut of dear meat–thus the general reluctance in to antagonize this sonabitch.

Accosted by a different sort though that fourth. A young man. Said he was a student of Indian life. A doctor of some type from back east.

"A little late *Tahlee*," young Kuy replied ironically.

"Well," rejoined the smiling young man, "that's why I am here. From your dress; I would wager that you are a Kiowa."

"Kudwa!"

"OK. What I mean is–can I ask you some questions?"

Kuy discovered that the young doctor wanted to ask some questions about the *Pioniyo* religion. In response, he went on to quote an old Washo man,

'Peyote is like a Bible to us here Peyote is our Bible When I'm with this Herb sometimes it is like a book. Like turning the pages in a book.'

Wooed into a couple of hours' worth of talk Black Wolf found himself inside a dark cafe sitting at a small round table and sipping bitter coffee. From the shadows. He watched that white man with a practiced eye. Strange fellow. First offered him whiskey for information but Kuy curtly dismissed this. After an hour of banter the stranger's sincerity and questing manner dampened his suspicions so he agreed to tell a few remembrances for hot *tsoye* and a meal.

It took a while to find a place where they would both be served and later stirring fresh cream into his coffee followed by six sugars, Kuy spoke about the Sun Dance and as he recited the other young man opened a notebook and took out a yellow pencil to take notes with as the Kiowa, unused to speaking in english for any great length of time began,

"Before dark years–bad years many great gifts of healing and hope came from Sun Boy. Sun Boy was a great hero. He was a magician who roared out of the afternoon skies with fire and wind. His generous blessings were given to Arapahoe and Kiowa medicine peoples. These holy gifts were separated into ten portions gathered in *tipis* called Grandmother Bundles. These wonders brought much good and continued to spread health and bounty until the power and evil brought by outsiders challenged and then defeated our great strength and goodness."

The Kudwa paused. Then continued, "Long ago. A man–perhaps an Arapahoe. Shared another of Sun Boy's gifts with us. This was our *Tamie*–a sacred image; he hastened to add before the young doctor could interrupt.

"The *Taime* was the center of our Sun Dance. When joined with other figures or sacred images the power to shake and stir the darkness was in OUR HANDS!" he exclaimed, "and the Old Woman Under the Ground and *Seni* anointed the Sun Dance with great blessings"–

Quick on the draw for once, the doctor interrupted his recital, "Who is Old Woman Under the Ground? How do you spell *se–ni*?" Kuy looked at the young man. Cleared his throat and answered, "Old Woman under the ground is strong medicine. *Seni. Pioniyo* or peyote is a holy fruit from a cactus. Strong. A very powerful aid! How do you say? A sacrament? Opens doors. Hell! Opens your thoughts wide like a tepee swept by a new bride."

As the doctor frowned in concentration and copied his replies into his notebook the Kudwa continued, "The Sun Dance drew us together. When encamped. We begged buffalo ghosts to stir from mount scott and rejoin us. This dance mended our dying customs and traditions like rawhide thread." Smiling at his turn of speech, Kuy drank his coffee, stirred his cold beans and then took up his recitation once again, "All lasted for ten days. Six to make the lodge. We had tests of courage before dedication. Deathless battles. Bloody tests of skills," he added with a smile of pride, "four days for dancers to seek grace. Our *Taime* granted us foresight and wisdom–to crack the line between our world and the spirit world. Cutting our flesh. Breaking fingers and burning ourselves to seek spiritual insight. Vainglorious power or favor from ghost worlds. Listening, speaking to theses quiet, solemn and aloof messengers milling about us unseen and unlooked for–"

Despite himself, that young man looked over his shoulder prior to correcting and excusing his actions with a shrug. Later scooted his chair away from the table and leaned forward before turning to a new page as the Kiowa continued, "Our woman joined in and afterward, refreshed or chastised our camps were broken up as men went off to hunt."

"Flagellants–we had them in our religious history but long ago–"

"The inquisition!"

"Well that was under the Catholic Church. Can we get back to talking about your revival moments?"

"Wovoka? I have nothing to say about him! Back to your inquisition. Torture. Burning people alive–"

"As I said that was another time and place."

"Wounded Knee?"

"Ah come on Chief!" The doctor cajoled, yet apparently chastised, or flushed with guilt slowed down for a moment.

"Please. Do not call me that–" Kuy complained.

"Sorry. It's George isn't?"

"Yes."

The younger white then cleared his throat and stirred his coffee before continuing, "Your people use Peyote to prepare for ritual or spiritual matters. Isn't this a crutch to ignore true spiritual awakening and fulfillment?"

"The host, the wine, and the sermon!"

"Yes but Catholics do not drink to the point of intoxication," he stated then added with a shy smile, "least while in church!"

"But their priests hold the keys to heaven no? We realize that there are many doors, windows and keys that can be used by anyone willing to look for them and learn to use them," Kuy spoke before asking, "You know about messiahs?"

"Yes! Which messiah? Christ. Muhammad. Buddha. Joseph Smith?"

"Haw! Most are false or passed on long ago. With *Seni–* we do not need to chase after the words of dead messiahs or hearken to the probable lies of the new. With *Seni* we can see for ourselves the truth and then decide which path or paths to follow."

"Ok," The young doctor agreed. Moistening the tip of his pencil, he then asked, "You're very knowledgeable about history and the world. Where'd you pick up all of your edification?"

"Pardon?"

"Learning–"

"Oh. I attended university in florida–"

"Which one?"

"Fort marion!"

Listening. The young man frowned in concentration as he tried to remember when he had heard this reference before. Then recalling a salient fact. Next looked away embarrassed before remarking, "Order 88?"

"Yeas–"

"I'm sorry."

"Don't be."

"Why–"

"You do not even in the least favor president grant."

"Ok–What happened to your Sun Dance?"

"The dance was our song. When our voices died. The dances passed also." After his last statement, his voice hardened as he continued, "After the battle of Adobe Walls and others–our last battle leaders were sent into exile and broken. All but the most brave or foolish buried their weapons or sold them. Once a fighter has no opponent or cannot destroy those who seek his destruction. There is often a turning inward. The knife is turned against the hand that wields it." he said still carried away with the power of memory.

"I know this," he next reminded his audience," Strongmen often break with no roots to support them. The worst of all are the damned americans," this said, he apologized to the young man before continuing, "and their false promises of new sowings. Useless tracks of land stolen from us are given back ungraciously like pocket scraps grudgingly returned to the host of rich banquet by a former beggar.

Alkaloid soils fit only for scrub and stock not fit for anyone. Promises and dreams evaporating like shallow pools under the burning sun." while speaking he opened one hand for emphasis; "Often no one has skills for the earth or the learned patience to nurse thin shoots to maturity under icy rains and burning days. From where would these skills arrive? Government men even if honest and dedicated are often too hard pressed with too large territories to cover and too many clients to serve. The crooked ones whisper bad advice or ply the unwise or desperate with promises of good living in the towns and cities for fine Indian folk dispensing advice in the back rooms of dark saloons with grand ole american whiskey to sweeten the evenings followed by sour mornings bringing new owners with star wearing men with hard knocks and voices demanding access to their newly won property," he sighed and then stopped.

Throughout that evening the young man demonstrated that he was interested in many aspects of Kiowa beliefs and practices. "Tell me more about your people," the young white asked.

Irritated by insistent questioning, Kuy turned the tables, "Yes but first. I have a question."

"Go ahead."

"What about Little Red Riding Hood. What is the meaning of this tale?" Kuy asked with a crooked smile.

"It's not a myth; it's a story for children."

"What about its hidden meanings?" he pointed out, "For example, the grandmother. Eaten yet jumping out later alive and what–pardon–damn how do you say it–yeah got it–is the significance of the color red?"

With a sour expression; the young man looked away for a moment, then yawned and tried to answer his informant's question, "Ah my Kudwa friend. You see. These two German brothers. The brothers Grimm were folklorist and they collected old German folk tales."

"Just like our stories," the Kudwa replied.

The doctor looked at him again with a wry youthful grin, "You trying to cut a shine?"

"No. Just asking questions. Perhaps you should study your stories. Maybe you could learn something?"

"I have some more questions. Are you a peyotist? If so—"

Kuy refused to answer more, "Listen! All you do is rob the dead."

"Now wait a minute!"

"No it's true. I have seen the belongs of our dead stacked ladder high in new york and washington. How would you like to go into a great hall and find you grandmother and grandfather's corpses sitting under a lamp or even your parents–surround by their chintz? Rugs. Maybe the family bible placed in front of them. Religious and personal stuff strewn everywhere–perhaps a locomotive and a covered wagon to set it all off," Kuy roared.

Before getting up to leave he added firmly, "As for *Seni*! This is of the present and not to be picked over like old bones. Thanks for the meal and coffee. But I think it's time to hit the road!"

Despite the young man's cajoling and promises of compensation, after saluting him with a touch to his brim, Kuy went out into the dark boisterous night.

Relishing the memory of turning the tables on that young doctor, Black Wolf smiles with satisfaction. Now more seasoned. Less bitter and ornery he wouldn't mind chatting with him now. There's so much to explain. What if peter and paul discussed their cantos with roman or greek philosophers? Would christians now enjoy an improved, more tolerant faith and creed truly incorporating that carpenter's from galilee vision?

Arguing only for the sake of argument. Holding forth as if the young anthropologist was sitting beside him rather than the fitfully sleeping Mandan, Black Wolf recounts the hardship brought about by reservations, "When our ways fell there was nothing to fill the hollowness of loss. Dances of sun and ghosts were noble dreams costing hundreds of lives," he pauses. Then continues, "Bitter failures! Woman without husbands wandered with thin children into white towns and sold their bodies either as cheap labor or whores. Old men faded away to the shadows. For young men it was worse."

Kuy knew from his own experience. As he was also forced into exile far from home with remnants of his military clan brothers sent to rot in the barren florida pine forests.

"Hell. I was not even 18 then," he reminisces aloud as Billy wakes up.

Rubbing eyes and yawning. Walks into Walls solicits their general location, "Where are we?"

"On the way out of texas. How long do you need a ride for?"

"Well. Are you heading anywhere near green county?" Billy asks as he scratches his chin.

"Yes. I am passing that way."

"Well thanks. If you don't mind; I will just ride with you a spell!" All said, the clown looks around the Hercules's interior. Noting the peyote buttons riding in the back and the Kudwa's particular dress. Intrigued, hazards a question, "You're a *brujo*?"

Though the Mandan is wary. The Kudwa reassures him. Stating, "Well. I'm roadman or a road chief."

"Well. I was listening to a little of what you was talking about as we drove along. You were a fighter. You fought them damn whites?"

"Yes."

"Do tell! I wish I were a little older! I wanted to fight!"

"It was pointless. Be glad to be alive now! The past is dead and those years were damn hard!" Black Wolf stresses his point looking at the Billy's exhausted face and worn clothing, adding for emphasis, "harder than now."

The rodeo clown wrinkles his nose and wiggles his ears and laughs dryly–doubting Kuy's point of view.

After a long stretch of silence. This hitchhiker begins another topic. Perhaps wishing to ingrate himself or at least forge a rapport with his benefactor, "I headed up to South Dakota after I heard about Wounded Knee and Drexel Mission–"

Upset by this turn of conversation, Kuy turns with a pained, angry expression and curtly asks Billy to drop the subject, "Please. Let us not talk about it–"

"I'm sorry–"

"Life's heartbreaking at times. With its deaths of wives. Children. Family and old friends. Horrific events like Wounded Knee. I have buried deep," the roadman solemnly reproaches, "And threw away the key–"

Not wishing to discuss the massacre where many innocent. Men woman and children. Scraped frozen from the blood–crusted ground and pitched into a mass grave. A terrible event. Sending shock. Despair and discontent throughout Native American communities everywhere as the murder of nearly three hundred Lakotas spread by conflicting published accounts. Self–serving whitewashing (no pun intended) committees of inquiry and by word of mouth. Revealed the brutal actions of the army. Disproving once and for all the american government's lie of integration and peaceful coexistence.

Left to his own devices for a time. Billy stops talking. Bored. Watches nothing and no one pass.

Later, a family of rabbits streak across the highway interrupting their discussion. Quick as silver shadows. They disappear into the night while just in the nick of time, Kuy slows down to avoid hitting them, before speeding up again.

Down the road say forty miles or so Billy rejoins the waking world and with the instrument panel's green light shining in both men's eyes, they start anew with a related thread.

"I'm sorry for cutting you off Billy. What were you going to tell me?"

Billy grins before answering, "Oh not much. I never did get no further than Kansas City where I met up with a nice gal or two–" he pauses. Then continues bitterly. "But I really wanted to go up there and do something. Anything! But what was I to do? Army had already rounded every one up and suppressed the Ghost Dances and Wovoka's words and his disciples' sermons. Anyway. It was long over before I had a chance–"

"Billy. Don't regret. At least in your heart–you were determined to fight their injustice. The first act of rebellion is to wish it–"

"Ok. Maybe you're right. But I feel that I have missed out on too much. What did you do after you got out from prison?"

"Billy. I was lost. Damned. My inauspicious return from detention where wild saw grass and spanish oaks sheltered ghostly bands of defiant Seminoles was harsh. They kept us closely confined. In my damp cell. I could hear the ocean but was not allowed even a glimpse of it. Can you believe this?"

"Oh. From them," the rodeo clown replies heatedly, "I can believe anything. Anything at all!"

"Sad but true Billy! Despite yellow fever and malaria. I returned eaten up with hate like a rabid coyote or wolf–"

Walks into Walls nods for he knows the price and baggage of hate.

Black Wolf suddenly laughs, and slaps his new friend on his shoulder, "Get this son! One day an old horse officer looked me in the eye and let me know one fine spring morning as I climbed out from a gray boxcar holding me and other former prisoners,

'If it's one thing in the world that makes me wish for the old days it's a loaded Springfield and a savagerous unrepentant injun.'

"Watching us stumble around clad in army surplus blankets reminded me of hooded and clipped hawks."

Billy pantomimes. Mimicking the motion of an eagle flying. Then asks, "Got a smoke. It's been a stretch."

The roadman shakes his head, "No but take a pull on this." he suggests while reaching into a bag under his seat and handing his passenger a bundle of black licorice.

The clown inspects it and then sucks on the candy contentedly as a five year old while outside, night passes with only an occasional light from a rare ranch house or passing vehicle.

Cut off from the outside world both stare ahead.

Fighting sleep the roadman continues, "Sometimes I talk too much Billy. Like an old widow. Usually alone; this keeps me from falling asleep while driving."

The rodeo clown shakes his head as the Kudwa continues, "What I witnessed saddened, and embarrassed me. I used to bite my fists helplessly: old men begging for handouts outs in the rain. Their eyes blinded from drinking poisons sold only to the People at fort sill. Listen. One candle light in particular still dogs me *thali*. After a long day–a young mother was selling herself to buy food for her sick child wrapped in an old blanket. When I protested and offered to help. She curtly dismissed me. Asked what I could do without even the price of tinned milk. I had to walk away. Embarrassed for I had no coin. Hell. I was glad my close kin were dead. At least my father was not shamed and forced to beg for food even their soldiers would not eat and with the army occupying and herding us into forts and onto the Bad Lands near fort sill oklahoma. I realized that I had to do something!"

Billy interrupts, "My mother told stories like this before she passed. About how hard those days were. Times are hard now brother! I hope I am mended up to catch another rodeo circuit soon. I know of one coming up if I can tide over. You know how it is. If only it was more like the old days. Eh!"

"Yes. It's hard all around but even before it wasn't all buffalo tallow and berries! What with mourning battles. Blood clans. Revenge. Feuds and the pure joy of theft and sometimes just bloody murder between different Peoples. Those days were in some ways just as evil as today. With the same empty. Boastful histories!"

After all this talk, both sigh. Then remain silent for a spell till Billy breaks the quiet with a comment, "A big one's starting up in Europe. Probably going to be a daisy of a war! But I heard old man Wilson promises to keep us out of it!"

"Presidents–we can always trust their word no?" Black Wolf adds cynically, "How more grand, wearisome everything is now as if all of the colors have washed away from triumphs and failures and yet compared to what came after us it's as if a children's scuffle grew into a bar room knife fight between several men."

Billy laughs. Encouraged the roadman continues, "Perhaps if we were more inclined to unity and not rollicking independence and I mean all of us–perhaps we would still be free men and woman!"

The Mandan remembering his mother's accounts agrees but bushed from listening to his host and hungry, hastily asks a more pressing question, "Got eats?"

"Yes. We will stop soon and eat and then I will let you go your way. Since I am going up into the hills here to visit some of our settlements. Brother–it's hard times for all!"

"Ain't that the very gospel?"

After his rejoinder, Billy sits back and closes his eyes. As any one used to hardship and privations. He conserves his strength when possible. Yet with a promised meal, ride and companionship for a little while, thing's aren't so bad he admits while turning on his side to get comfortable Billy silently deliberates, "If I was in better shape would I rob this man?" But figuring this Kiowa is dangerous. He is not up for it at the moment. "Also," he rationalizes, "Listening to his yarns. It's as if I'm listening to an uncle," Billy reckons, "telling me about what has passed."

Biding time. The clown closes his eyes. Soon he's lulled to sleep again by the Hercules' rocking motion.

Watching Billy slip off again the roadman comments silently, "Poor bastard! He's on his last legs. Judging that Billy's tough son of a gun in better times. Black Wolf wonders if it would be wiser to drop him off soon after suggesting that they share a meal before parting. No use taking more risks he warns with a tired shrug.

Stopping to take a long needed call of nature. Black Wolf stands by his truck on the road's crumbling shoulder.

A coyote calls nearby as he pisses into the dark relishing the strong stream leaving his body. Wagering that this is one of a man's greatest pleasures. Black Wolf smiles and then buttons up his black britches. Hearing the howl again-asks, "Spirit or just an animal? Perhaps there's a last soul or two waiting out there!"

Frowning. Remembering several recent unpleasant omens or warnings, Kuy asks, "I dreamed of a waiting dark man. Why? Is it because I have killed?" Having asked this unanswerable question, he pauses, then beseeches, "Or is it really that all I loved are dead and waiting."

Staring upward now. Stars shine but with light both old and far away and little good to him stitched to this cold lonely ground.

"Loved ones and friends though. They're the ones that come for you! *K'ou–m–tou.* Spirits wearing the forms of owl. Wolf. Bear and coyote or even more frightful. Mixed up critters shuffling along on moonless nights–if the deceased were of mixed race or tribe–to call on the living."

Worrying. Years spent encircled with elders and attending lectures and sermons about owl spirits and the terrible. Lonely dead. Whom when living mated outside clan boundaries and in death must wander alone. Black Wolf considers their fate with a sorrowful comment, "Poor wretched souls neither fish nor fowl and what about the american dead? Do they hang around as if waiting for a train," he wonders while standing by his truck still dawdling bent ear'd.

"What was that word that young doctor used, "hy–brid," he mutters uneasily with wary contemplation, "Mixed ghosts. *'Ata*! Especially on this night swept mesa. *Yuh*! Best move on!"

Not having the time or inclination to gossip with spirits or other lost wanderers taking a stroll and hungry for company, Kuy checks on his passenger.

Billy?

Soundly undisturbed slept.

Letting sleeping dogs lie he closes the cab's door behind him and sits for a time gathering sounds and impressions wary as a sentry on duty.

Figuring that a presence or two might be adrift just outside the truck's cooling cab. Waiting. Soliciting notice or perhaps company to pass time. Jealous. Drawn to him and the sleeping Mandan for warmth against unimaginable cold, hunger, and desire.

Given a hard stare night stares right back yet frankly his heart isn't in the contest. Vouched by his unbraided hair standing straight like a hog bristle brush even as unexpectedly there's a sharp crack behind them like a tree branch snapping and then a tap. Followed by someone's hard rap on his front hood.

All this hullabaloo wakes Billy, who bolts upright with more than a dash or two of wild panic in his eyes. Evidently not knowing where in thunder he is.

There's few more taps. Scrapes and other diminishing noises. Then all is silent as an unmarked grave.

After this, Billy gives his host a long thoughtful cast of blameworthiness that Kuy hasn't seen a finer example of in many a year. But otherwise, Billy doesn't say a word. Just listens with his ears pricked till the sounds fade away completely and the two men are alone.

"Shit. I had a dream! One in a million brother."

Black Wolf listens but doesn't respond. Instead looks about. Then switches on this head lamps before attending to his passenger's outburst.

Nothing outside except an old mesquite half dead from lightening. Its left side blasted and withered. In the sharp relief of the headlights–an old thing–a stark brooding entity best left to its own devices perhaps.

"*Yuh*! You were saying Billy?" Black Wolf prompts.

Answering. Billy first looks over at the night swathed Kiowa and then outside through the bug splattered windscreen. Wetting his cracked lips, finding his thoughts–starts off in a husky, hushed tone, before continuing in a near whisper as if he's afraid of being overhead or drawing attention to himself, "Had a bad dream!"

"About–"

"Being beat up!"

"By men?"

"By———a couple at least," Billy admits worriedly still looking around as if they are indeed close at hand and ready to attack them any second.

The roadman deliberates a minute before suggesting, "Pay heed! Watch out Billy–"

"You reckon?"

"I reckon!"

Billy nods. Afterwards suggesting, "How about we get out of here! Place gives me the creeps!"

"*Tambien!*"

This thought voiced in the otherwise silent night. Black Wolf. Paying no heed–napeacrawl by none too subtle witch's feathers–opens his door. Gets out. Bends down. Cranks and then gets back in after a long plaintive whistle. One of challenge. Or counter sign. But unanswered.

Not meeting Billy's eyes or his unvoiced questions, Kuy starts up and drives away hoping that the time and place for his reckoning will be of his own choosing when they come for him shrouded in familiar forms.

Later, steers by headlamp along a flat and featureless road. If alone he would pull over. However, not wishing to awake alone, stripped of possessions, including perhaps his truck far from kin–no sir–he drives on while Billy, evidently battling various visitants, omens, or just evil *suenos*, snores anew.

***

Not daring to relax yet, debates if nonviolence and outward acceptance of federal control over their lives was the correct choice, "Perhaps," he bitterly rejoins, "I should have died with a gun in my hand!"

On his return from federal stockades, there was nothing left for him since his past was dead as a cold campfire and besides backing and filling, he reckoned he had a need for a quick retiracy before he was arrested again and shipped away, and there was no need for him to watch the burial of his nation.

Like other fighters, his weapons were cached away in the hills. If the times turned in their favor, many men swore, oiled clothed rifles and pistols would be uncovered.

But not this year or next.

During this period he had no goals but survival. Except for mission school. Its demands for total sundering of his past: clothing; hair, speech, religion and a thousand other subtle commands to mimic. There was only the ashes of a stillborn present and sterile future.

It was futile to even try. A simple case of,

"You're damn if you do–you is dammed if you don't!"

The more adaptive Kudwa were mocked. Ridiculed openly or guardedly by those they sought to emulate. Truth was that Kiowa men or women aping whites would be equally derided by their own people.

Disgusted, he left reservation life to work on stock ranches. Kuy was a good rider. Knew horses and was gifted with other animals.

At first he was ruthlessly ribbed and belittled by the other hands but through hard work and pure outright grit and stubbornness, Kuy persevered. Later gaining a hard won grudging respect from the men around him.

On nights off. Whether in a crude bunk house or camped on the vast plains, George, as he was called, was left alone by the cowpokes and varied ranch hands.

Listening to their lonely collective boasts, he didn't try to join beyond what was necessary yet most young men if given a smile or a hand up will remember it and return the favor. Even the most barren emotional fields grow with friendship.

George Black Wolf was a fighter. Foolish hands that crossed him regretted it. Sometimes lashing back cost him a job. A stint in jail but it was worth it. Though he acquired the reputation of a troublemaker that outweighed his natural talents.

Undisturbed, Billy stirs and whispers, "Lupita," then bends toward morning.

Stop to eat on a wide strip of sand. The clown doesn't help much, just watches like a feral dog with eyes fixed upon Kuy's preparations.

The roadman takes out contributions given to him by his last congregation, corn bread, and puye bean with dried red peppers, squash blossoms, and places the food on tin plates. Serving everything half cold since he has to break camp once more before sleeping.

"You eat good man," the clown observes.

The roadman studies his table mate before commenting, "When you work are you paid?"

"Yeah sure. Sometimes. Anyhow, if a show is bad or rained out we get shit!"

"Well. This is all I get from the families I visit. I am glad for it. Except for gas money. This is all they can afford. Dig in. Later Billy boy. You're on your own!"

Billy agrees. Knowing what Black Wolf is thinking. The Kiowa is reluctant to camp with him. Billy does not try to persuade him otherwise because he might be tempted.

Later as they eat surrounded by silence. Billy, Black Wolf ruefully notes, eats more than his share but the roadman ignores this breach of manners, "Man's hungry, that's all!"

Eased by warmth and food, the Mandan leans back and points to the stars above.

"*Ts' pîmi–bei kuocdl*," the roadman remarks also looking up toward the stars above.

Grinning, the Mandan translates, "Everywhere!"

Interested, the Kiowa later asks a question, "So your mother was Mandan."

Billy looks across the now roaring fire and simply states, "Yes she was. One of the last of the full–blooded."

"Terrible what happened to your people!"

Billy shrugs. Then replies in a thin, dry rage almost choking his words off, "Hell Kuy! We went from having thousands and living in nine cities till we were wiped off the map by small pox. Maybe twenty to thirty left in a land of the dead. Had to mix with our neighbors to survive the coming winter."

Without a word between them they reflect on this tragic history of the Mandan people with bitterness and anger. But whither anger's outlet when the act of destruction or genocide is almost complete. Leaving few if any to seek redress or revenge. Where's the lament of carthage or the moors and jews of spain?

Billy, obviously holding on to a great deal of anger and sadness states, "Well Kudwa! I am one of the last. Mother always called me little lastman when I was a tot. Since there were so few of us left. She often said she was lucky to meet one of our folk every five years or so and this was only because they deliberately sought her out trying to keep our language and culture alive."

Settling down, Billy then slicks back his hair and starts another thread. One more light hearted to stem, perhaps even cast away the melancholy settled around them, "Listen *Honcho*. Once your People crossed a sea of grass till they found a stream and stopped for the night. It came quick and they were uneasy knowing that their old enemies the Bear People lived nearby. Truth was they smelled and marked the camping Kudwa by their campfires.

The Bear People were starving since the Buffalo had left."

Billy pauses for a minute, to scratch inside his boot, before continuing, "Seven young girls from the Kiowa camp went out to gather food one evening along a stream. Suddenly several Bear warriors attacked. Frightened, the girls ran until they came to a large rock and climbed onto it. Their pursuers followed so they prayed and begged for protection. That rock was old and lonesome. It had never heard the human voice before and it was charmed when them girls prayed to it so it stood up and reached toward the stars and the seven also rose up and raced along with him toward the sky. Well my! Those Bear folk seeing their prey escaping sang their songs and also reared up taller and higher against the growing rock.

A shadowless time. A moonless hour.
Mist rolled and lantern eyed. Thin
laughing, silhouette. Resentful, distant canyon walls hunkered buddahavis-
ta slouch across billy's maiden aunt
crisscross woebegone hand warming outline

Those Bear warriors tried to capture them but they had sprung so far away that they could not reach them. Angered, still hungry, they looked down and saw the lights of their homes growing smaller and smaller so they decided to return hungry and bitter rather than getting lost forever and as they lumbered back toward their homes still far greater in size than normal the Kiowa saw them and panicked," Billy stops and glances at his acquaintance, chiding him, "Hell. Even your people would run if they saw great biiiigggg bears running after them!"

The roadman laughs, "True. I know I would."

Smiling Billy continues, "They fled the great prairie. Burning with guilt and shame. They told themselves that the seven missing maidens were already eaten and beyond help to assuage their loss and sense of shame and thoughts of revenge. Later. They named the towering mountains behind them Bears' Lodge. Or—"

Here, the roadman interrupts, "*Two' Ai*."

Nodding, the rodeo clown smiles, and starts again, "Well those girls were mighty scared because they saw their people pack up and flee. Frightened they sang again. This time to the stars and they mind you. Heard their sad voices and reached down and placed the seven amongst them."

"The Seven Sisters. My father told me this one but you tell it better."

"Thanks partner," Billy says, taking another sip of coffee. Before finishing, "Every night the Seven Sisters pass over the Bears' Lodge both in gratitude to their friend the mountain and because they are lonely—always looking for their people. Helping them by lighting their way."

"For such a fine tale. I believe you deserve an extra portion."

"Don't mind if I do," the clown replies. Reaching for his tin plate again, eats his last forkful of grub.

Finished, the Mandan hands the roadman his cooking gear cleaned up as best as possible with parched grass and water and later thanks his host for his ride and the food.

Unattended, their fire attracts large moths and other flying insects. Risking all, Black Wolf observes. Circling unconcerned with the bravest or foolish singeing their wings off and falling into the flames.

Peacefully Billy too watches the pageant. Silent. Learning nothing. Mute, yet grateful for its warmth.

With a start the Mandan turns away from night's empty pitch asking, "Say? I tell you about a stretch I did in Yuma?

"No," the Kiowa replies. Resigned. Figuring that the Mandan's averse to being cut adrift alone and penniless into night and like that lady staying the hand of fate every night by yarning another tall tale–although not in a similar pickle–this here boy's desirous if you please for a helping of human company piled high steaming beans and another chipped cup of coffee. Not much but when your stomach's empty. A good tightner. Cup of Joe. Someone to pour out life's miseries and joys to with a spoonful of understanding is priceless. Especially in hard times.

Not too sure of his audience's interest, Billy promises merrily, "This one's a toot"

Listening. The roadman weighs several considerations while looking over head and settling on the hour while Billy opportunes another slow drawn query like a quart of good beer, "You're not a church'n type are you?"

"Your question Billy depends on whose church you're asking about."

Mildly exasperated. Expressed with a bottom of the pickle barrel frown. The Mandan challenges the Kiowa's droll comment, "Come on man!"

But the Kiowa just smiles adding easily, "If you mean to ask me if I am easily offended. The answer is no son go ahead."

In turn. Billy lets fly a wide grin and then starts, "Met up with this fly blown *Berdache*."

The roadman caught off guard by Billy's sudden revelation. Asks for clarification, "You mean a *mihdek*?"

Considering the Kiowa's question. Billy turns away for a moment searching for the right translation before nodding. At the same time. Black Wolf gives the younger man a hard probing glance from his side of the campfire and asks. "Beg your pardon for asking but you ain't one of them, "Miss Nancies" are you?"

Billy nigh ruffled by this accusation. Battens down any discourteous reply before assuring his companion that he's as far as saturn when it comes to having any propensities in the direction of acting sissy, "Listen man!"

The roadman gestures with a shrug before adding "Go ahead. I am all ears."

"Better be *hombre*! This one's rich. Ripe as tripe and red chilies," Billy warns. Starting, "It was last october–"

"Near this time of the year?"

Billy stifles his annoyance at his interruption and then begins again, "Anyway Kudwa. It was around now. I was cold and desperate. Didn't Have a Tail Feather Left. I was backing out of Yuma. Did not want to stay there anyway. Mean sort of place! I reached the last of the adobes when I noticed this older gal or so I thought trying to unhitch a horse that was a might cantankerous."

The roadman silently encourages his telling; glad all the while for this entertainment before driving on a league or two more before morning.

"Well. One thing led to another and this old dame. Guess she was lonely. That's why she invited me for supper."

The roadman suppresses a rude comment but just.

"Inside. She had a nice comfortable house. Real homey–"

"I bet!"

"Now there! Who's telling this story?"

"You are."

"Damn straight!"

"Sorry!"

"No need to mentioned it. Anyway. She dished out a big plate of tamales and beans."

"Then what?"

"Well. We fell to talking. As I sat there in an old leather chair and watched and listened to her in the lamp light and glow from the fireplace. I je'ged that there was something off kilter about her–"

"How so?"

"Well. Her hands and shoulder were broad for a woman. Plus she looked to have a five a clock shadow at candle light."

"Hmm–"

"Well as I was saying. It started to snow again and I was disinclined but understandably ready to hit the road again when she suggested kindly that the weather was too ornery to send any child of adam out into so–"

"So?"

"I was offered a place in her front room or pallor on the floor in front of her small fireplace to sleep on. So I jumped like a flea on it."

"What next?"

"Nothing. Slept like a log to morning. Next day. I was the first to wake up. Took a look out the window. More snow and cold as presbyterian's heart. So I built up the fire. Sat back and read a little Emerson till she showed. I was going to get but again she asked me to help her cart some medicinal remedies cross–town when the weather calmed a little. Said I could help around her place in return for a place to sleep and eats. So I did. She had kind of barn back of her. With a horse and a milk cow. Time and again. Men visitors paid a visit. Then she and he skedaddled for a while. Other sorts came around. Woman mostly. For something else–"

"What?"

"Hattie was her name. Hattie was a medicine healer or herbalist. Hell man. Her whole house and barn was stocked with dried grasses. Herbs. Plants and whatnot. Smelt to high heaven but it was warm as I was saying! Well after a couple of nights the unavoidable happened and she invited me to sleep in her room."

"Take her up on it?"

"No sir! As I said. Was something mildly–well displeasing? Anyway I rejected her invitation."

"How did she take it?"

"Not hard. Resigned I'd say."

"Then what Billy?"

"Stayed on the floor out of trouble and harm's reach. Noticed as the weather got worse fewer people knocked on her door. Things got tight. She started to complain and get demanding. I was about ready to high tail it when she suggested a business proposition–"

Kuy shifts position to get comfortable and then returns his attention to the unfolding tale.

"It went like this, 'Billy dar'en. You and I need to come to an understanding.' I was dreading any demands you understand. So I just sort of hunched down and folded my chin inward. But she was on a different trail altogether. Hattie told me that this time of the year was hard. When the weather kept her customers inside and only a few brave man or women knock. I seconded her. Well then. She fastened a look on me that would have frozen spit before she continued. Hattie asked me plain and straight, 'you particular how you slip a dollar or two into your pocket?'

After I shook my head, Hattie went on. 'Well. Then. Come here and listen.' Turned out to be a plum of a plan. A little crooked but then what isn't right?"

"The crook?"

"O dress up as a missionary couple and solicit funds for imagined food. Bibles and classes to make honest citizens out of their savage and reluctant Indian neighbors. Hattie had a gaggle of nieces and nephews borrowed to parade in front of je'm christian souls to help us squeeze a dime or two out of their skinflint hearts. Well they bought our ham act hook line and sinker. Things were swell as May."

"What happened?"

"Well. Hattie got greedy with the collections. Spent what we took in in hand over fist. Yuma's a small burg. Not much happening during winter so her newfound spending habits attracted attention and one day. A church committee knocked on the door and forced their way in. Far as the eye could see there were bottles. Fully dressed turkeys. Clothes and other finery strewn about."

"Well?"

"Righteous indignation. Hell. They swelled up big as turkey cocks seeing how us "skins" lived high on the hog–"

"Then?"

"More came around. Not saying much. Just giving us the EYE! Then one day a deputy came by and took Hattie and me to the caboose. I lied about my name and age and got three months but Hattie had a lot bad feelings stacked up against her."

"I imagine."

"Yes sir! Plenty of wives did not like her attentions to their menfolk. The town's doctor and dentist did not like her competition under cutting their monopolies. Especially since a lot of Hattie's remedies worked. All in all. It was just the plain facts of her being."

"Well. She being what he was. What happened next?"

"Don't know. I high tailed out of there as soon as my cell door was opened. Stopped by her joint. It had been fleeced by her god fearing law and order loving neighbors but we had buried some silver in the barn–"

The roadman digests the tale and then asks simply for clarification, "Did you take all of it?"

Billy looks away for a moment. Then with his jaw set in reply answers the question, "Every last dime and half penny!"

The roadman nods. Then offers a short comment. "Them. Like Hattie. Should not be dishonored."

Billy corrects the roadman, "Him!"

The roadman grins sadly, "We should not let white prejudices seep into us and blind us."

"How so?"

"They're two souled. Sacred. Having spirits of man and woman. Moon and sun."

Billy looks at his companion for a minute and then shrugs. "Maybe you're right. But who would ever know?"

"You for one," the roadman suggests evenly.

Billy snorts, "Me?"

"Yes you! And others like you!"

"Yeah. But once we're gone?"

The Kiowa in turn ponders Billy's question and spreads his hands helplessly, "Pass it on!"

"To who," Billy demands.

"Those who come after us–"

After listening to the roadman's suggestion, Billy shakes his head before opining dryly, "They really don't give a tinker's damn about these old ways Wolf. You know this!"

Sadly the roadman agrees yet suggests nonetheless, "You know a lot of old stories. Tales."

The Mandan hitches his shoulders. Yawns. Dismissing his sincere but impractical praise, "I'm just a tumbleweed. Sooner or later–"

The roadman doesn't reply. Simply adds a final log to the flame. Stirs the pot for the last time considering Billy's story. A cautionary tale but as to a moral or point he's at loss.

This night. No moon. Dark as pitch away from their small dying fire. So Kuy decides to move along. Slip Billy a half dollar. Camp separately. The safest course to take alone on these empty roads and plains.

Before parting company, the roadman asks Billy a final question, "Where will you go now?"

"Well. I will keep this fire going for a while. Sleep. Tomorrow. I will try a town always near here. Might meet up with a carnival or rodeo crew I know. A hard. Risky bunch sometimes but you know how it is."

"Luck," the roadman wishes.

Billy smiles and shakes his hand with one last question, "Have you ever read Emerson?"

"No. I have not."

Warming to his theme, Billy says, "Well. At night I like to read him. Puts me to sleep. But I lost my only copy," he adds sadly, though with a dry chuckle before making a pretense of gathering up more grass and scrub than possibly needed for a night's brief fire.

Before they part Kuy gives Billy an enameled cup of spring water. "Tonight if you are thirsty drink this and here is a pinch of coffee for tomorrow. You can brew a cup for yourself tomorrow. So long."

"*Adios. Suerte!*"

This said, Kuy cranks his Hercules and drives off down an old rough trail. In his rear view mirror the clown's fire dims like a distant star.

With the strained camaraderie of the Mandan behind him, Black Wolf judging that he has placed enough distance between him and the Mandan, pulls over and without delay falls into dream.

Chapter Ten

Adam alone. Dogged by hail and hard rain Kuy hunted a turnoff to grab a quick sabbatical and afterward when sky relented a prairie minute, stretched his cramped legs, aired boots, wiggled his toes as thunder stampeded overhead like yesteryear's bison.

Unconcerned, opined that oklahoma and texas suffer more weather in a day than most other states and territories witness in a month and as if accenting his point, eavesdropping upstairs, a mammoth rainbow arcs the long narrow valley as P'ay threshes drizzle into a gauzy mist curtaining the highway.

Checks for hail damage and later grabs a long clean blade of saw grass to chew on while keeping an eye on the changing weather.

Rain left sunshine right. Enlivened, arrows through warm cold light and cold warm water holding his arms away from his sides like a scarecrow. Each pool disputatious across outstretched palms concurrently. A brownie could snap his flabbergasted, tear streaked features if finger quick. Why the whole act might as well be staged solely for him. See anyone else about?

Tactile ghostlings. Mysterious? Or most assuredly ordinary if viewed from the correct optical or spiritual lense?

"Boy. If Old Smoke or William Little Buffalo could see this!" Missing two old *Gwa-kelega* road chiefs and friends situated near fort sill the roadman opines, "They'd label this is a spirit rain. Well, perhaps so it is! After all. I have never seen the like. Have you?" he asks his truck.

Don't answer. Nor anyone or anywho else. Well at any rate as with all mysterious curiosities, abruptly the phenomena ends as it started. Still engrossed by the pageantry recalls an old wish to visit a sea or ocean one day and walk along its shore but not this day he reckons or the next, "But before I pass hopefully," he pledges–striking east, unconcerned singing, "Niagara. O roar again–"

Tardes. Afternoon warm. Thirsty Kuy wishes for cool water to wet his whistle but having shared most of his water with Billy, there ain't any and now hot enough to fry eggs and a rasher or two of bacon even with open windows–drives without stopping into singular sleepless intervals. Halting only for gas, eats snatched from behind the wheel and without acknowl-edgment, slowly transforms into the quintessential new american.

Though tires fail, windows crack, and engine boils, Kuy persists and after thirty or so hours at the wheel he parked on a slight rise and ex-hausted by the heat, naps on his front seat. Serene yet not picture perfect because outside his open door and window. Choking and laughing like bankers on holiday, a family of black vultures gorge on rotten steer. Little if no attentions paid to them even though the shifting wind carries the odor of their banquet but he's too tired to drive away.

Merely tosses and turns on his front seat. Hunting forty winks.

Evening mounted rancher passes and asks questions but gets no an-swers. So rides away disgusted and put out by being ignored by a lazy skin perhaps later runs off to the sheriff's with a tale or two to tell.

Quien Sabe?

But this is of no consequence. Black Wolf roams far away on knife's edge watched above by P'ay while wise carrion eaters feast on top of his cab unconcerned and undisturbed.

Croaking birds sentinel until shooed away by evening with chang-ing banners, colorful standards, and darkening heralds. Later a rare eve-ning breeze raked yellow tired scrub backward and forward beside the Hercules accompanied by the pop and crinkle of cooling metal where deliberations pull and lengthen like taffy as heat's banished by shadow.

Dusk.

Awake recites prayer for eventide cached from—

Hunted and
dead disciples' unprinted scripture
churched on
wind, empty plain and lonely mountain's
Sermon

Borne away on watch fires, pass
furtive councils, locked cells' deprivation,
and the missionary school lie

Forming a litany of hope for those without

Embodying
Seni's spirit to
contrast
warrantless argument,
spirit's defeat…

Apostles-jailbird bishops,
elusive cardinals, and outlaw priests

Administer and kneel at
transitory alters, nomadic sees,
offering the bitter host,
sanctioned resistance, and mutinous prayer
windowing hope, and Dwk'i's love

Though lacking chapter and verse. Grasping at difficult truths. Reaching for the all too brief reprieve of conviction and principle. With the majority of their original apostles dead or engaged in small, degrading, and compromising battles for survival, Kuy wonders if their trials and tribulations will be collected. Codified. Written down.

Yet cautioning. If this goal is achieved. Their faith may lose something of its free unregulated spirit. As did the christians when they rode the elevator up from the catacombs.

Stopped afterward under pale moon. Declaims; "Hope began as a whisper from imprisoned leaders of many tribes. Many of us were locked up in fort marion. When we were released, our faith spread." After clearing his throat continues, "We held ceremonies and councils were called. Not many at first. Scattered meetings of haunted men and a few women!" Though women were usually excluded from these early ceremonies. Yet no Kiowa could forget the first of them—Peyote Woman.

"Many rejected us because they were frightened and stung by the cold hopes left behind from Ghost Dances and other empty guarantees mouthed by discredited prophets and they turned against us. Labeling us. Outlaws! Fools. *'Ccdlk'cce–dcc*! What with our long hair and wild clothing!" he adds remembering how bold and arrogant they were. Burning to counter missionary deceit–"The hapless against hopelessness." Recalling with pleasure this period. After all. They were young with nothing to lose and filled with an overriding purpose that escapes all but the fortunate or cursed.

Many were the troubles caused using *Seni* without council or forethought. Lacking the foundation of new and old traditions. Disrupting frayed. Splintered authority and challenging white notions of acceptability and progress. *Seni*. Sometimes a curse. Not a blessing. Yet when used wisely as by these stout, brave fellows, though hunted men. Great men— Santana, or White Bear. Big tree and Apiaton—named for his wooden lance. *Seni* paired with these men offered salvation based not on a broken past or white promises but on truths threshed from the mission school and christian lies and older knowledge from the deserts of mexico that coiled and waited like bright serpents to strike through darkness and fear."

"*Seni* opens a new path or beginning. Even if it demands walking into terrible and wondrous fires." Moved, Kuy continues, "We can achieve this victory by casting away the bottle's devils. Cheap mission clothing and empty words. Only by following this path can strength be rekindled."

All said and done, stated and stacked neatly, he still needed a codicil to plank loose ends and for once coming up empty on the necessary word, turn of phrase, timely thought or expression, reverently quotes a pledge revealed to Quanah Parker to plug any gap, '

Lay down your arms. Quanah Parker. Your solution. As is the solution of all creatures. Is personal. Turn your energies toward conquering the self, only through this will you and your people have a freedom that exceeds the white man's. I have planted my flesh in the cactus Pioniyo (peyote). Partake of it. As it is the food of your soul. Through it. You will continue to communicate with me. When all of those with the skin of red–earth clay are united by Pioniyo. Then and only then will they once again reign supreme. The white civilization will destroy themselves and the Indian will return to nature. Master over himself and at peace with all.'

Powerful words! Other teachers on the great unfolding *Pioniyo* way echoed this wisdom. Men like the wise Sam Lone Bear also called Leo Old Coyote, who paid for wisdom and resurrection with harried pursuit and white men's jails.

Later, devils slain and put back in their boxes for another day, Kuy stretches and after sitting up, discovers that it's almost night so opens his door. Disturbed, the vultures reluctantly take flight stumbling toward last light drunk on flesh.

As P'ay sets Black Wolf remembers his wife's red lips and with this and other, cheek–to–cheek, private thoughts, grows wistful and later reaches into his pocket to take out a few sticks of black licorice to kill hunger and thirst. Shamefully the candy also slakes his craving for whiskey and human companionship.

***

Not everything from the americans is *mal*. If only we were allowed to pick and choose freely what we desire rather than what they shove down our throats. Bounty they have stripped off us as we once butchered animals.

Here doubt pricks him like a horse army surgeon's probe. "What happened? Among the People it is a great and painful mystery why we have been forgotten or allowed to fail as more and more americans take our land, "What promises have we forgone? What wrongs did we commit to be so humbled and broken? he reflects minding his slow ascent and answers, "Only answers come from the Way. We must reforge our strength in order to win the right to answers." Soothed by his own sermon, Kuy drives on though mindful that doubts are not always so easily tamed. Sometimes. Usually late at night and after driving for long stretches he confronts bitter memories. A few so debilitating that he has to pull over. Way–sided by jealous and lonely evils stalking these empty highways, "St. Anthony in a pickup," he often mockingly referrers to himself.

In the past before graced with redemption Kuy was lost. Haunted by loss with no cross to lean upon. Whiskey couldn't sooth bitter accusations, "What about the death of your only son?" Though he pressed corn meal. Elk into his boy's mouth. Tending his burning fever. Ignoring the rumbles of raw hunger.

Doubt mocked and scorned him, "Healer–you could not even nurse back to health your only flesh and blood. Failed priest. Liar!"

Fumbling at reply, challenged by the memories of his wife and son's painful death and the death and despair of his brothers in arms. Faltered. Remaining silent under continued accusations, "They died and you lived. Fattened on the white man's corn," and, "what can you do? You cannot bring the food. Medicine and clothing your people desperately need. You cannot bring them good housing or warm clothing." This true? A few days ago after stopping at a stock pond to ponder these charges while filling his radiator, he fretted away an hour or two watching altocumulus clouds ripple like speared fish miles away and arguing with himself, "I bring empty promises. Hollow dreams," he admitted, "My flesh is weak." Not even a bird sharing his solitude.

No eyewitness to his sudden frailty. Knelled on hard ground. Pulling clumps of soil and lance grass. Thorns cut his hand and his blood pooled and dropped to the ground like dark tears. Mocked. His own unwashed stench. Heat and thirst. Standing. Faced his accusers after calling upon *Pioniyo*.

As with the teachings of a difficult master. It could take days to understand what lessons were offered or problems solved and which sins absolved. Why pilgrim? *Seni* is hard. Often harsh and demanding. Terrible. Not suffering the foolish. The weak. Or cowards. Ware the fool who came to their ingested altars with petty needs, selfish or foolish desires. This loving teacher can turn terrible. Remorseless. Watching supplicants on fallow or unworthy paths. Warned not to return to the holy sanctuaries. He once witnessed a man fail to return from his quest. Young man. Judged and sentenced.

Day almost over. Night close. Thoughts regress to matters at hand. Rains again. So switches on headlights. At a crossroad, realizing that they're precarious. One does not always know what awaits dusk. Shooting forward into night.

Next morning a small hard river swollen by a flash flood blocks his way. Dead steers turn. In brown wash under threatening sky.

"Must have been caught when the downpour began." Watching a single span brave surging crests, mutters, not at all pleased, Complains. "Heck! This will cost me 50 miles!" Back to his Hercules to consult his maps, ruefully notes more hail damage. His headlight now squints at an odd angle.

"If I did not discover those cottonwoods to nest under. I might have lost my windshield as well as the rest of my paint," he remarks grimly.

Sitting in his cab rain–washed prairie clean as a whistle tempts but he studies the folded and creased map on his front seat with his door open and after a hasty consultation, discovers that there's a railroad crossing only a few miles north from his present location.

Railroad bridges are built with company money and are usually built better than county maintained roads. Aware of this fact. He risks a further delay and heads north toward the crossing printed on the map.

Trestle's intact. . Below it a river churns loudly and soddens his clothing and after crossing over to the middle of the span and jumping up and down a few times, turns to survey the brunette, wet cat furred prairie and as first drops wet his face like a whore's kiss, later kicks a tie or two as well. The weakened span's haw from the flood's impact is a fitting challenge, "Fit enough," he essays. "Though tricky. The only problem with train trestles is trains. Hate it when half way across and a train comes at me on the opposite track. Well. No other choice for it!"

No sign of an oncoming train. Instead quick as spilled ink a storm lashes closer.

Beyond present concern a buzzard or vulture roosts on top of a leaning telegraph across the river. Head out his driver's window Kuy spots his way slowly across. To the fore lighting threatens. Moving his way. Before the squall hits. Guns his engine.

Out of nowhere a rough provincial wind shoves him to the right half way over the middle of the trestle but he neverminds. Presses pedal, pilots his truck forward to safety.

Afterward, what's really perched on the telephone pole is revealed. "No bird but a man!" Alarmed, Kuy opens his window and shouts, "Need help?" But the old man sitting on the crossbeam ignores or cannot hear him. "Hey there!" Kuy yells again but here's no response from the great coat wrapped bare foot a dangle mystery.

Under thunderstorm's continued assault the roadman gets out thinking that this old fellow was treed by wild dogs or coyotes and can't get back down.

Folding up his collar ran over to the wooden post and looked up and while shielding his eyes, shouted upward, "Hey there! Hear me? Big storm coming! Get off your perch before it strikes you dead!"

Old man angrily retorts, "Who gives a tinker's damn? Care for a bro-tus—a bottle of sassafras?"

"What? No!" Kuy shouts.

Seventy if he is a day the roadman wagers. Unconcerned the stylite looks at the coming storm. Straightening, recites loudly,

"'He woke up. Rebuked the wind and said to the sea. Quiet. Be still! The wind ceased and there was a great calm.'"

"Maybe so partner but not this time!"

Rainstorm. Closer.

Frustrated as a polecat suffering from irregularity, Black Wolf readies to climb up and get the fool down yet finally hesitates, doubting this course of action, "And who am I to break reveries on wind and prairie's altar? Old fool! Must be touched," he decides while noting the fouled ring around the stylite's post banked with shit streaked pop bottles, wrappers and other detritus forming a sizable ring around his perch.

"This bird has nested here a while!" Black Wolf concludes.

"Lord. Oh Lord," the fool moans. Standing. Flapping his long arms like a crow. Deigning to notice the roadman for a second time, "Expected along a night or so. Get gone! Get along little doggie!"

Kuy looks up against the pouring rain, resignedly asks, "By whom?"

As with most oracles there's no reply. "Come down? Truck's dry and warm."

Fool hesitates as the wind and rain walls him off. Interrupted by a strike of lightening both men shudder. Later teeth chattering perched oracle adds another plea, "Christ don't leave me in this darkness. You who gives us light today and you who gives light to the night. Our lord illuminated and made the moon set in heaven. Illuminated the stars!"

Dodging this and other discharge, angered, Kuy shakes his fist and quotes Obadiah,

" 'The pride of thine heart hath deceived thee. Thou that dwelleth in the clefts of the rock. Whose habitation is high; that saith in his heart. Who shall bring me down to the ground?'" Pausing threatens, "Verse three, and never mind your tomfoolery! Get down or I will climb up there to get you!"

Getting him down in this deteriorating weather might prove difficult so Kuy ignores the fool's howling prophecies, mutterings, and avoids as well hawks of snot, hurled candy wrappers, buttons, dead crows and a spray of limp roses thrown at his head while the stylite's only response to further entreaties is "Dixie," hummed loud and off key.

Closing his eyes with frustration, he blesses the old man at the crosses. Watching the rain whip along the coal dark sky and lighting strike nearer than god to thee. Glancing up, Kuy notices a large devil's darning needle hovering by the old man.

Dodging the heavy drops it seeks shelter.

Stylite allows it to perch on his palm. Then cups it with his fingers. Guarding it from the hard–hitting rain.

Witnessing this kindness, Kuy asks, "*Ts' p'mi–bei kuocdl?*" Yet exasperated draws up with final deliberation, "What is shall be. What would make a man nest atop a telegraph pole is beyond me. Seen cantankerous foolishness before but–" and prior to skedaddling, tips his hat. Hurrying back to his truck but first something splashes in the mud at his feet. In the poor light. Isn't distinguishable.

Bends down to pick it up. It's a cross.

Back into the cab of his truck. Sits out of the pouring rain and examines leisurely what was tossed at him. An old Mexican silver crucifix. After another benediction for the man outside, kisses the worked silver and then ties it around his neck along with other talismans and protective amulets already noosed.

"Where have I seen that face before?"

Snapping his fingers, answers his own question, "Oaxaca. Of course!" Where he witnessed a Mayan festival in a lapsed catholic iglesia. The crowded spanish relic. Filled with boughs of fresh fragrant evergreens. Crops. Enough incense to choke on. God almighty yes! Seer on the pole resembles that waxed and weathered john the baptist nailed to their wall.

Drying off. Recalls. Their god was surrounded by censors, candles and young virgins dressed in white standing underneath the saint's naked painted feet.

No longer possible to see that crazy fool out there in the rain and not wishing to waste any more concern for the futility up there, Kuy gets out, cranks starts, gets gone. Thinking all the while about warm. Distant mexico.

Chapter Eleven

Kuy crossed north from el paso texas to the mexican state of coahila riding high chaparral like a ghost. Crossing the arid plains of northern san louis potosi he threaded his way through the sierras de catorce and the sierra los picachos del tuanlillo highlands without catching sight of another man or woman till a lone shepherd's fire beckoned and he begged leave to sleep against its roaring flame.

As days passed and later weeks, he felt neither a kindred bond nor alienation with the tribes' people met tumbleweeding past border towns and lone haciendas keeping his eyes open and his ears cocked.

Each state's inhabitants were as different to him as a scotsman was to a german and unlike the tribes of the north this land's original inhabitants were not forced into reservations. Instead, they clung to their tiny slivers of land between vast estates; sandwiched between mountain and vale. Each village had *la Santísima Trinidad*, one small *iglesia*, una *cantina*, and a *tienda* to sell basic supplies to tend to the needs of spirit and flesh.

Trails between scattered pueblos were only washed out riverbeds or perilous mining trails. A slip equaled injury or death. It was a different world atop raw mesas and ragged hills and yet captivating, with tiny villages set among towering crags and seemingly endless, windswept gorges.

Often Kuy marveled at the deep canyons stretched before him across lands with few bridges while he galloped silently cross endless highlands hemming flat constricted rivers stretching toward far mirage haunted horizon.

Between bouts of shivering and burning up. Black Wolf discovered that the climate changed drastically within the range of one or two days on horseback and that settlements were few and far apart. Had to rely on old mining maps or upon passing strangers to point his way south. Usually. These guides were small and furtive men expressing only guarded fellowship with hardship–gap tooth smiles framing their broken conversation. The locals called him Apache or *americano* but he didn't mind their address long as his destination was reached.

He rode through one thinly populated village to the next. Often camping with a bedroll and partial tent on stark and lonely sierras astray and unaccompanied. Wind played against his clothing and ruffled the fur of his rawboned horse's pelt.

After his american horse died. Kuy rode tough, local unshod ponies. The mules and donkeys of his guides fought each other just for the sake of argument. Striking without warning like snakes. Gouging chunks out of the unwary.

Though coming from horse people, he had never witnessed horses worked so and felt for their mounts well as the haunting; disturbing cries of freshly broke-in mules staked out on a rainy night. Surely the saddest and loneliest sounds ever heard–even this hour many years later.

At this time, adrift and with what goal? To escape american tyranny? To save himself? *Quien sabe?* When locked up in fort marion he debated the value of peyote rituals with other young and middle aged men lost as he, after release, hearing vague rumors of old rituals down mexico way, he wagered that southern tribes had not lost everything though the spaniards had their foot upon them far longer than the oppression endured by his own people. If they found a way to survive. Why not others he reasoned before traveling southward to discover first hand if any of their prison scuttlebutt was true.

Learning that nomads such as the Huicholes practiced wonderful and strange rituals but were furtive and not welcoming outsiders, young Kuy sought answers instead among half–castes in smoky little cantinas scattered throughout those bright, cool highlands. After stumbling upon a dying mining town in the high northeast he rested for a week.

In real catorce the spaniards and the tribes' people shunned him. The natives were interested only in his coin and the spanish not at all in this wild american.

Mines failing. There was little work. Many were leaving. Only by asking persistent questions and listening to wild, often improbable stories told inside low beamed adobe hovels crowded with the over ripe odors of pungent tobacco and too close bodies, he learned piecemeal what he sought.

Chasing rumor. Often no more than provincial wisdom trotted out as the gospel truth. He slipped and skidded down torturous trails of loose shale and gravel. Aside deep perilous gullies or *barrancas* leading to small dusty and lonely *rancheros* searching for clues.

After spending a week with a family of trusting *mestizos*, he followed a limping *brujo* to a cold empty *chaparral* accompanied by three other men also on quests. This old *mestizo Don* instructed them in the rudiments of gathering and using *Pioniyo*. *Señor* also warned them that one does not choose peyote. The sacrament chooses you.

Cactuses ranges in size from that of a silver dollar to a small plate and grows in the shade of larger plants around it. Its coloring a light gray. Successfully camouflaging their appearance. Making the cactuses hard to find but before ingesting any cactus the gray bearded *Don* cautioned them not to eat or use liquor before trying it.

Since Kuy had neither. That night camped in a gravel–strewn arroyo; he ate *Seni* for the first time on the bottom of a dried gully.

It sheltered them from cold and discovery. Above shooting and sentinel cactuses–towering yuccas. Scrub and dried thorn guarded them.

As each pilgrim retreated into separate stations of waiting. He walked east to an ancient aqueduct arched above a washed out narrow gulch. Under its shadow. Wind grew chill. Evening deepened. He waited cross legged under blood red sun setting above distant mountains. No more than cloud–covered shadows bending down. Stirring mirage.

Parked above effaced. Washed out stones. He used his barrow knife to cut portions of *Seni* into bite sized chunks. Like cutting the fruit of an orange; he thought while separating the fruit from the rind.

Peyote tasted. No, this was wrong. It had no actual taste–just an impression of acidity.

His first sensation was of light falling below the horizon. Filching russet crown from distant sierras. Leaving only blue tinged shadows behind deepening chill.

Color faded. Darkness filled the arroyo and echoing, bitter winds swayed thorn and scrub around him. Alone. Braced under the broken colonial arch, young Kuy watched, listened, and waited.

Solemn evening ended as hue and tint decamped toward the laps of awaiting mountains. As none of the others were in sight Kuy felt abandoned as evening dimmed and grew colder.

Old broken aqueduct served as both guardian and warder.

Occasionally laughter, shouts, hell even howls broke out beyond his line of sight. Later gradually near dusk dead faces bubbled up around him or if not actual features of dead men and women, then perhaps ritual skulls, followed by the masks of the ancients who once lived here, whose only trace were broken shards of pottery and worked flint scattered around.

On surrounding stones fleeting symbols scratched black and red in bold script. Abandoned secrets? Keys to his quest? If so! He had no wish to leaf through these static. Etched. Traced whispers as wild wind sighed and whistled through arch's mouth.

Later–stone swirled. Altered. Forming into the curved spine of a coiled dragon. Reminding him of the mysterious symbols found outside *TsHenej–kiH* laundries and chophouses.

Afterward, wrapped in a borrowed blanket he waited revelations while light failed and temperature dropped. After many an hour, realizing that these lessons weren't for him. That these secrets belonged to others. For a people no longer living. What he desperately sought. Did not desire wisdom this abandoned land whispered. Barely discernible. Over the brittle cutting wind's–lost songs. Forgotten rituals. Tired magic cast long ago. Now grist for dream and nightmare.

Feeling as if he had reopened a musty tract from a shelf–a recital of dead words, Kuy steadied himself, ignoring cold's bite, demanding, "Why am I here?"

Voiced delirium replied. Echoed in languages not understand until not unlike like a phonograph needle sliding into a record's groove, an icy gust stammered in Kiowa, "Hungry for answers but like a wolf do you know the answer swallowed?" it whispered laughing and mocking.

"Did I blunder into the wrong lecture?" Kuy brooded.

"Run along Kindred," whispered wind.

This he heeded. Listening attentively as it spoke for the last time contemptuous of his retreating steps."–amid light amid darkness a man must hunt," it chuckled with indistinct delivery. A faltering lisp that pinned his ears back.

Crouched now in dark. Recalling the hundreds of miles traveled to reach this lost, gravel–strewn gully, Kuy demanded, "Was it just to shiver under this old arch? Is this "*Seni*" speaking? Or am I just too dammed cold," he deliberated, trying to keep his teeth from chattering too hard.

Later called to help gather wood for the night's fire, he turned away from the growing shadows and too subtle schooling.

Feeling a prick of fear on the back of his neck like a schoolboy sulking away from a stern instructor.

Little choice. Cold chilled to the bone. Having no gloves. Stuffed his hands in pockets. Gathering firewood exposed his fingers and they cramped and grew numb quickly.

"Damn, that was a cold night for everyone! Huddled around their fire."

They listened and spoke to each other with rapturous. Bedeviled necessity. Or sullen listlessness. Each entrapped in their own heaven or hell. Employing broken spanish. He listened to his comrades' fragmented and hesitant tales. Chasing divination that long bitter night. Without fire's warmth they all would have frozen.

"*Yuh!*" Even distant coyotes cried for warmth and when too dark to gather more wood or thorn brush for their fire, their bonfire was reluctantly allowed to die as each man sought what shelter he could. Having the makings of a rude tent Kuy crawled inside. Throughout that night, wind tore at his rough shelter and rough thorns raked his rude tent like the nails of a Senile witch.

Alone in the icy dark. *Seni* turned on him like a snake. Drying out his mouth. Tying his stomach in knots. Listening for voices. He sought revelations but nothing came. So Kuy cursed, dreading that perhaps he had missed his only opportunity for enlightenment.

Later parceled up in a rough horse blanket, juddered like a bowl of suet, he had to smile and shrug asking what price wisdom?

Stronger than Seni was cold. Nature can never be eclipsed. She's a force of her own and how he struggled with heightened awareness! Every stone and pebble pressing upon him new realities as he tossed and turned from one equally uncomfortable station of the cross to the next reinforced only one lesson. Earth's power is strong. A lesson recollected while gripping his steering wheel harder and peering ahead.

Peyote is no open door to greater wisdom. Nor is it an automatic gateway to salvation. "*Seni* is similar in a limited way to white churches," he grasps shifting gears. "One can enter into its sanctity. But it is what you strive for in the encounter that counts. Have you come to mourn? Pray for loved ones? Seek answers? Then the responsibility of gaining enlightenment is yours! Unlike the Christian host. You and you alone shape or forge your experience; Wisdom is gained only if truly sought."

On the final morning of that long ago day. Their guide returned to gather each woebegone men. Later every one gratefully returned to his crowded adobe house for a meal of tortillas. Bean and rice. Washed down with cups of steaming coffee.

At the wheel of his Hercules the roadman contemplates this past experience. Weakened by cold and hunger. His fledgling self—realized that morning that *Seni* was only part of the solution. The main answer lay within. Would *Pioniyo* help him to answer these questions? If so. How? Southern folk possessed rituals and ceremonies that did not articulate outside their fires.

He needed answers yet they evaded him. Were the mask and skulls of his brief vision a warning? He had no idea and had much to learn. Who could teach him the lessons necessary to master the knowledge and arts that he sought?

The old ways of attaining *dwdw*. Spiritual or supernatural power were discredited. Almost abandoned except for by a few older men and women and they in turn were wary of sharing what remained as if well sustained yet surrounded by a sea of starving.

That long ago night under mexican stars. He fought his losing battle with the deepening chill. Too miserable for sleep. Got out of his shelter and looked upward: the bright stars overhead manifested the beauty of this world. While fatigue and deepening chill illustrated his flesh's weakness and returned to the frost laced chaparral and collected as much peyote possible. Vowing to find answers and teachers whether spiritual or human. If unable to answer his questions. Then at least he could hopefully discover his own questions and his own answers.

Chapter Twelve

Under blue and pink hued sky. Returning to here and now, the roadman sighs, "Mexico's neither here nor there!"

Ahead train unloaded a gaggle of gaily–painted wagons and a handful of trucks. Intrigued. He drives over, stops and then strolls over to a group of men unloading wagons and crates from the train. Must be a circus or a carnival Kuy figures. Deciding that he just might be able pick up a few dollars working as a general roust about for a few hours or even a day or two, Black Wolf walks over to a crowd of workmen unloading wagons from flatcar with cable and pulley or snubbers.

Sighting one fellow directing rather than unloading, the roadman asks, "How do?"

Dressed differently from the men around him. This bold fellow, Kuy surmises, must be the lot manger or owner tarted up in a rather citified clothes.

The dandy's black hair is slicked back over his balding crown framing his eyes. Both brown and expressive like a child's sizing up an older relative for a stick of candy or a special boon. Addressed. He turns away from his inspection and studies the roadman with a calculating. Easy smile of the lip though not of the eye. "Just fine Mister and you?"

"The same. I was wondering if you needed an extra hand around here for a day or two."

The man looks at him with a broad grin, "Already have a brave in our revue. Chief. But I notice you have a truck. Have a new wagon lacking a team to pull it. Pay you five dollars to tow it."

"To where?"

"Not too far friend. About twenty–five thirty miles or so down the way. A long haul town but we'll be there in time for supper and you will be helping out a fine family."

"Five dollars? Make it six."

"Your drive a hard bargain. Eh Mr.–"

"George"

"Nice to meetcha. George. I'm Mr. Manoliadis. Tell you what stranger. Five and a half with a cook house good dinner and breakfast thrown in."

"Done."

"All right," Manoliadis agrees and then calls over one of his razorbacks unloading the train.

"Fred. Come here. Meet Mr. George."

The roadman and the circus hand shake hands. "Fred show this gazoonie where the wagon is. You know that new fortuneteller's trailer and mitt camp." This said, Manoliadis turns away and goes over to over-see the offloading a troublesome tandem wagon filled with the roar of unhappy, road weary animals.

Fred looks over the Kiowa and with a curt nod. Then follows him back to his truck and asks, "Nice truck! Must have cost you a pretty penny."

"No actually I traded for it."

"For what," Fred asks shyly, "if you don't mind me asking."

"A life."

"A life. I like that. Ok. Drive straight ahead. See the funny wagon just yonder with the roof like an old hat–that's the one."

Kuy drives over to the wagon and jumps out.

Fred follows.

In front of it a small family of dark, somber clad people wait expectantly until Fred introduces the roadman, "Mrs. Satorina. Here's the man who will tow your house to the next gig."

Before saying a word, she examines the roadman, and then hazards a guess, "You're an Indian. No?" with a heavy, lilting accent.

"Yes," Black Wolf replies, "a Kiowa."

"Well. Glad you came along. We have just joined this–association and our horses have *gripe*. Had to leave them behind in case they infected the other animals and come back for them later when they are better."

"No problem," the roadman answers her. "Glad to lend a hand."

With Fred guiding him. The roadman backs up against the wagon's hitch, stops. Then gets out. Later, both men heave the heavy hitch and pull the wagon upright. While the roadman strains with the weight. Fred ties it down against the Hercules's hitch.

Now free. The Kudwa helps him lash the wagon to his truck. Satisfied. Fred directs the roadman to take his queue forming behind.

Black Wolf nods and invites the Gypsy woman and her family into his truck.

He starts off slowly after gauging the caravan's weight and draw and then circles back to join the rest of the procession.

Shortly. The caravan forms ranks besides the waiting black locomotive building up steam to roll away. Waiting for them ride off toward their next show. The roadman leaves his truck for a moment to step over to the puffing and hissing engine.

Trains have never been a favorite of his–equating them with destruction of the buffalo and forced displacement rather like the great wall of china he had read about with every inch laid with blood and sacrifice.

Its crew are warming up like the boiler in front of them. Wrestling with switches. Checking gages and shoveling coal. Eyes fixed ahead down the track. A little talk–office scuttlebutt drifts around in the super–heated fall air, "Well. At least we got them unloaded and on their way."

"Yeah but it will take months to get rid of the stink from those animal cages!"

"And them some–"

"Think that old college professor will keep us out of the war."

"Well he promised didn't he?"

"Yes. But he's still a politician–"

"And they have a habit of forgetting their promises!"

Black Wolf listens for a minute or two. Then interrupts, "Gentlemen. Pardon for the interruption. But I would like to ask a question."

"Yeah go ahead," the engineer. A short compact man says with a slow nod. Though surprised by Black Wolf's sudden appearance. He's seemingly in a genial mood, though slightly distracted, necessitated by watching a large gauge as the steam builds up.

"Know anything about a particular fellow piled on top of a telegraph pole back west about 50 miles."

The engineer. Fireman and brakeman glance at each other in consultation as if they asked to divulge a weighty secret. Then with a slight frown the engineer answers Kuy's question, "Oh. Old Pete. Yeah. You're asking about Old Pete! We know about him! He's been up there for years. Under the trestle like a troll or perched on his pole; the boys and me slow down or stop when we pass by and throw him some food or pop. All of the trains on this line do the same."

After listening, the roadman explains his interest in Old Pete by relating his encounter.

"Yes. Sound about right. You're lucky he didn't take a bite out you!" the fireman chuckles, "There are a couple of stories about why he's up there. One's that he was a preacher who either killed his wife's lover or his wife and family or ran off with one of his parishioner's. Or something thing or the other to this affect Mister—"

Kuy curiosity satisfied, thanks them for the information. Afterwards walks back to his truck and waits. Within a few minutes. There's a general hullabaloo, hubblebubble, followed by a raucous whistle from the lead vehicle. An ornate wagon painted with about every imaginable color. As the line pulls taut, lurching forward to match the first wagon's pace, Kuy starts up and follows.

Later toward dusk they round a narrow plain hedged by hills. A sign proclaims a hamlet ahead boasting a population of three thousand souls.

Each wagon and truck put on a brave show entering the small, windswept prairie town with as much fanfare as the tired performers and workers can muster.

Children happily flank their progress as the town's fire and cyclone siren heralds the troops' passage through and down the main commercial street.

Black Wolf laughs as several kids climb up on his running boards screaming excitedly before just as quickly jumping off.

Leaving the excited. Waxing weekender crowd behind. The carnival caravan follows a series of red arrows and a trail of handbills laid down by tack spitters to the town's outskirts–near its stockyards. Once stopped each follows a mapped out plan, breaking into separate but interconnecting encampments.

Black Wolf cools his heels until directed. Later a back yard boy helps him unhitch and set up the fortuneteller's caravan and when finished he wanders and helps where he can while asking questions and taking in the unfamiliar sounds and sights till Manoliadis finds him and offers him a few more dollars for a couple of odd jobs. Including taking a group of carnies back into town to buy needed supplies and pass out handbills and post posters.

Kuy agrees since it is too late to hit the road and he could use a night's diversion and a rest so he loads up as many people as possible and circles back to town. Not wishing to lose track of his passengers, he stays inside his truck until one by one they return worn and tired. With everyone clutching bags of beer, pop, cans of tuna fish, oranges, candy and whatnot return readily to the carnival with only muted and disjointed conversation passed among them and not at all to the Kiowa.

On return, out on the empty. Grassed plain. A city of lights now saddled the horizon in a rough horseshoe pattern. Ablaze like Baum's city of Oz.

After parking. Kuy investigates. Taking in the magically altered site. Aladdin's caverns and ghostly attractions beckon now where once only prairie stood.

One full circuit. Then he's assigned more jobs. Muscle work. Helping to erect gaff banners. Lights. Electrical

Half-erected Ferris wheel and other rides beckon with the promises of fevered shamans or cautionary tales of demon encampments tempting the unwary wiring, pulling like a sailor at long ropes to host wires and canvas into place. That plain's winds play soon as they're hoisted above the ground.

Everything runs on juice now, so the carnival pinches electricity. Placing a mexican harness onto the wires. Works swell unless there's a short or too great a load. Followed by a brownout. Or blackout and the sheriff will pay a visit. One that only a charitable contribution to a local charity will soothe.

As moon rises and the hour grows late most workers finish their tasks and cluster into small groups based on status. Performers hobnob with fellow working acts. The Strong Man. Magicians. Contortionist. The Human Dynamo. All joshing. Lying. Betting. Courting acrobats. Knife Throwers. Cowboys and Indians. Half and Half's. Missing Links. Sky grifters. The girl from the Girl and Gorilla show. Aunty Sally agents. The Geek drinking dinner. Razzle Dazzle Men. Bozard and Kootch show girls.

While the roust abouts. Shills. Talkers and touts lounge around with a beer or two or a lazy game of cards as general workers. The shovelers. Stake drivers. Drivers. Sweepers. Booth and concession kids gossip or flirt with their own.

The main performers, the "Royalty of the Road," retire early except for the few animal acts seeing to their chargers before having a drink or going to bed.

Shortly lights snap off one by one and it's dark and quiet except for the occasional bray of an insomniac mule or argumentative voice.

Tired as the rest Black Wolf ignores bunkhouse accommodation and walks back across tire treaded, wilted prairie grass lit by torch to his truck Bedding down for the night, he is a little uneasy with all of the unfamiliar sensations draped around him. A wailful wind. Creaking canvas. Opening and closing doors. Heated whispers. Snores. Well as the heady scent of animals. People. Closely packed vehicles. Food. Gasoline. Leather. Animal forage and droppings. All wrapping him in sleep picketed by a watchman's footsteps.

Before first light Kuy awakes. Pocket of carnies astir as well. Up and bustling. Amid protesting animals, phlegmatic washing and cooking.

Kuy joins later a queue to wash up and eat only to find out that he's too early.

"Cooks?" some busybody asked.

"Sweating out last night's hoot and holler," a passing dwarf insists.

So folks will just have to wait a while since no one messes with the cooks. Not as long as they are still eating at the show's one and only hash barn.

An obviously hung-over roughy passes by and gives the workers the lay O,

"Ok! We're all a little hungry and crawling for coffee. No problem. I wallop on the sons of baptists' door and roust them out. In the meantime. You all know what you should be doing. Right?"

Bleary–eyed men and woman reluctantly nod. With few asides packs of troopers, wander off knowing where they can at least find a cup of java while on the other hand, "forty milers and green peas" just cough or scratch their heads before heading off to find a work boss or assistant lot manager for orders.

Hungry. But used to it. The roadman follows their example and joins others at their appointed tasks. Mostly setting up false fronts empty as the promises within.

Later Manoliadis finds him and offers him a week's employment based on his work so far.

Kuy declines. "Would like to but have to get along."

"Yeah. Figured. Where to?"

"East."

"Old Oklahoma!" The lot boss pauses. Then asks the roadman with a serious. Focused. Tone. "What are you Chief? Not an everyday joe cut the way you are."

"Meaning?" Kuy asks.

"With your clothes and all. Hair–"

"I'm a Kiowa! A roadman."

"Well. I gathered you were some type of conjurer or something of this nature. I have one of your people here working for me."

"A Kiowa?"

"So he boasts."

"Where?"

"Down on the left. Next to the pinheads and nature's oddities. White Horse is his name. Bunks with our Geek." the lot manager curses, "Two of a pair! They're probably still asleep. Like the bottle."

"That you provide?"

"Hey. Who am I to object to what a man like or does not like along as he pulls his weight! So you want stay on?"

"No!"

"Ok. See me before you leave and I will pay you. Prefer coin or alfalfa?"

"Come again–"

"Paper dollars"

"Coin."

"See you later then. Work usually starts in about half an hour but every things a little topsy-turvy right now with all the new hands we got so scratch what I just said. Breakfast's as soon as possible."

Despite being more or less english fluent, Kuy suspects that when Manoliadis opens his mouth he's speaking some other lingo altogether. Therefore he shuts his own and waits for more–"And don't worry being paid. This ain't no red light job but a full nelson!"

Afterward with his head still spinning follows directions till he finds a battered caravan without paint or slogans. Knocking on its door. Waits.

Within a minute or two. There's a muffled reply, "What do you want? I'm not on till tonight sonabitch. Go away!"

"Open up!"

"Who's there?"

"*Khoam!*"

"*Khoam?*"

A throat clears. To Kuy, sounds masculine but unwell, followed by cursing and hurried dressing before the caravan's small oval door opens on its sagging, rusted hinges.

A haggard face peers out. A portrait in dissipation if Kuy had ever seen one.

"A Kudwa? Well what are you waiting for come in?"

Ducking his head, Kuy steps in. Inside a rank, odorous smell hits him. Almost makes him puke but catching his breath. He sits down on a wooden rocker, trying to ignore the tiny room's reek of vomit, gin, and sweat. Studying his host instead.

A tall, if bent man with hair longer than the roadman's. Darker faced. Worn and pitted with acne scars. Late middle aged, Kuy guesses and ill–used by circumstance.

The caravan holds two rumpled beds. One's still occupied and the other empty well as tiny kitchen swarming with flies. What little light seeps in comes through two curtained oval windows shaped like those Kuy had seen in drawings and paintings depicting ships or cabin boats. The caravan's only notable feature is a tumble of bottles of all shapes, sizes, and colors stacked and piled in every corner.

"He smells about 80 proof," Kuy complains, pointing over to sleeping man.

"Shit. That's nothing," the other Kiowa exclaims, "wait till you catch his act!"

"Don't think I wish to!"

"Oh. Jimmy's Ok. Our Geek you know. Gets drunk in front of the crowds and bites off the head of a chicken or two!"

The roadman looks at the sleeping man. Then shakes his head, "Hell of a way to make a living!"

"Buys the grub!"

"And you?"

"Oh. I'm *Isa–tah*. But here I'm big chief Dohasan."

"White Horse. Glad to meet you. I'm Kone-gyah-daw-kue' or as my family and friends call me, just Kuy will do!"

"Black Wolf," the other translates. "Get comfortable," White Horse suggests. Pointing to a chair cushion.

"Dohasan. Hell of a way to honor his name."

"Well anyway!" White Horse replies with a slight frown, "What brings you to my door? Passing through on the way to strike it rich in california? On to the way to see prospective clients. Selling railroad futures or you a recruiting sergeant for the army and navy?"

Not blind to sarcasm. The roadman smiles at his witticisms, realizing that he had been too judgmental, "No. I'm on the way back to fort sill to hold some ceremonies. I'm a road chief. Got my truck loaded with two crates of peyote for my church."

"One of those. Figured from your dress. Anyway want some coffee?"

"Sure."

The other Kiowa gets off his bed and slides over to a primus stove next to a dry sink full of dirty dishes and empty bottles. Watching his preparations. The roadman notices that he's crippled and has to use the trailer's fittings to walk upright.

Makes a pot of coffee and afterward suggests they drink it outside. Free of the caravan, White Horse points to two wooden folding chairs leaning against another trailer. Black Wolf grabs both and sets them in place so they can sit and chat awhile.

Sitting down each watch P'ay climb while late shift workers rise. Take in clothing. Still children's cries. Shake out dreams like dirty rugs. Read papers. Gossip and start their long day while main acts continue sleeping till last call for breakfast sounded by sculleries beating pot lids together.

White Horse starts the ball rolling in a low, whiskey edged voice, "I'm main talent. Work my show. Now Jim. He's different but the boss man doesn't make him do any general work anymore. One can be either the Geek or a workman. But not both! Believe it or not he was a professor back in boston."

"A professor–really–of what subject?"

"Math. Said it wasn't the teaching that made him go to the bottle but all of the rest. Organizing. Playing politics and the rest of their bull crap–"

"Yeah. Tough life! But back to you–"

"Oh. I was north of you probably. Up near the kansas border. I'm a *To–kinah–yup* man and little older than you I reckon. Notice my legs. Got polio a while back. Now. I'm not much of use to anyone. My wife died from it."

"I'm sorry."

"Don't be. It was like a fire. It passed and left only a little. You 're not going to stay on?"

"No."

Relieved. White Horse sighs. "Good. There's room for only one of us around here!"

Kuy laughs, "You don't think that I would stand on a stage playing for whites do you? '

Isa–tah gives him a hard, questioning look, before stating, "Don't be too quick to judge. Before I lost the spring in my step. Maybe I was a little like you. But now. I'm lucky to be here. We move around all the time. Everyone here accepts one or another–more or less–or they get out or are forced out. Manoliadis is hard but fair unless he can see a way to take advantage. More to the point, where else would I go?"

"You could come with me!"

"Where?"

"Fort sill."

"And do what?" White Horse demands.

Kuy takes off his hat to best consider his question. "Well. You have me on that one. Guess I am too quick to jump the gun! Comes from being alone all the time. Talking and thinking too much on the open road."

"When you leaving?"

"Tonight or early tomorrow morning. With what I'll earn here. I'll have enough to gas and stock up on some needed supplies."

"Ok. I want to invite you to my show–"

"Yeah. Might drop in anyway but I was never was a sucker for the greasepaint and stage."

They continue talking as morning stretches from its beachhead across the plain to their encampment.

In daylight the carnival grounds suffer noticeably from a lack of charm. Puddles of dirty water and litter wait for the broom and bucket and the show's garish paint looks tired and worn.

Tired of yakking the roadman yawns, hitches up his pants and waits for the cook shack to stir and start brewing coffee, fry eggs and flip flat cakes as fast and hot and as many as wanted.

The other Kiowa keeps the conversion going because he's lonely. Telling Black Wolf he's mighty glad to meet one of his own folk again, "It's been an age; we had a Mandan here for a while. A rough one!"

"Was his name Billy?"

"Yes. I believe so. Know him?"

"Yes. A nice young man if you keep an eye open. Knows a lot of our tales. Sings for his supper."

"Billy?"

"Walks Through Walls."

"That's him!"

"Do tell! Small world and all!"

The roadman relates how he met Billy. Before going on to other subjects near and dear to them both. With the sun high. Enough to read the broadsides scattered around. Black Wolf gets up and excuses himself/

"See you later–Guess the flags up!"

"Want breakfast tumbleweed?" Isa–tah teases before adding a warning, "Say there–watch out for Manoliadis. He might try to get you drunk to cheat you out of what he owes you!"

"Let'm try," the roadman responds angrily," I don't drink and I need the money."

The two men shake hands. Then White Horse goes back inside. While Kuy strides off to hunt breakfast and later a roughy or lot boss to discover his duties for the day.

***

Later by the hour it's early evening and still not a cloud in the sky. Unseasonably warm. Not a breeze in sight to break the doldrums. Riled Kuy swats at a hungry back fly before finding a spot of expanding shade to watch the crowds start down the carnival's Broadway. First just a few scouting parties. Followed by eager pioneers. Then gawking tinhorns and eager beavers even though its (excuse me miss) just too blamed hot and sweaty for October!

"Indian summer," he jests. While following the flocks from the nearby town crowding into the darkening midway. Shunted like an invading army under barrage. They're hit with every enticement guaranteed to elicit a smile. A laugh or two. A rumble or turn of the belly. A whoop of pleasure. A guffaw of disbelief. Loss's sigh or the thrill of a momentary victory.

Smell. First casualty's the nose. Assaulted by the collywobble scent of an autumn country carnival. Carried lazily on the warm–stirring air. Fall harvest. Church bazaar. Halloween. Barnyard odor rekindling youth. Adventure and courtship as faded freckled hands, grasp, and pull toward the elusive beguiling odors of popcorn and peanuts. Johnny cakes with maple syrup. Sausages. Hot dogs. Hamburgers. Cotton candy spun out by magic. Don't forget candy apples. Corn dogs. Pop. Beer on tap.

All in all, an old, though beguiling shake down. Emptying pockets. Wallet and coin purse with well–rehearsed ease.

Listen. Ears' turn next. Organ music. The soft shoe shuffle. Twanging guitars and banjos. Soprano. Baritone and tenor. Sweet Adeline don't you know. Barkers promise. Touts challenge. Spin the bottle. Town shoe and county boot shuffle old Joe Clark while Vienna trained fingers pluck the hoedown, the arms akimbo and pigeon toed waltz.

Watch. Eyes later. Whatallready? Well for starters a thousand burning colored lights. Hot as candles. Entrap with a penny's wonder–a transitory, whatchama–callum. What–not mutable world consisting of decorated wagons. Painted men and women. A tattooed man. A bearded lady. Two headed sheep. An authentic Indian chief. A real life swami from calcutta.

Even an authentic marvel or two swishing out whiskey from their breath and trying to gulp down soup and hold it down before first curtain call.

Work done. Black Wolf. Watches cotton candy vendor spin out miles of candy. Buys a bag. Then walks down the midway.

Town and country mill about. Scouting the sights. Later splitting up into smaller groups.

Many are spellbound by the whirligigs rides. Arcade games while others part coin for the freak shows. The exotic dance pavilion or the Wild West show with its exhibits of embalmed dead outlaws. Original Indian songs and dances led by Big Chief Dohasan. Last of the Kiowa warrior princes or so the play bills passed promise.

Alone. The roadman heads toward the carnival's candy coated heart.

Might be a lesson here if he had the time and patience to unravel its subject matter yet guessing that it would take more consideration than he is willing to invest. Lets the matter drop. Moving on. Ogling the sights. Content to eat his spun sugar floss. Gawking at the unfamiliar grab joints. Ten in one booths. Question mark shows booths. Watching families excitedly going from stand to stand. Watterdogging soft drinks. Bitter. Strong coffee. A beer. Even whiskey.

At a junction he finds White Horse's pavilion. Waving to the slick out front. Slinks into the show tent. Inside joins a small group of men and women watching a few dancers and singers on a tiny, ill–lit stage. Keeping toward the back. Not wishing to be noticed.

On stage Isa–tah rides. Crooked legs akimbo on a painted wooden horse pulled by actors. He has a tomahawk upraised in his arm. Spinning around. Chasing two–faded actress costumed as settlers beset by Indians.

Pausing momentarily. White Horse turns to his audience and makes a short speech, "Ladies and Gentlemen: here before your very eyes. We will reenact–"

The crowd bored. Restless. Boos.

One man. Half–drunk. Steps forward. Shouting at the stage, "Heck. What type of a gyp is this? Throw that cripple off his hobby horse and let's see some naked squaws or some good old fashion American mischief on this stage!"

Seasoned players, Isa–tah, and other actors ignore the drunk. Hearing the same night after night. Attempt to play on but a group of young men well–oiled and urged on by hecklers, empty their pockets of old vegetables and rotten eggs, lobbing them at the performers.

White Horse and his fellow recitalists stand for a moment under the barrage. Then hurriedly retreat behind a patched curtain.

Angry. Black Wolf grabs. Then carries the older heckler outside. Helpless in the Kiowa's unforgiving grip.

Green pea carnival hand noticing the row. Whistles. Within a minute the local toughs are ringed by angry, threatening carnies and after a steadying hand falls on his straining shoulder Black Wolf spins around as Manoliadis bawls,

"Whoa there Chief! We'll take it from here!" Quickly. Without additional fuss, the troublemaker on his shoulder is roughly manhandled off into a local constable's custody while his fellow town's men are forcefully herded off.

"Sorry sport. It's nothing personal or unique just some drunks looking for a bit of release at our expense. Like I said. I could use one of your sort–"

Dismissing his offer. Kuy thanks the carnies for their assistance before stepping back inside. Within. Watching the truncated. Heartbreaking show till embarrassed and disgusted by its pathetic and desperate attempts to please its diminished, suckered audience. Files out. Deciding to leave tomorrow morning after he's paid.

Afterward. Wondering if whites and Kiowa differ all that much. When it comes down to basics. Watching their flushed expectant faces. Comparing them to his people when playing *Tho Oyeon*.

"We like to play. Losing ourselves. Running from responsibility. Failure and sadness like children–then how different is the cloth from which we are cut?"

The roadman. Encouraged by a passing roughy. Joins in several games of chance. Baseball. Bottle. Hoop toss. Shooting gallery and other quick ways to sucker marks. Luring men and boys to part with their buffalo nickels. Liberty dimes. Quarters, half dollars and occasional dollar.

Screams from the rides and the lights of the Ferris wheel attract his attention so he walks away from his pulpit. Watches silently until Mr. Manoliadis finds him again.

"What do you think of our Simp Heister Mr. George?" Manoliadis asks pointing to brightly lit Ferris wheel before adding, "Changed your mind about staying on for a bit. I like the way you handled yourself back there."

"No. Rousting drunks. Hecklers isn't my line. Have to be on my way tomorrow."

"Fine. We open at seven a clock tomorrow. I'll have your money ready for you. Find White Horse?"

"Yes."

"A little old and rusty for my show. Starting to drink. Acting so bad he's becoming a pickled punk. Hell! I could put him in a jar a charge admission and he would bring more percentage to the house than he does now. Tell you what. Take his place. I'll give you double what he's pulling in now. Expanding my Wild West revue. Make you a main attraction! With all of these dime novels coming out and Nickelodeon westerns so popular. I believe western themes are going to be very popular. If this war doesn't take peoples' minds of the good ole US of A."

"Mr. Manoliadis let me make this very clear. I was born. When white faces were rare. Only fire light. Nights long and dark. Hunting. Gathering brought in food. Kept people honest and strong because the weak and untrustworthy were shunted aside. For me gadgets; electric lights and all are a marvel but this gimmickry–is just a temptation–like a candle to moths. Tomorrow. I get back on the road and go from congregation to congregation ministering to my parishioners."

"You're a priest?"

"Well. Call ourselves roadmen or road chiefs."

"Hmm. Mighty different religions aren't there? Me. I'm Greek

Orthodox. Jewish on the Saturdays. Major holidays. Here out in the high weeds and sticks, I might as will be a headhunter!" This said Manoliadis strikes a match. Lighting a cigar. Offers one to the roadman but it's begged off. The lot manger shrugs. Then holds out another inducement, .

"Care for a drink?"

"No. No thanks but I have a question for you if you don't mind."

"Go–ahead sport–"

"Are you going to keep him around or kick him out?"

"Well. We're a large crazy family. Maybe. I will have to freshen up the act a little–make it more realistic. See you around Mr. George."

"Never know!"

Manoliadis noticing his interest in the rotating amusement ride. Offers Black Wolf a free ride.

The roadman considers it. Then with a wary grin accepts the boss's generosity.

Passing the ride's attendant Kuy exchanges a curt salute as he is sat in the next free bench. Clinching his teeth while the ride's minder clamps a metal bar down in front of him with,

"Have a good one brother!"

Lurched upward with sudden exhilaration. Breathing rapidly. Laughs. Then frankly brays.

Breathtaking. The Carnival's lights. Seen from above.

"Heck! If this is for chumps. Then enroll me the fraternity brother!"

Once on top. The ride comes to a shuddering halt. Feet a dangle. Kuy stares ahead. Marveling at this tomfoolery harnessed just to titillate and thrill–

"How these people come up with all of these crazy distractions is beyond me," he admits.

Jolted again. The Ferris wheel creaks to a new vantage. A wind picked crow's nest threatening his hat and nearby ladies' headgear. Rocking pre- cariously. He uses one hand to secure his hat while his other resumes a death grip on the forward bar. Till full circle.

Looks for Velvet. Wondering if he can locate her place set. Recalling that one can only see for a range of twenty–five miles horizon from horizon. Reluctantly gives up.

Aground. Walks away on shaky legs. Fighting the temptation to get back in line for another go. Instead. After sober reflection. Decides instead to return to White Horse's Wild West show to solong. Close to last call. The crowd is as thin as government tinned milk and after walking back to the impromptu stage finds Isa–tah slumped against a stack of old fruit crates.

Catching sight of Kuy, White Horse mumbles one thing probably meaning another, "Saw you watching my show. We were a little off to-night. Those critics were rough! Too bad you didn't see me some time ago. Town sons of bitches!" After taking a long snort from a bottle of whiskey, rolls his eyes and coughs prior to passing the gutrot.

Kuy declines. Instead helps the performer to his feet. Half carries, carrying — all the while. warning his friend, "Listen. If you think you can trust your boss!"

"He offered you my act. Didn't he?"

"Yes."

"Did you take it?"

"No, as I said before–I have other plans."

"Yeah–That sorry greek son of a gun. He' s always threatening to use me like a bounce and put me in a jar of tea!"

The roadman laughs. Then trying to ease his friend's mood says, "Listen. Can't trust this white man. Tomorrow I'm going. Last chance! Care for a ride?"

"No. Tell you what tomorrow. There's one of us–maybe half Cheyenne or something to that effect but–guess what–"

"You tell me."

"He flies."

"He what?"

"Flies. He's got a plane and does acrobatics. Takes people up for ten dollars or so a shot."

"Do tell."

White Horse stumbles. Almost falls. The roadman steadies him. "Sorry–had too much–"

"It's all right," Kuy reassures with a calm, dry confidence.

"Brother. You know. When I was a young boy. In them old days. There was a big prairie fire–"

"–the Long Fire?"

"The Big Burning! You remember it? It's good to have someone who remembers those days to talk to. Listen–afterwards. Everyone was in an uproar. We were hungry. Burnt off our hunting lands. Looking for lost family members and friends," suddenly saddened, he pauses. After the space of a minute or two, with his eyes tearing, and face clouding, White Horse continues, "One day–an old buffalo blinded and burnt by the fire wondered in our new camp. It walked slowly over to where my mother was cooking and drank from a bucket in front of her like an old pet."

"What happened to him?"

"We ate him of course," White Horse says with a bitter smile, adding "I'm a little like that old bison so have a little patience."

"There's a word they have Isa–tah," the roadman cautions.

"What?"

"Nostalgia! It's a word for remembering too much the past. I suffer from it. You too I guess."

"What should I do? Focus solely on–" he pauses, clearing his voice, "This?" he asks resignedly. Looking down at his ruined legs. The bottle in his hand.

"No. But the past is as buried as those we grieve for. Those calling on lonely nights–"

"Sssssh. Don't speak of them! The other night–my late wife stood outside this caravan–calling like an owl. Even Jimmy heard her and woke up," White Horse whispers. Changing the subject after turning around to ask another question, "Hey listen. Want some sport?"

"What kind?"

"A girl. A woman. I have a gal. Dances in the jig show."

"Jig is a bad word isn't it?"

"Ok pilgrim. What are you any way a Lookie–Lou? Or a whistling gopher hunting the key to the midway? Anyhow. We had a carnival marriage–rode the merry go front wise Her and some other girls got a notch joint cook'n tonight."

"What's that?"

"Woman selling–no listen to me–what I mean–"

"Don't buy it and right now not looking for it either."

"Ah Come on! She's not a lot lizard. She and I need money to break out of this joint and join up with a different show. That greek and I don't see eye to eye. I'm not going to take Jimmy's place and leave him behind on the lot like a bug ripped out of its shell!"

After reaching White Horse's den Black Wolf glances up at the ripening moon hanging clean and cold overhead. Then decides that he'll flee this carnival. That one nelson is all of the work he will do for this show and he'll leave tomorrow come what may.

After stumbling inside his trailer, White Horse returns with a small piece of printed paper, "This is my pitch card. Something to remember me by." Kuy gives it the once over as the drunk explains, "I can't read. But Jimmy says it's a good autobiography."

The roadman scans the small cardboard card, and afterward places it his front jacket pocket. "Photo isn't half bad either. Listen. You have been struck down–I understand you–at least you have a place–goals–but I have to leave tomorrow. If you and your woman need a ride–look me up otherwise look for me east."

"Thanks sport. Listen. No hard feeling!"

"No hard feelings!"

White Horse takes an envelope out of his shirt pocket and hands it over to the roadman. "Listen. I have a sister near fort sill. Her name is on the front. Will you give this to her?"

"Sure."

"Don't say anything about me to her. She's sick too and I send her money from time to time."

Black Wolf takes the envelope from him. Then straightens his friend up like readying a child for church service, "I'm out of here. But I make circuit through here about every three months or. Save your money. Next time throught–"

"We'll ride off into the sunset–"

Kuy smiles a crooked. Hard smile. Tips his hat and walks away toward the moonlit field where his truck is parked.

"Alone, White Horse goes back inside to find Jimmy. Then returns. Crawling into his possum belly to hunt another bottle. Once found, standing back outside crookedly, he stares at the moon. Why? Old people promised he remembers that you can see faces up there of the dead if you look hard look enough.

***

Scratching. Tapping on his windscreen woke Kuy the next morning. He opens one eye against the glare and sits up. Outside. Isa–tah and a tall black woman wait.

Stretching after getting out, the Roadman asks, "How do?"

"How do," White Horse replies yawning. "Listen this is the gal I spoke about. Black Wolf, my wife Mary Ann Corbett."

After smiling politely, Mary introduces herself, "Glad to meet you! Are you another of these wild and crazy Kiowa men Mr. Wolf? Lordy. Oh Lordy ain't you fine as a Georgia pine. All tall and dark!"

"Afraid so–"

"Ah shit Mary! Don't get started on that old song or dance or this time I'm really going to hit the road," White Horse threatens.

Impatient the roadman interrupts, "Come on. I worked late last night!" Yet afterward, slightly intrigued, studies White Horse's wife. A tall. Oak brown woman with long black hair down to the middle of her back. Black Wolf clears his voice and introduces himself formally, "My name's George Black Wolf." Then lazily scratching his back, studies Mary a little longer as if cribbing for a spelling bee or boning up for a geography quiz.

She? Strong oval face. Offset by heavily lashed. Large set green eyes. Mouth most would call overgenerous but suiting her just fine.

Mystified, Kuy compares White Horse's broken two–step slumped posture. Gin soaked demeanor with Mary dancer's grace and is a little confused by the juxtaposition of the two. All the while smiling inwardly at the strange match they make. Wondering what glue binds them together! Can't be money Kuy fumes. Isa–tah has little and what he has. Drinks it up as fast as he earns it.

While wishing them well and willing himself gone the roadman turns and checks the brightening sky for a hint of this day's weather prior to Mary turning toward him. "Black Wolf–you another of those all too interesting. Mind–stretching names? My goodness but you look like someone out of a dime novel or a children's history chap book and well I know because I use to keep school down east in Waycross Georgia for poor little Black share cropper children."

Kuy yawns. Doesn't reply. Just looks at them. Questioning silently why they're here when it's too early for carnie folk to be out and about.

"True as the gospel Mary," White Horse adds, "We never were worth owning. So we poor ignorant Indians came with names like Beef or *Wo–haw. PHesei'n* or Five Cents! Maybe it seems like we're pure crazy and ornery but to us Indians–not named after some plantation owner–"

"Now watch that hating sugar. Hating makes my honey dry up!"

"Ah shucks. I'm just joshing!"

"Better be love. Night's long hereabouts and there's no shortage of lonely boys and men about looking for a little brown sugar when darks all around and souls feel'n lonely!"

"Ah Mary," White Horse whines unhappily.

Black Wolf coughs loudly and raises his voice to ask Mary a question attempting to hide his disbelief in her statement about former employment, "As I was trying to say–you taught school?"

"Did! Couldn't stand to see what whites were doing to my babies with their old mangy books. A real leaker of a roof and sagging floors. So one day tired of all of that bow'n and yesirren shit and the sound of them gators nesting under the school house and when a carnival came through town–not this one mind you. I hitched myself to it–"

"Now Mary–"

The roadman watches their exchange for a prairie minute. Then interrupts, "Hitting the road with me?" he demands, "or staying on?"

Isa–tah shakes his head. Mary on the other hand, remains silent but expectant. "No. I wanted to say goodbye to you again before you left and introduce Mary. Listen. I saved up some money to take a flight and I want you to tell the folks back home that I have ridden the sky and danced with P'ay!"

"Up there?" the roadman asks pointing upward.

"Yes!" White Horse exclaims. "I want to see if *P'ay* and Sun Boy really are up there!"

As White Horse continues to explain why they're out and about early. Mary looks at her husband with a bitter smile before adding,

"Hmmmm. If it isn't enough that I shake my ass in a nasty revue and sell my tail on the side. If it isn't enough that we need to get away from this lot before Manoliadis either throws your sorry redskin ass out of here or you become the geek of the week!"

After her outburst, she shakes her head and stares at the roadman, "Can't you talk some sense into this crazy redskin?"

"What can I say? I have always wanted to fly. Who hasn't? When my mother was alive. She always dreamed of flying."

Mary turns away, muttering under her breath, "Crazy sonabitch Indians. What's a girl to do?" Then grabs White Horse by the waist, "Well if we're going waste ten dollars and the day. Let's find this airplane man and get on with it."

They walk away from the carnival grounds toward a separate collection of tents and trucks under a fluttering banner in the morning's listless breeze proclaiming *O–uh–oh's* Flying Circus. Mary after studying it turns toward the roadman asks, "You're different from my man. How come?"

"Mam?"

"You know. The way you hold yourself. The way you dress all in black like a fetish or a conjurer man. Seen your like all my life in them Georgia backwoods and swamps. So I ought to know!"

"That right?"

"Sure enough. You have that smell or poise about you. Charged like– summer lighting. Waiting to strike!" Mary comments wistfully.

Listening. It's hard for him to determine if she is being flirtatious or just honest in a down–home, country porch sunday manner. Deciding upon the latter, favors his new friends with a broad smile and states for the benefit of both, "You sure have got you a fine–amazing wife here. Not of ordinary acquaintance."

"Yes sir! Now listen boys," Mary demands after just the barest acknowl-edgement of Kuy's compliment, informing them with a tone brooking no disbelief or backtalk, "Ole Mary now. Why I'm descended from conjurer men and root doctors on both sides of my family." Studying the roadman for a moment or two. Warns him in a voice so low that's almost a whisper, "Best you move on hon. You have business up ahead."

"So I have been warned–repeatedly."

"Listen now. You two buffalo hunters take Mrs. Sanatoria. The lot's chief hussy. Gypsy queens my ass! She can't tell a fortune from a bad hand of twenty–one. But honeys," she says proudly. Challenging both men with a stern–proud look. "I sure hell enough can!"

After this last exchange they walk over to a large tent beside a small plane.

Studying the flying machine. Kuy's caught up in conflicting reactions to the O so graceful machine resembling a dragonfly. A brother or sister to the one the stylite sheltered from the wind and rain in his veined hands and while walking around, takes in its functional marvel and design, pleased as if it was his special day.

White Horse and Mary watch him then stroll over to a group of men drinking coffee and enjoying the late autumn warmth.

Black Wolf notes that this camp is set up differently from the carnival. Instead of men and woman reluctantly going about their tasks with a driven air. These men wait peacefully until the moment when they need to start work. Not because they have to but because they are a brotherhood. Not of a religious order but never the less a group of men in love with flight.

A breeze. Rich with dying foliage. Dried expectations sweetens the air. Otherwise occupied with ruffling canvas, banners. Stirring dying flowers. As October sunlight slants past the tent. Thawing the ground. Easing morning aches with just the right degree of hoarded warmth mechanics and road crew smoke pipes, cigars and hand rolled cigarettes. Enjoying first cups of coffee.

Buzzing like hornet. Pilot is a tall man. All in tan whipcord. Markedly Cheyenne. Broad faced. Offset by eyes that may often dream.

Eagerly. White Horse shakes the pilot's hand, "Good morning. I would like to fly."

After returning his shake the pilot sleepily banters, "Go ahead. I'm not stopping you." Used to being the butt of many a joke. White Horse merely smiles. Then rephrases his request, "Very funny. What I mean is that I would like to take a flight if possible this morning!"

"Better. You Kiowa always like to beat around the bush or play with words," the pilot states while stretching out the last of his morning kinks. "But that's Ok. Wouldn't have it any other way! It's a little early but in say—an hour. It's a go. Ten dollars a head." Noticing Mary, he makes an additional offer, "Perhaps two for the price of one. You folks work back on the lot right?"

Mary nods then gives the pilot a hard stare. "Sure enough. Listen my man is crazy to fly but me. No sir—re!"

"*Nátséhéstahe* by the way," the Cheyenne smiles and introduces himself, "But call me *O–uh–oh*."

White Horse translates, "Soaring Eagle."

"Don't laugh folks. Ever since I was a boy, had my eyes upward. Learned from white children how to build and fly kites–learned machinery. So became a mechanic. Next learned to fly. Never looked back and anyway in this business. There's really only the moment–"

More than a little concerned Mary asks, "Because?"

"Let's not talk about it. In an hour. Ok?" Looking at the roadman, the pilot asks, "What about you?"

Black Wolf shakes his head. "No. I'm just here to see my friend off. Then be on my way. She's beautiful. I would like to fly someday."

Noticing the pilot getting ready to snap another joke, Kuy hastily amends his comment, "In a plane–can't do it on my own though I have tried when I was younger."

"Me too. Broke a leg when I was around nine. As to my plane–Oh she's a beauty! Built most of her from a wrecked frame out of a crash at a California air show about four years ago. Some say this is bad luck but so far–"

The roadman nods. "I have a truck. I know a little about mechanics. Leaning as I go along."

Interested the pilot asks, "What kind?"

"A Halk Hercules."

"What kind of engine?"

"Straight six–" Impressed, the Cheyenne whistles. "Sweet. Stick around. I would like to check under its hood."

Kuy regrettably shakes his head, "Sorry but not this time but maybe the next occasion when I circle back."

"When might that be pilgrim?"

"Oh a month or two. I pick up peyote down the mexico way then return to my parishioners near the wichita mountains and fort sill."

"You're a spirit man?"

"Yes."

"And a Kiowa?"

"Yes indeed friend," the roadman replies. Then introduces himself and his friends. I'm George Black Wolf–"

Interrupting him, the pilot jokes, "Do you howl at the full moon?"

The roadman chuckles. Used to the response his name sometimes engenders. Continues, "And this is my friend White Horse and his wife Mary."

"Glad to meet you all," the Cheyenne says. Every one smiles and shakes hands. The pilot satisfied that propriety's demands have been satisfied, turns to the roadman and requests a favor, "Will you say a good word for me and bless this day?"

"Happy to oblige."

Kiowa and Cheyenne cross the field where the plane rests under a green tarp with a handful of mechanics following them. O–uh–oh pulls the covering off and with a showman's gesture and introduces his plane, "I call her *Okohke*."

"What does her name mean?"

"Crow. Because she's black and flies and is a little mean spirited at times."

"Hold a blessing here?" the roadman inquires with a sweep of his arm over dying oil stained grass smelling of tar and gasoline.

"It's a good as a spot as any."

"All of you?" Kuy hesitates after noticing that the mechanics vary in hue from black, white, red and yellow–and is concerned that a chinaman or korean and may not appreciate a "heathen" rite celebrated among them.

"Why not!" the pilot argues; "up there no man or woman is different on the ground!"

Thinking this over, the roadman smiles, asking, "Ready?"

Responding affirmatively they kneel in front of the plane as the roadman performs a brief benediction. Isa–tah and Mary participate. But only White Horse displays any real interest in their brief moment of spiritual unity.

With his blessing over the mechanics fuss over the plane and manhandle it until it points north.

Figuring that White Horse is nervous, the pilot reassures his prospective passenger, "Nothing to worry about in a milk run like this. With no acrobatics or stunts. Little to fear."

"What if the engine quits on us?" White Horse nervously asks.

"We glide down like a bird. Flight is the way of the future folks–it's too bad that with this war breaking out in Europe–planes are most certainly are going to lose their innocence and be recast as killing machines."

"Think so?" Mary ventures, "Sure why not. Remember the Chinese and gunpowder?"

The pilot agrees, "Same thing is going to happen to flight. Fact is it's already starting over there!"

"Too bad," Kuy says, "More of the shame really–that another way of killing has commenced!"

"It's the way of the world," Mary suggests.

Afterward the Cheyenne and White Horse climb in.

Isa–tah, since he cannot climb in by himself, is helped by the others even while the ground crew starts the plane. Turning the wooden prop till the engine starts up with a cough and rattle. Quickly building to a roar that shakes its canvas frame down to its small bicycle wheels.

Nervous. Mary grips Black Wolf's arm. Watching the wooden blocks removed from the front of the plane's wheels before it tears away from the grass strip. Climbing hard and fast into perfect, pale and clear October sky.

Black Wolf watches the take off with a wide smile. Noticing the look on White Horse face. A gamut of expressions. So conflicting. The roadman laughs despite himself.

Below. Mechanics split off. Watching the plane in worried, boastful groups like mothers watching a fledgling's flight.

The roadman and Mary stay put. They're too entranced by the sight of White Horse airborne to pay any mind to where they are standing.

Looking eastward Kuy unhappily discovers that the sun is higher on the horizon than thought so starts to walk back toward the carnival's main office to grab his pay and get gone. "You know Mary," the roadman declares after pausing for a minute and facing her with a solemn look of appraisal.

"What have you got to say me now you smart ass Kiowa?"

"You're really a wonderful extraordinary woman. Take care please."

"Goodness Gracious Man! You two are strangest men I've ever seen!" she exclaims with a wry smile before shutting up.

"Mary, I need to get going."

"Aren't you going to say goodbye to White Horse."

"We already said our goodbyes."

After tipping his hat, asks a final act of kindness from her, "Take care of him will you?

"What if I was to come with you?"

Black Wolf looks at her and then back up into the sky. "Do you really want to leave him?" he asks pointedly.

Mary sighs and watches the plane again before answering. Satisfied that the plane and its passengers are safe for the movement she walks over to the roadman and takes his hand, "Feel this," she directs. Referring to the strong current running between their fingers and shooting up their arms toward their hearts. "I guessed it! It's a strange sensation that I get sometimes every few years or so for loners. Lost men. Hunted men—strays. God knows why?"

`Last waltz. Someone waits and will wait as years pass and shadows grow longer`

"Yes. Peculiar isn't it. But I feel it too—working inward. I wouldn't know what to do with a fine gal like you," Black Wolf says warmly. But gently loosening his entwined fingers. "Listen, I am a roadman. I'm always on the move—going from congregation to congregation like the wind—"

"Like a lot of hot air you mean," Mary adds with sarcasm "Listen. I get about a lot myself."

"I know but—"

"What am I–Snakebite? Or something–" Mary complains. Emotions. Feelings pinned up like Saturday's wash for anyone to see. "You sure have some strange notions. Let me coil up to you one night wrapped safe and warm in my little caravan with the wind outside and we'll see just how afraid of snakes you really are!" she promises, "But as you said. You have to be moving along! It would probably kill that old coot if I took off down the road however short and sad with you. Besides. I would have to ride backward on the carousel and screw the lot. Keep in touch will you? He's very lonely. Brontosaurus or some old thing left high dry and alone. The last of his kind."

"Well. Mary we really are!"

Silently. Mary unhooks a worked silver carnie bracelet from her wrist. Gently taking Black Wolf's arm. Places it on his wrist. Then kissing him on his cheek. Walks away.

It's five–cent polish is worn and chipped, yet like Mary on this sunny day, shines brightly.

Chapter Thirteen

Past a junction. Two heavily dressed figures approach. Kuy makes a snap judgment. "One's a woman-another's a girl child." After drawing abreast. He slows down. Makes out yet a third. They are not "People." First. Intending to get gone. Instead brakes hard. Why? Guess it's that old rule of thumb on lonely, open plains and foothills, it's normal to help others. A sensible precaution. Well as a ritual of concern and propriety.

After he stops, the woman pulls her coat closer against a sudden gust. A younger child cradled in arm.

"Where are you going?"

"Next town. Mister. My boy is sick. I am taking him to a doctor."

She's blond with two little towheaded children behind her.

"What's wrong with him?"

"I do not know. He can't hold anything down. He's got a high fever."

"I am going that way. Get in!"

She hesitates only briefly then gathers her second child into the back of his depot car. Then sitting down with her sick child in her lap in the front.

Mother pale. Long hair piled into an unbecoming bun. A few straggling stands frame her face.

In the cab's darkness. Kuy can't tell too much about her children. Little girl's a miniature china doll copy of her mother. Her son in his dark clothing and little boy boots. Is only a shadow resting in his mother's lap.

Later, to break the tension, the roadman introduces himself. "My name is George. How are you called lady?"

"My name is Tryphosia Clemens."

"Like the writer?"

"Well yes. But we are of no relation I know of," she adds nervously, "but my friends call me Phosy. This here," their mother says pointing to her lap, "is my boy August and in the back is my girl Kelley."

Young girl expresses her gratitude politely, "Thanks for the ride Mister; it was dark and very cold."

"Nothing to it! *SyH–n*. Glad to meet you all," Black Wolf replies. Relived formalities are over. Even with a hitch. It is a good distance to the next town so looking away, he speeds up to reach a town where a doctor might be found.

Except for whispered questions from the girl and the muffled endearments for her sick child, their ride is quiet lit only by his dash's sparse light.

He's uncomfortable. Not knowing how to talk to a white women. Having spoken to few. Usually missionaries or reluctant sales girls treating him as a novelty or a nuisance. Kuy's silent. If she were one of the People or another tribeswoman he would ask her for news and gossip yet cannot because of the gulf between them and if asked he would take a look at the child and determine how sick he is but peering ahead relying solely upon his headlights to guide them, instead only drives on.

Years ago. He might have harmed this woman or allowed others to do violence to her as well. Yet in this uncertain present. The powers he represents. Or professes to serve. Tempered by age and bought with wisdom. Would not take kindly to cruel acts against three tired. Defenseless travelers. Thus smiles. Hands the children and woman some candy. Passes his canteen. Makes a wry face when they refuse his proffered water. But he expected little else. White woman are cut from different cloth!

"Hell son. Remember that little old german girl you danced with long ago in the back of that saloon?"

Hell yes he remembers!

***

With no prospects. Rode in sullen silence. His last greenbacks buttoned into his ironed calico shirt pocket. Seeking a dance hall for misery's sake.

The Old Union it had no white only door policy. Fact. Known for its policy of amalgamation. If you had the coin be you black. White. Red. Brown. Or yellow. Long as you paid in full. Tipped. Were not troublesome. There was a place when not a damned blamed thing soothed one's ruffled soul.

Horse and weapons. Left with a mixed Apache hosteller he trusted. Rest of town closed to him. Not only barred but dangerous on nights when men washed away sorrow with whiskey along narrow filthy alleys swollen with dram shops. One or two 'hotels' filled with whores and the Old Union. All on one stick. A thin artery overflowing with hookers. Drunken revelers. Cutting up diodoes. Kicking up a ruckus.

"Watch out honey," a corned cowboy dancing the Virginia Fence warned his escort. "Don't get scalped. Brave on the warpath! Waaaaaa–hooooooo!"

`fice dogs sang for supper and were kicked for their trouble`

Kuy ignored him and later when women beckoned or tried to pull him away off the dirty back yard trace into tottering shanties and doggeries huddled together at the end of the dark alley–their desperation. The smell of piss and vomit made him regret his coming and hurry onward and through the Union's doors.

It was a Saturday night. Packed. Inside. Cavorting ditties pounded his ears like Osage war cries. Contesting Fiddle, and piano, joined a long wail of a harmonica. Howling like a ring–tailed devil caught in a tornado as couples shook the saloon's wooden floors circling each other caught up in feverish merriment.

To the side. Under pale lights. Solitary men. Garish hostesses lurked in murky shadows or sat alone. Bolt upright. An empty bottle or mug in front of them. Eyes averted. Corned. Awaiting judgment.

Kuy knew that lonesome ranch hands paid to have girls sit with them for silver. Loneliness. A big business for women working the saloon circuit from the californias to the stockyards of kansas city. Solitary cowpunchers sometimes looked for an ear to pour out their hearts and soul. Hell! If they wanted more the girls were willing.

To his ears that night's music lacked rhyme or reason. Just noise without any sympathetic vocals and drums joined in accord. Raw notes. Strings. Sharp as whiskey. Carrying–ons. Wild and unprincipled.

Adjusting to the bedlam, young Kuy pulled his black hat down. Scouting the dim ballroom, caught sight of a couple of Mexicans and a Pawnee ranch hand named Will Two Blood. Boys he had worked with a while back.

They waved him over even as Will shouted, "*Ven cabrone*!" Moving over a chair for him to sit. Later filling a glass with amber colored whiskey.

Which after taking a seat Kuy downed in one gulp.

"Take a seat Kiowa and have a shot of this good old Kentucky anti–fogmatic Will suggested.

Across the table Lupe and Juan nodded greetings but otherwise spoke not a word.

The House's piano player accompanied by fiddle and harmonica provided melody as wild and as fast as the dancers' drunken pace demanded.

Conversation almost impossible. Yet bending nigh. Will managed to ask a question, "How's things?"

With so many responses to this open–ended question Kuy didn't respond. Instead he glanced away toward a group of dancers in the bar's center gathering his thoughts like horses. After a few moments reflection, he finally reply in a tired, confidential manner, "Bad all around. Hell Will! Let's not talk about it! I just want to have root–roaring–gosh dang time!" Spoken curt as rawhide. Drawn on their mutual. Rather extensive repertoire of giddiup cowboy lingo.

Bending ear. Will patted Kuy on his back and pouring him another while sympathetically stating, "I understand! Hell I *sabe*." and yet later grinning wide and impetuous as a coyote's yawn Will added an off the cuff suggestion, "Want a gal? Sometimes a roll with one of these girls puts a man's thoughts to well–"

Abashed. Black Wolf asked, "A white woman?"

"Hell," Will reemphasized, "here most of these girls don't give a cat's whiskers color your money is. I know one. Sweet little girl. She's huckleberries above a persimmon. From overseas. Says she likes Indians and told me *that we "bloods" smell like wood smoke.*"

"Hell after what they done to us. Why not?"

As they batted this notion around the joint's musical trio started again. This time racing nonstop into a fast paced version of "Buffalo Girls".

"Buffalo girls won't you come out tonight. Come out tonight and dance by the light of the moon—" led by the piano player slightly ahead of the fiddler. Raw notes flew past every idler and dancer. Finding accord only at the end of each stanza. The harmonica player followed his own soulful rhythms between belting out the vocal to the melody in a heartfelt, rough and ready rhythm known to only him.

With a break in the musical onslaught, Will seconded Kuy's take on the matter. "Why the hell not George!" Later adding, "hold your horses for a minute!" Then he pigeon toed over to a group of painted, scented woman sitting and laughing between dances. He bowed. Then opportuned a girl. One dressed darker. Differently cut cloth than the other "hostesses."

In response to Will's solicitation. She smiled. Looking over at their table. With a quick nod. Followed Will over with a flurry of dark, rose tinted crinoline.

No slouch. Will presented introductions with a flourish, "Greta. I would like you to meet some good friends of mine. These here are the Hernandez brothers. Lupe and Juan."

Shyly the brothers nodded their heads as Will continued making introductions, "And this is the hombre I spoke to you about. A real life–full blooded Kiowa! George Black Wolf. Say glad to meetcha Greta. Say glad to meetcha George!"

Faced with Will's prodding. Tongue–tied, Black Wolf didn't introduce himself. Instead just blushed. Bright as a lantern.

Noticing his friend's discomfort. Will road to the rescue. "George's almighty shy. Why don't you just sit down beside him and get to know each other!" he suggested.

No what she did. None of Kuy's here to then short life had prepared him for such an encounter and his heart melted fast as deer tallow on tongue.

Will and the Hernandez brothers faded as this sweet smelling enemy sat next to him and breathed softly against her constricting corset.

His for a gold dollar.

Favoring Will a weak grin, Kuy took the girl's hands into his. Gazing into her enormous green eyes above a red mouth bright as a wanderer's star.

"What's the matter cat got your tongue?" she playfully demanded.

This witticisms glanced off his shy superciliousness.

Still reeling under this glib assault Kuy shook his head and asked, "Like to go somewhere quiet? Away from this hullabaloo!"

Whore hesitated. Smiled. Then suggested without a hint of impropriety. Least to his ears any way, "Off the reel?"

"Yes," he rejoined.

Pleased (on the clock), she nodded her head in reply and then took his arm and led him through a drunken carnival of reeling forms.

Even at the wheel. He recalls the catcalls raking their progress. "Watch out Greta! Hold on to your scalp girl," and other less polite remarks meeting their pull–footed advance to the back of the dance floor.

"Follow me Hiawatha." Words sweet with guile. Sharp as old honey.

"I'm Black Wolf–not–"

"Pardon?"

"Black Wolf. It's my name!"

"Don't be such a calf!" she laughed. "Come on slowpoke," Greta said. Pulling him by sleeve down the hallway out past other lovers and romantic couplings to a flight of wooden stairs leading upward. "Sorry there is no light," she later apologized. "Let me light my lamp!"

"I see in the dark," he boasted.

"Really?" she asked, amused.

"Like a bob cat!" Unused to strong drink. Kuy felt unwell and a little uneasy.

"Are you going to ravish me?"

"Pardon?"

"Make love to me," she whispered as she closed her rickety wood door behind them with a snap. Bending to light her single lamp. It burned like a nova in the room's darkness above her iron bed–

***

"Excuse me?" Mrs. Clemens asked half asleep before twisting in her seat, straightening her skirts.

Snatched reluctantly from reverie, Kuy casts her a brief black look prior to asking, "What? What were you saying Mam? Sorry. I was thinking about someone met up with long ago."

"I hope it was a pleasant memory."

"Yes. It was. Just something to keep my eyes open. Nothing important."

His passenger. After listening to his reply. Returns to her original comment that broke his root–n–tootn daydream.

"I was just saying. Excuse me if I am being impertinent. It's just that I never rode with an Indian before. I mean in a car. Never saw one drive either Mr. George."

"We drive–would more of us if we had money."

"What do you do?" Tryphosia asks quietly.

"I'm a priest. But not a christian!"

"Why do you wear a cross?"

Hesitating before answering her question, yet sensing that Phosy and her kids are no threat, he answers her readily enough, "This cross," Kuy points out, touching its tarnished silver, "well Mam, it's a story for another time. What do I do? Well. I am a road chief. You would call me a preacher."

"Of God?" she asks hesitantly. Nervous. Not wanting to upset him since it is a lonely land they travel.

159

"Of many!"

His passenger mulls over his answers. Turning to stare into the passing night.

It's close to an hour later before she speaks again out of sudden necessity, "Mister! I hate to bother to you but Gussy is worse. I need to stop!" she pleads.

He's reluctant to stop because this small stunted basin is an ill–advised place to linger for spiritual and ritual reasons. Secondly Kuy is reluctant to break routine. It is easier to go on and keep looking for a white doctor. Glancing at Phosy's face, barely illuminated and ghostly in the dash's light marring her strong features croaks, "Ok" in a bone–dry whisper.

Stopped. Phosy gets out. In the back seat Kelley whimpered. Disturbed in sleep. Her veined eyes tracing dreams. Scrutinizing inward projections.

Silently standing guard because this is a bad land with *Batl–sai–an Badl–sai–ya–don* or stink weed fencing them in a ring.

"Watch," he warns. "Listen!" At the same time observing stars overhead. He marks a retiring planet. A shooting star. Passing overhead. Another key for interpretation.

Slightly annoyed, the roadman wonders what she is doing.

Before Tryphosia asks him, "Got water?"

"Yes. Not a lot. Wait a minute!" Grabbing his canteen, he walks over to where the sound of her voice came from. "Here," he says carefully extending the cool, silver metal into her waiting hands, "How is he?

No answer. Then after a minute or two with a nervous lilt, she responds, "Real sick. He`s burning up!"

"Let me see," he orders. Feeling the boy's narrow forehead, he jerks his hand back in reaction to the kid's fever, raising his voice just short of a shout, "Why didn't tell me that he is this sick. He will die if something isn't done!"

Startled. Phosy snatches Gus back. Pleading with the dark figure in front of her, "Please help him. What can we do?"

Kuy? Grouses. Telling her to place August in his arms. "You will have to trust me! Get back into the wagon and don't stray. Listen and do what I tell you please. This is not the place to take a walk and do you understand me? No matter what you hear. See. Do not get out of the car!" Finishing, takes her chin roughly into his hand to make sure she understands him.

Nodding her head, Phosy returns to the truck.

Alone with the boy in his arms, Kuy plans his course of action. No traditionally trained healer. The death of his wife and son had soured him on holy medicine folk. However., Kuy had returned and asked to be taught a brief. Truncated course of study.

All of this is of no great shakes but there's no firemen or other spirit warriors to aid him here and in this place more evil than good has occurred Black Wolf judges even as old and lonely powers coil around them. Some familiar. Others best avoided. Though possible allies if sufficiently bored. Seeing as no one knows what tricks they will try Black Wolf focuses on the task at hand.

Builds a strong blaze in a derelict fire pit half filled in by sand and time. It's comforting to know that others have stopped here in the past.

"Have to break his fever. But how with only half a canteen of water?"

Regardless, Kuy takes out several oiled packages, laying them out on the cold ground in front of him, in the sputtering light, carefully examines his patient for an appropriate diagnosis. Most probably the boy suffers from elf owl fever. From either tainted water, milk or hastily prepared food.

Carefully placing the child next to the fire on a heavy horse blanket, he takes several buttons of *Seni* from a rawhide sack at his feet and stirs selected medicines into his kettle over crackling flames.

Taking out a peyote button he bites deep swallowing the acid–tasteless cactus and then eats several more.

Then grabs the boiling bubbling mixture and pours it into an old battered tin coffee cup. Cooling it with his breath much as his mother would have. Taking it over to the sick child. Gently forcing August to drink it down.

Calling spiritual healers, "*MiHndei–dcc'ts–Hidoc.*" and with his harsh yet vibrant prayer sounding beyond the fire into the darkness. "O spirits. Angels and holy allies of Peyote. Please aid me to drive this sickness from this child August. This defenseless child. Though he is not one of us he is innocent and will die if not aided."

Shrivel tongued wants to spit but hesitates. Not daring to soil this alter as he gently takes Gus cradling him is his arms. Imitating eagle's cry. Passing the boy over the flames. Careful not to singe him. After the fourth pass he places August back on the blanket. "Devil," he commands, "Leave him!"

Strong. Familiar foe threatens. Kindred to his wife's killer.

Fanning healing smoke toward the child. Aware of hidden colors. Unveiled. A mourning widow transformed into a riot of color by spring's advent.

Tryphosia. Aware only of shadows moving in the darkness: wind dancing with scrub and dry thorn. Twisting and gamboling. If witnessed by an unschooled observer. His actions and cries would resemble plain ole lunacy! With foaming lips and intelligible speech to human ears.

Waiting.

Lone coyote listening in the cooling distance reckons not. Whining uneasily. Moves on.

A rattler nearby decides to find a better spot to hunt.

```
Chest pains. Bad as if a hot coal was
buried there. Glancing upward, the road-
man wonders if this is how it ends.
Dancing with ragged panting steps over
this dying boy. Singing healing songs.
Desperate to hold gathering spirits-
drawn like buckaroos to a saturday night
fight to watch-at bay, startled by a sud-
den hissing wind tearing through willow
scrub.
```

Overhead. A large moth grows fearful. Changes course.

Hearing it passing overhead. The dohate Kuy is well–nigh deafened as he cocks his head aside. Listening to the vast withering menagerie of dry hill and plain around them as uncanny cogency pools.

The fears of the boy's mother. The dreams of the Kelly in the back mourning her missing kitten.

Shielding the boy, wondering if it's an evil spirit passing close. Places his canteen over the boy child. using a good measure of its now precious contents, mops Gus burning forehead with his calico handkerchief. Sopping his brow with cool brackish water.

"If only I had more water!"

Casting aside petition. Snaps his fingers. "Of course!" Inspired by a hunch lifts the boy in his arms. Crossing back over to his truck. Lays Gus carefully on the Hercules's hood.

Ignoring his mother's frantic silent entreaties, Kuy opens his cab, digs under his seat for a spanner. Next desperately loosens the radiator's bottom cap. Later scraping out a hasty depression before taking off his jacket and lining his shallow pit with it. Since made of treated canvas. It should hold water.

Grabbing Gus. Gently places him under the radiator. Water. Cool now. Pours downward. Subsequently soaking the boy. Screaming for his mother.

Jacket holds water like the rough, impromtu tub many men in faraway europe are splashing around in learning to make do

Before all of the water rushes out, Kuy recaps the radiator. He'll just have to leave early or drive this night before the heat returns and his unprotected engine boils over.

Gus twitches. Moans. Yet despite the boy's protests, Black Wolf pins him in place as he screams for his mother again. This time. Phosy gets out of the cab. Witnessing the Indian's apparent rough treatment of her son. She panics. Tries to snatch him away.

Unexpectedly assaulted from behind. Kuy growls. Shielding Gus from her frantic tugs. Warns his mother to get back inside and stop hitting his back, unprotected shoulders with significant force.

Holding the boy with one arm, reaching around and grabs the woman's thick, well–muscled calf, Kuy pulls her leg out from under her.

She falls with considerable fanfare as he turns back around shouting,

"Get back inside. Or I will drive out of here. Leaving you three here. Understand!"

Sitting up. Phosy stares at the excited Indian. Seeing the determination in his eyes and jaw well as Gus wrapped like a soggy pupae, she breaks into sobs of frustration and fear. Not speaking or moving.

Kuy grabs her again by her foot. Pulls her close, and explains, "It's the only way. Get inside and wait!"

Phosy hesitates. With no other option. Reluctantly picks herself up. Beats the clinging sand off and with a huff and an hmmmrph returns even as bid.

Black Wolf, figuring that boy has soaked long enough, picks him up. Unwrapping the shivering child, places his forehead against the boy's. The child's fever is broken and normal.

"Son of a bitch," he hisses in triumph and exhaustion. Falling to his knees. Wondering how much of this passing experience is alkaloid poisoning. Imagination. Or raw providence. But as any men or women of faith after the censor cools and the host put away. The Kudwa can only measure with conviction what has passed.

For a white child
For an innocent child
For revenge

Dwindling power smiles. Forces him to stand. Soothing boy's face with a cool, passing breeze. The other-whipped good and proper-jangles and prances afore rising to neighboring branches of prickle and barb crying uncle. Exits.
Afterward winner fades following the course of a fixed star or planet without further word, sign or as those frencies would have it, ado…

Striking the chill from his body. Kuy finds the sleeping boy and gently picks him up.

Temperature normal, boy dreams peacefully. The roadman stumbles back on shaking legs to his truck and hands August roughly to his mother. Knowing no more. Night serving as a rough blanket against cold's caress.

Chapter Fourteen

Dreams. Fine house. Children. But as to their number, gender unsure. A wife or even wives.

During elaborate dinner. Cries outside. Along with the toll of bells ringing in alarm.

Coyotes stands down from nocturnal dog-watch. Joining the subdued march of day Winds catch dry sage, sparse grass with skittish cat paws while spiders frolic in a singular drops of dew

Servant enters hastily without decorum demanding that he pause eating and follow him to the roof of his manse.

Does.

Up steps, passes handsome pictures. Ancestral portraits gilt somber.

On leaded roof. His servant points nearing glow. Looks where directed. A fire. Sweeping storm raging across countless roofs and walls. A great river. Like a sleeping serpent. Where many boats and a thousand or more milling people flounder, lacking order or discipline,

Alarms. Both vocal and belled. Peel. No authority's manifest or acted upon. Urged. Returns downstairs. Retainer in arm. Grabs a padded leather jerkin. Thick boots, opens his great door despite his wife's desperate pleas.

Outside. Horses. People. Slew panic and fear. Driven concern—escape.

Buttoning up heavy coat, turns to servant, gainsays his determination before racing opposite roasting surge—two fowls on a spit—

***

"Hey Mister. Are you all right?" Tryphosia asks concernedly. Afterward, when she returned with his water. He sits up shielding his eyes from raw morning sunlight and taking several deep drafts of air. The water helps dispel throat's soreness but it also threatens to push him back into nausea.

Noticing the look of concern on Phosy's face. He waves her back to the truck. Watching her depart he wonders what he is going to do with her and the children.

Spotting wisps of stratus trailing east he stands up and stumbles over to a gully behind a small barren ridge to empty bowels and take stock of their situation. After absolutions. Cleans himself with fragrant grasses. Reflecting on the situation at hand. He cannot simply leave the three of them here but since there is no need for a white doctor now he will drop them off at the first village or post they come to. From there. Hopefully they can find a ride.

Returning to the truck without a wasted word, Kuy speeds away from this fated valley. Not looking back. Experiencing a perilous prick in the neck.

***

After pulling over the side of a road while his passengers slept in the hot midday sunlight. Black Wolf hiked to a distant clump of willows and leaned back against the trunk of the largest. An ideal spot for an idyll. Picnic or nap. However, Kuy chose to recall a pleasant memory instead. A journey made with his father when he was a boy. Perhaps five or six years old. Doesn't remember why. But it was a bad time for the People. Some said the end of times near.

They left on a full moon. Not arriving 'til next. Perhaps father sought to save him. His mother had already slipped away amid nightmares and childish longing.

His father Iron Knife needed to go on a trading mission and decided to take his last remaining child. They traveled by foot to the texas panhandle. The real purpose of their journey lost. If it ever had a compass or goal perhaps it was to contact distant kin yet unbroken and scattered.

Lands traveled were unfamiliar. North near the canadian river. Where old, haunted cliffs and abandoned pueblos offered possible clues to a distant past. Given whispers of their people still graced the empty ruins and jagged caves.

A day crisp as an apple after a full morning filled with the hardship and joy of bartering, meeting new and old familiar faces. His father borrowed a horse and took him to what was promised to be an ancestral place. Site of distant grandmothers and grandfathers not known to every Kiowa yet a part of their history related by the *Q–gop*; important tribal families and spiritual leaders.

Perhaps one of the original homes of their people suggested his father sagely that day.

Day dreamt of evening when they arrived. Captained by wild winds. Billowing cumulus clouds. Sailing by. Shadows brushing the ragged cliffs washing color from earth and sky.

Burnt earth. Dry stunted growth. Bitter with tang of lost silver. Keenly observant he agreed with his father these ruins were a special or sacred region. His very soul acknowledged its uniqueness and its daunting patina of age and history.

When they tied their horse to a dead hackberry tree. They walked toward the cliffs feeling a palpable stir of familiarity and belonging.

"These are the *toows* of our grandfathers. Very old houses," his father related. Pointing out a series of crumbling, dun colored cliffs. True. What at first seemed to be only the handiwork of wind and weather proved with closer inspection to be cobbled walls of fired brick and fallen chambers of worked stone.

Iron Knife next took him by the hand. Leading him to a rise beside the cliffs, pointing out details, dragging relics and artifacts for his inspection out of the warm, rusty red soil. Hard nodules of worked and unworked alibates flint. Broken bits of pottery. Some of which he said, 'were from other pueblos since their workmanship was too colorful and detailed for the Kudwa.'

Iron Knife also traced lines of abandoned homes and walked the outlines of old ceremonial centers while below them abandoned fire pits lay where ancient witches once sang against drought begging for rain.

Placing his hand on his shoulder, his father said, "I know you think pueblo people differ greatly from us and act odd. But let me tell you little man—we were once like them. Something came. Taking us from here. I do not know what. War. Hunger. Sickness. Yet we were kindred once to the folk farming and caring for the land here."

"That day was clear and sharp as this moment!" swears Kuy leaning against the giant willow while unbidden recalling how father and son spent the rest of that clear fall evening climbing down ventilator shafts, broken, brittle stone deflectors, sipapus—long unguarded and eroded ki-vas with broken vaulting. Abode only of coyotes and rattlers.

Sighing, "A pleasant memory," wishes his father was alive.

Weeks after returning from those very same ruins his father was killed

`Memories are bridges to sorrow`

Owing to this fact, he laments, "I have had no one to help ford time's passing jests," yet remembering his father's face, cracks a rare smile, and then heads back to his truck and the folk waiting inside.

Chapter Fifteen

Back on the road Black Wolf steers lost in thought.

Tryphosia sighs. Looks away from the passing sterile plains and scrub. Eyes locked on passing dark. Calling to mind her marriage. Hurried. Necessitated by mere survival. Desperation. Loneliness. Tryphosia's family was large. Unsettled as recent frontier land.

Father old for his age. Mother worn out. Both passed away some time ago.

At home. Children were expected to make their own way as soon as possible and not to let the door catch you on the way out. Half of her older siblings had already run off or married. Her turn. She had few options. Though a quick girl Phosy was not favored. Boys in school never fought for her company. Her friends few. Girls at school took little notice of her and she kept quiet.

Husband. A small farmer. Wasn't suited to land and their marriage was a low comedy of errors. Every move made was not in tandem. His joys were not hers.

He drank heavily to escape the near animal burden of work he subjected himself till broken and they did not conjoin each other's sentiments.

After their second child. August was born. He became even more beleaguered. More desperate–a distant wraith of broken hopes and private sorrows.

Fighting bitter battles without resolve. They slept under the same roof yet pleading and dreaming of release from the life that ensnarled them, though joined in a hollow marriage, they were not joined in spirit.

At night. Each remained vigilant against the unspoken sallies of the other. Before sleep or fantasies. They wondered how their marriage had come to be. Fallowness. Granted a false fecundity by their children.

Phosy breaks off from these bitter memories. Looking down. Straightening her daughter's dress and smoothing her hair while Kelly sleeps on her lap and Gus in the back.

"My little ones."

Only her children gave respite yet caring for them taking on more and more of the burden of farming crushed her.

One day her husband did not come back from town.

The following days and weeks there were no real answers to inquiries. He had simply left as so many others caught in broken dreams and the dull daily routines slowly strangling life's merits.

Hopes of escape are built upon the flimsiest of dreams and often as unsupportive. Winter came. She could not keep the farm and had to take to the road.

Now? Sister in Texas might take her in for a while. But she is also married. To a stranger. Not liking to have three extra mouths to feed and clothe.

When a girl. Playing with hand made dolls; she would have never dreamt that she would someday be riding at the mercy of a stranger. A man she barely would have tolerated to hire on her farm or sent away with worry for her pies if seen from her roughly dressed window.

Their highway winds ahead. Illuminated only by the Hercules's headlamps. One lamp is out of line. Its errant light does not shine onto the lane in front but off into the hostile. Empty land. As if to illuminate her other option. Least. Inside this car. She can rest for the moment and let tomorrow cares rest till day's rising inquiry.

Chapter Sixteen

Remembering this land before its disfigurement. Black Wolf passes a rusted and bullet pocked tin sign proclaiming,

DOC PRICE'S WATER. EATS and GAS:

LAST CHANCE

ONLY 25 MORE MILES

While ruminating over this new america traveled over. In its dusty flyspecked cafes. Dry goods stores Kuy is at best given perfunctory service, or in the worst case, ignored or ordered off the premises. Since many cafes and stores have a

WHITE ONLY

policy. Posted or generally known. The Kiowa knows whom to trade with. Who to avoid as most traders and local business people disdain the native trade except as marks and suckers.

Tryphosia and her children sleep. So much the better Black Wolf decides. Wishing to find them a ride to the gulf, he wants to get rid of them as soon as possible. This country has too many needing healing and there is not enough good medicine to offset the bad.

If their roles were reversed. Would a white woman driving a car stop for a sick or injured Kudwa and his family? Making a decision Kuy plans on letting Phosy and her children off at the next trading post.

When he cuts off to a gravel laid path to reach the next stop, concerned, Tryphosia asks, "Where we going?"

Cold faced Indian watches the highway for a minute before replying,

"To take you somewhere. Drop you off. So that you can get to where you and your children need to. I cannot help you more."

"I thought you are a priest," she replies with incrimination."

"Yes I am," he counters, "But not a white priest."

"Then how are you different?"

"Listen," he says, cocking his head toward her,

"The white man goes into his church house and talks about Jesus; one of the People goes into his tepee and talks to Jesus." Then tapping her shoulder for emphasis, Kuy continues,

"If you take[a copy of] the Christian Bible and put it out in the wind and the rain. Soon the paper on which the words are printed will disintegrate and the words will be gone. Our bible is the wind." (Carol R. McGrath)

"So. You do not believe in God and Jesus?"

"Him?" Yes. God. Or *Dwk'I*. The maker. We believe in and give him thanks. We have many spirits. In the hills and valleys there are many—you would call them spirits all around us. Some are bad—some uncaring—some good. When I fought for Gus's life—a few helped. But I would have lost if not for insight and medical learning I gained over the years—"

"Well, I'm sure am glad you happened along. You saved August's life—"

He cuts her off with a quick evasive comment, "A life for a life—"

Phosy studies him a moment before inquiring,

"What do you mean?"

"Years ago. When I was a settled man. My wife and son died in a typhus outbreak," he relates, keeping his eyes on the stony road ahead "No one could help them. Our healers. White medicos. So I promised myself," he explains quietly, "that I would learn how to heal and when the opportunity arose. I would use what I learned—"

"Thank you!" she adds with true heartfelt gratitude.

After acknowledging her appreciation with a nod Kuy falls silent. Pensive. Wishing to confide in her more. But hesitates. The gulf between them is wide. He will be rid of her. Her children. Returning to their white world and singular god.

Later eagerly follows hand–lettered signs leading to a roadside cafe and post.

Joint isn't inviting. A one and a half storied wood and plaster building with an older section atilt under a higher–pitched roof.

"Place is as bent and crooked as a witch," Black Wolf remarks silently. True. Unsure. Meandering light. Accents its ramshackle appearance.

Ignoring deprecation. He gets out and stretches. Before going inside he warns her that they should not be seen together since it would only create problems.

Nodding, Phosy gathers her children and enters the trading post first.

Watching. How different they are. How vulnerable they look. Waiting before following, Kuy checks the dusty lot for trouble but only papers. Dead weeds blowing in no-account, footsore wind meet his eye. Inside smells of stale fried food, sour mash whiskey, bitter spices and old tobacco interwoven with the sweet, acid taint of dried sweat and winter smoke.

Within he pointedly ignores the woman and her kids, "I have done for her. Now. Let her own kind take up the burden." Afterwards, Kuy steps to the back where there is a rusty bell on the counter a sign reading,
RING BELL FOR SERVICE

The old rusty bell. Ain't got no clapper. Only a bare, rasping sound escapes from its shell. Minutes pass before there's a response. Someone singing a tune from somewhere out of view in the rear.

"SOMETIMES WHEN GOD DOESN'T WANT TO GIVE. YOU'VE GOT TO TAKE WHAT THE DEVIL OFFERS." Followed by coughing and a harsh voice asking him to, "Wait one minute! God dam–nit. One–minute. I am coming. Don't give any credit here. Cash money or barter!"

From a back aisle store's proprietor tilts into view. Middle aged or more with long gray hair topped by a soiled railroad cap.

Man's dark eyes frame questions. Form suspicions studying Kuy. Satisfied after a long stare, the clerk or owner's thin mouth cinches. Mumbling one word,

"Indian."

Quiet. Waiting to see what this white will do. Kuy asks himself, "Will I be served? How will the woman and her kids fare here? None of my damn business," babbled even as the clerk or owner snorts a sally.

"What's that? Speak up good. Can't hear you boy!" Kuy reaches into his jacket. Handing the attendant a list. Then waits as the proprietor picks up his scrap of paper with a smirk.

"Well. Got most of these notions. Take me a little while to gather it together. Sent my help off on an errand so why don't you sit yourself Mister in the cafe? Want some old orchid to wet your whistle being it's kind of parched outside."

"No. Just my list."

"Well. I don't care beans. Had a grist of dust in these parts."

Kuy remains silent.

The owner scratches his chin and mumbles under breath, "After I see to them," he states pointing to the woman and her children, "I'll see to you. Coffee on the boil. Five cents a cup. No milk. Sweetener on the table."

Nodding, Kuy walks away from the counter and sits down at a rickety table as far as possible from his former passengers. Sparing them not even a glance. Following a dying horse fly's antics against a window instead.

Attempting freedom. It strikes the glass. The window is resolute–pitiless. "Uneven contest." the roadman assays.

Day's heat bends into slow crematorium so looks away.

Across, Tryphosia loiters. Nervously looking around. Avoiding glancing at the strange Indian. Obvious wanting rid of them.

Doesn't blame him, "It isn't like we're kin, and he did help little Gus!" Yet answers to her dilemma are not forthcoming. She has nowhere to return. Nowhere to go. Sister in Galveston might take her in for a while. Yet getting to coastal Texas without money and food stretched before her milling thoughts. The Gulf is a world away–a world away.

The proprietor. Muttering. Slowly walks over. Spreading his hands, places a stiff smile on his face before speaking, "Hello. Well. What have we got here? Some pumpkins. A Bub and a Sis?"

Looking up at the man, Tryphosia asks timidly, "Do you have milk or lemonade?"

"No Mam. Not today. What else can I get you?"

"Well. We are not hungry. What we really need is a ride to Galveston. Do you know anything about service through here?"

Questioned. Man's eyes narrow with suspicion. Then he coughs into his hand. "No Mam. Don't run a coach service. Might be a ride through here now and then. But none that I know of at the moment. See here. We're a little off the main path here. Kind of off on our own little selves."

Phosy listening, timidly looks around. She does not know what to say or how to say it. Desperate. States her problem hesitantly, "See here! Kids and I need a ride. Got us just a little bit of money and had problems back home. So we need to find a way to the Gulf where I have a sister who will help us out."

Studying her. Man looks around with a sly jerk of his neck. Spying the Indian in the corner. Both his eyes light with a crafty. Shiftless shine before he pitches his voice into a mellow. Reasoned tone,

"Well now. Got a notion or two might help. There's always a way if there is a will. I've heard! Might need a little help around here.

This big busy cafe and all. You and the kids be able to stay around till a ride comes through."

Not sure how to respond, Phosy sneaks a peek over to Black Wolf. The Indian. Seemingly very disinterested. Seated far as can be from their table.

Laughing dryly. Owner fondles August's greasy curls. Handing a condensed milk sweet to each child. An act played with hearty chuckles.

Taking stock of the situation, the proprietor beckons their mother toward the back of the store. As she follows, he takes a last surreptitious look before closing a door silently behind them.

Restless. Children. Left on their own, turn away and stare outside. The view from the window. More interesting.

Windblown tumbleweeds. Papers gusting outside as solitary birds dive. Rise in steeply concentric circles.   to catch invisible prey. Hoping for sustenance.

Suddenly a shrill scream. Followed by the sound of a slap. Rivets eyes. Ears. Toward the back.

After a door slams, Tryphosia runs out from the kitchen.

Hair in disarray. Speeding past. Phosy gives the roadman a startled look grabbing her children. Running out through the cafe's front door. Banging it shut behind her.

"What the hell," the Kiowa snarls. Not knowing if he should laugh. Take offense, or come to her rescue.

"All–fired!" Even as the fat proprietor returns without cap. Hair wild as witch's fancy. Looking around with a sullen–sheepish frown. Peeking out a front window, grunts,

"Beat the Dutch! Damn woman!" Wiping hands on his greasy apron and fixing more than a fair measure of undeserved scorn on the Kudwa, "What are you looking at," the now embarrassed man asks.

Eyes narrowing as he strokes his now unsheathed bowie knife against his shin. Kuy returns the man's stare. With contempt. Answering hotly,

"Nothing. Looking at no one. Going to get my supplies or do I buy else-where? Not looking for trouble. Just want what I need and be gone. *Sabe*?"

"Sure. Sure. Give me a moment. I was trying to help out that crazy little thing. Got the mitten. Sure enough. Guess she had a fit! Sure tell."

Afterward still angry. The roadman stands up. Looks out of the dirty window.

Phosy and her children wait by the side road.

After half an hour, the proprietor returns with his goods. "Got most of what you wanted. Here's the bill."

Studying bill of sale Kuy figures he is being overcharged. Yet not enough to throw the supplies in the owner's face. Therefore pays with the bulk of the money earned working at the carnie and stalks away.

Stopping halfway out asked a surly. Suspicious question,

"Got anything to do with them folks outside? If so tell them to get off my propriety!"

Turning Kuy spits on the man's floor. Addressing him,

"*Ch'i*! If you are man enough to take liberties with her. Be man enough to tell her!"

Out of the store to his Hercules. Throws his goods into the back. Starts to get in. Hesitates. After glancing at the woman. Two children nearby.

Night's close. Chill wind blows off of the valley floor as Kuy weighs several options while driving a cigarette butt into the hard ground with his boot heel. Since no clear solution is reached, he shakes his head. Calls out.

"Ma. Get in. I will take you somewhere else!"

She nods gratefully. Gathers children. Gets in.

Inside the store. Its owner stares at them with a miserly flinty gaze. Coveting individually none of the people outside. Only the fact of their association. Opposing camp to his will.

Spitting. Turns back into the shadows with a final exasperation,

"A damned Indian. A white woman. What's this world coming to?"

Innocent of this final bigotry the four ride across darkening valley. Toward blue tinted hills. Lost to sight.

Boosting fallen spirits with a promise, "Wait to you see the hills at sunset. You've never seen anything like them!" Black Wolf reaches for a bag full of licorice. Handing some to everyone before turning his attention back to narrow road. Encroaching hills.

Chapter Seventeen

Comanche blows into his kerchief. Then readies sermon.

Respect's due. No don`t grovel. But do doff hat. Ain't that kind of church! Not a white man's. Snaring you as you're weighed. Adjured by your sunday's rig. The cut of your family's gilt. Hollow eyed con's quick abasement. Brother. Pass the collection plate and fork over that shining liberty dollar.

No sir. This one's vault is starry night. *Burning sun.* Distant cloud enveloped by cold passing winds. Unfriendly, impersonal, eager to be off. Far from this itinerant pastor.

Sharp eyed. Hungry lacking ease. Might act up presently.

Get gone wouldn't you?

Moss covered cow skull ringed by wild sorrel and yellow rose of the prairie alter. Host? Wilted field gray peyote. Murdering outlaw. Scarred by knife. Time and merciless occurrence. Officiating padre.

Smell him? The dickens you say? He's near. Well as a passel of crudely featured mestizo saints just outside convention. Exquisite. Cruelly raked limbs. Blood rendered like bright jewels. Incised wounds and stigmata. Pigeon toed. They decamp on tiny gilded sandals. Woven maize husk. Hundred yard stare. Ghastly eyed toward Aortic star.

Him sigh. Howl! Pass anger like a stream of galled piss. Then draw up tall. Eager. Malicious. Scorpion's sting impatient for the matinee all gussied up in filched boots. Shirt of pale calico. Midnight black cattleman's hat. Hunting coat chased by silver. Set with inlay. A chief's sheathing—smirks at though at this,

"Chief who and of what? Chief of nothing! Fool?"

Instead fastens on another designate–

"Killer!" Well howdy. This he accepts.

"World presents two choices:

Kill or be killed!

This not so? Once it's down to it.

Man to man or woman to woman with only one prize for eager greedy
hands?"

Spirit's ill.
Consents diagnosis.
No remedy.
No rest.
Weary
Tired

Where do old ways prevail?

And not ten cent emporium copies.

Away from jimmy crack corn and I don't care

Tin Pan Alley odium.

Shrugs. Eyes hard, "No place. I most sincerely regret.

Rebel.

Last of a kind?

Murderer!

Rapist?"

Dogs growl. Whine. Paw. Relieved when his boot heels recede. This
wolf's head droving a diminished pack. Skirmishing against railroads,
stocks, bonds and manifest destiny.

Hunt's drawn nigh. Trap's set. Baited.

"Go'na nail your pelt to the door of the american way you tarnished
star!"

Now friend. I'd say that's either a
threat, promise or a wish and so not to
be taken without a grain of salt

Chapter Eighteen

After their disappointing and disheartening encounter with the cafe's proprietor, Kuy builds a brushwood campfire.

Watching. The children's eyes catch the fire's reflection.

Later. Hearing coyote or wolf howl. Both nestle closer against their mother's skirts.

Earlier at the store. They were shaken by their mother's encounter and her reaction. Naturally! Far from their own people. Familiar folks. Now huddled around the fire built by this strange man.

Old life far way–perhaps never to be recaptured and yet children are very resilient like bones. Unbeknown to themselves. Kelley and August are adapting to furtive campsites. Rough food and cold nights. Huddled together on the gasoline–powered *thoowngul's* benches. Smell of ripening. Drying cactus bringing to the fore feral dreams.

Truth be told, Tryphosia's little family do not fear the roadman. He's still an unknown factor from the wildwood or a fairy tale summoned by striking flint with iron or perhaps the Kudwa is simply a good–hearted lost stray drawn by laughter and warmth.

Their mother is wary of the tall dark stranger. But no longer afraid of him and as her children watch his clever shadow puppets cast elongated menageries on the ground before the flames.

Tired, fretted out like an old worry wart she fears she is becoming, Phosy hushes her kids. Turning to listen as the fire crackles, pops and is later harnessed to boil coffee, bake corn rolls, and cook stew from goat jerky so her kids can eat the otherwise indigestible dried meat.

Supper started, Black Wolf wipes his hand on a bunch of dry sage. Clearing his voice, captures their attention circling his hands around the campfire.

Smiling, he pours the coffee and stirs the food while wolves howl again, stars fall and night deepens.

The roadman crosses himself. Then passes tin plates around, after adding a brief benediction—recited softly as not to offend any passing jester.

Afterward with a shy glance around their campfire, he closes with, "And an even bigger thanks for the good company around this fire."

Across. Phosy and her two children mirror his infectious beam and inviting manner yet later both children make wry faces during their frugal meal. Taste for goat meat is learned and old friend hunger aids each lesson.

Kuy glances upward at moon. A gossip with portents to tell. She's mum at the moment with not a word or sign free for the taking.

Meal finished, Tryphosia cleans dishes. On her return discovers her sleepy children wrapped like two peas in a pod under a shared quilt watching the bright fire, entertained by its changing patterns.

Turned sideways, Kuy gathers a handful of sweet dry brush. Throws it on to the fire.

It explodes with a whoosh. Startling both the woman and her children. Making the roadman laugh.

"Scared?" Reaching for the coffee pot. "Okay. Before sleep. I promised you a story. Want one or are you too tired?"

Boy looks at sister. She looks at brother. Nodding their heads as Kuy starts.

"Listen now! This story is old. I'm not sure when I first heard it. Don't know if it a story from my people or yours. It's a story from long ago," he promises, before placing more brush on the blaze and later continuing, "There was a family of three. An old couple and their adopted grandchild. They took the boy in after his parents were killed. All lived happily near a great forest. Never cleared.

Ringed by yellow prairie. Forest was like a fort.

Sometimes the boy's grandparents traveled half a day's walk to trade. Old. Traveled together for protection. When the boy was very small. They carried him. But no longer. Now knee–high he had to walk the whole long way and it was too hard for him. Despite their concern. His grandparents left him behind with very stern instructions. Brooking no infraction.

Old *Pa' hy* waxed and waned–"Moon to you," he translates. Pausing a moment for their enlightenment–"Winter faded. Snow melted under spring's return. After frost and ice withered. A considerable she bear crossed the family's clearing roasting her bones.

Still chilled from long fast and sleep. Bear once fat. Now thin. Skin loose. Her once rich coat bare and dull.

After waking. She bore a cub. Born during the general hush of evening. The other animals pronounced the birth of this new prince with admiring silence.

Even the crows.

Named little man." Black Wolf pauses, addressing the boy, "Maybe a good name for you too," the roadman suggests. "Little man clumsy. Weak. Helpless as a blind kitten. Soon, though, was covered in a thick coat the miniature of his mother's. Healthy. His mother's heart swelled with pride at his merry play and childish nonsense. As spring gained, his mother showed her heir off.

He had many enemies but under his mother's watchful eye slim cause to fear. Panther. Wolf and coyote knew whose heir he was and as royalty, granted much favor. His mother taught him many lessons. The most important was that of silence but like other children. He loved to play and make noise. This was Ok at night or early morning in their warm home. A deep narrow cave. But in the wild bitter world such behavior could not be brooked.

Silence was necessary when hunting or being hunted. Fire Starters were the only creatures feared by the cub's mother. They could use fire and shoot pain and death from a distance. His mother told him in a hushed voice that they. Unbelievingly as it sounded. Hunted them too!

Meanwhile. Human child's grandparents were busy getting ready for another long winter. So their grandchild often wondered alone. A visual map and compass carried in his head. Keeping him from mischief.

One golden day he discovered a bear cub trying to climb a tree. The animal climbed up with all his might. Only to slide down again. The boy laughed at the other youngster's ungainly and increasingly frustrated efforts. Noting that little animal's carryings-on were beyond his allotted strength.

As that day ended the boy witnessed a larger animal of similar hue and kin collect the little fellow. He thought they were dogs. Hearing his grandparents calling him for supper. Boy then raced home only as boys can.

At supper they sat on the clean swept floor of their house under flickering candles of elk tallow. The boy told the old folks about the puppy and its mother.

His grandparents were alarmed.

"Dog!" His grandfather sputtered, "There's no dogs round here!" Unfazed by his grandfather's mitigation of the plain facts as he saw them. The boy again described his experience.

"He means he saw a bear," his grandmother suggested. "Everyone knows dogs can't climb trees."

After his grandfather cleared his voice, he gave his grandson a stern warning, "Listen! Bears are dangerous. So listen or I'll fix your flint! Bears with little cubs are as nervous as your grandmother making flat bread. Don't go anywhere near this bear and her cub!"

Boy promised and later safely covered by his mother's blanket, dreamt peacefully of great shadows padding silently on the forest floor."

Shifting position. Kuy pauses. Gets comfortable. Checking on his audience. Their faces are rapt. Blue eyes aglow with expectation.

Satisfied returns to his story, "The bear family at first did not wander far. But the bear's mother knew that her child had to be strong so their journeys became longer. Often her cub was tired out and would roll on his back. Refusing to take another step. His mother tolerated this only for an instant. Then would ignore his small upturned waving paws. Little pink tongue. Forcing him to get up.

He would cry like a boy child full of self–pity but soon the cub became stronger. Welcoming their daily jaunts. Sometimes. Eagerly awakening his mother. Urging her to get up.

"Why mother–the day's wasting! The cub was eager. Over eager as you will find out!" Black Wolf warns.

The children look at their mother. She shrugs and they turn back to listen to his story.

Yawning prior to continuing, the roadman lowers his voice, "Let me see–where I was–One day the cub was rooting alone. Not far from his mother. But out of sight. He nuzzled sweet smelling plants. Chased a bee or two and watched a jay hop from tree to tree building a nest to woo a wife.

Suddenly the little bear smelled the most delicious scent he had ever known. Sweeter even than golden honey. So he followed his little wet nose to the savory scent's source. In a hollow. Beside a large tree. After circling trice taught, little man ashamed he couldn't count any higher but the mouthwatering scent emptied his little head of all of his mother's stern warnings.

Like any child he saw only the promise and not the actuality

"What is it?" he asked eagerly.

A bit of gamy elk roped with white fat.

"My! What a treat!" he said. Not noticing the iron sharp tooth holding the tempting morsel. His little paws tried to grasp the delicacy.

His moist tongue curled from his mouth like a schoolboy with a weighty problem

Not too far way, hearing screams, his mother tore through the brush. When bear came to little man. She knew he was dead.

Licking her child. Moaned. Yet try as she might, could not free his small torn body. Grieving. Would not leave him for days till nearly dead from hunger. Finally, left his little form buried under fresh heather.

Weeks later boy was walked alone. Day bright. Strong breeze swayed the trees and through misstep or evil chance. Boy became lost. No matter how many times he walked through the undergrowth and traced what he thought was the right path–it was not and as the sun began to sink below the tallest trees. Frightened, he began to cry and call for his grandparents.

The sounds of his sobs and thrashing were loud in the silent forest and traveled far. Many heard them. One form. Not far away. Froze in her tracks because the soft sobs of the lonely lost boy reminded the she bear of her own dead little one. Edging her toward the sounds.

Nearer. A sleek yellow shadow astride a bridge formed out of dead trees also circled back to the boy's cries. Driven by hunger and hope of an easy meal. Panther crept silently from branch to bough until spying boy.

In a glade the child stopped. Glad for its ration of light and warmth even though his face reflected recent events. It was dirty and tear streaked.

Without warning, the forest stilled. Hushed. Even crows. Knowing he wasn't alone Boy looked up and down. Sucking his thumb with concern even while Panther slid forward. One an inch at a time.

Child was almost his.

Crash of brush and tree. Bear appeared. An intimate of the forest. She immediately smelled the big cat and knew what the old rascal was up to. Spotting him. Knew boy was intended prey. Rushing toward the child, she reared to her full height. Her commanding roar challenging the stalking cat.

Panther brave. Hungry. Knew his place. If this child belongs to bear. This meat was not for him–Panther reasoned. So with a curt snarl. He turned on a dime, vanished. One shadow amid others.

The boy. Not frightened of the bear as she sat down and gave this other little man a friendly cuff on his back. Knocking him down.

Upset at first. Yet guessing the bear was joshing, he laughed with

He had not yet placed himself upon the crown of creation as lonely Adam yet he knew the she bear meant no harm her and rolled in play and later as the forest grew silent. Still and dark. The boy. Tired from adventures. Slept besides the great beast. Her fur warm as his mother's blanket and just as a soft.

The next morning. The boy's grandparents. Frantic with concern searched for him. Both had bows and arrows. Grandfather also carried a great fighting ax, his long knife and spear. The old couple had no idea what had happened to their grandson. They had found the glade where the bear and boy slept and were terrified at first. Petrified that the bear had slain their grandson. But as the morning's light grew stronger. They saw him sleeping rosy–cheeked and lost in dreams cradled by the bear.

Old man hushed his wife and called out softly to the bear. She startled and the boy awoke.

'Grandpa. What are you doing here?' The old man said nothing. The bear weary of Fire Starters with their long bows looked at the little man and knew he was now safe. Jealous. She rolled over softly and rose. The bear had already lost one child. She didn't want to lose another and wise mother that she was, knew that his fate was not with forest folk but with his own kind and with a mild roar she lumbered off to hunt breakfast.

Watching the bear rumble away. The old couple felt as if they had witnessed a legend first hand of the sort often told on nights just like ours!" the roadman suggested.

"The boy ran and hugged his loving family. Asking his grandmother. As a boy will, 'What's for breakfast grandmother? I'm starving.' " Finished. The roadman turns away from the firelight briefly.

Glint in his eyes. Tears or just firelight?

Morning after camping, everyone is sore and flummoxed but Kuy, mumbling as Phosy and her children are slowly herded back inside the Hercules after a hasty and cold breakfast.

Quarter mile down the highway, morning pools like shirred mercury on the Hercules's hood. Temporary blinding everyone. Kuy lowers a leather visor while Phosy woken by the sleepy protest of her cradled daughter mirrors his action.

Below in a valley, indistinct figures cross the road. Dancing and spinning mirages imagined into gulls or other birds, later retreating before gentle waves or dancing, warming shadows. Once actually on the valley's floor, a congregations of flat–faced sheep block their advance while dust heralds their forward press. Blending with the waning smoke of night's fires.

The shepherds guide their flocks of gray, dusty sheep across the narrow two–lane highway as dogs of many breeds not far from their mutual consanguineous with wild coyotes and wolves challenge with seditious cries. Forming whirling vanguards, curt bastions urging bleating flocks onward.

Led by joyous barking, yelps, joining rude flutes echoing cries of sheep forming a pastoral melody old as cain.

Their sheep marching forward at a brisk pace are descendants of flocks the *pastores* brought to texas and oklahoma long before historical record.

Fenced land, claimed, and bonded with rusty barbwire. Water rights jealously guarded by the gun and the hard stare yet these shepherds follow old paths through barren hills and hidden valleys traced long ago by people forgotten or scattered by invasion and deadly incursions

The Kudwa knows something about their history and practices from his ranching days. These shepherds follow the old *transchumante* system of moving flocks annually between summer and winter ranges learned from herders of the last century. Spring the sheep are spread out during lambing and are later herded back to arid valleys to be sheared.

Kuy sadly realizes these herdsmen are the last of their kind. Their fate. Foreshadowed by the fortune of other pastoralists. Will be that of clipped birds. Caged and haunted by memories of lost freedom.

Getting out of his truck, the roadman hails one of the sheep herders while suggesting to Phosy that she and her children stretch their legs a bit and get some fresh air until the last flocks pass.

Interested in news the herders carry. Kuy darts among them. Why?

Nomadic herders carry the news of what is before as well as what is behind.

The herders narrated tales and gossip in soft arid voices watching morning's horizon expand and fill the landscape around them. Speaking of bitter winds, sour grass, drought and hail big as fists. Lightening. Wolves and coyotes, as well as cursing mealy–mouthed anglo–ranchers with their guns and hate and yet they continue arriving from the dawn of a new day and stepping into its night at day's end.

"Your fires are fewer these days," the roadman sadly remarks.

"It is the same with all of the People. They come–we pass," bemoans a grizzled herder.

Yellow-hued man with a scared face and a friendly gapped tooth smile echoes his companion's sentiments,

"Yes. We fail and our land is swallowed up. Cattle everywhere–fences. I fear that we are the last" the nomad bewails. Later spitting before taking another plug of wild tobacco and continuing. "Hope this year is better. Many mouths and many miles. Will you bless us?"

Black Wolf assents. Sharing the strength of his heart singing aloud old blessings of power. Making a wide cross of benediction over the herders heads and their skittish flocks, "Please oh *Seni*ors–spare these fair folk the bitter water. Poisoned weed, grass and may the wolves, snakes and coyotes not savage their flocks. Bless the children and mothers of these people. For they are close to you. Never forgetting it is you that brings the rain. Grow the sweet grass. Seed the spring lambs."

They ask him for medicines and tonics. The Kiowa agrees. Trading his craft for smoked meat jerky. A little milk. Hard cheese.

After this quick exchange, they warn Kuy that the way ahead is not friendly.

"Nor is the way behind. *Aahoow!*"

Guiding their diminished gray, dusty flocks over the next ridge, the shepherds become distant, unsure mirages again.

Phosy watched the herders pass. Then turns to Kuy as he approaches.

Later handing her food and milk, while saying "Take some for yourself and the children. This is very good milk. Sweet and nourishing. Drink it before the heat turns it."

Afterwards there's not a sign of the herders' presence except the tracks of their animals and a quickly diminishing shroud of dust. After a strong wind from the north. Within minutes. All sign of their passageis swept away with a solemn finality.

***

Tired. Dusty. The roadman and his passengers hit the outskirts of another hickville. Drawing stares for a variety of reasons. One. It's Sunday. There's not a lot competition for entertainment. Secondly. Kuy and his Hercules present an unusual sight. Indigenous man. Driving new automobile in a part of the county seeing few. Three. Present company is mixed. This draws amused and disproving eyes. Setting tongues wagging. Mouths to whisper.

"Look at that trash coming to town Nadine!" old woman mealy mouths. Pointing her bony arm toward passing station wagon. "Pure out and out trash. What type of white woman ride with Indian?"

Realizing. They are a source of interest. Before reaching the main cross street of the town, they stop.

Keeping his eyes peeled on the growing crowd around them, Kuy makes a suggestion. "Now listen Phosy. Being in this truck together is trouble. Pay attention please. I have to go to a village and hold a ceremony. People need me. It will take all the rest of this day and tomorrow–I cannot come back before. On the following morning. Two days from now–around eleven I will look for you at this same spot. Please see if you can find someone to help you!"

Gazing into her expectant face and her eyes of alien blue, he continues, "I will not leave you and your children stranded if nothing comes. But I cannot bring you with me for the same reasons that I have to leave here."

189

Kuy temporarily annoyed by the inconstant honking of a ford truck behind them, motions the driver of the vehicle to go around before Phosy asks meekly,

"What should I do?"

Kuy suggests, "There are some good people here. People like Quakers but a little different. Do you know who they are?"

"Yes. I do."

"Good! They have a lodge at the other end of this street; they help all types of people. Go to them and see what they can do. Please remember Mrs. Clemens. If you have no help–be here by this store and I will give you a ride to another town. Understand?"

"Yes. Thanks a million mister for your help. I know that we have been nothing but trouble–"

Phosy's interrupted when the Kiowa takes her hand. Solemnly suggesting "Take care of them kids Mrs. Clemens," before turning away so she cannot see his face's expression.

After gathering her children out of the depot car. Tryphosia. Not wishing to embarrass Black Wolf further. Ushers them toward the front of his truck.

Before walking away, Gus shakes the priest's hand.

Facing the roadman with a mature look beyond his years he adds, "Goodbye Mister. Thanks for–helping. I have never been that sick in my whole life–"

"Don't think of it. Take care of your mom and sister for me will you?"

"Sure–don't worry about us!" This said the boy digs into his left pant's pocket and takes out a gift for the roadman. Keeping it hidden behind his back.

"Oh but I do. You and I are bonded now!"

August doesn't reply. Instead. He steps over. Handing the roadman an old bent penny.

The Kiowa takes his gift into his hand and examines it, "What's this boy?"

"My lucky penny sir."

"Lucky penny. Well shouldn't you hold on to it–for yourself?"

"No Sir. I want you to keep it for me. You might need it someday."

"Might, son. One never knows what's waiting out there down the road–Thank you!"

The roadman studies the good luck piece. Then places it carefully in a small vest pocket while August looks awkwardly at Phosy. Stepping beside her while his sister, Kelley timidly takes Kuy's hand in her small one and gives him a hard squeeze before rejoining her mother and brother.

As his farewell gift, Kuy gives both children a bundle of licorice and presses three silver dollars into Tryphosia's hands.

"I can't take these," she protests.

"Ah. Don't stand on ceremony Mrs. Clemens. Children cost money! Besides," he points out, "you and your children taught me a lesson–"

"Which?" she asks.

"Don't judge a book by its cover!"

"You know Mr. Black Wolf. That is true," she agrees. Glancing at him again, she adds wistfully, "Very true. I was afraid of you! You know. Dime novel Indians and all!"

"And I of you! People are often foolish are they not?"

Afterward she takes a piece of paper out of her pocket and hands it to the Kiowa. "By the way, here is my sister's address if you ever come that way–"

The roadman glances at her note, then takes off his hat and addresses them for the last time, "Goodbye Phosy."

Unfazed. Mrs. Clemens straightens her skirt. Looks around at the unfriendly. Questioning faces watching them and gathers her children. Taking them in hand and quickly walking away behind a small herd of cattle toward the center of town.

August catching sight of another boy kicking a hard red rubber ball runs ahead to join him.

"August," his mother calls out, "August come back here!"

Back inside his Halk Hercules Kuy watches them for a minute with a solemn, enigmatic look. Until his reverie is broken by a harsh voice demanding, "Hey redman! What were you doing with a White woman?"

The grate of this rough voice, unbidden, captures the Kiowa's attention. Looking around until locating the irritating voice. A fat mouthed, portly mechanic.

After lighting a cigarette taken from his front pocket of his soiled overalls, the man dangles it from his lips. Giving the Kiowa a look his mother would not be proud of as a few concerned citizens watch their exchange like dogs looking for sport.

Before any other exchange breaks out. A rough looking character. Dark featured with perhaps a little of the "blood" in him, frowns at the mechanic with a slight challenge, demanding,

"What the hell do you care Ollie. No woman. White. Dark. Or Red would spend a minute with you unless you bought her!"

The mechanic frowns. Then darts a glance backward.

But the Indian has absconded.

Denied a spectacle, most of the town's people go back to their business. The mechanic after a brief consultation with a couple of toughs around him swears. Watching the depot car until it turns onto a side street and is soon lost from sight.

Feeling the rough neck's stare. Black Wolf promises,

"Wish I had the time but I have more important work to do. Those days are gone. Lucky for you fat man," he adds, a smile framing the street's narrowing.

Chapter Nineteen

Preparing an important ceremony, Kuy kneels inside a ceremonial lodge. Readying himself in front of a crescent alter of sand facing west before lighting another fire east of the main altar.

Outside new moon parts the clouds while his congregation assembles at the east side of the lodge. Later entering clockwise sitting in the swept *towdowm* inside.

Mantled. Adorned with painted or stitched sunbursts, their chief drummer and cedar man seat themselves on colorful blankets on the ground west of the altar. The fourth official, the fireman waits by the entrance posts as three other spiritual leaders join them.

Smoke, clean water, sage, and oak acorn bless each dohate and every ritual object used tonight.

Large water drums. Bird–tail feather fans. Gourd rattles. A staff. Dried *Seni*. Tobacco. A peyote button centered on their altar complete their array of the necessary ritual objects.

Readying ceremonial bundles of tobacco, water oak leaves, Kuy whispers a silent prayer. One for himself. Another for his fellow priests. Gathering the power and courage to represent grace greater than himself to the hungry, sick, and needful.

"Let my prayer come like sweet incense before you."

Sanctified, Kuy passes a burlap sack of *Seni* buttons clockwise as each participant takes four buttons of *Seni*–corporeal prayers to eat at the proscribed moment.

Kneeling. He holds a long staff made of *zaip–gwawt–'ko–ya–daw* while in his left hand a fan.

Another priest shakes a rattle and sings hymns accompanied by the main drummer.

Midnight the first part of their ceremony ends.

Parishioners tend to mundane needs outside with a dash of gossip and fellowship while raptors hunt in the cool autumn dawn.

At first cock's crow the cottngregation returns to sing accompanied by rhythmic drumming, music and prayers until dawn.

At first light the final ceremony begins; a meal of corn, meat, fruit, and water blessed and passed clockwise. Each man and woman partaking ritually of four measures of food and water.

Kuy later pours water from the dismantled drum on the sand altar, extinguishes the ceremonial fire and in silence and joy ends all.

Just perceptible like a sigh behind a screen of exhausting exuberance, if keen and observant (as Kuy), a sudden loss or bereavement is experienced by not a few when benevolence rejoins dancing siblings on morning's edge.

Kuy plans to stay with friends. Accept donations. Catch up on local gossip, events before returning to town and amid his own worries, hoping Mrs. Clemens and her children have found help since only part of his fate weaves through theirs.

"Or entangles," he adds with a note of reflection after a wry grimace.

Glancing back again at the now empty ceremonial lodge, Black Wolf blesses his benefactors who had set him upon this road rather than one of darkness and loss that almost swallowed him as whale jonah.

***

"*Goam Khoat.* This storm blows hard now!" No Oats. An old soldier and friend of Black Wolf complains. Calling attention to bitter winds howling outside, he knocks a log deeper into the fire's greedy heart.

Indeed cold outside this night. Ever since a wayward Autumn storm moved in, marring what had otherwise been a perfect fall morning and afternoon.

Along with Black Wolf a few men, warrior society remnants, grouse going on about how brave they were. How they knocked the shit out of them soldier boys long ago. How many virgins they stole maidenhood from while waiting for the door of this age to close.

Facing a limited present, they retreat from aches, pains and sorrow to bask in the warmth of remembered youth.

"You fart like the wind No Oats," William Little Buffalo jokes adding to the general laughter.

When the merriment quietens, Kuy starts another story to help all pass this cold night, "It wasn't just their numbers," he argues.

No Oats. William Little Buffalo and Pete Old Smoke listen and wait. Rough old men with eyes smoldering like muted coals around firelight.

Still feeling the chill outside despite a now blazing fire, Little Buffalo slides closer to its smoking heart before complaining,

"*Tou*! Damn it's getting colder!"

Agreeing, the others nod.

After being interrupted again, Black Wolf throws a few more logs on to the fire. Watching it grow, brighten and chase shadows around the pitched ceiling.

Then resumes, "Some of them white and black soldiers could fight and one of the bravest men I ever saw was one of them son of bitches!"

"Oh yeah," No Oats asks, "Got more of that black licorice Hawkeye?"

"Yes. Might have a stick or two Hiawatha!"

Each pass Kuy's gift around as their friend continues, "It's all true! Look at this scarred old arm of mine Billy," the roadman insists baring his long limb. "Old wound. Got it from being knocked off a good horse years ago. A hard fight with mounted troops. Most of our battles were small. Not even worth a colored flag on the white man's map. But they were important!"

William Little Buffalo nods silently in agreement while sucking on the black candy like a contented young boy.

Eager for diversion, No Oats also takes some licorice and sits back to listen.

"Hope for wives. Children and nation was what they were," Black Wolf says, finding his tale again, giving the slumbering fire a poke while outside angry wind howl at the lodge's door trying to get in.

Listening. Kuy ignores it. Only glancing back at the fire. Warming his hands. Side tracked by private concerns, petitions silently, "Know what the wind wants–does anyone?"

For a time Black Wolf sought such answers dreaming beside fires on lonely nights and empty roads or by taking part in countless ceremonies, yet no solutions were found. Just more foreboding.

Even surrounded by fellow roadmen and road chiefs, feels a providence or fate, malevolent and expectant closing after a long chase.

"Let it come," Kuy mutters, then, "is there a spiteful presence outside? Or my imagination? Perhaps it's just a bit of under cooked potato?"

Belittling concerns to offset his unease, the roadman recalls how an old friend. Big Timmy O'Tool a mixed kid with an irish father. Told him one dark night listening to the wind scream and call,

'That it's only the shriek of banshees.'

"Hell. We got enough ghosts of our own around here with importing any," he nervously comments. Wondering if the ghosts of different tribes follow their migration to new lands.

Before resuming his tale, demands suddenly, "Who calls? Is it trouble from saving that boy?"

"Kone-gyah-daw-kue', off hunting buffalo?" Little Buffalo asks sarcastically.

Deep in thought. Black Wolf ignores his friend. Turning away. Most troubling, Kuy recalls a recent dream of a dark man.

"As you were saying about 1874? When you were a boy with one of our bands fighting to get free of the reservations!" No Oats demands. Pulling the roadman back to the fire; to his story, to the present.

Kuy shudders. Not from the cold. Then resumes, "Just saying–We were poorly armed. Made up for better tactics and scouting. We Kiowa unlike their soldiers lived off the land. Hell. The land was our mess tent. Gave us lots of *kii*. Deer mostly. Many of them soldiers were city people. Not only could they not shoot or ride they were blind. Without Indian allies. They were like blind woman lost on a saloon's dance floor."

"More like a drunken white man on his wedding night!" Old Smoke adds with a jeer.

The roadman grins and continues, "Hush now old mule before I forget my story. During this battle. I lost my horse. So shot from the ground. Killing one soldier and nicking another. Now another wounded Blue Coat yelped like a kicked dog. His white pony was splattered red with blood and terrified by the smell and noise. So I knocked this wounded soldier off his mount with my rifle butt. Smashed his face in like a pumpkin. The boy spit teeth like seeds. His eyes sought mine before they closed in pain and his face purpled up.

Soldier's horse was a good one. Trained well. I used him to ride over his former master until he stiffened and lay with a stream of black blood running from his ruined head.

There was another Blue Coat ahead of me in a small defile. A large man. Dismounted as well. This one could kill! He had already shot one of us through the head. Being a fool that day. Decided to ride this one down too. It was a mistake. He roared like a bull and used his rifle as a club and broke my arm. Slicing it open to the bone. It went numb on me. Bit through my tongue it hurt so badly. Made me mad."

"I bet," No Oats, laughs..

"Steadying my new *tsain*–I circled around flanking him. The man's rifle hit my horse's head. *Tsain*–reared. Screamed like a girl. Threw me off onto the ground. I rolled upward cursing. Using my good arm to hold my rifle. The big soldier was remounting a big bay with heaving flanks. His eyes were bright and his blue uniform was splattered with my horse's blood. Quite a picture. Eh?"

"One of us shot the big bastard in the shoulder; he was forced to let his horse go. Then screamed a curse. Not English. Some other tongue," again thinking of O'Tool and the frequent oaths of his drunken father,

Kuy adds," perhaps irish. Anyway! He returned fire. His bullet hit a scout named Old Crow in the thigh. Old Crow spun around and presented his horse's flank as a shield. The soldier was taking aim again when I shot him through his chest before that rascal turned and shot at me. Just missed too!

Old Crow returned fire. The soldier was caught in a crossfire. Kneeled down. Picked Old Crow right off his horse. Me? I crouched down to get a final crack at him.

Other white soldiers flew by. Except for screaming out suggestions to run they offered the big man no aid. Other Kiowas broke off pursuit to circle this lone soldier.

He fired several times. Wounding another man.

I hit him in the arm.

He turned firing at me. Missed.

A hunting arrow caught him in the neck. Rifle dropped. He pulled his Colt. Firing with manic precision.

Another bullet tore off a piece of his head. He continued to fire until Twin Snakes' horse rode him down.

Since we were in a hurry. Since he was brave. Two Snakes shot him in the head. Except the loss of his weapons. Boots. He was not molested. Biggest soldier I ever saw. Least he could fight!" The roadman exclaims carried away by memory.

"We sure were some wonders back then. Kuy; you sure were a marvel. A real hell getter!" William Little Buffalo chuckles, slapping the road-man on his back. "We *Pa' hy–dome–gaw* men could dance on or off the battlefield!"

"Vanity. All is vanity," Black Wolf sadly concedes. "Where now the laurels of victory?"

Wiping away a tear. No Oats proclaims emotionally, "Those old days make me mighty sad sometimes."

Laughingly bitterly. William Little Buffalo interrupts, "Don't worry man. Custer died for their sins–"

Patter. Fellowship. Remembrance followed as the wind kicks up outside. Rocking the wooden frame and roof of their meeting house.

Glancing upward. The men smile, continuing in the same vein trying to ignore the elements outside.

"Wounded Knee–"

"No. Little Big Horn!"

What about Chief Joseph–"

"You mean, *Hinmuuttu–yalatlat*, don't yah?"

"Yes sir! Tell it true!"

"Bear Paw Mountains."

"–they had no choice!"

"Who? The Crows–"

Frowning, Black Wolf falls silent while the others continue.

"Well. We killed ole yellow hair at least–"

"Did it plank for the Washita River?"

"Who–Morning Star?"

"Yeah. Him!"

"Hell. We Kudwa missed out on the little Big Horn!"

"As I said, *custer* died for their–"

"Oh yeah!" Black Wolf exclaims dismissively, countering their ribald, empty boasts, "But they didn't notice this fact of atonement did they?" Shrugging, he adds indignantly, "Just more fuel for the fire–"

"Hush then!" Chiding, William Little Buffalo asks, "Want a laugh boys."

Responding in unison, the men shout, "Yeah. Why not!"

Billy takes out a couple of framed, laminated documents and passes them around,

"Feast on these boys. A real good laugh! Or two."

"What's this?" Old Smoke inquires.

"Why just the best damn constitution ever written by mortal souls! I ripped it of the wall from a post office; hell it belongs to us doesn't it?" Billy boasted.

"For shit!"

"No listen," Billy urges, "this is good,

'Establish justice. Insure domestic tranquility–secure the blessings of liberty–'"

Listening each veteran grows solemn. Knowing that good ole US of A's promises for the most part, though well phrased, are like the love talk of a young man to a jilly– after the act–they are just fucked and forgotten.

Afterward, a young man named Deer Fingers comes in. Hesitant and shy in front of the older men. He keeps silent until locating Kuy.

"Well. It ain't much Kuy. But it's all we can spare. There's more than enough to get you gassed and gone. A little supply money. *Aahoow* Father. Where's your road taking you?" Deer Fingers asks. A might uncomfortable. With the aged men around the fire remind him of goblins and spirits his old grandmother gabbers about.

Accepting the donations with a heartfelt thanks, Kuy replies, "Oh. Got a ways to go yet. Congregation in need. I will see to them. Lots of backsliders. I got to light the fire under them before they lose every damn thing and are scattered to the winds."

Later as ash and dying embers fail, Black Wolf bids everyone farewell in the hot, stuffy room before joining Old Smoke outside to take up a discussion that he and his older friend had started earlier,

"*Haun-day gaht p'haydle-doe.*"

"Yeah. *Naw haun-day baht p'haydle-doe?* About your next err–parish. Listen! They get lickered up in town so bad they lose a lot of stock to white men. Woman folk from nearby ranches complain to our wives. It's *'n–hH'–dei–mH–e–*Bear Above fault! Hell. He is raising his boys as if we were still at war. They know next to shit about farming or stocking. Just get crazy, bored and look for trouble in town. Believe me! Towns around there are nothing but trouble!" Old Smoke warns.

Listening, the roadman shakes his head. Knows these troubles. They're everywhere. With nothing but failing herds and scrubland. Young men's thoughts run to the distractions found in small towns. Where the assorted snares of drink, gambling and whores wait for the unwary and after digesting all that his friend just said, Kuy changes the subject to something that has been bothering him,

"Listen old friend. There's a man. Guess it's a man tracking me. But I did not see his face!"

"What kind of man?"

"A dark man. A witch perhaps? Or a *'H'dei–kiH–*"

"Watch out," Old Smoke warns. "Keep your face to the wind–old friend. Sing only strong songs. Sing of life's goodness. You know. Sometimes trouble walks behind us!"

"Hah! Trouble has to have a long stride to catch up to me!" Though his boasts rings hollow even to his own ears, Kuy tilts his head. Then gives his friend a careful, considered look, before straightening his black hat and raking it to his favorite angle above a brave smile.

Noticing a glint of silver around his friend's neck worn over an old military gorget. Old Smoke asks another question, "You got a cross around your neck. Why?"

"One of their holy fools gave it to me during a rain storm."

"Wear it friend. Can't hurt."

"You're probably right. Say–"

"What else has got you by the tail?"

Black Wolf taps his head. Looks over his shoulder. Then confides in a low voice, "Listen–"

"Go ahead!"

"Two things."

"Them being?"

"I want to leave most of the peyote here with you."

His friend considers his request. Then asks with a worried frown as a gust of wind threatens his hat, "Ain't you coming back Kuy?"

The roadman shrugs. Looking away toward the horizon before answering, "I figure to!"

Old Smoke wrinkles his eyes, "Figure too but–Ah hell Kuy! But nothing!"

Black Wolf steps closer and grasps his friend's hand with a firm grip before adding, "Another thing–"

"Shoot!"

"There's this gal–"

"A woman?"

"Yes!"

"A *dulce* of yours?"

Again Black Wolf nods.

Old Smoke crinkles his eyes, "A woman?"

"Said yes!"

"Name of this woman?"

"Velvet Horn!"

Old smoke rolls his eyes this time. "You mean that–"

"Yes! The healer. Medicine woman. Whatever you want to call her."

"But she's–"

Black Wolf holds up his hand.

Old Smoke catching his friends' smoldering look, kills any more out of the hat comments. Then waits with hard earned patience for his friend to finish.

"Anyway. If she sends word or letter. It will be either to you or to William."

After listening Old Smoke asks, "What then?"

"Forward or hold her letter for me."

"Then?"

Without replying Black Wolf digs into his pants to bring out an old leather purse greasy with age and wear and then fishes out handful of bright golden coins handing them over to Old Smoke.

Old Smoke examines the coins. Then separates one from the others. "What's this? Seems real old?"

"It is. Roman."

"Roman? Now. Ain't that a wonder?" he comments while turning the ancient metal over in his creased and worn palm.

"It's worth a couple of hundred. Say about two."

"And the rest?"

"Two hundred more."

"Why are you giving me these coins? Who do I hold them for?"

The roadman explains quickly, "Sell my roman coin. There`s this shop in oklahoma city–downtown–named Einstein's."

"Spell it!"

"E.I.N.S.T.E.I.N'.S."

"And?"

"Man inside has the same name. Fair man more or less. Sell it. Take what you need for there and back again."

Old Smoke considers his friend's request and then nods.

"And the rest?"

"If Velvet Horn sends you a message or writes that's she with child–"

At this Old Smoke starts. Then grants his friend a long look of wonder. "With her?"

Again Kuy nods. "Anyway. If she sends word. Means she's with child."

"Yours?" The roadman just grins. "And give her the rest. Including my truck if it comes to that."

"Many gone already Kuy. You thinking about joining them?"

"Not if I can help it!"

"Then why all this solemn leave taking?"

"Just in case!"

"Just in case?"

"Yep."

"Ok. *Hermano*. You always have been mighty pernicious ever since we fired your house and you rode off into that blizzard!"

Black wolf clasps his friend by the shoulder and admits, "I was running. Running from myself. From the death of my family. Even from you. But I am through with running!"

Old Smoke stifles a sudden flow of tears.

Naw. He would never cry.

Black Wolf too fights strong emotions. Then turns away for a moment to battle them. When mastered, continues, "Got a few more odds and ends to burden you with–"

"Them being?"

"Got this letter to deliver. But Bear Above's troubles forces me to run off tomorrow. Could you see that this gets to this woman?" After asking Kuy fishes into his coat pocket and then hands a yellow envelope over.

Old Smoke takes out a pair of worn, patched bifocals, reads the address and then whistles before commenting, "Know her. Knew her brother too before polio licked on him a little and killed off his wife and children."

"Didn't know about his kids."

"Oh yeah. Sad story! He was a real buckaroo back then. But after their deaths and his own sickness. He changed. Became a lush and walked away from everyone. Where did you run into him?"

"Back west. He works in a nickel and dime carnie show."

"Well. Times change. We can only roll with the punches," his friend suggests. Then fastening a knowing look upon the roadman adds, "He was like you Kuy. But broke. You didn't," Old Smoke points out. Alluding to a specific night, before emotionally reminding his friend with a mournful comment, "I still remember that winter night–"

"So do I!" Black Wolf replies reluctantly. Not wishing to talk about the night he burned his house down with his wife and his in–laws' typhus stilled bodies inside. "No. I didn't. Don't know why. But you were there with me. Like a father," he recounts with his voice pitched low, "Or a brother!"

Old Smoke. Saddened by their shared memory. Hesitates before replying. By and by though, finally, wishes his younger friend a safe journey, "Take care. Watch out–"

"That's for sure old friend. *You* take care–too!"

This said Black Wolf clasps him on the shoulder, then picks up his saddlebags and walks away.

Part Two

La prestidigitación

Chapter Twenty

Kuy departs with morning. Had hot coffee. Corn bread. Thick bacon before first light, and afterward at peace, experienced a profound sense of contentment stemming from the loving support harvested from yesterday's ceremony, with the positive reaffirmation of his personal values and his commitment to faith. Now rekindled. Made him if not stronger. Then. Perhaps similar to an old oak kissed by a brief passing spring—a little contemptuous. Later returning to the market town where Phosy and her children might wait, parked and waited in a reflective mood. Watching breeze blown trash roll and play in front of his parked truck.

Frowning, comments sourly, "Wherever they. Trash follows."

Waiting, wafting, filtered sunlight fills his cab and warms him. Forming a conspiracy of drowsiness.

Kuy pulls his hat brim down and naps.

Asleep. Struggles to retain feelings of contentment and purpose cradled from last night's ceremony yet sleep is broken by discord pulling him back to this dirty street within this small town and waiting vigil.

Awake, he realizes that he is not as settled as he had hoped. Unlike a good number of souls under the sun, moon and star he does not abide and trust whispered, veiled promises. Empty sermons. Cheaply printed tracts. Or revival tent hosannas. Thus his disquiet. Under his sanctioned. Inward piercing altar of peyote. Miscellaneous blessings and brief glimpses of other vistas or worlds spin chaotically. Autumn leaves in a whirlpool. Answering ambiguously or not at all, leaving the penitent unsure unless time is taken to unravel what was shown and what walked before or behind veiled eyes.

Rolling down his window, Kuy decides that this isn't the time for self-reflection. What will come is beyond his scope. "I am small man. A simple man. Let my tasks be equal to my strength. I have many people to care and mind—"

Till noon waits. Then no sign of his adoptive family, Kuy drives away grateful that they must have found someone to help them. Undeniably. Part of him misses them. August especially, due to the intensity of his struggle to save him, crowding into his ark of loved ones.

At a crossroads, he searches for an old cohort. Headsoverheels toward a scattered collection of western relics; wagon wheels, mothy blankets and other residue from the recently closing past loitering in sunlight and shadow awaiting perhaps a touch if for only a moment to arrest rust, warpage and the unwanted attention of carpenter bees and white ants.

Standing at bay like a robed priest king, an old *tsH–'H–ga* hauled here year ages ago waits forlorn. Menaced by clinging scrub.

Resigned. Facing west.

Kuy bows and later speaks, "Poor old father. Who dragged you here?" No answer. Only the rustle of field mice or rats burrowing within as the buffalo stares forward with eyes of yellow glass solemn and commanding.

Moved. The Kudwa places his hand upon its scuffed, woolly head and splintered horns, requesting forgiveness and a blessing before turning toward the hand of providence.

***

Hours later, the distant wichita mountains far away on horizon break the seamlessness expanse of grass and occasional strands of trees sloping into the gentle folds of oklahoma.

Kuy rehearses how he's going to council *An–hH'–dei –mH–e* and his family. Especially his older son Running Legs. A troublemaker and a constant thorn in his parents' side. After all of its particulars are hashed out, carefully ticks off the folks he would like to look up on his next circuit.

The people who have joined—if inadvertently—his growing congregation whether they are privy to this fact or not.

Chapter Twenty-one

Man stands with his thumb out hoping for a ride on an otherwise empty road.

Catching sight of him, Black Wolf slows down and studies the hitch-hiker–a young brown skinned man dressed in a neat tan suit coat with matching pants. A Panama hat worn at a rakish angle and two musical cases. One resting at his feet while the other. Slung over his shoulder.

Kuy calls out, "Hey there. Need a lift?"

"Sure as a month of Sundays Mister! I need to make it to Oklahoma City quick as fried okra!"

"Get in then!"

Needing no further encouragement, the musician grabs his two cases and hurries inside.

"Thanks for the ride. Oh mother may I. Rides are rare around these parts. Flagging a ride is mighty tough if you're slapped with paint."

"Pardon?"

"Black–Negro. Indian or the like! Where are you popping off to Chief?"

Kuy visibly bristles at being labeled with honorarium never applied for. Gritting his teeth, saying not a word. Figuring that relations between a Kiowa and a black man ought to have a better footing than passing animosity.

The musician notices that the driver didn't cotton to being called "Chief" so he changes tack, being a quick study dependent upon passing strangers. "Sorry. My name is Charlie. What's yours?"

"George Black Wolf."

"A nice name. Lyrical. Better than just plain ole Charlie."

"Where are you heading Charlie," the roadman asks.

"Around Oklahoma City. First to look up some relatives. Then I need to kick around the nation to hunt up some of my folks for business."

The roadman glances at his passenger. Judging from the young man's appearance. Black Wolf guesses that he has some tribal blood so he digs deeper, "You're of a Nation or at least part. Which one?"

"Yea You Right. Cherokee. Grandmother was full–blooded. Now it ain't no mystery about that is there? Now you're a–"

"Kiowa."

"Fighters and buffalo hunters!"

"Were."

"Yea You Right! The MAN came along and put a stop cold to your people's freedom–"

"That's the truth–!"

"Sure enough! Can I have an Amen?"

"A what?"

"An Amen brother!" Fathoming his request, the roadman complies, "Amen!"

"That's a whole lot–better. Now we're rolling with steam! Now we get'n down and truly spiritual. Lord Jesus yes!"

Another question, "You're a preaching man Charlie?"

"As God's my testament. I surely am!"

"And the Guitars?"

"Oh. I play the devil's music and preach God's holy world at the same time! Might be what you call a contradiction but ain't we all?"

"More or less," Black Wolf concedes all the while laughing before looking at Charlie with a graver expression. "Listen–"

"Yes?"

"I have wondered a lot up and down many roads from mexico. Texas. Oklahoma and more and I have met a lot of people."

Charlie butts in, "Like me?"

"Yes like you and I have discovered something puzzling–"

"What may that be Captain?"

"No captain but plain George–anyway–it's strange that even in english. There are so many ways of expression. Many turns of phrases. Slang and cant–"

"Yea You Right–Oh I got you George," the musician acknowledges happily. "For instance when I talk to white folks. Unless they're ignorant country trash. I talk real proper–minding my p's and q's and when I'm with Negroes and other Colored folk–well I talk natural–kitchen talk. Rhythm and blues. Boogie woogie and rag time. But when I sit down with musicians, ain't color bar usually unless they're one of them solarium or parlor room pianie types–well we just cut a rug in our own language's olfeggio'lo–get me George?"

"How so?"

"Well George. Music's a language unto itself. For example. Suppose I asked you to play D natural in the fifth bar of a B flat blues note–could you?"

Soliciting clarification Black Wolf asks, "Come again?"

Responding, Charlie flashes the Kiowa a beaming smile worthy of a grand pappy gator before answering as well with a flash and driving verve that's almost magical, "See what I mean Chief–I mean George. We all got dissimilar sides–like a cut diamond. Contrary facets–though spoken in our own way," he emphasizes with a snap of his fingers, "Different. Yet all of the same cloth–like a prize quilt sowed by many hands–then joined together!"

After digesting, heck, translating the musician's words, Kuy exclaims, "Well Charlie. Not only are you a musician–matter of fact what you truly are is a philosopher–"

"Yea You Right!" Charlie acknowledges merrily with a further aside, "No sir! We's in Church. Just plain honest speaking between two men with no nonsense or fear, just the way it should be!"

"Amen," the roadman seconds.

Later, for the sheer hell of it, racing down a hill, each lets loose a rebel yell worthy of Bull Run or Shiloh.

After settling down, Charlie asked, "Been Reading about the war going over there?"

"A little. Here and there! Read from an el paso rag recently. Sad news for a sad time.

The musician smiles bitterly before continuing, "I think a lot of whites are going to catch it in this one!" Charlie gleefully point outs.

"Maybe. But as I was saying. What's going to break out over there is going to be the show of shows and the king of kings' ultimate retribution–"

"Amen!"

"–and it's going to spread. No one can believe a standing president of the united states on any real point of truth!"

"Amen to that!" Charlie shouts.

"God almighty he is loud," Kuy complains silently.

And that's the truth! His voice is a muted roar, oft filling the cab and hurting the roadman's ears even as he lassos the conversation back to a sustainable level, "Of course my young friend. When the grease hits the fire the big men in washington are not particular about color and creed," Kuy states sadly, prior to redirecting their conversation, "Would you serve in their army?"

"No siree!" The musician says with a snap of his fingers. "Don't get me wrong. I like to fight as well as the next man. Maybe even more but I have a calling–"

"–preaching?"

"–yeah you're right. But even more than this–I'm ashamed to say–"

"Well. What then?" the roadman demands impatiently.

"The blues. I filled fit to busting with that old black magic!"

"You'll never find peace–then–unless you follow your gift–"

"Amen to that–"

"–and find contentment."

Charlie nods and agrees. Snapping his fingers, changes the topic, "You got the vote don't you?" he asks.

"No! It's the states that decide."

"We had it after the war with their version of freedom too–O Lordy! Forty acres and a mule–but every time those old rotting planters and captains get together they try to take it away–though they have to give me a second look or so to see what side of the Color line I stand on and brother. Now don't get me wrong! This can be a real help when I'm tooling around. Why? Sometimes those sons of bitches can't tell if I'm colored. A Native. Mexican or whathaveyou! Sends them into a tizzy! Not knowing and all and sometimes–now listen George–this is the kicker," he adds with a deep, laugh, "I can't tell myself when I have a few good glasses of gooood liquor and have a fine doll or peach in my lap–and a few dollars in my pocket. Now don't take me wrong friend–I have a nice little wife and daughter but when I am on the road–it's time to dust my broom!"

All said Charlie supplements his thoughts with a soft, embarrassed comment, "here's something I started to work on but right now I too busy since I have a whole passel of other songs and tunes. As if to make his point, Charlie clears his voice and starts to sing an echoing and mournful tune,

" *'I'm going' away to a world unknown–I'm worried now. But I won't be worried long.* "

Then, "Name it Boss; blues–any old kind–hillbilly. Saturday night, dances of every kind and together with all of the musical mischief you can throw a hat at–I play it!"

"Well. One thing's sure–you sure have a fine set of pipes!"

"Thanks! Ain't no bragging man but I sure play!"

Silent later, both watch the countryside pass outside. It's dry and dusty day then evening as well.

Dry grit and the day's warmth makes them thirsty.

"Got any water?" the musician asks.

"Sure!" Kuy says handing him his canteen.

The younger man takes a long drink and passes it back to the Kiowa who also takes a swig. No longer parched, Charlie, catching sight of a landmark known to him ahead, asks the roadman to slow down, "Hey George. Could you let me off at the crossroads ahead? That one!"

"Up ahead?"

"Yes sir. There's someone I want to meet ahead!"

Mirrored, shadow cast doppelgangers whip away toward an old lone oak-eerie majestic as a bent sovereign

After they stop Charlie grabs his instruments and with a quick shake vamooses fast as he joined the roadman's company, vanishing surely as a last sustained note.

Chapter Twenty-two

After dropping Charlie off Kuy heads due east judging that rain might break soon but after a little consideration changes his mind.

Notes hereabouts land's free of obstacle or even a shadow to hook eye`s interest. So allows a wind to capture his attention.

Unbidden two red headed boys alike as peas in a pod stumble ahead of him hand in hand across a dried out riverbed.

Windblown and sunburned they stare at him slowing down. Wishes he could aid them. All the while puckering a furrow or in two inquiry. Its assayed outcome's without a doubt will never be revealed. Leastways here and now as opposed to later and yon as stage actors pose between a quick nip or two.

"Do moments have tantrums? Outbursts?" he wonders since there is so much unknown or assumed until too late?"

Slowing down Kuy opens a window and asks the obvious, "You two youngsters lost or just out taking a long stroll?"

They reply not a note unlike gabriel and his horn. But do stop their unsteady advance to rubberneck.

Under closer inspection they prove moon faced and if not exactly vacant gazed. Lost in consideration not freely open to examination by causal trespass.

He tries instigating a dialog but they just gape. Plenty far away from any habitation that he's aware of.

"Just got rid of one family. Don't need another!" Yet stops. Opens his door. Whistling as he walks over asking, "Boys? Taking a stroll, taking the air?"

Each goggles at him with veiled or perhaps innocent smiles. But without any other response.

"Maybe just shy!" he opines observing the same time that they have odd, elongated eyes like the *TsHenej–kiH* well as swollen features. Together with thick lips. Heavy jaws, broad foreheads surmounted by thick glasses, matched by heavy clothes and brogans below.

Smile might do, "You speak?"

"Yes," they answer lazily. Only partially distracted by a large moth or butterfly. Diving toward them. Simply a foil against wind. It soon recovers and is gone.

"You do. Great! Ok amigos. Live around here?" the roadman demands, taking stock of his surroundings. Seeing neither hint nor daub of man's presence. Doubts it.

"Yes."

"You do?"

Both look away smiling their engaging woebegone smile.

"Where you off to then?" he asks again.

"Grandmother's house!"

"Grandmother's house. Now where's that?"

The boys smile again. Then point vaguely in several directions, answering in unison, "Arkansas!"

"Arkansas! Might far for two young as you!"

Don't answer. After acknowledging politely his presence both strut away. Path's clear and mutually decided upon ahead without obstacle.

Black Wolf scratches his head. Tilts his hat and follows after them. It's not hard; his lanky stride is worth two or more of theirs. He catches up in a shake or two and inquires politely, "Say there fellows. Want a ride?" Now there's a quiver. He's got their interest. Mercurial as a firefly's he reckons; however they now look directly at him.

"To Arkansas? In a Car?"

"Truck actually! But not that far!"

"Car!"

"Ok car. Want a ride?"

Nod both.

One of the boys has a cardboard card tied around his neck. So Kuy gently reaches down and steadies it. Then reads the sun faded and rain splashed note.

'Dear folk.

These are our sons Clive and Castor. Please care for them since we have come to painful the conclusion that we can't.

God bless them and you.

Betty and Lou.

G.T.T.'

Unties it and folds it carefully. Placing it inside his shirt's front pocket and buttons it safely inside from wind and occurrence.

Before escorting the children inside. He cranks and then gets in after them. Changes gears and heads toward the nearest burg not too far off of his route.

Kids silent. Black Wolf's positive they are more than just a bit mesmerized by the sensation of mobility. Twins surely. But even something a might more particular. Sad though. Since they sit like two hounds. It's no concern to them where they are going just that they are.

"Yes sir! Picked up some sights time and again but these two!" Wondering what's wrong with them. Obviously they suffer from a malady outside the normal day–to–day variety. But as hard as he tries. He cannot recall any affliction like this hoping as well that it's not catching.

Heading smack into the town's meager outskirts, flies toward the sheriff's office. Parks out front. Gets out and suborns the boys to follow him.

Inside a lone deputy types away on a big monster of machine. Picking with two fingers like a man possessed by great industry. Only looking up when the Kiowa and the children intruded. Afterward shaking his head unconcerned, returns to his typing.

Used to being dismissed unless fitting the description of a general warrant, Black Wolf Shrugs at this veto, then clears throat,

"Deputy."

"Yes!" Says man. Pausing his typing long enough to look up at the Kiowa with a frank dislike and outright dismissal that almost simultaneously wilts Kuy's habitual hard crust a moiety.

"What can I do for you? Since you're of one mind to interfere!"

The roadman in turn motions to the two children behind him, "These two—"

"What about 'em?"

"Found them wondering alone. Thought I had better gather them up and bring them in."

"Bring them to whom?" the deputy complains. Looking despairing at the tall pile of papers before him.

"Well. To you!"

Again, deputy smiles a sour; half grin. Before giving the Kiowa a further scowl, "This ain't no orphanage. No foundling home. This is a sheriff's office Chief!"

Though tired. Weary. Itch'n to be back on the road, Kuy tries again to pierce this man's density and prick his official vanity, "Pardon amigo but isn't the welfare of the community a concern of this office?"

Unwillingly. Deputy stops typing. Gets up with a long sigh, "Goddamn! I knew we should a posted a sign against this! Christ Chief! Get it. Sheriff's not here. Just me. I got clerking duty form this morning till long past evening. Now that I'm jarring away with you. My hours behind this devil have increased in increments equal to the time I spend wasting with you."

"What about these two boys?"

"What about them?" the deputy testily demands.

"They're lost. Maybe cut loose by their folks!" This related, the Kiowa reaches down and unbuttons his pocket and unfolds, presenting the boy's note to the deputy with expectancy that the deputy dodges like a spent bullet before grudgingly grabbing it and reading it.

Later put out at least a week by the Kiowa`s refusal to take no for an answer and fade away as one of the Vanishing Americans should, deputy steps around him and takes a long look at the boys.

"Hell. They're t'eched or something!"

"They're what?"

"Retarded. Do I have to spell it out for you?"

Stepping back. Kuy wonders why he's wasting time here. He had thought beforehand that if he brought two white kids to white justice. They would be taken off of his hands.

Deputy sitting back down. Fixed a long. Dismissive look at the three of them and then offered this advice, "If I was you mister. I would just take them back to where you found them and forget 'em. You don't want to be charged with kidnapping or any such do you?"

Kuy weighs the man's words. Finding them wanting in both wisdom, well as far from reflecting any sense of duty or office. "Can't do that! Look at them. They are half–boiled from sun. Obviously tired out and worn down by thirst and heat!"

Deputy dismisses his comments, took another sheet of paper from a tray and feeds the typewriter all the while suggesting,

"Ok Chief. Listen. I do not know these two kids. Got no circular about missing children. Maybe they are new to these parts. Maybe their folks did just drop them off. I wouldn't lie to you chief. Honest Indian I wouldn't!"

Before more's said the office's door bursts opens and a short man strolls in.

Tall as broad with a short blistering haircut that must have been swiped off a photo of a Prussian officer. Man stops dead in tracks after catching sight of the Kiowa and the two boys. Bugged eyed for more than a minute before turning and giving his deputy what goes on here penny ante place your bets gentlemen whatdasamhillhellnow expectancy concurrently sucking hard on a wad of chew. "And?"

"And nothing sir!"

"What then?"

On the carpet so to speak, Deputy hastily explains the dilemma.

Nonplussed. His boss hawks and then spits a bolt into a metal wastebasket,

"Jiminy Oscar! Can't you handle the office when I am out on the rounds? Was up north dealing with a lot of crazy Mormons out of Utah. Then at the Frazer ranch and now," he pauses and holds up his hands as if Job before spitting another shot of cud while standing in front of the Kiowa with a dime store smile and a click of store bought dentures, "Ok Chief. Tell me—"

Kuy relates his discovery. Points to the deputy; the deputy in turn grimaces again and hands the children's note to the sheriff with a shrug.

Sheriff takes a pair of gold–rimmed glasses out of a case and then gives the note his attention. Finishing reading it, sighs and later turning toward the roadman admits, "Clear case of abandonment. This is a different kettle of fish my find doughty friend. Therefore—"

Out of earshot. Both lawmen confer as if Back Wolf was not in the room or at least shy of english or the sense to follow their conversation,

"What we do?"

"No so loud—"

"Why?"

"Him's a blood. Can't let white children be ferried around with some redskin. No matter if they'd touched. Or retarded. They're still white and he's red!"

"Gotcha Chief. So now what?"

The Sheriff ignores his deputy`s question and walks over to the roadman. Taking his hand, gives it a brisk shake, "Hell Chief. Thanks a million for bringing this problem to our attention. We'll see to its solution sure as sundown."

Kuy frowns. There's a hurt. Some lesson. A miss step going on here but it's too abstract or broad for easy interpretation and guidance. Perhaps too far–reaching for him to fathom and pick out the how and why of it and act accordingly as he should so he sighs, pulls himself upright and makes another stab at it!

"What will happen to them?" he demands worriedly.

"Well Boy. Seeing in ain't any of your concern amigo; we'd rather let the wheels of justice and procedure course along proper and such–"

"Being?"

"Knew right off that you're an Indian with more than two cents aren't you?"

"Listen! My name is George Black Wolf. I am a resident of this state Sheriff and I know the law."

"Figure it was such or another mouthful. Anyway. Good–bye Chief. See you again someday. But between now and then. Don't let the sun go down on you in these parts since we have a low," the Sheriff warns, pausing to glance at his deputy for support and confirmation, "but I got a mighty low tolerance for Indians who don't know their place!"

Kuy looks at the men. Dismisses both with a cutting look. Then walks over to the boys and places his hands on their shoulders while asking, "Want to stay here with these two–men or go with me hons?"

One boy looks at Kuy first, next lawmen before taking his hand and saying, "Go!" Kuy looks down at the other boy. Who after studying his brother. Echoes, his prior sentiment, "Go."

After this, Black Wolf informs the lawmen in a broad troubling af-front, "They want to go with me."

Shaking his head, Sheriff replies, "No Son. They stay here. You got no legality on your side. No sir! They stay put. Might find a place for them at an old spinster's in town till we can sort them out!" After this mouthful, issues a sharp command.

"Oscar. Run over to old Doc Spruel! If he's not too deep in his cups. Tell him to get his fat behind over here on the double! Then head over to O Dell's and order them boys supper before everything closes down!"

Poking a long finger into his nose. Deputy whines, "Who is paying?"

Sheriff scowls then spits again before wearily adding for his deputy's edifi-cation, "And tell that O Dell to charge the county and not stint on the fixings either! Hungry looking things. Sure as hell hope they're house broken!"

Wishing he had had the patience and concern to sort their boys' problem out himself instead of handing them over to an impersonal, unncaring future, the roadman asks himself, but what would he do with them? Take them to Bear Above and Emma's. They have enough trouble with their young ones and don't need more. Despite the fact if asked. They would care for two more until he could figure something else against their law. A growing. Spreading odium of writs, ordinances and probations.

Fed up, Kuy, tips his hat. Wishes the boys good–bye.

Before leaving, takes out wrapped packets of licorice and gives each a fair measure.

Each child clutches his hard–callused hands, while Kuy looks away, exiting expected anon, and summoned ahead as lead actor without script or notes as to particulars.

Chapter Twenty-three

Drawing near to Bear Above's spread, Black Wolf takes account of his encounters with the boys and men like Charlie–with himself as a prime example. Solitary travelers–will–of–the wisps if you will–moving from place to place as opposed to all of the characters. Fine folks and odd balls met over the years with particular destinations or goals such as Phosy and her children, only momentary uprooted, all the while seeking once again to be lodged or potted regardless of the depth of soil or eventual outcome.

Many men, woman rove like wind and rain while others wait stationary as tree or flower. Immobile. Others fleeting. Never meeting except for monetary. Infrequent encounters running the full gamut of human actions and emotions. A sudden kiss or a quick stab in the night unmediated. Disordered actions based on whimsical turns of thought or feeling as unfathomable as a wind's jest or waves toss.

Company rare and thankful for the sporadic and delightful hue and tone companionship presenting itself. A soulful eyed mongrel dog asking for a handout, a lame winged bird huddled in an old cigar box riding beside him, a colored cowpoke or a passing tramp. It does not matter form these allies against sorrow and loneliness take. Behind the wheel. His nights and days are long and often empty. An understanding ear, entertaining quip, or anecdote eases mile's passage and road's slip. Shifting and steering without conscious thought across a backdrop formed by rutted roads, abandoned homes, and barbwire.

Bushwhacked without warning out of the clear, unspoiled halloween

sky as if affronted by a stagecoach bandit from days long gone the roadman starts another set of topics. Attempting to settle numerous tenets
of faith and belief couched by silence the empty road outside his passing
pickup's shadow,

"Listen good *amigo*!"

"What?"

"Not what but who!"

"Who then?"

"Doubt dunderheaded fool! That's who!"

"As I was saying–"

Hijacked with not as much as handswhereicanseeem and monetary
blindsided. Finds footing. Hitting back with hard earned, earnest faith.
If conviction is needed, got it in spades bud!

"Yeah?"

"Yeah!"

Rational hierarchies rounded up from his free ranging clutch of beliefs. Punching 'em along sing song chinaman's,

'Get along little doggy, 'protesting, mooing toward a box canyon of
belief bedrocked with devotion, conviction, ropes and ties theses unruly,
dusty thoughts into a more husbanded and mannered gospel to dissim-
ulate to other men and woman lost without the benefit of any road to
follow.

"No Johnny Appleseed," he corrects with a wry smile. "But maybe.
Just maybe Peyote George or *Seni* George."

All said pulls off his hat. Gives it a quick brush and then sets it back
on his head.

Looking around with a sudden yawn, offers another mote of counsel
to his assembled audience, "Ponder well this! Ever see a child of peculiar
cut set among other yearlings? Say a group forming an association of any
spell. How long will this new comer last? So where this much touted
original sin?" He waits but there's no show of hands or impatient rejoinder from the peanut gallery.

Accordingly with a sad cluck of disappointment, returns to his theme. "This perceived innocence of ours. Gone a missing soon as we crawl and mouth a few words! Our fall from grace? Preached from every pulpit. Once everything was letter perfect and so it should since formed by an almighty and righteous god flawless to a fault and of course little ole us made in his image naturally are the crown of creation and everything other johnny come lately has to suffer as a direct result what we will!

Sorry folks but is the writ of the land! Listen. What instead if we are not failed. Fallen and foul? Ever wonder sometimes if what or who made us did their damnedest. An imperfect god or group rooting around. Playing with earth, sun, and water. Till they molded us as best as they could and then set us down here with the rest of their handy work. If we are indeed made in their image Mr. Wolf, wouldn't this explain a might rate better why everything is so–" and with this final comment. Kuy shuts up. Opens his windows wide as possible. Then steps on the gas, singing several old Kudwa songs taught to him by his father Iron Knife when just a little sir many years ago.

How his father would regard his present life wondering around like tumbleweed in a rich rancher's truck? Would he be pleased or would he instead caution, telling his son to chuck this wayward life, settle down with a good woman.

"There's Velvet! Couldn't find a better," yet Iron Knife never took to spiritual manners beyond necessary and good for his family. He was a warrior and son of the same. Member of a military order old as collective memory.

Kuy steers with a light hand since he's familiar with this route yonder toward scraggy high ground. Off the main road along a long curving track crowned now by distant thunderheads. Driving. Thoughts are consigned to the less secular or commonplace. Old passions and lectures queue up for his edification and contemplation. Spiritual questions and answers creating endless tracts on morality and service.

Some he will use. Others wrestle with him. Engage him. Inspire and taunt his travels. An odyssey crossed and recrossed into its passage forming a living sermon built upon dust, hope and mileage.

Leaving the road, last night and morning's events fade and today's theme is suggested by the living testament of the land passing outside.

It is an old tale with stories gathered and spoken by the earth. Attentive. Listening to endless cycles of legends and stories driving with windows open and the scent of each acre's diversity or dulling monotony flagging every mile.

Land is at war. No agreement exits between old battle grounds, hint of possible reconciliation or any hope for the grace for amalgamation. Out of many one their shiny coins proclaim. But this unity will come at the expense of his People and others of our kind.

Climbing higher into the hills even a fool could see signs of contested cultivation and grazing. "Indian lands!" he hisses. "Not much good bottomland belongs to us. Most of it was stolen piece–by–piece and lie–by–lie.

"Now we are allowed." this spit in contempt, "To squat on the fallow hills and dusty unwanted corners with bitter water. Where only the winds, harsh–fickle sunlight and cold rule."

Off the main road, climbs a shadow–etched prominence before appending,

"Hope Bear Above ain't in one of his crotchety moods. Need someone to talk to." Driving, orderly husbandry stretches as far as sight. Corrals, stock pens. Tilting jakes. Windmills. Occasional farmhouse. Barn or stable till abruptly hidden by cloud of thick dust from a great herd of passing long horns.

Forced to a stop, Kuy halts beside a large horse hitched to heavily loaded wagon also forced to pause. Atop, what surely must have been a cousin of methuselah waits impatiently for this sudden tempest to pass.

It's a couple of hot, watch the clouds minutes before a cowboy rides up.

After taking off his hat, he offers an apology to both men, "Sorry. But this herd's on the way to the railhead and then to Kansas City and big ole Chicago. So might take a while gents. Hell. She's about a mile long," he states with a proprietary grin, "And there ain't no brakes!" simultaneously pondering the tick of time, the trail ahead and chow down toward night.

Bored. With no other option for conversation. Black Wolf passes time with the cowpoke.

Slightly muffled behind his plaid kerchief worn to protect him against the blanket of dust kicked up by the passing cattle. The cowboy asks lazily, "Where you heading Mister?"

"East."

"Me too!"

Black Wolf judging that the young man is no threat relaxes while the cowboy sitting up straight in his saddle gazes over the multitude's wavering. Incalculable backs. Cascading like a slow moving river.

Satisfied all's in order. Man offers a little friendly advice, "Be a while yet. But there's a store up that hill!" he says pointing to an isolated hill or forked cone about a quarter mile down the road behind them, "Grab yourself a cool soda pop or a nice pull of taffy."

Thanking him for the suggestion Kuy locates the aforementioned distant shop. Making a mental appointment to mosey up there later if the wait proves too long.

Swearing and cursing. Mightily irritated by the dust but otherwise not moving or speaking except for the liberal use of red handkerchief rheumy eyed old man on the wagon takes out a block of wood and commences whittling.

Cowboy? With a sharp, "Hah!" disappears with a jab of spur and wave of hat weaving his way carefully through the brown and red dust caked steers.

Getting out to stretch. Black Wolf stands and warmly greets the other waysided traveler, "Heck of a wait!"

His nags up front half maddened by the near stampede, pull and jeri-their hitch, the wagoner takes one sharp look at the Kiowa. Then turns away to focus his sole attention on carving form from his block of wood.

Used to such displays. Kuy shrugs. Decides to hike up the hill and buy a bottle of sassafras soda. He'd rather walk toward a goal. No matter its merit than stay hunkered in his cab choking slowly on dust.

Force meat Contrastingly, old timer throws an occasional clod of clay or earth at the passing cows. An injustice. Since they neither toil for their own benefit. Or desire. But are only meat for the slaughter. Unwilling commerce. Sops for the hungry factory hand. Banker. Cop, whore and others awaiting breakfast. The savory chop. Sunday hash. The grilled patty. Porterhouse cut. Link of sausages. Lard for potatoes. Suet. Kosher dill pickle brisket. Liver and onion hangover cure–all.

***

Aforementioned store crouched atop a small rounded hill. To reach it. Kuy follows a worn. Dry grass edged path to its summit and surveys the land. A small smoothed hallow. Split down the middle by a narrow and crumbling ravine of raw, red clay with a lone pine leaning at an angle from its anchorage.

Ruefully asking who would start a business here. But at lost to the endless tragedy or triumph of human endeavors. Shakes his head and later kicks a stone down the side of the hill. Watching its rapid descent, he's satisfied that ole newton was right about sumpton after all.

Joint's round. Made of rough–hewn planks. With a low. Wooden roof. No windows. Just a wide door fringed by long lather strips to fend off flies.

Ancient, gender unsure, rocks slowly in a padded rocker, letting sun warm bones. Soaking rheumatism in the late daylight.

He says "Howdy," then studied the figure in the rocker.

Poor thing, it's a dame after all. Blind with cataracts. Maimed by a stroke or similar malady, turning her into a choking and spitting machine with an occasional bark or distempered whimper.

Inside there's a small front room stuffed with the usual merchandise. Canned food. Dry goods. A bottle or two. Pickles. Kerosene. Lye soap and other useful products, all covered in a film of dust as if customers rare or overly particular.

His every step after he entered had been closely watched by an enormous woman with displeasure or unease sure as an excise tax stamping her meaty face.

Big girl had little or no femininity aside from secondary sexual characteristics, equally denied by the roped muscle on her bare arms and the heft of her bulky shoulders.

In a beat up crate. Young child. Maybe two or three plays with a rag doll made of a torn sock or scrap material. Suggesting fecundity. Yet on closer inspection Black Wolf doubts there is any link between youngster and woman waiting silently behind the counter.

Geetchegood. Child pays no mind. Maybe it's afflicted too the roadman infers sadly before turning his attention back to the proprietress to ask for a bottle of pop.

Blinked eyes but served up no other reaction except a sour smile and the 'get thee gone in a heartbeat—we don't serve your kind here' well as other, yet equally tangible signposts of bigotry, and racial hatred and as if to emphasize her line of reasoning, the proprietress points to a crudely lettered sign over the door that he had failed to notice before.

NO INDIANS OR COLORED SERVED HERE!

Kuy ignoring her and the sign calls again for a soft drink to slake thirst as the interior's dappled light, cut by a cloud's passage, flattens, filters, and darkens into solemn failure like a failing wick.

Proprietress? Ignores him and stalks away to stand by the front door. Shooing flies way from the old woman.

Given the cold shoulder—and partial to grand finales, Kuy exits leisurely after a quick salute. The older dame's muffled cries following downward like the lament of an evil spirit.

Horizon? Least a good twenty—five miles or more away and the wichita mountains are now only a blue haze, marking his goal.

Off the hill with about a quarter of the herd still yet to pass, Kuy finds a gentle slope and sits in its shade before snatching a blade of grass to chew on. Contentedly watching dust clouds write anew across otherwise a clear blue sky until the last of the herd cleared the two–lane and he returned to his truck. Beside it, on the wagon's buckboard, the old man snores while at his side as if sharing his *siesta*, a half completed figure study of a nude woman resting in her bedding of shavings.

Realizing that this great herd possesses enough meat to feed all of his people for years, perhaps even a decade and that this long train of cattle is but a day or two's partial rations for chicago and the large cities of the east he bows his head asking,

"How could we have thought to oppose so many," prior to answering his own question, "What other choice did we have?"

Chapter Twenty-four

Subtle signs denote change of ownership. White farms to land owned or leased by his People or other tribes. Stock fewer in number. Whites like fat animals needing a lot of feed and range while the People favor tough, stunted animals that live on scrub and little water.

Native land is tilled differently as well. Whites like order and straight lines. The People follow nature's guidelines. Disliking straight artificial geometry scarring the land.

Nor throw anything away. As with the animals hunted and herded–butchered–utilized, even the sinews, teeth and for this reason a broken wheel or harness is a resource needed in the future.

Scrutinizing homestead coming into view framed, by early evening's gentle light and a warm haze, the roadman slows down to better study his friend's ranch.

It's a wild and unsettled–though solid smallholding surrounded by gardens. Fenced by dwarf, wind twisted pines. All in all, his old friend's accomplishment commands the crest. Resting as a jewel in a king's crown.

Feral dogs arching their mangy backs. Bark. Whine as his Hercules passes the ranch' gates.

Not to be left out, nanny goats and tawny limbed lambs stir from boredom to watch the proceedings, well proud roosters heralding too his arrival.

Moreover, milling children end game, adding to sudden, startled vigilance. Wary and hopeful, for trouble comes from the road, yet did the rare breaks in conformity and dull routine.

Smiling. Black Wolf grabs his saddlebags, gets out, first soothing dogs.

Mongrels. All sizes and colors, wagging tails (if luckily still possessing), waving hot pink tongues.

Two kids. Twins. A sister and a brother. Flock over hungry for novelty—lonely for company since they have known and loved him from his past visits.

Conscious this visitor usually carries (if only black licorice ropes) store bought candy in his big saddlebags both children pout and prance for attention.

"Where's your papa," the roadman asks.

Hickory stick thin and just as tough, kids don't answer until the girl shyly glances at her brother answering softly with her dark eyes focused somewhere beyond them,

"Oh him. Kone-gyah-daw-kue'! He's back in the barn with a sick horse. Want me to go and get him for you?"

"No, don't bother. I will go back there and see if can give him a hand."

After more shy glances, Sister asks for candy. Black Wolf hands over a bag of licorice for both to share. Then straightens his hat and waves them on, heading toward the back of their house down a trail of gravel bordered by tall weeds, giant and gaunt sunflowers, rusted toys, empty bottles and various types of cast off farm equipment.

"Is this a taste of our future? A slow partial assimilation into otherness or will salvation be possible for our People? We are not like the Cherokee or Seminole. Never have been many of us. Woman got stuck and the Kudwa have paid the price ever since!"

After almost tripping over a pile of cans, angrily, he kicks a rusted tin can into a sumac bush with a curse, "Old damned metal!"

Later, "Let's see what Bear Above is up to!"

Walking up to the barn he shouts, "Bear Above. Are you around? Company!"

Before echoes of Kuy's shout fade, a harsh male voice answers,

"I'm in the back. Trying to put a cure on my mare's leg. Come on back!"

Following his friend's voice, he ducks through the barn's low doorway. Hard to make anything out despite light seeping in through chinked walls.

Locating Bear Above holding the neck of a large red mare, Kuy meets his friend's gaze over the arched back of large red colored mare.

"Damn horse has got a deep cut on her leg. Now she might lose it!"

Kuy gives Bear Above a rough hug.

He is a barrow shaped man. Head shaped like a block of hard wood sparing him a quick smile before turning attention back to his mare.

"Been like this for a few days. Nothing I know seems to do the trick. You were always good with horses. What do you think?" Bear Above asks, pointing to the wounded horse's leg.

Nodding, Kuy steadies the mare, carefully inspecting her flank. Soothing her with soft and caring endearments, discovers that there is a nasty gash on the horse's left leg. Looks dangerous. Very irritated. Bright red and blue with infection.

Whistling, the roadman pats the old girl and essays his opinion, "Well. Looks like she cut herself on some old iron hereabouts. You'll have to soak the pain and infection out. I have something back in the truck with me. I will see to it."

"Thanks," Bear Above says relieved at Kuy's offer.

"It was nothing. But you know I did not come here to see about your livestock."

"Don't jaw nonsense."

"I came to set you and your boys on the righteous path!"

"Kone-gyah-daw-kue'. You mean a ceremony. I never had much track with any religion white or red."

"It's more than religion!" Kuy retorts. "It is salvation. For me—for you. For your children. The twins out front. Emma and your other boys and girls! Perhaps salvation enough to last us until these hard times pass."

"Yeah. Well maybe tomorrow night. Can you stay till then? I got good deer laid up on a hook for supper—"

Asked, roadman watches Bear Above's eyes. Light and spark, displaying several emotions simultaneously like a hooded oil lamp on a gusty night. Layers of complexity hard to read or even acknowledge.

Ranging from ill humor to a suppressed friendship of long standing.

Satisfied his friend's words are heartfelt, Kuy replies, "Sure."

"Emma's not here at the moment but she will be along shortly. She's bringing up some apples from an old Indian orchid down the road on the sly since its ownership is contested between me and another rancher—more about this later. My wife is probably gossiping with one of our lady neighbors. Confound them! I suppose some of her fretting made it back to those old army blankets you call friends—"

The roadman shrugs, remaining silent.

"Well don't believe half about old woman's gossip you've heard—like I'm on the warpath or that my older sons drink up a sergeant's bounty every night in town. Not true!"

"Glad to hear it!"

"You betcha! Please see what you can do about the horse!" Bear Above implores and after shoveling his large hands into his pockets. Adds, "Getting chilly. October can start off mean around here with those wichita winds blowing of their tops and coming down here this time of the year. I'm going to lay a fire in the kitchen and start seeing to supper."

"Ok. Where are your doctoring materials?" the roadman asks.

"Over their on that shelf to right," Bear Above answers, pointing out the direction. Kuy nods and gets to work as his large friend walks out the door toward the main house.

After fetching additional medicines from truck, Kuy tends to the mare's leg while outside, a stiff wind springs from nowhere rattling the barn. Its sudden draft makes him shiver. Setting down a bottle of iodine, pain shoots up and down his left arm followed by a general numbness on the same side.

"Must be old age knocking." Ignoring the discomfort, returns his attention back to the mare since she surely must be in worse shape than he is.

Afterwards tired from driving and horse doctoring sits on Bear Above's wood and stone front porch with a mason jar of cool water watching *Pay* set and blue foxed shadows seal the valley below.

His left side feels particular well as left arm. Numbed as if pain felt earlier scalded or branded him with its sigil. "Yet it eases and this too shall pass."

Early candlelight and his friend's children play in the glow of a swaying kerosene lamp, Kuy, remembering his responsibility, turns toward them beckoning the twins over. Once at his side they beg the roadman, "Come on, you gonn'a tell us one of your stories?"

Frowning in mock puzzlement, Kuy asks, "Stories. Do I look like a man to waste time with stories?"

"Yes sir!"

"Well," he says watching night chase day, "what type?"

"A scary story!"

"A sad story?" Bear Above's little girl, Small Flower pleads, shyly rubbing a long stalked cornflower on his knee.

"Hmm. Many stories here. Swarming around under here," he says tapping his forehead, "Let's see." While he considers, a breeze passes by. Says hello, bringing evening's deepening chill. Suddenly ice-cold, Kuy buttons his jacket even as the children close around him.

Of all of the yarns, which one should he recite? Something purely entertaining a waste of time. An instructional tale?

Beyond the windbreaks. Screech owl emboldened by dusk cries out. Ignored by the children. Owl continues to hoot.

The roadman exhibits no response but is aware of its too close proximity.

"Come on Kone-gyah-daw-kue'! Hurry!" the children beg.

"Ok. Listen chickabiddies! This is one of our stories from long ago. It's named. "How White Crow Hid the Animals." This stated, clears voice, sets glass down and begins,

Stories, myths, legends, tall tales, the lifeblood of a people and once lost or solely the property of collectors, no more than disembodied codification of everything they once represented like the mysterious imprint of an ancient hand stamped in once living blood-

"People starved. All of the animals disappeared. Cold winter near." A little like now the roadman frets, yet continues for the children's sake, "The People believed a *dohate* or medicine man was responsible. But who?

Among them was White Crow. A man who lived apart. Both good and bad he loved animals above all except for his only daughter. Had a stingy streak wanting all of the riches gathered from the animals around him.

Not ordinary either." Kuy explains. Fixing his eyes upon them, drawing out his words. "No. A shape shifter. Do you know what a shape shifter is *SyH–n*," he asks.

Little Flower shakes her head.

"Well," Kuy continues, "A shape shifter is a man or woman that can change their form. Explained, clears his throat, continuing "White Crow could change into a white bird and fly very high–seeing all and talking to all the buffalo and other animals.

Got worse. Village moved many times but bad luck followed. Desperate. They sought council. Coyote rejoined them. Wanted to talk– to smoke and gossip, tired of the endless prairie, too silent nights with only the moon and stars to chew the fat with."

Bear Above's children laugh at his imaginative invocation of loneliness. So he pauses. Beaming a smile of encouragement, rewarding their appreciation. Then starts again,

"At first. Had trouble relearning human speech. Few nights among the warmth of and chatter of the people. Could talk again. When the people asked him for help. He weighed their options. Deciding to help, asked for scouts."

All play acting stops quickly as a pin prick. Why? A burning numbness hits his left side. Well up and down his arm. Especially under his armpit.

Concerned. Cuts off the story. Catching his breath. Kuy continues. Hiding fatigue, soreness–

As this recitation continues, *'n–hH'–dei –mH–e* and his wife Emma quietly walk up to their children's side, listening to the end of roadman's story.

Almost as tall as her husband. Emma possessed the remnants of a gentle, delicate beauty tempered by hard work and childbirth.

Her dark eyes brighten when she catches the thread of Black Wolf's narration. Reclaiming girlhood memories of this tale told on cold, nights, she smiles and places her arms around her husband.

Kuy notices his host's look of disapproval but ignores it, pausing for a moment to great Emma, "I can always tell those who are fond of the old stories and those–," he adds giving Bear Above a hard glance, "have no use for them. I might have some of the yellow kid's comics back in the truck for your husband Emma; really more his speed!"

Bear Above says nothing. Merely frowns.

"How are you *Kone-gyah-daw-kue*?" Emma asks with a wan smile acknowledging her husband usual boorishness.

Before replying, the roadman notices that she looks tired and preoccupied. "Fine and you?" Kuy answers, including a courtly compliment, "and you are as beautiful and as gracious a hostess as always."

"O you!" Emma replies demurely. Embarrassed as always by chivalrous compliments, she deflects any attention directed toward her, "Really! You two men go on while I finish up supper."

Both men bow as she as she steps off the porch back into their detached kitchen while Kuy continues the conclusion of his story–

***

"Coyote was extremely angry. He shouted at Spider Woman. How could you allow our enemy to escape? Upset. She looked down at her long arms and noticed that one web was still attached to their fleeing captive.

Forgive me Coyote; I can bring him down and she did. Once recaptured there was no mercy. The villagers gathered firewood. Lit a great bonfire and roasted While Crow like a shank meat till he shrank and blackened.

Finally. People pitied him and released him.

As he fled into dark, moonless night, coyote taunted,

'Go no! But you are now without the power to harm anyone. Spend this seasons and every after scavenging. Always afraid–a friend to none–with all hands against you.'

White Crow sadly diminished and scorched by cruel fire. Croaked and then angrily flew away after a final curse–"

Delighted. The children immediately beg for another. Black Wolf shakes his head, picks up his glass and takes a long, needed drink. Looking away before adding, "Another time–children–another time. *GyH–heJteii–dcc*," he gently dissuades.

Bear Above clasps him on the shoulder yet there is no merriment in his eyes. "These old legends are worth as much as a Sears and Roebuck catalog out of reach in the outhouse."

"You didn't think or say such things when we were locked up together in fort marion. You know that these stories are the heart of our people."

Stifling a sudden yawn, Bear Above counters, "Yeah. Like those pictures whites take of us. Dressed up like the dead with our exhausted. Hungry faces pressed into smiles!"

Recalling similar occurrences, Kuy argues, "Right or like the stuffed animals in their exhibits that I once saw in washington. Listen. If we do not keep our traditions and language alive–won't we become like those poor souls in their photographs or dressed animals pressed behind glass?"

"Maybe. But I have a family now and all of our promises made in florida seem empty and from a time long passed. See friend. Emma as you know is a Comanche and white. So we talk english mostly. Our kids know a little of both of languages but to what point?"

"To keep our language alive," Black Wolf suggests sadly.

"Are right. Call me a back slider but–"

"I will!" the roadman chastises. "You know brother. I have noticed a funny–well a strange occurrence as of late."

"What?" his friend asks.

"I discovered that I have become a man of many parts or even different men depending on where I am and whom I am with."

"How so?"

"When I'm with whites. I act like them. Speak their words Think their thoughts! Recently. I worked in a carnival and later helped out a mother and her two kids. In both instances. I was less Black Wolf and more George. Each fragment of myself could interact with these outsiders and yet observe and judge all of the different. Conflicting emotions and thoughts tangled inside," he confesses while taking off his hat and smoothing down his hair before continuing, "And still return to me. *Néín*–myself and I."

"You're just adapting! Dodging like Coyote when he needed to pull a fast one."

"Ah, you listened to more of my story than you admit *'n–hH'–dei –mH–e!*"

"Your story!" Exclaims Bear Above loudly, "my mother told me that one–long before our sorry assess met in that tiny cell, besides," he reasons with a worried smile, "what other option besides blending in with them is there?"

"But I'm worried. I came across this broken down old gin rummy. A Kiowa but lives apart from any us. I spoke almost nothing but english with him and hardly a word of our language. If we slip and fall," the roadman frowns. Expressing worry and a deep fear. "What hope of our children and those that come after us?"

"I don't know. There's only so much we can do!"

"This is true but I fear that all of this will lead to the loss of who we are or were and once we lose our identity–there is no going back!"

"Too deep for me–"

Emma calls them from the kitchen.

Distracted. Both men fall silent yet still sticking to contradicting viewpoints.

"Hungry?" His friend asks before adding, "Let's eat! Everyone to the taaaabbbbble!"

The twins. Excitedly bolt toward the kitchen's soft light and warmth. Behind the two men glance at each other then single file into the kitchen.

A split pine room crowded by oak table, filled with the delicious warmth from a glowing cast iron stove.

Invited to sit at the head of the table, after glancing around the table, Kuy remembers that *'n–hH'–dei –mH–e*'s family eats in shifts because of the many children.

Outside, night grows cold fast as a falling man. But inside scented with white pine smoke, the stove spreads a delicious heat in contrast. With no electricity, kerosene lamps adding to the inviting setting with light, warm, hazy, with an impeccable radiance hopeful as a new sunrise.

Despite their fuzzy wicks and smoke, the roadman knows of no better way to get cozy. Nor food any better when cooked over a wood fire.

Settling down. Kuy didn't speak. Just listened to routine bustle unfolding around him. Happy to be among friends.

First. Bear Above's spouse, Emma and her daughters serve the men. Bustling to and from the wood fed stove to table bringing large blue enamel platters, filling the men and older boy's cups with fresh brewed coffee, before serving large bowls of roasted pinion nuts, pinto bean soup, deer meat tamales. For a final flourish, baked, red–cheeked apples covered with drizzled molasses and more coffee.

Meal's one for silence. The amount of food is a novelty. Reserved for special occasions.

Emma. Glad to serve an old friend her kitchen's best, lays out as much as her family and valued guest want without stint. So each tucks in saving words for later.

Smaller children watch expectantly from a doorway restlessly waiting for their turn at the table.

Oldest son. Running Legs. A surly tall youth. Laughs all too frequently at the roadman's questions slumped at the table with his brothers, wrinkling his eyes at his father and the priest when he's certain no one watches.

Running Legs bides his time to escape down the valley where other inducements to a free spirited young man wait.

Emma. Attentive to all of the nuances in her kitchen. Promises with a flash of her eyes and a stern look of disprovable to set matters straight afterward.

When the roadman engages him in conversation, Running Legs is evasive. Unfortunately Bear Above's other sons follow suit. Seeing how things are around here, Kuy sets his plate aside and addresses his friend's firstborn, "Listen. I want you to help me hold a Peyote ceremony tomorrow night."

Running Legs moans, "Those ceremonies are a waste of time! Right Pop?"

Bear Above looks away. Flashing an embarrassed grin before addressing his eldest, "Well. It won't hurt us any. Listen. Running Legs. With the trouble you have been rooting for. It can't hurt any!"

Young man laughs and gets up informing his father before leaving, "Have to see to the stock. Nice to see you again reverend!" he avers cynically before walking quickly out the kitchen door into the yard outside.

After he leaves, Bear Above turns to his other sons with a stern charge, "I expect all of you to be here tomorrow night!"

They groan but agree to stay around, hurriedly finishing their meal and clearing the table so the woman and children can eat.

Stepping outside, Kuy and Bear Above retire to the front porch. Chilly outside. Accordingly, Bear Above grabs two horse blankets, motioning the roadman to sit down in one of his hand carved rockers facing valley below. Lighting a lamp, coaxing flame till the porch is softly illuminated.

Stars circle in old dance. Unseen but sensed, long nosed bats glides across the porch into the barn's rafters while beneath a few lights glint and twinkle in upward swelling mists below.

Gesturing toward distant nearly hidden mountains, sloping valleys around them as twilight vanishes like a tired ghost, Bear Above points out a few landmarks around them, "That's mount scott over there. But you know that don't you storyteller. Wise man—*tsHhy–Hp–kiH.*"

The roadman nods, replying light heartedly, "Yes. But not as well as you!"

Retorting, Bear Above snorts, adding, "Out there. There's a lot of buried treasure. Comanche. Kiowa and even a hoard of gold and bank notes left by jesse james."

"I always admired him," the roadman adds, "Even though he and his brothers were white."

"Yeah me too," his friend reluctantly agrees. "Anyway. I once acted as a guide for teddy roosevelt when there were plenty of elk about.

"What was he like?" Black Wolf asks.

"Oh about what you would guess a shrewd and rough customer?"

"Shoot any?"

"A few. But I feel bad about that hunt now but I really needed the money! It helped to build this house and buy the first of my stock and our first milk cow. Hell! Emma and I really needed her when the first of our kids came around. A real thirsty bunch. Bear Above recalls with a happy grin before remarking with a change of topic–

"He's buried close–"

"Who are you talking about old cell mate? Jailbird. Felon–trickster– are you alluding to Lone Wolf's grave?"

His friend smiles bitterly at Black Wolf's jibe, then replies with a little sarcasm of his own, "No! Parker."

"My friend and teacher?"

"Yes and his great cabin."

"Star House?"

"Yes. It is not too far from here."

"Visited there though it was years ago. Parker and I differed on opinion on a lot of things. Unfortunately. I hadn't seen him for a spell before he died; now I regret it." Distracted. Listening to a night bird's call, the other Kudwa remarks abstractedly. Even as he again points to the shrouded mountains and hills cradling his farm, "Remember the time we found that dead wild cat's carcass?"

"How could I forget?"

"Yeah. The stink alone–we chased all the kids around–especially the girls–swinging it around like a war lasso–"

"Till the tail snapped off and the rotting cat spun off into a ditch," Black Wolf adds. Recalling that day, he contributes a further reminiscence. "We had them running around like a cyclone. Hell my daddy and mother did not speak to me or allow me to ride my horse for a week when they learned about our prank from other parents!"

Listening. Bear Above's smile fades. Stiffening he addresses the roadman with a long simmering grievance, "You changed a lot after sleeping on war shields and listening to old male witches–"

"I had lessons to learn from my father and other *Q–gop*–men"

"*Dwdw*?"

"*Doi*! You mean? Shield medicine bought and planked with pain."

"All of those vision quests and self–mutilation. Worth it?"

Black Wolf only nods as Bear Above continues, "All of which. By the way old friend–turned your head and filled you with a lot of nonsense. You're far from the man I once knew. A man I could share a drink with. Play cards. Go rooting for gals with during our bachelor runs," Bear Above accuses bitterly. "Left me hanging old friend!"

"So that's–"

"Yeah–"

"You knew me then. Remember who I was. What I was. Did I have another choice?" the roadman beseeches.

Pausing his harangue, Bear Above gazes at his friend for a long time before answering, "No. Not after your wife and child died and after you and Old Smoke burnt your farm down. I looked for you. But couldn't track you down! Besides, the way you were running yourself ragged. You would have either been hung by the neck or in one of their stockades rotting for life."

Abruptly. A large shadow whirls around Bear Above's head. Startled. He exclaims and swats at the unknown intruder.

Laughing at his friend's battle with their unexpected visitor. Black Wolf motions for Bear Above not to hurt the silent trespasser that on closer inspection proves to be a large ragged, chocolate colored moth fluttering by the kerosene lamp by their side.

Its wayward intrusion captures Bear Above's attention momentarily away from his contemplation. Tries to bat it away but hesitates when the roadman stops him with a shout, "No!"

"*Dwdw?*"

"*Doi*! Don't hurt it!"

Cupping the moth in his hand, Kuy continues, "He or she is old and trail worn," while gently holding it outward in his hand, "Take a gander!"

Both men examine the large brown moth crawling on the roadman's open palm. Its battered wings, marbled and thin as tissue are scarred by experience–a cat's claw, a cardinal's beak, possibly a rival's sudden lunge.

Later the moth slowly climbs the ridge of Kuy's thumb, very carefully with its feathered antenna sounding the way ahead prudent as an old warrior trying not to slip on an icy pond when fish are wanted.

"A great grandmother or grandfather. Many songs and battles it has known. Perhaps many children and grandchildren," Kuy says holding the insect close to his friend, "Would you kill it?"

Bear Above shakes his head. Then answers, "Not if you insist but it's a black witch. Unlucky thing to be hanging around–" he grumbles, adding, "and it eats clothes. Emma hates them!"

The roadman laughs at his friend's vehemence, "*Mariposa de la Muerte*. How could anyone hate this little foil of life–so beautiful?"

Bear Above always the most prudent of the two, switches their conversation back to more earthly concerns–by pointing out the dark, misting land about them, "Old mountains," he remarks knowledgeably, "Maybe some of the oldest around. Not getting any younger felon. Do you know that they reseeded the buffalo in these valleys around these parts seven years ago," he pauses a minute, smoothing down short grizzled hair. Before continuing with a dry chuckle, "Which is funny since our old people believe that the last of them hoary old bisons hid themselves here inside mount scott. There's still a scarcity of land here abouts. A lot of it seized by the government!"

"To hold in a trust?"

"Yeah but for whom? Not for us!" his friend remarks bitterly. Then, pointing to a few twinkling lights below, continues a confession of doubts and hopes, "See those lights down there?

"Yes?"

"They're electric. But the line ends down there. I want to install a windmill up here to power a generator. It would help the twins do their homework without excuses," Bear Above states determinedly, "and makes life up here a little easier. Read about how it all works and points of installation in a magazine–"

"Wind's always blowing up here," the roadman remarks off–handedly and then sits up straight in the wooden rocker with a long sigh.

"What's the matter?" Bear Above asks worriedly, "Feeling Ok?"

The roadman weighs his answer before replying, "Feel'n all used up sometimes. Heart maybe–"

"*T'ein–houdl–dH*? Like your father?"

"Hope not!"

"Well," Bear Above advises, "Find a doctor old friend!"

"A white doctor? White medicine. With their pills. Tonics and patent medicine swindles and dollar a bottle opiates–thank not!" Kuy argues, "I don't want to be one of those reservation walking dead sitting in shade taking another spoonful of medicine every hour or two passing the day away. I have too much to do! Places and people to see!"

"And if you die?"

The roadman shrugs, changing tack to explain why he's here sitting on his front porch, "Well. I didn't come for a geography. Or history lesson! And for the record–medical advice neither–"

"Yeah. I know, "Bear Above growls, "What did you come around for? I know you like Emma's cooking but when a priest like you noses around–"

"Time to set the china!"

"Now listen–"

The roadman interrupts getting to the point, "Like White Crow.

Your oldest is looking for trouble;" the roadman warns. Then asks softly, "What goes on here?"

Bear Above sighs. Then answers–"Well. You know how it is. They're young. Isn't anything here for them. They hate school! Everything they are or know is criticized or belittled; my oldest just feels all of this. Strongly! What else can he do?"

Sympathetically, after listening, Kuy advises his friend, "He must stay away from white trouble. They just wait and lay the pressure on. Like the old days when we would force game into an ever–tightening circle. Remember how the animals fought and trampled each other?"

Put out–Bear Above demands, "You came all this way to tell me this?"

"No. I am going to try to get your family settled here! There is a lot of talk–gossip–about trouble here."

"Well. This white rancher. Mitchell; a real hard case, claims some of my bottomland. He has taken me to court but his claim is so bad even our local judge threw out his case. But this has not slowed him any. Before Mitchell bought this land. The old owner was a fair man. He had no problems with me. We would cross his land–a short cut to town–but now–Mitchell just looks for any excuse to start trouble. He has a bunch of boys and girls too. Funny *Kuy!* When they were all children they all played and ran together. But when they got older.

"Trouble?"

"Yeah. Every week! Sometimes I do not know what to do."

"Well. You have to hold on. What other choice do you have?"

"I know but–"

"Listen; there is no way to fight this rancher. The law is his. I am surprised you weren't ruined in court. I can only help with a blessing. Prayers. You have to find the strength for you and your family to resist. You and your boys have to learn to step around trouble. Not through it."

"I know. But it is hard. My daddy had this land since Red River days. It's funny. He would not bide the reservation. He was one of the first to jump at the agents' offer for resettlement. Now look at me!" he carps, at the same time indicating the land around them with a broad swing of his right arm.

"Quiet! You are doing well. I left hunger and sorrow behind and others of our people have nothing!" and to emphasize his point, the roadman spreads his hand in a wide arc before stating, "Look at all that you have!"

Bear Above nods before pleading, I know. But can I hold it for my children?"

"Yes. If you find the patience and calm down. I will help you. Well you have a ceremony tomorrow night?"

"If you insist."

"Then we have hope. Hand me your blanket. How's your straw?"

"Fresh and turned yesterday."

"Goodnight."

"Thanks for coming. Tomorrow. Feel better—"

Chapter Twenty-five

Oftentimes Night is beautiful, not only to its poets but for its renegades as well. Stung by serial betrayal and long spells of wasting regret. Men and woman. Fate's stalwarts. Horned and whetted by loss, sometimes acquire or grow appreciative of what the more fortunate ignore.

"Much as a girl's throat, night's sleek and long—" the Comanche says, and then focusing on nightfall. Not wanting to be overheard sprouting claptrap. Why thoughtlessly contradict an otherwise hard as nails façade Twice Born asks, cutting such fiddlefaddles with an open ended chuckle, "Not calm. Nor at rest. Night's hungry. Whether for food. Sex. Violence. Or just outright murder!"

Afterward this longhaired, scarred, slouched hatted errant shuts up. Then takes out a rolled, roughed up journal out of a sack while overhead sun slowly extinguishes like a five dollar lamp with a failing wick.

Unrolling his special entertainment for the evening, a copy of the British medical magazine the "Lancet" stolen from a druggist's magazine rack. He regrets that it's too dark to make out better its illustrations and all too rare photographs. O he's a caution all right! Most men get a kick and a holler glancing at half nude or postcard dainties, given the slobbering stare like reticent larking mooncalves. Not he. No siree bob! Something about detailed illustrations and black and whites of various maladies or diseases give him a drunk in clover thrill. Especially newer photos showing war wounds.

"All mighty," he muses, "Maybe I should have been a doc, handy as I am with the blade and saw!"

Nearby, shrouded by day's ghost, a few small brown featured birds turn, roll, and hide from each other like children at play. Later they land at his feet expectant, unafraid but having nothing to offer them. Not even a smile; Twice Born watches them for a moment. Then grunts, turns away.

Following additional soundings, memory clamps jaw, creased into a long cruel smile, a lick of dry chapped lip and narrowing of eye quick as passing shadow equal to their swarthy cousins dancing behind his veiled eyes,

"Dark and pretty notions," Twice Born mutters, setting deliberations on cruelty gone a skidder. Too much hate and acrimony. Odium consuming untended fire or undiluted lye slewing questions like riled hornets.

Tribes furrowed under as if never except for well-crafted flint chanced upon after rains had softened the fields. Or a well-made basket. Woven blanket. Mold darkened and eaten by hungry worm.

Suffered his family. Extended. Clan as well. Older brothers dead and better so. Mother taken by a fever no one had a name for. Father locked up and the key thrown away till cast into a urine slicked alley like a spindly legged slunk to die. Handsome uncles? Tambien! Racked by coughs. Pool sticks on a billiard hall's wall.

"The dead," Twice Born summarizes," walk elsewhere!" This said, with a roll of wary eye, changes the subject, "Feel more alive when everyone's asleep!"

Alone or with his band of brothers and sisters. Night is silent, blurred shadow larked by day.

Later. Carefully balanced on the balls of his feet. Twice Born stalks down a dead one street town lacking even a candle's flicker hint of habitation. Just as well since he and the town's sheriff have a long and bitter history between them. If less proud and ornery, he would avoid this dead on a stick hamlet altogether.

Hating piss fenced lockups more than average. Incarcerated, simply stares ahead. Baited by occupants. Expresses contempt with a barely suppressed snarl. Sentenced to hard labor in lieu of fine. Just grins. Disappearing the first or second day. There's not a man that can track him.

Up ungentle hill the ramshackle township recedes as brisk up moon sneaks over his broad shoulders with a peekaboo glint. Another of her assorted tricks.

"Never liked her much! Why? Tell you why! She's a rich man's friend. Always on the lookout for mischief and trouble!" he adds, "Night's best when absolute. Without even a spark to mar its perfection."

A trip by steamer to sweltering new york city carrying former prisoners on a "shock and awe tour." Its purported purpose to introduce newly freed indigenous prisoners of war to the civilizing aspects of american culture and society, though its actual slant was grinding their faces into their unworthiness and ignorance. While hoping to amaze and disconcert them with the might of their conquerors' workings.

Gathering makings of fire, Twice Born recalls that day a thousand or more evenings ago.

A tour of museums. Musical revue.

"The Works," in other parlance followed.

Twice Born, unlike his companions, wasn't dismayed. Swayed. Or given to even a sliver of awe. On the contrary. Viewing what was before him from the steeple of trinity church. Lights thicker than stars. More people than fleas on a hound. Endless buildings like forests. He formed a resolve that come what may, he'd stop this even if it killed him.

Dickens is that he entertains several affinities roughly based on half–truths and penny dreadful writers' notions. Centering on slide and pitch patterns of advancement and retreat.

Zigzag, counter clock patterns repeated frequently to the dismay and eventual disdain of companions however brief of duration. Doesn't care a tinker's damn really. Concentrates catching fragments. Battle savvy. Stealth. Evasion techniques, detained by swollen jointed sinews, thinning, brittle connective tissue, and aging synapse passing from collective memory until sparked into remembrance by porknbeans, a bottle, sometimes just a morsel of companionship or quiet solitude on a cold barren night.

Walking. Sketches a tentative outline for his proposed guerrilla movement, religious crusade against assimilation's slow withering, genocide and condemnation.

Later paused against a large boulder, eyes expand yet close. Evening's dimming off. Turning inward toward richer, if slightly selfish, secretive dominions shadowed by desire and revenge.

While like a good and industrious clerk, tallies his ledger of debits and credit with a hard–edged smile not cruel but calculating under furrowed, creased brow.

An aggressive wind, no friend to a lone man walking on a darkening night, springs out of nowhere.

Shivering. He steps into a grove of wind bent trees, unslinging a bag from his shoulder. One carefully placed a considerable distance from him after weighing it with two large rocks.

There's a hushed stillness. Or expectancy within followed by a brief warning rattle.

Man smiles. Gives the sack a quick, vicious kick with his boot. Along with a warning equally daunting,

"Rest now or it is rattler chili since it's cold and my belly's pinching my backside."

True and for the hundredth time he longs for a cup of coffee. A smoke. A decent meal. A woman. All put aside for redemption. Not one christians would recognize or even label as so. One older. Darker. Couched on blood and sacrifice. Burnt offerings, darkness, and not the light of day, outlying, unseen by waking men and woman, excepting visions, dreams, and nightmares.

After grabbing a handful of dandelions, pulls wilted flowers off their tops. Brushes the dirt away, eating the stems with noted lack of enthusiasm, his jaw stubbornly chewing and swallowing the dull, slightly peppery bolus before gagging.

The half masticated mass comes back up but he mulishly resists and scoops the flowers up and chews them for a second time till they obey and are successfully swallowed.

Sharp as vinegar. Wind draws his fire away. Wishes he could have seasoned his supper with it but now it is too late.

Gust cries with many a voice. Songs and tales but he chooses not to listen. Not for him. Instead. He shrugs and looks away into the gathering darkness shouting angrily,

"Why I am barkin' at a knot?" Posed with a quick frown, knotting of fingers and finally a sharp tilt of his head as he comments sadly, "Most tribes have had the dander and fight kicked out of them!"

That's so?

The Comanche takes a deep breath. Then essays on the matter,

"Dress white. Talk white. Try to act white! Never the less we are never accepted as equal unless it is for some onerous task such as filling the ranks of khaki clad cannon fodder freighted eight tiered to fight the Spanish or Moro!"

Lightly veiled by passing clouds or dark blue mists. Moonlit trees rattle and sigh with each passing gust. Something old here. Not friendly or welcoming. Probably why it is deserted. He's aware of this but Comanches have always been pragmatist when it came to religion. Almost worshiped the horses that gave them freedom to roam unhindered but then did not. The sky. The hunt too. But no. Not even the land. Which shaped them.

Commenting sagely, "Them old greeks had a notion or two worth considering with their god pan. Ole goat would probably feel at home in a place like this," he suggests while watching the wind shift toward the north without even a goodbye or a catch you later.

Now sicked on another track, ignores magician's tricks to concentrate on a more immediate campaign,

"This Kiowa. Wonder if he and I will agree or have to slug it out. Early christians. Did they wallop each other over points of contention? Argue reverent questions and answers. Then coil and twine over questions of faith? After all of their effort what did they achieve? A loving embrace of humanity?"

Responding, doubtfully shakes his head, "No. Something else altogether! Hypocrisy. That's the word. Unending. Ideology leading to a mass grave or imprisonment behind barbwire. Why Friend? No matter what the act. It is forgiven. Krist. Excuse me. But how can offer themselves as standards of peace. Love and compassion–shit! Ole Paine said it true,

> "*I do not believe in the creed professed by the Jewish church. By the Roman church. By the Greek Church. By the Turkish church. By the Protestant church. Nor by any church that I know of. My own mind is my own church. All national institutions of churches. Whether Jewish. Christian or Turkish. Appear to me no other than human inventions. Set up to terrify and enslave mankind and monopolize power and profit a final question.'*"

Finished quoting he scratches his nose making a final statement, "What they done? I might! Take a page from history and use peyote as a foundation to start a crusade. Start off small and timid. Then roll down on them with an avalanche of holy warriors stewed to the gills with *Seni* spoiling for a fight!"

Bright prick of light,
Small fire
A man and a family
Under star and moon

Bites off his slough of pity and sadness. Straightens his shoulders. Stops hands clawing earth. Eyes keen as they often will stalking. Starts a small fire before taking out a handful of Seni. This night's second course, swallowing a couple of mouthfuls. Will bring thirst later but still hunger and dehydration.

Squints at a fleeting vision of listless dusty scrub framed by fire and smoke. Wrinkling eyes, almost cracks a smile singing an old prayer of hunt. Finished, softly whispers so as not to be overhead by the grove's resident spirits.

"Rain soon. Get a move on!" This said, gathers belongings slinging them over his shoulder leaving the fire behind to light his way downward.

Chapter Twenty-six

Kuy doesn't know where he is but the fresh scent of straw jogs his memory. Sitting up, clutching a blanket folded along his length because there's a light autumn frost inside.

A strand of straw to clean his teeth. A bucket of night-chilled water nearby allows him to wash his face. Rinse mouth. Later rude toilet completed he stands up. Knocks sweet straw off his clothing.

Outside tang of pine smoke, aroma of fresh coffee greet him.

Morning's chill bracing. Not much light. Ample to find his way to the main house.

Inside kitchen. Bear Above and Emma sit at the table. After he steps inside, Kuy discovers that both hosts are deeply worried and careworn from lack of sleep.

Concerned Kuy asks, "What's wrong?"

"Running Legs did not come home last night," Bear Above answers.

"Where is he?"

"Devil knows? Can guess where he went though. Have some coffee and grab some biscuits; will you come with me and the boys to look for him?"

"Of course! Want to look for him in my truck?"

"No! The trail is too rough. We will have to use horses. I will saddle one for you."

Outside Kuy waits for his friend and his two older sons to round up and saddle horses.

Bear Above's wife and her younger children mill about uncertainly.

They have faced trouble before the roadman surmises. But they seem lost this cold morning.

Emma whispers to her husband, demanding to ride with them.

Taking her hands in his, big man gently consoles her, "Listen old gal. You have to stay behind and take care of the rest!"

Emma complies but with a look on her face promising hell to pay if anything goes amiss. Silently, she gathers her children watching their older brothers and father with quiet concern and forces them to eat breakfast.

John Little. Bear Above's next oldest son bridles a gray mare for the priest and brings the horse to him.

Out of practice with saddle, Kuy grunts swinging up and onto it, yet once securely seated, darts off to his Hercules, dismounts, then quickly grabs leather bags stuffed with medicines. Ignoring rifle. Instead, ties medicinal supplies under saddle horn, and using an old blanket to cover them.

"Ready?"

Kuy nods.

Bear Above then points toward the distant valley. Reassuring his friend, "Ok. Perhaps there's no real trouble. My boy strayed before. But with all of these trials and tribulations hanging around."

"I understand," the roadman, acknowledges, "Let's move."

"Yeah. Fast as shit through a goose's ass! Let's do it!"

They ride. Line of order as follows. Bear Above point. Two sons trailing. Roadman bringing up the rear.

Glum.

Even with *Pay* climbing slowly above the horizon. Behind them. Emma's lamp casts more light than partially hidden primary.

Not one word, down old rutted trail, winding behind barn. Their combined pace a slow canter.

Stunted trees shake, stir with bands of wakening starlings past a line of dusty cottonwoods. Their harsh cries score a somber ride otherwise interrupted only by snort of a horse, pull of leather, jangle of iron and steel, cresting a hill, riding slowly down toward hazy rim below.

KiH-hiH-t-

Shaking his head, Black Wolf watches his friend and his sons ride ahead silently down into the quite valley with only a hawk riding morning's gusts as an escort.

In the distance fence and bunkhouse or cook-house fronts a group of larger structures so he slows down, circling back to his party.

Sighting him. Bear Above orders his sons to stop, "No use putting all of us in danger! I want you boys to wait here."

They argue but he ends it. Then turns to his friend, "We will ride down to the main house. With me?"

"Sure."

"Come on then!"

Taking rein, the two old friends move forward toward a group of mean looking ranch hands watching idly standing by the ranch's main gate. Cut into its top post in bold black letters. Three M's.

How men can name the land when the land gives the name and soul to the people who are granted the grace to live upon it.

Imprisoned. Black Wolf studied bricks and stones of his prison cell. Individual blocks. Walls of his cell seemed uniform. Without individuality yet upon further inspection. He discerned that they were individuals. With flaws and strengths separating one from another.

Such is the case with all men. Some hard. Well molded. Others. Flawed.

Only when grouped together can the inhomogeneous project an image of strength. Separated. They often crumble or break.

Hailing men by name.

"Lucas. Pete. Rojas. I'm looking for my eldest. Have you seen him?" Bear Above demands.

Lucas, the tallest of this bunch glances at his companions for support.

Spitting a wad of tobacco, before answering, doesn't look Bear Above in the eye or meet the roadman's questioning gaze,

"Yep. Looking for trouble last night. He and Beth were fooling around. Well. Old Mitchell got wind of it and–"

"And what?" Bear Above exacts.

"Well–trouble–with a capital T," Lucas reluctantly adds.

"Tell me about this trouble!"

"Yeah–well–"

"Come on then!" Reluctantly complying, the ranch hand turns sulkily walking to one of the out buildings–likely a barn.

Roadman and Bear Above follow after them silently.

Kiowas' horses do not like the odors and sounds around them, so progress stiff legged like thoroughbreds on parade.

Cantering forward Kuy watches men and his surroundings carefully realizing that one does not need to be a brujo to smell trouble brewing.

Bear Above starts ahead but Kuy grabs his reigns and stops him,

"Listen," he warns, "This is a matter for the law!"

"What law?" Bear Above shouts, snatching the reigns out of Kuy's hands, "Mitchell's law is the only one around here!"

"You said that you won in the past."

"In the past. But now?"

Before Kuy's question is answered, Lucas halts. The other ranch hands form a rough semi–circle around the main house while from its front porch, a tall, weathered gray–headed man steps forward. Green eyed. Curious. Weighing as well. Nods at his men before addressing his angry neighbor,

"Listen. I warned you. I warned your son! He came around here try-ing to flirt with my Beth. Well!"

"Where's my son?" Bear Above demands.

"He's locked up in town. Sheriff Wilson locked him up."

"I want him out!"

"Well. Keep him away from my girl and my land!"

"Now. How do you expect me to do that Mitchell? They grew up together!"

Listing, Mitchell pauses. Trying to explain his point of view, "Listen. I know that. But can't you see they cannot and will not have any association! Any mixing at all. It will not do!"

"Why. Because he's a—"

"Hell! You know how it is!" the rancher wearily retorts.

Stung. Bear Above angrily informs the rancher. "Listen Mitchell. This is not over by a long shot!"

"Well. Watch out Mr. Bear. Next time!"

"Are you threatening me?"

"Yes. See you in court!" Mitchell threatens.

"Yeah. See you in court!"

Fearing for his friend, Kuy grasps Bear Above's saddle horn.

Noticing Bear Above's companion, Mitchell asks roughly, "Who's this joker?"

"No joker Mitchell. A friend. I'll take this up later," Bear Above promises.

"See that you do. Keep that son of yours off my spread or I'll see you in court!"

Bear Above does not reply. Instead rides away cursing, with the roadman and his sons hurriedly following behind. After catching, they cut him off, refusing to let him ride forward in a blind rage.

When Bear Above calms down, spotting an opening, Kuy offers to drive all of them into town, "It would be faster. Safer. You should see these town whites react when I drive my Hercules into a town it makes them turn cartwheels."

"Cartwheels. Yeah. I can picture that. Ok. Everybody move!" Bear Above orders.

Within the hour after leaving his Hercules near a small Sheriff's office at the town's edge, Bear Above's sons try to counsel and slow the big man down but to no avail.

At the Sheriff's. They learn that Long Legs will be released in two days' time with no more charges pending if he stays out of trouble.

Nothing else to gain by arguing with a lone, disinterested deputy, who new to the job, does not brook with anything not "ordinarily, routine."

Outside the roadman suggests, "Could have been worse!"

"Might well be next time," Bear Above cautions. "Listen. Why don't you come back in a week or so? Then we will have that ceremony."

"In a week?"

"Yes. It's a promise," Bear Above says, turning away. Then remembering that his friend is ailing, faces back around, and scolds him,

"Listen. I know you! See a medico. *Pronto.* If not for yourself then for the people who need you–"

"For instance–"

Grinning bashfully, Bear Above points out what should be obvious,

"Me. Emma and our kids. This enough? Or are you above gratitude?"

Black Wolf smiles, answering his comrade succinctly; if a bit off handedly,

"Fair enough! Not at all! I wish to thank you and Emma for your constant hospitality and welcome. See you shortly–"

"*'Ata!*" Bear Above exclaims. Irritated by his friend's footloose. Roving ways, he picks up a large stone and tosses it at Kuy who jumps aside just in time to avoid being hit in the head. Relenting with a understanding that come what may whether here or afterward they will meet again and with a final question, Bear Above lets the roadman go unhindered, "Pilgrim! Where you off to?"

"*TQ–bH 'H '–yiH.*"

After this enigmatic reply. Black Wolf indicates the mountains toward the east with a wave of his hand.

Sighing. Gently shooing sons toward waiting horses, Bear Above with a curt, fond and resigned farewell adds a final, stern admonition,

"Well you mangy jailbird. I'd better see you sitting on out porch soon–or I will come looking for your sorry set of britches!"

Smiling. Black Wolf promises and then without another word as they mount up and head home, Kuy walks back to his truck and waits till they ride away before driving off alone.

Chapter Twenty-seven

Keeping a death hand's grip on his wad of crumpled dollars sweated from a two bull, no account rodeo and liquored satisfactory, Billy staggers from one alcohol broadened face to another where his overly bold gaze is met and sometimes returned. Often simply ignored by the varied, red rimmed, unsympathetic eyes sawdusted with a star spangle banner kick up your heels mixture of hate, amity, indifference or just plain ole don't bother me mister unless looking for a fight.

Whooping it up in a railroad burg fed railway dollar like a fat tick on a steer's rump. A seasonal blue moon prosperity supporting occasional levity-festival, fairs, or rodeo.
Rodeo skedaddled leaving behind a skein of buckle bunnies, broken men, cashiered detritus. Billy, poco lame. Can't bronco and dint amid the kicking, hoofs and massive bucking, tearing, animals quick n easy enough to solicit Ooohs and Aaaahws from the eager, needy patrons amazed, grasping at quick last minute escapes and near misses, silently praying to jesus for a slip or fall-before lunch to spice up otherwise all too placid afternoons.

Ergo the dancing. Leaning. Or sitting. Raged against the fall of another day without regard for tomorrow since it usually takes care of itself. Even long tongued, long winded Emerson if not dead could palm off a second rate romanesque elocution on its inexorableness.

Shrugging. Billy takes a crack at it since as previously alluded to Waldo rests for the ages, "Day's just as assured as the heavy tread of a deputy. Rent collector. Or loan due," he offers freely to all assembled before turning heel and humming a few bars of, "The Cricket on the Hearth," tackling, "I'll Change Shadows to Sunshine," afterward.

Unbidden Black Wolf's locution against drinking whiskey resurfaces before returning to a deeper brine unmourned,

"Wouldn't cotton to my present state. Though he`s now far away riding in ease in his shiny truck while little ole me–Ah stop feeling sorry for yourself!"

Slowly it dawned on him that he's not exactly preferred company midst this mob of rodeo riders and stockmen. Least of all, it's how he is perceived between the nod and wink of another two fingered shot of whiskey.

Honestly. Most. Though not all rodeo folk are more opened minded when it comes to race mixing. Since they in turn are either idolized by common men or women or regulated to shiftless wastrels by less tolerant society.

Witching hour Billy is outside, catching a breath of clean if chilly air wishing he could lay aside drink. Get right with jesus or follow in another's footsteps and yet shot through with a malady of no easy remedy and royally fed up, sighs and turns his attention to appetites other than juicing for the rest of the night while a dollar or two is left in his back pocket.

Satisfied that a course has been set, Billy back inside shouts, "To a prostitute then," winning a brief and scattered applause. Solicits later but put off the price of a rut. Just as well since this *puta* raised her price hoping that he would skedaddle and dangle his sweaty legal tender elsewhere. Complies though in compliance trips over a timeworn relic passed out on the lush–crib's porch. Rustled rudely old geezer meets Billy's jaundiced eyes with a heated warning,

"Hell son! This burg's so odorous with law you'd had better watch out! They's on their next round. Ware young fellow or you might find yourself inside their lockup!"

Billy mulls this over while older lushington continues unabated,

"Ashes to ashes. Dust to dust," in a staccato wheeze.

After a brief hesitation and hiccup Billy breeches a quick rejoinder, "Amen to that old timer!"

"Listen son! Do a man a favor?"

"What?"

Old coot. Three sheets to the wind. Shoots Billy the fish eye before timidly fishing out his wallet. Picking out a sheaf of small bills from their larger cousins, slips a few into Billy's itchy palm.

"For?"

"Boy! Get me a bottle of red eye since them dried ass scuts. Hussies and upturned noses inside say they won't serve me no more! Can you imagine son! And me with enough money in my pocket to fire the place!"

Billy takes the money. It's more than enough for a few rounds of straight hell. After promising this ole goof he will bring back a bottle in a few, methuselah nods and pulls out a dollar coin and clamps it into his hand,

"That's for you pal. Have a snort on old dominium!"

Palming the old man's money, Billy after dusting off his faded jeans, walks back inside and bellies up to the bar once more admitted to society since he is an integral member with minted specie to prove it.

Billy fondles a glass bottle shoved into his hand, then unsteadily weaves his way back outside only to find his patron fast asleep with tongue out, false teeth on lap and glasses folded by his side.

Looks around and with nary a soul about, deliberates,

"Got a nice fold of green there." That's said hungrily and right needful as Billy slips practiced hand inside old man's striped suit coat to fish for dinner and a room to sleep it off in but stiffens before the deed. Muttering,

"Ole Kiowa poisoned me with his sanctimonious nonsense. Now what am I going to do till sunrise?"

Pockets empty, after a hasty, silent conference, Billy hurriedly limps to the nearest junction.

The tracks of the Cheyenne Short Line Railroad and the failing Chickasha Terminal Railway to see what's doing.

Looming whistle. Eerie. Highlighted by a fast approaching beam slicing clean. A scalpel, fore a fast dangler thundering, wheels a sparking, puffing, huffing, smoking. Fine as any dragon. Wind's east. Iron and steel giant whistles by uncaring. Running double track sixty or more miles an hour past Billy's feet.

Mandan. Editorializing. Offers offhandedly a self–directed threat,

"Just a step–ole boy and we's gone brother," yet no annakarenina Billy just smacks caboose's gilded lamp roaring past.

A brakeman mouths a comical O as the train whooshes past almost sucking Billy behind in its shuddering wake.

Spared to sing later for mulligan stew, stale bread, cheese, a dash of sardines spiked with hot sauce or whatever else is on the menu, woebegone dusting off his clothes, shuffles off.

Lacking tokens of admission, worried about reception in view of fact hobos and transients have grown mean and particular of the company they keep, not especially welcoming to tramps and other denizens from a vast uncategorized bestiary looking for a safe flop, warm fire or just company for misery. Billy takes stock and is not a little troubled by his innovatory. Tallied up, lonely as horny toad emerging from seven years of sleep, wishes he was somewhere and someone far away.

Spying two mendicants struggling ahead a long trestle spanning darker still, Billy skips to the loo my darling and catches up with the wobbling pair.

Lacks right leg one. Tied to the other's great coat by a thick leather belt broad as a man's hand. Other'n steps in tandem with partner, carefully shuffling along as if participating in a two man sack race.

Desperate for company and stalwart companionship, Billy picks up the pace willing to risk falling upon a hard lot if the possibility of forming a brief dalliance opportunes.

Introductions offered, they sniff each other making sure there ain't unburied grudges with a sharp knife or straight razor to itch a beef.

Middle aged, respectful enough for the gutter's edge, both tramps, shaved, nicked by a barber's hand recently and encased in two officer's great coats are alike as two peas in a pod.

Holding hands them two, Billy takes their measure and with articles of their association patiently obvious, finds himself without a widow's hope on this score, so decides sail in their wake wishing for the best. Hoping that the old phrase, "there is safety in numbers," rings true on a night like this pealing with the echo of passing freights, whippoorwills, deep throated bull frogs and an operetta of insects.

Descending, fast and terrible as a bolt of lightning, premonition strikes. Scart. Billy summons a line to ward off anxiety by that old transcendentalist Emerson,

"'We worship in the dead forms of our forefathers'–

"Old Waldo said it best when he told them stiff necks that–" Billy opined to no one and nothing.

Offering. Bending. Suck for a buffalo nickel or standing liberty dime

Beneath, boastful exchange, masked by shadowing mist, twink of furtive light, beckon below. Bonfire shining merrily as a candle set in a window.

Snaking unsteadily down a worn and reedy trail beneath a hollow under the bridge, Billy helps the others slide down, ignoring a warning prick in the neck and a queasy hitch in his gut.

No stranger to trouble or to danger Billy slows.

Impatient for their good fellows lording it over high muck a mucks with good fire, fiery beverages and steaming goulash or irish stew, stolen rooster, even wild cat or puppy if slim resources demand, momentary companions look at him with an areyoucomingcomeone till a cold wind strikes, ruffling hair and clothing suggesting retirement below where a balmier, more "accommodating" clime waits.

Shrugging. Billy grabs their shoulders and continues downwardly resigned. After half sliding, half climbing down they reach an established jungle shielded from prying eyes by ramparts of poison sumac, elm, and large brooding willows swaying overhead not denuded by season's change. Here warmth holds a wary court protected by flanked earth long after winter triumphs above.

A fire's lit. Loaf several. Close ring around it. Even a woman. Wild looking. Drunk. Eventual fodder for every ticket holder when fire lulls and bill's presented.

Billy's willing as anyone else to take his place in line after the queue breaks down and there's no sure account left of who gets firsts, sloppy seconds, or thirds. All he's really known since ten and a run away. Wouldn't have it any other way despite the roadman's firm opinion that there's a dollar or two worth left in him.

This true? Billy can't bank on it. Or use it for surety. So what use of it is it? Besides. All he knows is scuttlebutt, rumor, outrageous nonsense and lewd bawdy scribed from hobo junctions, work camp, or rodeo stalls from olympia to the florida panhandle.

Hastily made companions? Welcomed as honored guests.

Billy on the hand is given a feral sniff,

"Hey there Son."

"Hey yourself!"

"What's doing?"

Billy shrugs. Looking forlornly at their smoking and ascending campfire, asks plaintively, "You got a good fire going; can I sit and get myself warm?"

Tall man. Rough as ash and cinder looks at him with a hard, squinty flash of dismissal, demanding in a low growl more than a few steps from polite address,

"Got anything for pot or cup?"

Billy shakes his head.

Next pressed with a straightforward leer, "Accommodating?" shyly nods.

"Get comfortable. We'll see. Depends what the others want youngster!"

Billy dispassionately shrugs like a door to door salesman with his foot half inside settling for egress, shuffles over to the fire. After exchanging a nod or two. He squats by its side knowing full well that his tales. Knowledge.

Carried, applauded by the roadman. Will not serve him. Here, he's just a drunk troublesome injun by the looks of him. Favored crowd Billy from fire's innermost ring to exile beyond the choicest circle of purgatory where washed out hobs fancy a quick threesome but he's of no mind to dish out freebies when there's salt pork, beans, rich gut busting mulligans and pot luck dished out for those with the price or the will to appease.

Woman who danced merrily around the fire, corralled further away to a ring of spindly trees. O don't get me wrong. She laughs and is joined by laughter but not enjoined or in tandem. Hers, shrill indifference–others' hungry, jibed.

`pulling-unbuttoning-jerking`

Arguments. Slew of 'em. Who's first, last? Lust, need battered around matter factually. Listen. Like all democratic sentiments the right of the matter is decided by who gets there first with the most. Exemplified by the tall man captaining here roaring, pushing everyone back, then grabbing the woman's legs, pulling her dress off of her shoulder, splitting it down the middle, fragile underthings next, spread her like a compass, mounting uncaring of reception.

Too drunk to mind. Dozen doyens crowd around her watching eagerly as darkness and milling number allow.

`Cruel insect world tumble sprawled akimbo heaving bodies thrusting, and squirming limbs with an occasional wink of light on metal or gold filling to startle or delight the eye`

Thin albino's next. Grabs her by her long lank hair, straddles roughly. Shoves sex in her mouth while another fat deacon of a man enters her like a cork screw from the rear. Thus punched, forced, and prodded from three different directions, indiscreetly lit by the dying and distant fire, she rides, abiding until a train of a different nature without timetable or clear destination lines up behind the shuffling and gyrating cluster of moaning, cursing forms.

Good things come to end. Hark her as enthusiasm thins, cools. Sputters as she coughs up more brew (sobering spark). Aware now enough to perceive the faces and forms fucking her. Toothless mouths. Ravished faces. Hands with fingers missing. Crutched limbless torsos. All somehow still fanged with sexual need. Mostly–unfortunately, the organs to–

She? Attempts–protests though muffled by cock and cunt.

A man bit, howls joining her shrieks. To no avail and much too late since time, tide, and lust wait for no one.

More considerate lovers mumble protests and drop out of the line but just as many or more eagerly take their place and thrust back her lips taught till they crack and bleed like a bitch hound forced to bite down on hickory moaning and fretting but no longer if ever reflecting pleasure, O say not friend and her now bloated face what's seen anyway between an occasional flash of legs, arms, is now cast in a rictus of pain.

Watching, half desirous, sickened, Billy mutters,

"Don't no mores feel any inclination?" and after this distress'd damsel screams not for the first or even the second chorus, he grabs a large branch reserved for the fire and swings and in less than a white man's minute clears her admirers off.

There follows a cluster of complaints and enraged oaths, honestly even Bill curses himself for this sudden impromptu stupidity. Breathing raggedly, the target of justified wrath errs much by helping the woman numbed now and unable to stand on her two feet and how could she with clotted semen and blood seeping from her wounded crotch and staining her spindly legs torn and tattered stockings like a festive pudding from a devils' merriment?

Spotting an opening with a practiced eye, the junction's captain stabs Billy with a foot long Carolina cane knife in the back just under the shoulder blades.

Likewise the two hobo(s) met above, kick Billy with three legs and heavily booted feet. Others join in. This too is an expected welcomed distraction enjoyed when the opportunity arises for americans are a sporting and playful lot and when the need arises for correcting unaccommodating, ill–mannered and unprincipled fellows, so herewith thank god for the historical precedents based upon the same quality of justice set in place by their hallowed forefathers.

Billy down, teeth missing, not able to defend himself well as too bloodied to see slips away under the ring of continued blows and kicks which start to feel as if they were raining down on another luckless so and so and not his leaking sorry carcass.

Bunched before his blue and black face thick with blood, a collection of his teeth sit on a red velvet display of blood and vomit like a town jeweler's display.

Staunching wound between shoulder blade's rightfully judged the most important complaint to refer to any available remedy. Failing. Slowly, painfully turns over after being dragged into to a clump of garbage, possibly keeping company with another body or two as well.

Screened by dry green shuck of cat tails breakfasting midges feast. Adding a small but nevertheless annoying agony.

Billy swats at 'em but they return, settling just as quick, thirsty, and hungry as a table full of reformed methodists, swarming and gobbling from blood crusted hands, face, back thick as hickory smoke but ain't are they?

River close, last breath forward remembering his mother's lessons in beautiful lost, Mandan Billy stiffening rolls over dead. How he'd go? Listen. Shrill wind rattled the cat tails, a soft rain hardened to sodden downpour. Even Emerson fails near growling, whining, crowding empty bellied ferals.

Maxana
Nunp-
Namini
Toop
Kixon

'It fell in the ancient periods
Which the brooding soul surveys.
Or ever the wild Time coined itself
Into calendar months and days.'

Chapter Twenty-eight

Regrets smothered, farewells tendered, Kuy crosses familiar country joined by stalking whisper and echo. A barren land bereft of tree. Possessing little to break horizon's endless line of march. Exception's a crooked and forlorn windmill singed and crisped. Burnt as a kitchen match after being struck by lightning last summer though hereabouts it's still the lone sentinel for many a mile and a convenient roost for a barber shop quartet of red clay rusted buzzards.

Presuming that trinity of *Seni*, peyote and *Pioniyo* lack more than a bushel of self–importance, pride and arrogance and yet are; the road-man turns off a main road onto a lesser used auxiliary fighting an attack of doubt with a hard earned and earnest conviction. Not without needing to settle a few nagging doubts, clearing up a few persnickety points of faith, perhaps most importantly try to determine who or what stalks him. His penultimate need at hand. It tore him from his old friend and his family. Drove him from Velvet's arms and from others in need. Nevertheless, all bets are off since he is snatching at shards of memory, dream, unclear oracle, and elusive prophecy, blurring at eye's edge, motes outside perception's gate.

Hell! Kuy might just as well stalk untamed winds whistling outside armed as he is with his uncouth, skinflint apprenticeship from outlawed seminaries founded on hard riding, prison, furtive instruction and hasty investiture instead of ferreting out mysteries that the best of the lot just took a flying fuck at instead of these crazy peyote tricksters distilling a raw and sharp as turpentine gospel, creating derivatives pure as raw honey concocting a balm for their people's ills.

And it's not just Kiowas or other tribes people but eventually a remedy for all willing to kneel far from sheriff and deputies' warrant and find peace or at least a shelter from what ails them.

Still questions linger, drawing thick as a summer's quorum of flies and so concerned on a particular constituent of faith the roadman smiles with a hard cross of his bottom lip recalling a discussion with another peyotist named Hungry Eye awhile back outside a dusty tarantula haunted *borracherya* in the mexican state of *cholula,*

"What instead they be tired demons stung with the pride of the fallen, on a lark or what have you kicking up a fuss to while away eternity for there are wars in heaven as mirrored on earth," his coreligionist posed in a trail worn voice while Black Wolf frowned and listened, "Certainly not all knowing and all powerful," he stated before suggesting instead, "This too folly Kuy or are these and they out of range of our limited ears and eyes?" Hungry Eye smirked before offering another thought, "or just a pack of feuding multitudes of contrary persuasions. Gods? Or solely a bunch of no great account *'bonito(a)s'* or *'mailto(a)s'* set adrift?"

Cry voiced, silent shadowy, motes of coded will and desire, perch and wait omnipresent as air picketing the chair where you sit, the tree outside, the crowns of your children's head, even your empty cold bed, hungry anticipant for the play to begin

After digging up the correct frame of reference stretching another long taffy pull of a question, Hungry Eye continued, "Are we not then made in their image? Cast in their mold like lead bullets?"

Shut up for a doggoneaminute to allow the Kiowa to pose counter arguments, nearly though not completely curtailed by the dusty brawl of wind, heat and twining shadows outside the swinging doors of that ancient, too close eaved smoke filled cantina and dropped their voices. Why? Witches were still burned thereabouts.

Hungry Eye sipped endless small thimbles of mescal and Black Wolf bitter tea till their symposium halted under the swinging arc of kerosene lamps. Later when their sleepy host draped by his family motioned for them to go after extinguishing the last candle and bolting the door behind them with a heartless finality.

Placing this memory away Kuy concentrates on driving.

Hungry, thirsty, reaching under his seat, grabs the last of his licorice. Unwraps it and thrusts a bunch into his mouth. The sweet and sharp bite of the confection helps him to think and clear his thoughts.

Mystagagus? Evening nearing. Rumpus of thunderheads turn southward washing the air clean, crisp with a scent of wild sage and prairie rose.

"Not the usual scents of autumn is it?" he asks, stating for his own edification, taking on a deeper, if equally seasonal theme, "We wear their tailored pattern and it suits us well," prior to pausing to check his bearings, Kuy resumes speaking glad for the company, "These notions hard to swallow? To get around your tongue? Well then. Look toward the nearest child of adam. How well does his or her inner nature and wellspring of heart and soul slip into your grasp. Allowing you to it read their fundamentals like a broadsheet or penny dreadful. No! Will then figure trying this out on these outlandish, strange, and unseen, "no see'ems," all around us thick as thieves. Just out of range of sight and sound except for a few unlucky men. Woman and animals. How far are you going to get on this bunch? Very? Don't think so! So the next time you pick up a holy script and ponder revelations rendered into sanctified writ ask yourself what are they saying and why are they saying it!"

Puteal Turning deliberations to more serious tracts, he continues, "Or is it faith and only Faith alone that guides us through darkness?" before halting sermonizing to clear throat and then carrying on in a surer voice, "Old gods. Heck. Didn't they fight like cats and dogs for both worthy, wicked, even spiteful and empty crusades known only amongst themselves and weren't heroes and heroines mustered to achieve these campaigns before being discarded by the very beings served?

That's right! One or two at of 'em got my number! Least enough to raise the hackles on my neck and wayside me," or so construed watching rustling dusk, rush of sand and a wind hailing from the east.

"Just want to save my people. Not much else a man can hope for is there? Can`t roll back time and give us all that we have lost. Maybe just maybe a place to bide away till what will come settles over the land and the dark times ahead do their damnedest. Spare as many the worst of it! I hope. Pray and cross my heart. Really not too much to ask! I mean lookie here. What are all those men and boys dying for over in europe for? Country. Nationalism. Pride. Military honor? All just sand in the eye leading people astray!"

Persistent and annoying as the hot sunlight stabbing his nape, *some* prickly presence hovers nearby. First Kuy ignores it. Then acknowledges it. Why? Listen if saul on the way to damascus. Joseph smith spade in hand. Buddha under tree. Mohamed secreted in cave, shut eye, and ear and then turned away. What then of our "sacred" books. Festivals. Places of worship?

A better world or one bereft?

`Victimarios-Victima`

As directed later drives to a distant hill barren of habitation with nary a tree. Scrub. Or thorn marring perfect symmetry. Old Hill, say ain't they all. Perhaps but this one was here before the other crookbacked Johnny—come—latelies broke through their shell and climbed toward *Pay.*

Raised by will.

`Bidental`

A scattered wise few declare that it isn't a hill but a witch mountain. A singular place. Where animals exemplified by white buffalo. Passenger pigeon. Giant otter. Timber wolf and giant elk are rumored and later storied to have entered to hide from white man until his day is done.

This true? Neither here nor there *amigo*! Certainly not worth the price of a half penny's argument. Though without the shadow of a doubt there's spirit here.

After parking, don't look, notice or concede evening's drain down night's funnel, now a star thick advent with muting fourth of july hue and cry. Attendants? Long gone or is hesheit around somewhere dusting their altars off. Filling the censors. Readying the long unemployed hosts once alerted by his boot fall.

Afterward, readies himself on summit. Building a fire in an ancient fire pit dug, reshaped, dug again legends say long before coronado with the inquisition perched on his mantled shoulder and his rusty ilk passed by looking for the seven cities.

Instead finding incomprehensible vistas, hostile or wary tribes peopling no map or even figuring into extant legends as these shopworn spanish passed and brought death with their wake—a prow of long pestilence—which they, the leavings of europe's slums, prisons and festering military orders embodied.

Along their march much of what they described was swept from the earth or diminished to the point that their chronicles of walled cities. Great pyramids. Vast networks of trade and teaming commerce. Festivals and the pageantry of war were later discounted or dismissed as latin embellishments from further south where the Mexica and Maya did.

After their heavy iron soled tread. Only sylvan glades. Fallow pastures and untilled gardens. Wilds grains. Thick musing forests. Tall grass remained with scattered bands of human habitation.

"THEM. Old Ones. The Anasazi came here ago as barefoot pilgrims tracing stars."

Right on that count they did. Seeding offerings to gods now without name. Whom never the less forlornly (feel them staring at the back of your neck. NO don't turn around) wait like tenders of a failed roadside enterprise for anyone. Anyone at all to stop. Even if it's for only a passing word or two. Quick silent prayer or sudden, startled awareness carrying a fragment of held remembrance.

Lights fire. Sings. Sacrifices. Weeping bitter glad tears and as flames lap the air like a stray kitten milk, Kuy takes out a bundle of peyote, cuts a good supply and with each pucker and sour choke, swallows till his spirit is sated. Needing nothing more dreams or dreams he.

Pass wife son friends enemies dead some with a few like Old Smoke living. Him? A worried expression on face shuffling along like an old woman in a heavy robe wondering why he was awoken. Isa–tah. Mary. Phosy. Gus also crowd his sleep. Billy? No. Elsewhere.

Velvet Horn. Barefoot. Not scared or defaced. Naked and full bodied, taking his hand and sprays his fingers, caressing each before inserting them inside her, rubbing herself against them and later smiling, moaning, arching her spine, before placing his hand over her stomach no longer taut as a drum, now pulsing with another heart.

His. Yet sadly realizing he will never see this child looks her full in her eye. Velvet nods and after a fearful glance over his shoulder and sad smile too is gone.

Just lonesome ole he with day rushing home rising from still smoking ashes ghost faced tripping on tripudium with a long whistle of awed complaint,

"What a kicker!" These visions he believes and perhaps even understands. Falling upon him not without the pang and regret of an isolated gethsemane. Well with the thin peal of alarm. One belayed and defused with a quick wave of hand signaling indifference.

Sourly slouching with a frown and clouded brow, Kuy shakes himself like a dog shedding fleas and looks up toward *Pay's* ascending, grinning light flashing across face says with wonder, "A child!" This revelation brightens his mood and gladdens heart though sad that this joy and burden's solely upon Velvet for the time being.

"Don't forget hard luck that premonition waiting aside an old adobe ruin."

No stranger. This specter. Not after investing that abandoned farm. Hitches his shoulders, tightens his belt and readies himself without another concern on this score.

Tastes briny sea, his hand though, not near even the dinkiest rivet. Sweet brine, raw tongue, she's savored until concerns and considerations crowd to the periphery love and life.

Now? Time to face death. Revel in it sing it embrace it like a former trade oiled, laid away unexpectedly, needed again when devil comes aknock'n,

"Death old friend. Are you ready?" Finished, dusts himself off, and heads down dawn ringing like a bell.

Chapter Twenty-nine

Two Cloud`s nervous. Velvet as well. As expected. Waiting as good hosts must for company to file past as they offer greetings. Encouragement. Salutations. Acknowledgments of loss and recent sorrow. Praying for the strength and fortitude to succeed this night while a small body of men. Fewer women. Step into the council house underused since acrimonious votes and infighting tore apart any remaining unity once they were dumped here a generation or more ago after any final attempts to break away from forced resettlement failed.

Velvet Horn coached her co-conspirators as well as possible in the rough gospel Black Wolf taught her before he will–o–wisped back to fort sill. Now on their shoulders rests the failure or success of this ceremonial launch. Shepherding each man and woman into a rough crescent or semi–circle arranged in orientation to the cardinal points and other spiritual armature and peyote nomenclature accompanied by drum. Pipe. Rattle and a small fire blazes center stage.

Reluctantly. Velvet keeps to the sideline since Kiowas' traditionally do not allow women significant roles in religious ceremonies. But this differs from clan to clan and different locales. Nevertheless. Remembering Medicine Woman. One of the first recorded peyotists and in turn her significant contribution as one of the principal founders of the peyote moment, Velvet silently invokes her name and revered memory as invocation or blessing for tonight`s ceremony.

Across from her. Two Cloud surveys his gathered parishioners. Wondering if white priests are made so. Rudely collected only three days before. Hurried through an irregular seminary. Forced fed catechisms and rituals and then set in place.

But a hardy fellow. Not too thin skinned or overly mindful of the opinions of others if not directed too harshly against himself or someone he cares for. Taking a breath. Braces for the enactment of ritual. Scattering sweet smelling *an–son–a* grass over the brazier. Readies the host. Settles into–if hasty. Yet practiced routine–ready, as he will ever be. Before glancing at Velvet. Nods to his suborned assistants, bending will to spirit and assorted alkaloid princes awaiting.

They start. Or he really. Praying. Next. Two Cloud performs a rough sketch of the ritual.

Always Sings an impromptu fireman. A younger man. John Wilkes Booth. Sergeant at arms and altar boy, standing ready behind Two Cloud, shining with pride and basking in the attention of his role.

Seni is distributed from the roadman's sack and divided among their small congregation.

Velvet keeping track of every move and reaction.

So far. So good. Everyone except Never a Smile and Long Tooth. If not freely participating and hoping for personal family or community salvation. Attentively follow instruction. Listening if not raptly to the sermon. Offering amen in the right places well as encouragement, if asked, also testifying, and unburdening perceived or actual requests for ministration and prayer.

Two Cloud isn't a christian. Never was or will be captivated by too close to collar, shorn lock, five cent attendance church supper hocus-pocus. Instead created much of the ceremony in his own heart. Velvet's over careful instruction and past practices based upon spiritual and religious truisms just shy of forgotten a generation ago, making a go at it.

After ingesting their hosts. Many parishioners experience a mild calm and a beneficial ease of spirit or flesh and fewer still enjoy a real emotional or religious stirring, followed by many tears. Sobs and heartfelt appeals for forgiveness are given and received.

Night's only sour note is a couple local toughs excusing themselves.

Their going almost unnoticed amid the general success of the meet.

Day break. They consume a ritual meal of corn cakes and raw honey. Afterwards. Smiles. Good fellowship and a sense of spiritual commune amongst each participant not seen in this township for many a year.

Saying goodbye. Extinguishing the ceremonial fire. John Wilkes Booth. Two Cloud and Velvet Horn step outside.

Horn grabs each man, thanking each profusely for their near perfect ceremonial finesse.

"Hell Velvet!" John admits, "I was scared out of my boots." Tired, distracted, he doesn't meet Velvet's eyes, yet behind his. Inward. Drifting consciouness. Follows an image of man walking barefoot and alone on a beach. Until his attention returns to the ceremony. Then shyly excusing himself, answering a call of nature outside. Their sole lantern's glow lighting only a few paces beyond.

Dawn only a blue tinged promise breaking east with usual expected fanfare.

The crow of cock—that strange welcoming animal's diurnal greeting and a host of insects regarding the dawn of another day with mutual expectancy and enthusiasm stilling for a moment their savage cycle's demand and execution.

As *Pay* rises. A pale innocent circle eastward. Two Cloud takes Velvet's hand and thanks her for selecting him, "Gal. I was nervous too!"

Velvet confides that she was also. Ecstatic at their apparent success, she excitedly recalls one or two of this night's successes,

"Did you see how old man Sky wept like a baby and promised not to drink more and beat his wives? Both smile at this memory of triumph. However insignificant to the world at large. It looms exaggerated in their collective memory since this notorious drunk habitually raises concern and disturbs their nightly peace by using his allotted government pension to drink almost every night and then beat his two, elderly, and resigned wives until they either flee to neighbors or curl up instead and beg for mercy.

Another success. Perhaps a new convert. Girl Little Woman. A three hundred pounder. Promised she would quit 'horring.' Eat less and pay more attention to her brood of ragamuffins who also daily add to their small collective community's disquiet and sense of failure and disorder.

Two Cloud hugs Velvet once more before going into dawn light heartened, enjoying *Seni's* benediction as its distorted colors and sounds crown him with gentle hallucination or divination allowing this quite, gentle man to step through and then step away stronger and more secure than many a year before.

Velvet. Now there's a case. Also flushed with success she straightens the council hall. Hoping with a degree of certainty that what was planted this night. Against the back drop of hopelessness. Idleness and general despair. Will thrive. Perhaps reaching others who did not attend. Either too bashful of innovation. Or caught by the traps of other. Enforced religions offering only supplication and not liberation.

Finished. She slips away..

Dawn assured cocks crow. Winds shift. Bats coast homeward overhead. Returning to their roost above her on silent glide paths older than memory.

Another cock crows as she moves across the treeless and grassless village square. Tilting her head, Velvet rips off her bandanna. Letting her sweat stained face breath freely. Hat also before sitting down and removing her heavy boots to continue barefooted toward *Pay* rising like an old friend afore sure of only that another heart now beats inside her and that its father is not so far away returning or no. For if called away he waits only for her eventual crossing to meet again guised in familiar form with smile welcoming and aglow with rapture.

Rooster again the only sound except a young dog yapping somewhere disturbing an otherwise still morning Velvet dances alone and unobserved under bright, unspoilt morning light.

Cloaked with retreating shadow and the first shy kiss of light, she's a beautiful. Joyful woman least till shadow returns and doubts coalesce.

Stopping in mid twirl. Gathering her hopes and fears, wills them toward last star. Gathering her clothing, returns to her sequestered solitude till meeting later with new converts to plan what course of action they should take to tackle their community's many shortcomings.

Chapter Thirty

Recognizing that human malady is beyond his or any man's ability to heal. Black Wolf regretfully turns his thoughts ahead. It's the times and not a task that can be helped by faith. Only a healing brought upon by a true future for their People and not simply believing that by accepting the man jesus from galilee, the peyote way or any other creed, one can cure hatred and poverty.

Roofed by closing black like a hungry mouth Kuy journeys over an arid land choked with amarillo scrub and thin sentinel pines gilt with the tongue of fossil sunlight.

Glimpsing a lone figure standing by an adobe ruin. Kuy slows.

In the headlights stranger's elongated silhouette conjures memory. Iron Knife's. One of this father pointing out a rock painting to him depicting a lone shaman or male witch slashed on a gray granite slab with rusty ocher and ash black.

```
Drive on or draw K'oo and get to
it since there's no peace until
this is settled once and for all
yet what if I am wrong and this
is just another foot sore woebe-
gone traveling alone from Alpha to
Omega down america's long throat
at out the tail pipe like the rest
of us
```

Scalp prickling Kuy shifts gears; speculates uneasily, "Dream's shadow?"

Realizing that only a desperate or malicious man or woman chances this road at night, deliberates —— "Witch? Or just a poor soul on this lonely stretch of road."

Rolling to a stop Black Wolf asks "Need a ride?"

Hitchhiker. Face dark, Eyes darker still. Answers. "Might. Waiting an age. Going far?"

"Not too."

"Get in."

Smiling stranger picks up his packs. Staggering under their weight he places them in the bed of the Hercules and climbs in.

Studying his new passenger Kuy makes few quick assumptions. A Comanche obviously, reminding him of another and what with his manner of dress man's a witch or a roadman.

Door is closed. There's slithering from the back. Kuy asks,

"Carrying snakes back there friend?"

"A couple of rattlers found asleep a while back yonder," the stranger explains guardedly after turning around. "Like you I also have cures and *pianyo*."

"Peyote," Kuy demands sharply. "You're a brother of the road? The *Piyano* Way?"

"For many years."

"Well. I usually don't carry snakes around but to each to his own! Listen I have driven since the early morning and I am only going another hour or so then I will camp for the night."

"Fine. It's damn good to find a brother to share a fire–rather than solitude."

"True. Well anyway. We Kudwa owe you Comanches a debt or two!"

"Do tell?"

"Well," Kuy adds with almost a smile. "Your people adopted one of us you captured and introduced that dog pony soldier to horses for the first time."

"That true?" the Comanche asks and at the same time, offers his hand in friendship, "Name's Twice Born. Yours?"

"George *Kone-gyah-daw-kue'*."

Both shook yet this gesture reminded the Kiowa of a white man's boxing match a silver piece was once wasted on.

Afterward, Twice Born replies, "Good to meet you. Sorry! It's has been while since I talked Kiowa. What is the meaning of *Kone-gyah-daw-kue*?"

"Black Wolf!"

"Black Wolf?"

The Comanche repeats the name aloud. Foxed eyes glinting perhaps with remembrance or association before adding, "Might have heard of you. While ago–spitting some peyote rinds at new light round cold fires. Dusty mornings. Are you truly a wolf brother?" he demands after fastening a hard, appraising look at the Kiowa.

Pondering, the roadman glances at the stranger, again entertaining a sliver of unease or doubt. Ignoring it. Banked with confidence merely states coolly, "Depends!"

Later as winds play their guarded fire the roadman adds dried buffalo grass to its diminishing flames. Stoked it roars and crackles happily as he prepares tonight's food. *Tooksey. Ahpuskey.* Spiced with red pepper and wild onions and sizzling flat bread while coffee boils. A feast by both men's shall we say, reduced and improvised standards.

Laying out plates, Kuy contemplates their path and the handful that take it, "We are so few," he laments silently, "Carriers of dreams and hopes. Seeds blown on a fallow wind." Finished, sets their rough feast.

Twice Born thanks him for the food. Then moves closer to the fire's warmth and light to eat.

Black Wolf studies his new acquaintance. Wishing to know what matter of man he is. Now only a broad shadow, banded with flickering, fire light.

The Comanche shorter than the Kiowa is longhaired, tough and gnarled as an old willow. Face's scarred. It's hard to tell if its wounds were self–inflected for ceremonial purposes or the results of some mishap or struggle.

Kuy decides regrettably. All in all. That it's not a face to inspire confidence or ready friendship yet Black Wolf, not wishing to judge solely by appearance, bides time. Allowing the Comanche to exhibit his own merits or disadvantages.

Aware that the Kiowa is studying him. Twice Born breaks the silence by asking a sudden question, "How long have you followed the Way?"

Kuy stares into their fire before answering, "Hard to say. Rode at Quanah's side a spell. Years ago. Knew him?" he quizzes.

"No. Not acquainted. He passed recently. Did he not?"

"Yes. I did not know he was ill till too late," the Kudwa replies sadly. "In their february." Remembering. The roadman relates a short personal history while tending to their fire, "He was another father to me. Taught me the road or as much known at the time. Between him. Fort marion and mexico. I owe who I am today sitting in front of you."

The stranger nods his head all the while watching the Kiowa closely as the roadman asks another question, "You know the story about Parker's mother?" the roadman asks.

"No."

Enlightening him. The roadman continues, "Remember. Not to speak names. But his mother. She was white. Named Cynthia Ann Parker. You Comanches captured her and gave her the name *Nadua*."

"Someone found."

"That's right. Many years later her original family. Or so claimed. Recovered her with the help of texas rangers."

Reacting to the name of the hated lawmen both spit into the fire.

As its flames recoil, Twice Born remarks suddenly,

"At Pease River!"

Black Wolf nods and then takes up the thread of his story, "Well. When he came to back to reclaim her he asked them, 'What right do you have to her?' He embarrassed them and was too proud to be ignored!"

Momentarily, a loud whistle beyond their fire startles both men.

Kuy pauses and turns aside, listening, "*Yuh*! Who's there?" he demands but outside their fire darkness fences all.

With ears cocked like a hound, Twice Born watches, listening as the roadman motions to remain silent. After paying attention to the diverse sounds around them both shrug and turn back to the fire and conversation.

"It was too late to rescue her," Kuy relates across the fire to his new companion, "Quanah's sister Prairie Flower died and his mother never saw her other children again. *Nadua* was returned by force to a life. Though per-haps–originally hers. Was now terribly different. Her original family though kind in their own way. Could not overcome her feelings of sadness over her husband's death. *Peta Nononca* and her other children's separation."

Twice Born interrupts, "She ran away?"

"Tried," the roadman, admits, "Several times but her family would not allow her to escape and return to her old life."

Choked up. Kiowa coughs. Stirring the fire again to hide any emo-tional shenanigans hiding inside. Continues, "His mother appeared to accept her new life as her old freeways faded and were folded away like, clothes in a chest. *Nadua* never spoke of her years with your people. Hell. Soon. She never spoke at all because knew that she would never taste again the freedom the open plains. Quanah said. His mother never knew again their raw nights with the wild merry stars above. Nor taste the salt tang of lathered horses on the sharp close of days." Remembering his old teacher's words, Kuy sighs.

"Poetry," Twice Born comments. But the hardness of his eyes and a barely smoldering glint doesn't match his glib words and Kuy no fool realizes it!

"Maybe. Sometimes a man just likes to talk. He was a prophet–and a poet. Been a stretch since I met one of us out here,"

Twice Born agrees silently. Familiar with loneliness. Remaining unspoken but watchful and attentive the Comanche watches the flames as Black Wolf continues,

"He loved his mother. Never forgot her. Quanah was strong but nev-er gained real peace," the Kudwa appends with bowed head and shadowed expression.

"Fated," Twice Born whispers.

"Yes. As a man. He learned hard truths. After time passed. As seasoned leader and a successful rancher in his own right he sought his mother. Only to learn of her death. Her passing was hard for him to abide. She had stopped caring. Would not eat. Starved herself after her daughter's death. Have you ever tried to take a wild animal and tried to tame it. Usually unless it is very young it is of no use to try–"

"Choked. Didn't she?" the Comanche responds bitterly.

Without hesitation Kuy replies, "Without question!" As the roadman continues Twice Born nods silently. "Not to name the dead. But he was grieved by her passing. Tried to hide it. Never could. He used to speak to me when like this around a fire at night. Remembering. Quanah once confided to me,

> 'I remember my mother smiling as rain fell and my sister gathered new flowers in her small fists. We ran laughing. Seeking shelter under dwarf cottonwoods curtained by a rush of contentment.'"

The Kudwa pauses and Twice Born closes his eyes as if remembering similar days before Kuy continues, "He couldn't leave her to a cold white grave therefore. *So* reclaimed her."

"Buried near Fort Sill?"

"Yes–with her."

"Been there?"

"Once. A few months ago. It's written there,

> 'Resting Here Until Day Breaks
> And Shadows Fall and Darkness
> Disappears is
> Quanah Parker.'

The Kudwa bows his head before adding, "Appropriate, and fitting–"

"He was a powerful man. But too proud. Too eager to take on white ways," the Comanche remarks caustically. "Didn't he die after over charging some poor family too much to cure their son?"

Black Wolf's face clouds with a trace of anger before answering, "True perhaps. I heard a couple of different accounts of his death. But if that one's true. I'm sure he regretted it. He once prophesied that his occasional greed would lead to his death."

"Well. Didn't the U–S of A washington on the potomac seal his high handed white loving ways with a shiny granite tomb?"

"He learned well! And I believe taught admirably also!" Replying, Black Wolf tried to keep his growing hurt and anger from edging out the possibility of fellowship this chill night.

"Might be the case I reckon," Twice Born concedes, "But I was never close to his clan and people. There are other ways to live. Fight and hate. His ways. Putting aside violence and revenge are only for the week and white lovers!"

Listening, the Kiowa studies his new acquaintance, wondering all the while if he made a mistake picking him up and offering his fire.

Raising his hand. Twice Born opportunes a hushed question, "Listen." Pausing to look beyond their fire before continuing guardedly in a confidential manner, "Some say he's an owl spirit. That he rides alone at night. Do you believe this story?"

"Who can say? Would a man like him rest?"

Stories finished and questions played out. Silence joins their circle, both realizing that this is no night to speak of the dead, they fall silent, watching the firelight stage narratives too sad for words camped in a forlorn hollow under a moonless star crowded night.

Witch fires overhead pointing to dawn, Twice Born stirs the flames for the last time as the roadman sips coffee. Around them night grows chill as a cool wind strikes down from the north. Later banking the fire, they move their bedrolls closer.

Unexpectedly Twice Born asks, "Who's waiting out there?"

Before answering, Kuy cocks his head and listens prior to making a jest, "Just the wind, *'H'dei–kiH*.*" Then attempting to change the subject states casually, "Like your boots Comanche."

"Well. You should. They're Arizonan Jaguar. I don't wear them often amigo. Roughening up my feet."

"Thought them Jaguars all dead."

"Well if they weren't," Twice Born replies with a crooked smile, "they sure as hell are now," spitting into the fire before returning to his inquiry, "Ha. Some wind! Perhaps it is an owl spirit hunting. We should be quiet. Not attract their attention," he warns standing up and easing a hitch in his back. While edging back from the fire he poses another question, "Ever kill any one Kudwa?"

"A few."

"Well. I wager one or two of them out there. *Puetuyai*! Waiting."

"*Kap–k*ougyH?*"

"Whites?" the Comanche hisses.

"A few. Had to. Their call!"

Twice Born nods before adding, "Wonder if whites have the same spirit laws? Men we kill in battle. Their spirits have no cause to bother us. Fair fight'n all! But they," Twice born frowns, his forehead crinkling pondering his own question before bending down next to grab a bottle from a sack at his feet and pull its cork out offering a taste to the Kiowa, "Want a pull? Good whiskey. Store bought."

"No thanks don't touch it."

"Never?"

"Not in a long while."

"Your one of the good ones? Never losing sight of righteousness. The straight and narrow?" this said looking away from the fire as if gathering a memory that's fleeting or hard to impart, "Might have crossed your path a while back."

The Kiowa's interested in this admission. Recalls that late evening back on the texas, oklahoma border when he briefly saw what he thought at the time was just another arrogant ghost well as a more recent vision atop that lonely hill. "Could be I have seen you under old moon also," he confesses. Remembering, he's not altogether happy with its implications.

Listening Comanche smiles with heartless mirth, "Sometimes amigo. Dreams ain't dreams but—"

The Kiowa interrupts, "Warnings!"

Twice Born acknowledges his contribution, "Right or the result of a dream walkers trespasses. Dreams come whether awake or asleep. Depending on their weave," and then pausing, rolls tongue adding, "Or for that matter their maker's heart! Them's like forays into no man's land one reads about. Check the papers pal? Big war's breaking out in Europe. Might take a little of pressure off of us just like the big war between the states did back ago."

Disagreeing the roadman shakes his head, countering the Comanche's argument with a sage tilt of his head, "Times were different then. There's not much left for them to deal with!"

"Maybe you're right," Twice Born concedes with a thin smile. Adding "Scared you that time! Didn't I?"

Nonplussed. The roadman looks up warily. Locking eyes with this increasingly puzzling man,

"When?"

"That evening!"

Unfazed, *Kuy w*aits for the other to continue.

"Come on! You don't remember seeing me walking by this same truck you got back there toward sunset?"

Black Wolf answers reluctantly, "I remember. Thought you a ghost. Leastways a foreshadowing. Or omen forewarning an evil occurrence."

"By the prick of my thumb. Eh!"

Kuy shrugs. Considers leaving. But not wishing to run away with his tail tucked between his legs, decides to stick it out a little longer as Twice Born resumed. In a slightly more menacing tone mirroring the naked greed sparking in his eyes hungry as a panther's stamped on his scarred face, "As I said before–heard about you. For years. About your abilities."

"This a joke?"

"No," the Comanche replies. Frowning. Explains his point, "Listen friend. Nothing's concrete. You and your road chiefs have growing traditions and ceremonies–but to what end? To keep what's left safe on reservations while the noose tightens. Safe and secure with you and yours in perpetuity. Till like the Lakota–settled. De-fanged. Slaughtered–"

"No!"

"Listen then! There are still a number of us. We that haven't been murdered or placed in camps and still kicking up a fuss. We're about the same age. Know I don't look it," he laughs. Tracing the scars on his face. "Lost a knife fight in torreon. Anyway. Listen. You and I were born free. The last of our kind so I got a proposition for you brother!"

Warily. The Kudwa asks with a tired. Impatient shrug, "What is it?"

"What say you if we don't let them just eat and shit us out? But make them choke on their greed instead? Hell. Peyote can be whatever we want. Dangerous. Revolutionary. Like a clean sharp blade in the hand– we can decide whether to heal or slay–Join us! We have other brothers and sisters–"

"Witches. You mean!"

"Call us what you will. We're spreading. It's the end of times for us surely as Ghost Dance prophets pledged. Haven't you heard the wolves' cry where we once roamed? Haven't you heard earth's cry. River's lament and barbwire's conceit?"

"Heard about you also–"

"Really?"

"Yes. Those Mescalero kicked your kind out. Didn't they? You were causing too much trouble; Peyote is a discipline. Not a warrant to–"

"Revel in sin and take all we can before we end up like the buffalo– Been east," he demands with a crooked sneer.

"Once."

"Like what you saw?"

"No. Never liked straight lines."

"That's our future from sea to shining sea. Soon there will be no place for the "vanishing american." Meaning us! Outside of penny museums. Wild West shows. Or flint hard reservations–" Sighing. Twice Born straightens up–then stops, interrupted by the Kiowa

"You're wrong. We'll survive–"

"You'll make a fine specimen. Noble savage. Medicine man. Kiowa–Plains culture–" Laughing mockingly. Twice born starts to say more but a sound like a snapping branch alarms them.

Startled both flinch. Then slowly settle back down around their dying fire.

Afterward, Twice Born watches Black Wolf as if the Kiowa was a rival in an unannounced match or secret game known only to himself. While in turn the roadman feels that their brief camaraderie has expired as much as the fading fire before them.

Returning the dark *dohate's* gaze. Waiting for the impasse to be broken by word or action and if not, Kuy questions whether he should sleep in the other's proximity.

Shifting uneasily on a bed of cooling gravel Comanche stands up, menacing Black Wolf with a low growl,

"Listen! I challenge you! We can't see eye to eye. So may the better man win!" Growing more belligerent, he threatened Kuy with battered fists before explaining, "There's no other choice. But to fight it out," he adds heatedly, pausing long enough to take another snort from his bottle.

Amused. Rather than frightened. The roadman objects lazily to his brazen dare. Having other plans, "A fracas now–at night–"

"Sure. Why not? Sing your songs and I mine."

"Think I'll turn in friend."

"I'm no friend old man."

"What's to stop me from just driving on? You!"

"Your call Kiowa!" Twice Born insists. Crouched away from the fire-light, the Comanche's deep set sockets smolder cold like sparked amber casting a covetous look at the roadman's possessions. Gathering them into an eventual sack of spoils. Enjoyed riding homeward framed by a gibbous moon for celebrations best not thought of at the moment–distractions from more immediate goals.

His rival's thoughts no mystery, Kuy hums an old tune debating what action to take. Has songs. Amulets. Coral and feathers to protect against men like this witch. Peculiar folk turned by hunger for power and prestige, who cannibalize each other's power and skill believing that this leads to earthly power and position.

After this consideration, having prepared for this very "eventuality," liking the word, decides to use it again somewhere and sometime, then shrugs, deciding to battle it out though his health isn't what it should be. Kudwa just hopes not to pass like his father. Iron Knife talked one moment and dead on the ground the next after a heart attack.

No great shakes to take this fellow in a fight fair or not. Kuy never sought an unjustified scuffle nor walked away from a necessary one.

"If it comes to a duel," he wolfishly grins, "So be it and let the best man win!" Then aloud, "Hold on and don't get in an uproar," while grabbing a couple sacks from his truck. Returning. He throws two of Twice Born's stained burlap bags at the witch's feet.

Without a word. The Comanche kicks one away ignoring its warning rattle and hooded lunge watching his rival unpack across from him, later grabs and opens the second of his own.

Meanwhile glancing at his truck resting dark as a lump of coal in the distance, Kuy wonders if he will ride off tonight or *manana*. Only one fact is certain—only one will leave here.

Inpatient to kill, Twice Born crows, "It's time you stepped aside Liliuokalani," before taking another drink from his bottle. Finishing the last mouthful, throws it over his shoulder into the fire with a final taunt, "Ready, or are you going to run away? Maybe go for your K'oo? A coward would. But have no fear! I have no weapons timid uncle," he promises holding his palms open for emphasis before grabbing another bottle, spitting out its cork and taking another adam's apple stretching gulp.

Black Wolf squats down. Takes out a large barrow pocketknife to cut his peyote buttons into several segments, chewing them with a careful and practiced motion. Digesting its bitter fruit tucked away atop supper, Kuy starts his attack accompanied by a small drum and a Lipan air.

Threading notes from own life into his steadily growing composition as the Comanche unwraps an old flute carved from a child's forearm across their smoldering fire promising he'll leave the buzzards Kiowa for breakfast.

Deadly serious. They begin. Crow footed baritone versus rasping soprano with murder in his eye. Don't fight with fists or knife. But with song and chant derived from opposite sides of faith's spectrum.

Given that *Seni* is dual natured and a deeply reflecting pool mirroring either light or dark depending on a soul's hue, Black Wolf considers that they're representative of this duality. Accordantly summoning,

–Remembered laughter of his wife and son

Snorting buffalo spirits to stampede hybrid ghosts

A boy's grateful. Convalescence sigh–and other forceful, strident pickets into his music's circle like a warm breath, alive. Proclaiming heart's command, like a deepening bell.

Laughing at Black Wolf's naivety, having counter–mined his own vein of occurrence; witch gathers several buds of cactus, swallowing them whole before joking softly, "Souls at twenty paces!" Taking up his flute, places it to his scarred lips, then snarls a fusillade of scales without beauty and tonal quality yet possessing unquestionable power opposing as a sudden storm to a summer's day,

Woven autumnal writs. Anasazi dirges–

Corpse music

Ancient before the Spanish–lisped glooms from abandoned pueblos.

Desiccated screams of sorcerers–

Plaited cold black ash of burnt marrow–

A collection of fell perceptions, witchcraft gathered from abandoned pueblos and sharpened from years of study at the feet of the old blind bruja discovered near Tucson left to starve and die alone to break her power and still her mischief until Twice Born rescued her from being pecked to death by a flock of mean spirited crows and later brought back to his darkening circle.

Before this bout got going, with the opportunity of finding a seat, an appreciative if unresponsive audience gather while they face off with eyes closed. Breath laboring. Clasping amulets for protection, praying for sanction invoking, pleading, *Seni* if willing, to abet.

Midnight, appeals answered, perception's straw is snatched away, winnowing like corn meal pigments funneled through reason's anointed hands, coalescing into tunneled riot behind veiled and hooded eyes introrse and introspective with concentration.

Afterward Kuy's gaze narrows, smoldering, darkening like emeralds as he changes tempo to match the other's refrain countering the Comanche's pricked dementia cold and deadly as a moonless blizzard.

Sidetracked. Twice Born's listening to whispering Night children is promised eventual spoils spun from the Kudwa's truck. His medicines, most importantly, Kuy's reputation pocketed like a pawned watch. Goading him anew to shape potent talismans. Gleamed deeds and sorcery cast with his strong, squat finger, into a second, powerful challenge as morning breaks like a jacklight,

—accusations of cowardice in death's duplicity.

Promises of a fallow wind
Empty tinned whooping Cough
And
issued smallpox blanket mirth—

Brushing fear away against deadly *Daw-gyah*, Kuy counters, pleased to add a little of Charlie's blues to the pigment,

Quanah's combative laugh
dying rodeo clown's final benediction
A silver crucifix's benefice against deepening shadow—
—*Seni*'s healing grace—

k'ɪн-t̂н'gyꞟ̄'-gyн   Exhausted, both *dohates* warily attend to the seemingly unfruitful, barren land around them. Wise. Least counting the bounty surrounding them both watch moon sated blooms fold, shy bats glide homeward counter clockwise closing toward morning.

Local residents. Undreaming these two augur eventual occupation, patiently await their departure and dawn's order to reassert even as Twice Born places flute to lip before owl scolds him in his mother's voice. Humbling the Comanche with a sudden. Biting memory of her fly kissed face turned toward death. Distracted, yet plays a final foreboding riff, striking the Kudwa down like a game counter.

Seni's healing grace
Anasazi dirges, benediction, laughter
whooping cough, buffalo spirits, tears—

Unattended, unleashed, their discarded music mutes, slipping silent and broodingly away.

Flushed with easy victory. Twice Born, unconcerned with provincial criticism—swaggers, hisses at raucous critics, a might rickety, shaking with exhaustion, struggles to keep his footing. Inadvertently brushing against moving, no longer slumbering shadows at his feet. Undisturbed. Emptying another bottle, danced a soft shoe shuffle off to buffalo accompanied on his bone 'til stopping abruptly with a bow, drawing a foot long bowie knife.

Kicked awake. Knife welding Comanche aiming to kill him. Kuy rolls over forcing himself upright. Ignoring a slashing pain on his left, reaches for his k'oo.

Yard or two away, . Witch pauses. Turns as if answering a question or summons. Stumbling, falling with nary a protest.

"Maybe just a case of disfavored collateral," the roadman opines. Anyway as any good pennydreadful yarn, Twice Born's crooked as an unpromising fetus. Dead as a dime store Indian.

Kuy a stickler for details locates dead man's flute crushing it with his boot heel. Grinding its tarnished bone slowly into the ground like a cigarette, prior to scattering *sengts–on* and *awdl–kno–bawg*, keeping wolves away from the corpse well as snakes and other critters slithering about in the chill, just before dawn's solitude.

Duel a tired memory, Kuy painfully makes his way unsteadily and boot heeled slow as a winged gunslinger to his truck relying on *Pay* to chase remaining shadows and cold away.

"Guess I spoke too soon!"

On the hood of his truck. Crow alights. Black with the rust of many a mile.

Tired, hurting, Kuy stoops. Gathers small pebbles, throwing them weakly at the bird.

It squawks and flies slowly away in a ragged circle.

"Snake bit?" said not without a deep, abiding, sudden hankering related to Twice Born's sudden demise, "or carted away?" No knowing, he slumps into his seat, grateful for his cab's relative comfort as first light filters through window in a widening spectrum gaudy as a whore's.

Again, crow circles particular in a cross–stitched gait proud and triumphant.

Impressed not a penny's worth, Kuy shrugs. Deciding to leave well enough alone, show's over after all, claps cotton mouthed, chinwags his last, "Good old truck!" Patting its warming dashboard adds, "forded many rivers together. Didn't we," as an owl lands beside him.

Ole crow, don't like this a bit. Who would? Owl flapping around daybreak. Ain't natural!

Flapdoodle, disturbed, pricks at breast, ruffling green and black feathers with a harrumph, gone before acknowledged.

Kuy? Startled. Grits teeth in agony.

Beseeching, astir-many emotions. All a rush, pinning him against day's ramparts. Solitary dogwatch's closing-light's beachhead, tidal remedy, night's end, life's passing.

Yet not resigned, manages, "*'Ccdlk'ccegyH–'cce. Dawkee,*" and when addressed at dawn countersigns, "*Ta'ta–'e?*" given that it presumes in his father's voice to still all he has yet to accomplish rising for final benediction ending.

Chapter Thirty-one

Get up! Unable to sleep Velvet pads down the hill from her small cabin toward her settlement's uneven, unmarked border into remaining night or early dawn. No lights. Little or no sound. Even dogs sleep and no one and nothing stirs.

Suddenly assaulted by awareness—a spiritual telegram or what have you, (never had one? Then you're lying or forgetful), presses her hand to her breast and moans, "Black Wolf!" shoving fist in shut cry mouth. How'd she know? Easy! It came to her unbidden as if borne upon a dying man or woman's last breath or by impossible gospel hard and undeniable as that which visited mary and muhammad (no not carny mary slow on the draw but the mother of krist).

Bay-ha Is it her body, starved soul and unquenchable loneliness that she pays assiduous attention to and not the man? Fated. Stalked and called to account, then summoned and mustered to serve afar.

Chickadee's kick mercifully rivets attentions to belly, stopping her campaign of hysterics woe is me momentarily.

Not knowing if boy or girl inside, acknowledges her first and only child before drifting over to the prairie's edge, sitting in a position old as first man and woman awaiting P'ay to anoint her and child, whereas beyond, unseen yet conceded, countless emancipated spirits ride over the high, windswept mesas, autumnal river banks and light shrouded forests, gathering seasonal harvests, reaping this year's while planting anew next's.

Chapter Thirty-two

Dam–'apk'onbH.

Shadow crowds Kuy. Gambreled can't stand or reach *k'oo*.

Apparition, solemn and demanding as three white devils combined, makes things hot for him until not insignificant radiance infringes forcing this malignancy to twist and fade as if assenting to its own demise. Leaving behind a lingering, terrible hunger possessing a tangible intensity rendering mere physical pain insignificant.

Before a voice out of nowhere, honestly nowhere–consoles,

Thoe-g;yah "Had compassion upon you son."

"Grandfather?"

Dressed in a young man's laughing guise, spirit mocks, "Why do you lie there?" Before stooping to pluck a white feather. An old penny. Carnie bracelet. Military gorget. Silver cross. Roman coin and other tokens of passage.

Examining each silently, spirit turns back to the roadman with a summons sharp as the snap of rawhide,

"Come with me!"

Pulled to his feet. Forward to stand alone before dark sea. Where cliffs. Bracketed below by a small cove. Stand sentinel.

On Tsahn bah Black Wolf. Desiring to walk barefoot pauses, removing his boots for he has always wanted to feel wave drenched sand underfoot.

Water lapping at his feet. Smiling. As would a child. He reaches down to pick up a shell. Gathering its peculiar arabesques into his hand, he studies its delicate, conchoidal grace while brine–warmed water decants from its pink heart and washes down his arm.

Curiosity sated. Puts the shell carefully down.

In the distance several figures shift and converge just out of perspective. Waiting poised with expectant longing. Tantalizingly familiar. Equally elusive. He walks toward them with his arms downward and palms extended.

Glancing at *P'ay* ascending, the roadman turns and steps to the fore at peace. Realizing that he has not departed but with great certainty returned.

’apk‘ąn-hę̄i

Afterward

Finished. Velvet places her sleeping daughter beside her until they are ready to leave after last night's ceremony.

Another awaits miles away. Later she turns toward a stack of peyote nearby and crosses around it to kiss Two Cloud's neck.

He smiled and after lifting their meager possessions into the bed of their aging Halk Hercules, turns toward her while Velvet clasps her hands over his and asks,

Shows over. Ready to get a move on?

He nods.

Reckon. I`ve already mapped out todays route. Love starts to move away but he catches her and plants a quick peck on her scarred face before asking,

Think last night answered any of her questions?

Velvet frowns before replying,

Don't know. Guess we will have to just wait till sleepyhead wakes up and ask her!

Afterward both pick up the girl stirring in dream and place her in front seat and then yet again.

Acknowledgments

First my parents. My father Robert Dean McGinnis for instilling a lifelong love for reading, history, stories of old and nearly forgotten legends, primarily through his own love of the identical. My mother, Elizabeth Jane Mitchell-McGinnis, whom embodied a cultural difference as a person of "Color," and her family consisting of Native American and other frontier heritage from Texas and New Mexico. Through her family's muted remembrances, a partial glimpse of knowledge, history, and awareness, was a cherished family relic passed down through previous generations, providing an inkling that my cultural heritage (as is true for everyone) was decidedly more complex and storied than face value.

My wife, Sandra Ricardo Guzman whom believed in me and most importantly, my work, and through her own sacrifices, helped it reach its aspirations, former professors of Anthropology and History who pointed the way, Darren Hedley, an Australian colleague, whom when I needed "Jestor Journal" access, sent what was required, or else "Roadman" might have taken an entirely different course.

Added acknowledgments must also go out to the talented Canadian Self-Portraitist-Caricaturist, Kristamas Klousch, whose "Rooftop Crows," with kind permission graces the cover of this novel, one lovely example of her haunting art, and additionally to Brad D. Blanchard, a close friend, and fellow writer whom has recently passed

The staff of the online journal *Aaduna* who saw promise in chapter 16 (now 11) of an earlier version of "Roadman," and published this element: William E. Berry, Jr., Publisher & CEO, Keith Leonard, Submissions Manager, Lisa Brennan, Executive Manager, thus providing hope for complete publication in the near future, and to Omer C Stewart, John

Peabody Harrington, Charles S. Brant, James Mooney, important linguists, ethnologist, anthropologist, historians, preservers of a fading past whose seminal works made "Roadman" possible.

The Kiowa, whose rich, fascinating culture captivated me and in turn, I hope that my work returns if only in part what entered my spiritual and creative life on that second class bus near Durango, Mexico watching a spinning dust devil cross a dry, valley, a dream or vision possessed, a passing tall surfer named (Peter or Phillip-sorry my resulting concussion renders full retention impossible) and a nameless lifeguard who rescued from drowning on a raw, decidedly dangerous Colombian beach and finally Donna Bister and Marc Estrin, who not only selected "Roadman," as an addition to their marvelous press but also spent considerable time, editing, proofreading, designing, and typesetting each page, constituting far and beyond what usually falls under the appellation publisher.

Native American-English Glossary

Please note: Though I have reviewed the Kiowa and other Native American words and phrases used in *Roadman*, I reserve the right to change and correct any entry where merited. Additional items: 1. All terms and phrase found below are from the Kiowa language unless otherwise noted. 2. The terms Kiowa and Kudwa are interchangeable. 3. FA denotes page of first appearance.

WORDS AND PHRASES:

1.   Saynday: a Kiowa deity. FA page 7.
2.   Pay: The sun. FA page 5.
3.   Paoyn: Dust. FA page 4.
4.   Pahy: The moon. FA page 6.
5.   Nᴜmᴜnahkahni: Comanche for a (related by blood or marriage) military or communal band. FA page 13.
6.   Napwat Tᴜed: Comanche for 'bare-foot ones`. A clan that habitually did without footgear. FA page 13.
7.   'Eit-dei th' peitgyH: Stars are falling. FA page 43.
8.   Da'kiH-'ei: Supreme Deity. FA page 25.
9.   Kayshaunt: Comanche, bad and good. FA page 34.
10.   Tovt-sar're: Comanche for Black Dog. FA page 34.
11.   Haits: Comanche, close male friend, FA page 34.
12.   Tuyaaitu: Comanche, to die. FA page 34.
13.   Eit-ma-han'it: Comanche. To do evil. FA page 34.
14.   Tovt-ti'vo: Comanche. Black man or, Negro. FA page 34.
15.   Tseey: horse. FA page 72.
16.   Ahoow: kill. FA page 72.
17.   Thalii: Youth. FA page 72.
18.   Pééy: Dead. FA page 89.
19.   K'oo: knife. FA page 76.

20.	Seni: peyote cactus. FA page 14.

21.	Tsowy: coffee. FA page 117.

22.	Kuy: wolf, FA page 56.

23.	Tipis: supernatural gift, or ritual device. FA page 117.

24.	Taime: supernatural gift, or ritual device. FA page 118.

25.	K'ou-m-tou: Spirits of the dead. FA page 133.

26.	Yuh: Interjection of fear or surprise. FA page 134.

27.	Doi: Power or spirit medicine. FA page 385.

28.	Ts' p'mi-bei kuocdl: Stars extending across the sky.
	FA page 140.

29.	Dwdw: Sacred power. FA page 385.

30.	Two' Ai': Bear Mountain. FA page 143.

31.	Berdache: French-Plains Culture individuals who acted,
	or lived as sexual opposites of their own biological reality.
	FA page 145.

32.	Mihdek: Kiowa for same. FA page 145.

33.	Gwa-kelega: Southern Kiowa who were allies with
	the Comanche. FA page 156.

34.	'Ccdlk'cce-dcc: To be foolish, or crazy. FA page 159.

35.	'Ccd 'cce-Km: a crazy man or outlaw. FA page 169.

36.	TsHenej-kiH: Chinaman, FA page 179.

37.	'Ata: An interjection of admiration or surprise. FA page 155.

38.	TsH-'H-ga: Friend. FA page 53.

39.	SyH-n: An endearment-Child, little one. FA page 51.

40.	MiHndei-dcc'ts-Hidoc: I am going to pray. FA page 247.

41.	Batl-sai-an Badl-sai-ya-don: "stink weed". Perceived
	To be a warning or a deterrent. FA page 245.

42.	Q-gop: The wealthiest and highest ranking families of
	Kiowa society. FA page 53.

43.	Toows: traditional housing, FA page 257.

44.	An-son-a: vanilla grass. Leaves sprinkled over a fire
	during peyote ceremonies. FA page 436.

45.   Ch'i: Man. FA page 272.

46.   Thoowngul's: Wagon. FA page 278.

47.   Nátsêhéstahe: Cheyenne. I am Cheyenne. FA page 224.

48.   Aahoow: Thank you. FA page 292.

49.   Towdowm: Place of worship. FA 299.

50.   Poue'ccpgccgy H-'ccdlk'cce-da'dei-'e J'mdoVpa'hmdoc':
        Lead us not into evil. FA page 300.

51.   G Qumdeip: The wind is blowing now. FA page 302.

52.   Tou: It is cold. FA page 303.

53.   Kii: Game meat (deer?). FA page 305.

54.   Tseey: Horse. FA page 307.

55.   Pahy-dome-gaw: `Under the sun men.' One of the
        principal Kiowa ceremonial bands. FA page 308.

56.   Gm-gyH Eyshi'H gyH-'R'bou: Last night I dreamt
        about a man. FA page 312.

57.   'H'dei-kiH: A medicine-bag man. FA page 312.

58.   Koc' gyH-ps'deidcc': I am going to sharpen my knife.
        FA page? 312 (edited out?).

59.   Zaip-gwawt-'ko-ya-daw: Bow wood tree. A wood
        used in ceremonial peyote staffs. FA 301.

60.   GyH-heJteii-dcc: That is all there is to the story. FA
        page 383.

61.   Néín: me, myself and I. FA page 379.

62.   TsHhy-Hp-kiH: Asker of questions. FA page 383.

63.   T'ein-houdl-dH: heart disease. FA 388.

64.   KiH-hiH-t-: One by one, in single file. FA page 403.

65.   Maxana-nunp-Namini-Toop-kixon:
        1,2,34,5 in Mandan. FA page 424.

66.   Numakmaxena: 'First Man'. A Mandan deity. FA page 424.

67.   TQ-bH 'H '-yiH: To hunt for a dream, or to hunt a
        dream. FA page 409.

68.   Tooksey, ahpuskey: Food. Original language and

specifics unknown. FA page 444.

69. Kap-k*ougyH: A shadow or spirit. FA page 451.

70. Puetuyai: A Comanche term for ghosts. FA page 451.

71. Da'-pH'e-gyH: A song. FA page 460.

72. k'iн-t̂н'gyн̄'-gyн : At dawn. FA page 461.

73. Sengts-on: Thistle. Traditionally used to keep wolves away from recently excavated graves. FA page 463.

74. Awdl-kno-bawg. Goose Berry. A plant both to treat snakebite and to ward them away. FA page 463.

75. 'Ccdlk'ccegyH-'cce: I have many sins. FA page 464.

76. Da'kiH-'ei: The Great Spirit. FA page 464.

77. Ta'ta-'e: My father. FA page 464.

78. Dam-'apk'onbH: At the end of the world. FA page 467.

76. αṕk'ɑn-hęį: Without end, forever. FA page 468.

Bibliography, sources & additional notes

"Roadman" started in Mexico's high deserts and finished in the Republic of Colombia's Caribbean coast under difficult and often extremely challenging circumstances. Except for Stewart's masterpiece, "Peyote Cult," I was heavily dependent on the World Wide Web for source materials. While researching details on Kiowa history, religion, culture, history, myths, and language, I was struck daily by the paucity of information available on these fascinating original Americans. It was only by shifting through a small number of web sites reflecting the hard work and dedication of individuals and concerned groups that I was able to build a creditable (or so hoped) armature to support the historical, linguistic, and cultural narrative of my novel. Since my research began in 2005, my listings may be incomplete or missing source materials and if this is true, I ask forgiveness for any un-cited (if any) source material.

Colin McGinnis

Print or Facsimile Sources:
1)   Stewart, Omer C., "Peyote Religion: A History." University of Oklahoma Press: Norman and London, 1987.
2)   Brant, Charles S., "Peyotism among the Kiowa-Apache and Neighboring Tribes," Southwestern Journal of Anthropology
Vol. 6, No. 2 (summer, 1950), pp. 212-222, University of New Mexico: Article Stable URL: http://www.jstor.org/stable/3628644.
3)   Harrington, John P., "Three Kiowa Texts," http://www.archive.org/stream/rosettaproject_kio_vertxt-1/ros. Smithsonian Institution.
4)   Harrington, John P., "Studies of the Kiowa, Tewa, and California Indians." Smithsonian Miscellaneous Collections 70(2). 1919b.
5)   Mooney, James, "Calendar history of the Kiowa Indians." US

Bureau of American Ethnology, 1895-6 Annual Report, 1900.

6)   Watkins, Laurel J., "A Grammar of Kiowa." Lincoln: University of Nebraska. 1984.

7)   Powell J. W., "Seventh annual report of the Bureau of American Ethnology, to the Secretary of the Smithsonian Institution," 1895-1896, Washington Government Printing Office, 1898.

8)   Harrington, John P., "Vocabulary of the Kiowa Language," Smithsonian Institution, Bureau of American Ethnology, Bulletin 84, "Washington Government Printing Office, 1928.

WWW Sites (World Wide Web)

1)   *Statement by an anonymous Native woman*, 2005-2007, "If you take the Christian Bible and put it out in the wind and the rain, soon the paper on which the words are printed will disintegrate and the words will be gone. Our bible IS the wind."

2)   *Kiowa Legend of the Devil's Tower.* 2005-2007 http://www.nps.gov/deto/learn/historyculture/first-stories.htm.

3)   *General history of the Kiowa Indians*, 2005-2007, https://tshaonline.org/handbook/online.

4)   *Legends/Bears-Lodge*, 2005-2007, http://www.native-languages.org/kiowa-legends.htm, http://www.firstpeople.us.

5)   *How White-Crow Hid the Animals*, 2005-2007, http://www.firstpeople.us/FP-Html-Legends/WhiteCrowHidesTheAnimals-Kiowa.html.

6)   Olli Salmi, 2005, *An Unofficial Practical Orthography for the Kiowa Language by Olli Salmi*, 2005-2007, http://www.uusikaupunki.fi/~olsalmi/kiowa.html.

7)   *The Kiowa People*, 2005-2007, http://www.texasbeyondhistory.net/plateaus/peoples/kiowa.html.

8)   *Chief Santanta*, 2005-207, http://www.historynet.com/kiowa-chief-satanta.htm.

9)	The Kiowa, 2006-2007, http://digital.library.okstate.edu/encyclopedia/entries/K/KI017.

10)	Kiowa Indian Chiefs and Leaders, 2007-2008, http://www.accessgenealogy.com/native/tribes/kiowa/chief.htm,

11)	Christine Musser, 2007, Assimilation of Native Americans, Kiowa Odyssey: Fort Marion, Florida, Oct 15, 2007.

12)	Kiowa Hand game, 2005-2007, http://www.kiowatribe.net/index.php?option=com_content.

13)	Kiowa Drawings in the National Anthropological Archives, 2007, http://www.nmnh.si.edu/naa/kiowa/kiowa.htm.

14)	R. E. Moore, "The Kiowa," 2006-2007, www.TexasIndians.com.

About Fomitet

A fomite is a medium capable of transmitting infectious organisms from one individual to another.

"The activity of art is based on the capacity of people to be infected by the feelings of others." Tolstoy, *What Is Art?*

Writing a review on Amazon, Good Reads, Shelfari, Library Thing or other social media sites for readers will help the progress of independent publishing. To submit a review, go to the book page on any of the sites and follow the links for reviews. Books from independent presses rely on reader to reader communications.

For more information or to order any of our books, visit
http://www.fomitepress.com/FOMITE/Our_Books.html

More Titles from Fomite...

Novels

Joshua Amses — *Ghatsr*
Joshua Amses — *During This, Our Nadir*
Joshua Amses — *Raven or Crow*
Joshua Amses — *The Moment Before an Injury*
Jaysinh Birjepatel — *The Good Muslim of Jackson Heights*
Jaysinh Birjepatel — *Nothing Beside Remains*
David Brizer — *Victor Rand*
Paula Closson Buck — *Summer on the Cold War Planet*
Dan Chodorkoff — *Loisaida*
David Adams Cleveland — *Time's Betrayal*
Jaimee Wriston Colbert — *Vanishing Acts*
Roger Coleman — *Skywreck Afternoons*
Marc Estrin — *Hyde*
Marc Estrin — *Kafka's Roach*
Marc Estrin — *Speckled Vanities*
Zdravka Evtimova — *In the Town of Joy and Peace*
Zdravka Evtimova — *Sinfonia Bulgarica*
Daniel Forbes — *Derail This Train Wreck*
Greg Guma — *Dons of Time*

Fomite

Richard Hawley — *The Three Lives of Jonathan Force*
Lamar Herrin — *Father Figure*
Michael Horner — *Damage Control*
Ron Jacobs — *All the Sinners Saints*
Ron Jacobs — *Short Order Frame Up*
Ron Jacobs — *The Co-conspirator's Tale*
Scott Archer Jones — *And Throw the Skins Away*
Scott Archer Jones — *A Rising Tide of People Swept Away*
Julie Justicz — *A Boy Called Home*
Maggie Kast — *A Free Unsullied Land*
Darrell Kastin — *Shadowboxing with Bukowski*
Coleen Kearon — *Feminist on Fire*
Coleen Kearon — *#triggerwarning*
Jan Englis Leary — *Thicker Than Blood*
Diane Lefer — *Confessions of a Carnivore*
Rob Lenihan — *Born Speaking Lies*
Colin Mitchell — *Roadman*
Ilan Mochari — *Zinsky the Obscure*
Peter Nash — *Parsimony*
Peter Nash — *The Perfection of Things*
Gregory Papadoyiannis — *The Baby Jazz*
Pelham — *The Walking Poor*
Andy Potok — *My Father's Keeper*
Kathryn Roberts — *Companion Plants*
Robert Rosenberg — *Isles of the Blind*
Fred Russell — *Rafi's World*
Ron Savage — *Voyeur in Tangier*
David Schein — *The Adoption*
Lynn Sloan — *Principles of Navigation*
L.E. Smith — *The Consequence of Gesture*
L.E. Smith — *Travers' Inferno*
L.E. Smith — *Untimely RIPped*
Bob Sommer — *A Great Fullness*
Tom Walker — *A Day in the Life*
Susan V. Weiss —*My God, What Have We Done?*
Peter M. Wheelwright — *As It Is On Earth*
Suzie Wizowaty — *The Return of Jason Green*

Fomite

Poetry

Anna Blackmer — *Hexagrams*

Antonello Borra — *Alfabestiario*

Antonello Borra — *AlphaBetaBestiaro*

Sue D. Burton — *Little Steel*

David Cavanag*h*— *Cycling in Plato's Cave*

James Connolly — *Picking Up the Bodies*

Greg Delanty — *Loosestrife*

Mason Drukman — *Drawing on Life*

J. C. Ellefson — *Foreign Tales of Exemplum and Woe*

Tina Escaja/Mark Eisner — *Caida Libre/Free Fall*

Anna Faktorovich — *Improvisational Arguments*

Barry Goldensohn — *Snake in the Spine, Wolf in the Heart*

Barry Goldensohn — *The Hundred Yard Dash Man*

Barry Goldensohn — *The Listener Aspires to the Condition of Music*

R. L. Green — *When You Remember Deir Yassin*

Gail Holst-Warhaft — *Lucky Country*

Raymond Luczak — *A Babble of Objects*

Kate Magill — *Roadworthy Creature, Roadworthy Craft*

Tony Magistrale — *Entanglements*

Andreas Nolte — *Mascha: The Poems of Mascha Kaléko*

Sherry Olson — *Four-Way Stop*

David Polk — *Drinking the River*

Aristea Papalexandrou/Philip Ramp — *Μας προσπερνά/It's Passing Us By*

Janice Miller Potter — *Meanwell*

Philip Ramp — *The Melancholy of a Life as the Joy of Living It Slowly Chills*

Joseph D. Reich — *Connecting the Dots to Shangrila*

Joseph D. Reich — *The Hole That Runs Through Utopia*

Joseph D. Reich — *The Housing Market*

Joseph D. Reich — *The Derivation of Cowboys and Indians*

Kennet Rosen and Richard Wilson — *Gomorrah*

Fred Rosenblum — *Vietnumb*

David Schein — *My Murder and Other Local News*

Harold Schweizer — *Miriam's Book*

Scott T. Starbuck — *Industrial Oz*

Scott T. Starbuck — *Hawk on Wire*

Scott T. Starbuck — *Carbonfish Blues*

Fomite

Seth Steinz or — *Among the Lost*
Seth Steinzor — *To Join the Lost*
Susan Thomas — *The Empty Notebook Interrogates Itself*
Susan Thomas — *In the Sadness Museum*
Paolo Valesio/Todd Portnowitz — *La Mezzanotte di Spoleto/
Midnight in Spoleto*
Sharon Webster — *Everyone Lives Here*
Tony Whedon — *The Tres Riches Heures*
Tony Whedon — *The Falkland Quartet*
Claire Zoghb — *Dispatches from Everest*

Stories

Jay Boyer — *Flight*
Michael Cocchiarale — *Still Time*
Michael Cocchiarale — *Here Is Ware*
Neil Connelly — *In the Wake of Our Vows*
Catherine Zobal Dent — *Unfinished Stories of Girls*
Zdravka Evtimova —*Carts and Other Stories*
John Michael Flynn — *Off to the Next Wherever*
Derek Furr — *Semitones*
Derek Furr — *Suite for Three Voices*
Elizabeth Genovise — *Where There Are Two or More*
Andrei Guriuanu — *Body of Work*
Zeke Jarvis — *In A Family Way*
Arya Jenkins — *Blue Songs in an Open Key*
Jan Englis Leary — *Skating on the Vertical*
Marjorie Maddox — *What She Was Saying*
William Marquess — *Boom-shacka-lacka*
Gary Miller — *Museum of the Americas*
Jennifer Anne Moses — *Visiting Hours*
Martin Ott — *Interrogations*
Jack Pulaski — *Love's Labours*
Charles Rafferty — *Saturday Night at Magellan's*
Ron Savage — *What We Do For Love*
Fred Skolnik— *Americans and Other Stories*
Lynn Sloan — *This Far Is Not Far Enough*
L.E. Smith — *Views Cost Extra*
Caitlin Hamilton Summie — *To Lay To Rest Our Ghosts*

Fomite

Susan Thomas — *Among Angelic Orders*
Tom Walker — *Signed Confessions*
Silas Dent Zobal — *The Inconvenience of the Wings*

Odd Birds
Micheal Breiner — *the way none of this happened*
J. C. Ellefson — *Under the Influence*
David Ross Gunn — *Cautionary Chronicles*
Andrei Guriuanu and Teknari — *The Darkest City*
Gail Holst-Warhaft — *The Fall of Athens*
Roger Leboitz — *A Guide to the Western Slopes and the Outlying Area*
dug Nap— *Artsy Fartsy*
Delia Bell Robinson — *A Shirtwaist Story*
Peter Schumann — *Bread & Sentences*
Peter Schumann — *Charlotte Salomon*
Peter Schumann — *Faust 3*
Peter Schumann — *Planet Kasper, Volumes One and Two*
Peter Schumann — *We*

Plays
Stephen Goldberg — *Screwed and Other Plays*
Michele Markarian — *Unborn Children of America*

Essays
William Benton — *Eye Contact*
Robert Sommer — *Losing Francis*

www.ingramcontent.com/pod-product-compliance
Lightning Source LLC
Chambersburg PA
CBHW061056190726
48286CB00006B/1764